Graham Anderson was born in New Zealand. At the age of eight, he was left with a family he'd never met while his parents moved to a remote island in the central Pacific. After rebelling and running away several times he was finally shipped off to join his parents, travelling alone across the Pacific by small 100 ton inter-island trading ship in the days before jet aircraft. He's never stopped travelling since, resulting in him visiting all seven continents.

His business experience includes sitting on a number of boards in both the public and private sectors and as an executive at the highest levels. His story telling draws extensively on his business background, combined with his many and varied travel experiences and a life-long love of history.

Fall From Grace is the second book in *The Elijah Trilogy* following *The Half-breed Boy. Elijah's Will* (due for release in late 2013) will complete the trilogy.

Today, Graham lives in Perth, Australia. He continues to travel and read history extensively.

THE
ELIJAH
TRILOGY

BOOK 2

Fall From Grace

GRAHAM ANDERSON

Acknowledgements

As with the first book in the Elijah Trilogy, *The Half-breed Boy,* a group of friends and family were instrumental in helping me with this second book. My thanks to them all but a special thanks to Nicholas for resolving all the computer problems.

ISBN: 978-0-9873819-1-0

Cover design by Damonza www.damonza.com
Formatting by awesomebooklayouts.com

www.graham-anderson.com

Read the other books in The Elijah Trilogy by Graham Anderson

The Elijah Trilogy Book 1 – The Half-breed Boy

In a world where money is everything, and corporate profits mean exploiting the natural resources of the outback, Nanderra Station in far western Queensland is under threat from the coal seam gas miners who covet the vast riches that lie deep beneath the remote cattle station. When environmentalist Libby Farnham is enlisted to help stop them, she's quickly drawn into the story of the mixed-blood boy, removed from Nanderra over a hundred years before and left with a Catholic mission.

An epic story of power and passion, greed, loyalty and betrayal unfolds as *The Half-breed Boy* traces Elijah Hocking's escape from the depravity of the priests to finding love on a remote *estancia* on the Argentine pampas.

When his wife and son are brutally slain, something snaps and Elijah embarks on a mission of retribution on all those who made his life a living hell. But peace continues to elude him and Elijah moves to San Francisco where he quickly learns that the path to power is through the manipulation of anyone who can advance his interests.

But who is Elijah Hocking? As he struggles to resolve the mystery of his ancestry, he must also come to grips with just who he can really count on.

Having been forced to leave the United States by Senator McCarthy and J Edgar Hoover, Elijah returns to his beloved *estancia* in the remote Argentine Pampas to lick his wounds. From there he plots his return to power, and his retribution.

Entering the armaments trade, he supplies both sides in the Six Day War along with uranium to South Africa, becomes involved in the Australian mining boom, and organises for his employees to be rescued from the Iraqi occupation of Kuwait. Vehemently opposed to drugs, when he discovers one of his closest confidantes has become a supplier against his explicit instructions, he views this as the ultimate betrayal.

A complex character as his many wives and children can attest to, Elijah has not yet played his last hand. As the tension mounts, so too do the rivalries and hatred as Elijah's children restlessly await his death and their share of his wealth.

For them the waiting has already stretched far too long, as finally the day dawns for the reading of *Elijah's Will*.

Family Tree

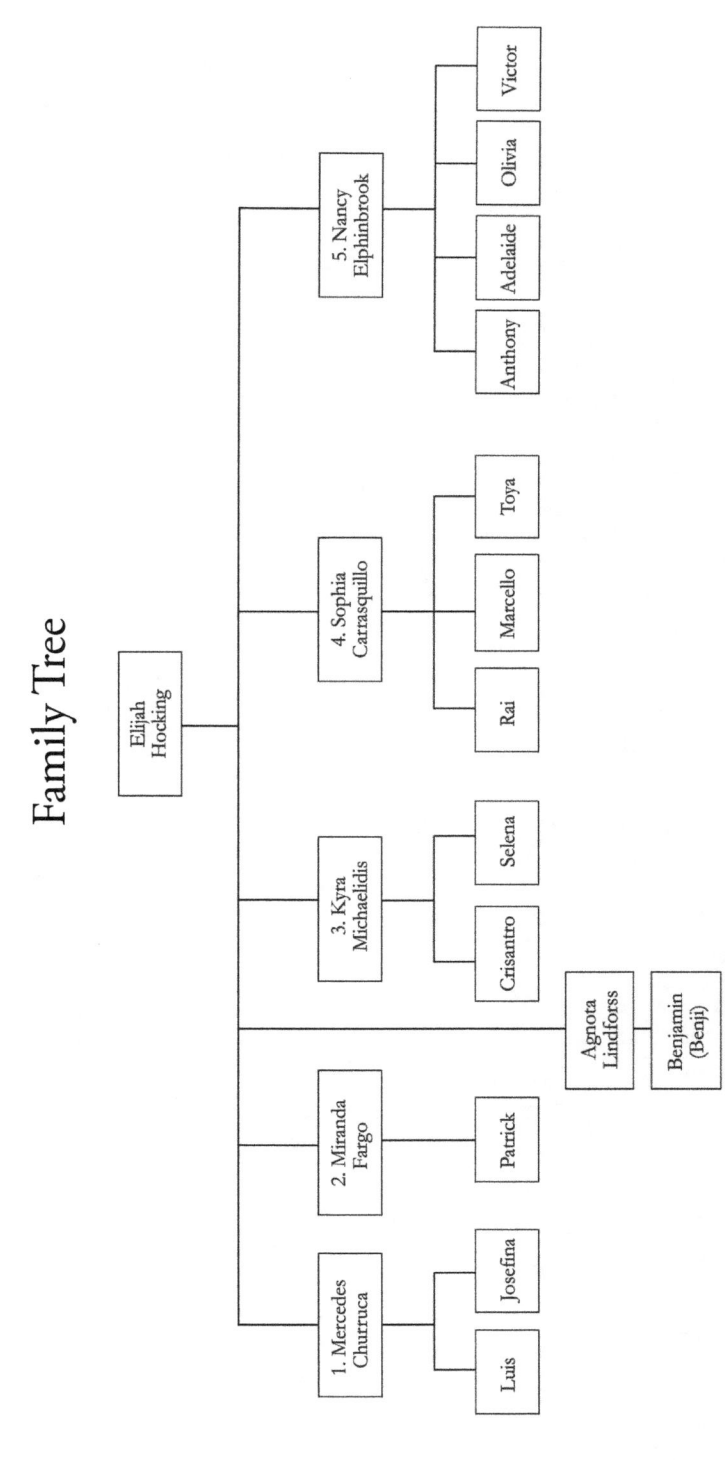

Prologue

Estancia Tierra de Abundancia, Patagonia, Argentina
June 1927

The lone figure stood motionless, silhouetted in the gathering gloom. He'd been standing there on the little hillock behind the *casco* for the past hour staring into the endless landscape stretching out before him. Being alone was not the problem, he'd faced that many times in his life. It was the loneliness he found hard to endure.

Desperately he sought her understanding, but instead it was her disapproval that enveloped him like a cloak, causing him to shiver despite the thick alpaca jacket he wore buttoned tight to the neck. Finally, he turned to face the nearest of the four marble gravestones as a large sigh escaped him.

"I've tried my love, I really have tried" he whispered.

The graves of his first wife and their son, the victims of that senseless killing six years before, lay alongside those of her mother and brother. Tragedy seemed to stalk both him and this place of beauty. When he'd returned to the *estancia* eight months ago determined to cease his aimless wandering, he believed the ghosts could finally be laid to rest.

Perhaps his biggest mistake had been to bring his daughter back with him, the living reminder of that tragic night. Josefina, beautiful ten year old Josefina, the image of her late mother, herself the most beautiful woman he'd ever laid eyes on. But while the young girl's physical beauty was there for all to see, mentally she would never advance beyond the age of two.

"She has to go back my love. Don't you see it's for her own good, for all of us?"

Far to the west, a fork of lightning lit the clouds followed after a brief interval by the distant rumble of thunder momentarily disrupting his thoughts. Tragedy it seemed was destined to forever be his middle name, the hallmark of his life. His own mother driven mad by the circumstances of his birth, his father who'd disowned him, both his wives snatched in their prime by the finality of death, his elder son lying here at his feet, his younger son for whom he couldn't find forgiveness for surviving where his mother hadn't ... and Josefina.

***

He turned back to the headstones. *"I'll be gone for some time. I will return I promise, but next time it'll be when I'm truly ready. Next time I won't rush it."*

It had become his practice to climb the little knoll each day to talk with her, just as they'd set aside an hour for each other at the end of the working day when she was alive. He knew she could sense he was restless, but as much as he loved this place, and her, peace eluded him. It was time to return his daughter to where she could receive the care, both medical and emotional, he couldn't provide.

But what to do with Patrick? God knows he'd tried to impart some feelings towards his younger son, but all Patrick invoked in him was the memory of his second wife buried on another hillside, far from here, overlooking the Tasman Sea.

"I'll be back before you know it with our son. I know it's going to be a son" were Miranda's last words to him – but in granting Patrick the gift of life, she'd sacrificed her own.

He reached down and touched the headstone, scraping away the moss that was forming in the lettering.

Mercedes Josefina Churruca Hocking
Nacido Octubre 28 1893
Robado en Esta Vida, Junio 4 1921
Mi luz, mi amor, mi todo

He could sense her trying to pull him back as he turned and headed back down the path to the *casco* but his mind was made up. Josefina would return to the Institution in La Plata.

Chapter 1

The child was curled up in a foetal position in the corner of the compartment staring blankly out the window at the featureless landscape. If he hadn't known better he would have the thought the limp listless body was that of a rag doll rather than a ten year old child. It was heartbreaking to watch her on two counts. That she was his daughter and didn't recognise him was bad enough. But what really broke his heart every time he looked at her, was that she was the image of her dead mother who he still loved passionately and missed so terribly. As they journeyed further north, drawing ever closer to the institution, Elijah couldn't be sure whether he was really returning her so that she could receive the care she needed, or whether he was banishing her in the hope he could finally expunge the terrible images of that night that continued to play in his mind.

Even though it was now six years since Mercedes' senseless murder by her deranged father, it still seemed as though it was yesterday. Josefina's presence didn't help. Once he'd delivered his daughter, there was no way he intended to return to the *estancia*. There was no solace for him there. Nor was returning to the lifestyle of the past six years an option. The days of bootlegging and living on the edge of the law were done. At least he could move forward from that. That was the one bright note.

Finally they arrived at the hospice in La Plata where he handed his daughter back to the care of the doctors.

"I know you warned me it wouldn't be easy, but I never expected it to be so hard. Is it possible she remembers the *estancia* as the place where she was attacked?" he asked.

"It's hard to know what she thinks Señor Hocking. She's reached her maximum maturity mentally, but yes, it's possible" was the reply.

"The tantrums and the screaming fits are the worst. Will she ever grow out of them?"

"Again we can't be sure. You'll recall me telling you when you first brought Josefina to us that medical science had made few advances in the area of mental health. What I can assure you is that she'll receive the very best care here. It's likely she'll settle better if she sees this as her permanent home. Her fits and tantrums are most likely caused by being moved from what she considers a secure environment. I remember your associate, Señor Perdido once commenting how she'd started to smile at him and reach for his hand when he used to visit her here. But remember, it was two years before that happened." The doctor paused. "Please don't misconstrue my next comments Señor Hocking, but it's possible she believes Señor Perdido is her father and she could be reacting to him no longer visiting her."

***

It had been nearly a year since he and Jorge had last met. They'd communicated often as was their habit, especially once the telephone line had finally snaked its way to the *Estancia Tierra de Abundancia* deep in the Argentine pampas.

What would he have done without Jorge, especially in those dark days following Mercedes' murder? His comrade had been the glue that held everything together in both his business and personal lives. The young articled clerk he'd first met when her grandfather, the Vizconde, had dictated his instructions for the control of the *estancia* until Mercedes received her inheritance turned out to possess one of the most brilliant legal and business minds in Argentina. Elijah had never experienced any regrets over his decision to fund Jorge in setting up Perdido and Associates following Mercedes' death and someone was needed to manage his affairs.

"This's a bit different to the old apartment in Calle Sargento Cabral" Elijah commented as they met at his trusted associate's luxurious mansion at San Isidro south of Buenos Aires.

"I guess the *estancia's* a little different to the mission where you grew up" Jorge countered.

"Touché amigo."

"How did it go at the hospice?" Jorge asked softly.

Jorge waited as Elijah fell silent and gathered his thoughts before looking up again. "I'm sure returning her was for the best" he said as he repeated the conversation he'd had with the doctors.

"And now...?" Jorge prompted him.

"I've decided to head back to America to start again...legitimate this time. I can't settle down at the *estancia*."

"I can understand that. I always thought it was too soon. Any thoughts on what you want to do?"

"That depends on what shape you tell me I'm in."

"I think you'll manage to survive for a while yet" Jorge started. "Barring some unforeseen catastrophe that is. Along with the property and share investments we've made in the U.S. from your liquor profits, all told you're worth close to fifty million dollars."

Elijah sat back looking stunned.

"Fifty million what?" he asked.

"U.S. dollars *amigo*. Actually, it's really only forty eight point nine million" was the answer accompanied with a grin.

"Fifty million dollars" Elijah repeated quietly to himself.

"Nett after debt" Jorge added.

Elijah shook his head. "Who'd ever have thought the half-caste kid...?" He stopped, stood up and stepped out onto the deck overlooking the Rio Plata.

"But if you're determined to return to America, then we're in the wrong place, or more specifically, I'm in the wrong place" Jorge continued as he followed him outside. "I need to be where you and I can get together easily. I need to be closer to the action. Since we've already moved your money to Switzerland I'm suggesting I headquarter myself there. There's also the added advantage that their banking laws allow us total anonymity."

"What will Elvira say?" Elijah asked staring across the muddy expanse of water towards the horizon hiding the distant Uruguay shoreline.

"Let me worry about that."

"Why not America?'

"Europe's awakening. We've already invested in Sweden and with you in America and me in Europe, that's a good split of our talents. Telephones and telegraphs make it easy for us to stay in touch these days."

"What's with investing in Sweden?" Elijah asked turning to look at his companion.

"Europe's largest iron ore deposits. In the main they go to Britain and Germany. As both countries increase their industrial production, they're going to need iron ore. As it happens, we picked up a small struggling company called Porjus Mineralämnen Aktiebolag."

Seeing his friend's face, he started laughing before he added "Don't look like that *amigo*! Even the Swedes have a problem saying it. That's why they call it PMAB. It's the smallest of Sweden's three major iron ore miners. Anyway, the major shareholder died midway through last year and the company looked like it would fold if they couldn't sell it. The Swedish government showed some interest but I jumped in first and took an option. If you're unhappy with the decision, we shouldn't have any problem unloading it again pretty quickly."

"No you did right not to wait if the opportunity was there" Elijah responded. "We've always got to be prepared to work that way."

"Frankly" Jorge continued, "I don't see how Europe can keep going another twenty years without them all being at each other's throats again. Everywhere you look you can see the war stirred up a hornet's nest that's raising more problems than it resolved. In my opinion, the situation's worse now than it was in 1914. Iron ore could be pretty important if they start re-arming."

He stepped back into the room and picked up a sheaf of papers from his desk. "I have another proposal I want to float *amigo*. You'll have to excuse the pun" he added with a grin as he told Elijah of an idea he'd been working on for a while. He believed there was scope to become the predominant Argentine shipping company and outlined a plan to build three 17,000 ton passenger liners to enter the burgeoning Europe – South American market in competition with the British and European lines monopolizing the trade. It would mean going into debt to finance their construction but Jorge was confident that he could negotiate subsidies from the Argentine government. They were already providing accommodation for up to twenty passengers on their freighters sailing from the United States and Europe, but this would be their first major sortie into the passenger trade.

Elijah took some convincing, but while he finally agreed with the plan, for the first time he found himself questioning his colleague's reasoning.

They finished their meeting by agreeing to inspect the Swedish operation as soon as possible. Since Elijah had already committed to spending Christmas in England, the two men decided they'd meet in Switzerland in the New Year and travel from there to Porjus together.

***

The country estate where Nancy and Montague lived was about thirty miles north east of London near Chelmsford in Essex. It was a year since he'd last seen her when she'd help unmask the truth about his father.[1]

Met at the station by an ancient liveried chauffeur driving an equally ancient Rolls Royce "shooting brake", Elijah wasn't sure whether he was expected to sit or lie down in the vehicle, it so resembled a hearse.

1 The Elijah Trilogy Book 1 – The Half-breed Boy

The chauffeur resolved his dilemma by opening one of the back doors to allow them to be seated before loading their bags in the rear.

The three-storeyed sandstone mansion was set amongst several hundred acres of grazing land, approached by a long tree lined drive that emerged into traditional manicured lawns and gardens surrounding the imposing structure. Elphinbrook House comprised over one hundred rooms, added to progressively by successive generations since the first structure was built back in 1572.

"You are the first guest to arrive sir" he was informed by the butler. "Her Ladyship has asked that you join her for tea in the conservatory. Dinner will be at nine this evening as his Lordship is not expected to return from London before seven."

"Elijah, it's lovely to see you" Nancy exclaimed as he entered the conservatory. She was sitting near a full length bay window and rose to embrace him. "Where's Patrick?"

"He and the nanny are in the nursery. She felt it better he was put to bed after all the excitement of the trip."

"Of course" she said making no attempt to hide her disappointment.

"This's quite a spread. I thought the house in Sydney was impressive, but this..." he said.

"Come and sit down over here" Nancy said waving him to a delicate looking brocade covered settee perched on impossibly spindly legs near the window overlooking the expansive gardens. She sat down in an adjacent chair and rang a small silver bell on a nearby table as she crossed her long lithe legs.

"Montague has been delayed in London but will be with us in time for dinner" she told him. "Our other guests will start arriving tomorrow but tonight I wanted you to finally meet him and for it to be just the three of us."

"I was beginning to think this mystery man of yours doesn't exist" he laughed. "Meanwhile I have you all to myself."

They reminisced about his recent search for details of his parents as the butler supervised the delivery of tea and thin crustless sandwiches served on china that was so thin it was almost opaque.

When he returned to his room to change, Elijah found his clothes unpacked and pressed, his dress suit laid out for him to change into and a bath drawn for him in a deep ancient bathtub in the adjacent bathroom.

"I feel as though I've known you for many years old chap" the booming voice greeted him from across the library where they gathered for drinks before dinner. The twelfth Marquis of Elphinbrook was a similar age to Elijah and very much the product of the old school aristocracy. The two men warmed to each other immediately.

"There was a time when I wasn't sure whether I was still running newspapers or had branched into a missing person's bureau" he laughed. "Nancy had half the resources of the company involved in searching for that ancestor fellow of yours at one stage, but I have to say I'm delighted with the outcome" referring to the recent search for Elijah's namesake.[2]

"You know we may have cleared up who my father was, but we're no closer to clearing up the mystery of my mother" Elijah said pensively.

"Why do you say that?" Nancy asked.

"Adelaide's letter to Amy where she talked about losing her child is supported by the annulment papers stating Hargreaves and Adelaide never had children. On the other hand we know that Rosie had a child around the same time as Adelaide lost hers but we have no idea who the father was. All we know is that Rosie's child was taken from her, but she steadfastly denied it was me right up until her death, long after Hargreaves was any threat to her."

"Good Lord, does this mean we're starting again?" Montague asked in mock horror.

Elijah shrugged and took a drink of his sherry. "Somehow it doesn't matter any more. I've lost the drive to find out. It's not going to make any difference to my life and I might be better off not knowing."

"Poor Elijah. I couldn't imagine not knowing who my mother and father are" Nancy commented as she took his arm and led him into dinner.

***

Christmas passed quickly amongst the small knot of guests who joined them. With unseasonably good weather for most of the time, the men engaged in outdoor activities with Elijah taking part in his first hunt. The biggest surprise was the arrival of the Prince of Wales accompanied by Thelma, Lady Furness for two days between Christmas and New Year.

"I know Buenos Aires well Mr Hocking" she said seated next to him at dinner. "My father was United States Consul to Argentina for a number of years. I recall meeting your wife's parents at a function. I was quite young at the time, but Señora Churruca stood out. She was so elegant. It was only later that I found out she was Spanish royalty."

"It's quite delicious isn't it" Nancy said later. "He only takes her to a very few places where he feels they won't be spied on or talked about. Her husband's Lord Furness, you know – the shipping tycoon. The Prince really is quite handsome isn't he?"

That wasn't the way Elijah viewed the diminutive heir to the throne. He chose not to tell Nancy he was sure the Prince wasn't just fixated on the ladies.

Chapter 2

Zug, Switzerland
January 1928

It was late January before Elijah left Chelmsford and headed across the wintry European landscape to meet once more with Jorge; this time in the old historic town of Zug south of Zürich, where his associate had established his headquarters. Jorge had leased an office in Poststrasse near the railway station in the old town, and purchased a house in Lüssirainstrasse high above the lake on the slopes of the Zugerberg. The views from the house across Lake Zug towards the Alps were breathtaking and Elijah wholeheartedly endorsed his friend's decision.

"Elvira's at me daily to find out what your plans are for Patrick" Jorge asked on Elijah's arrival. "Are you planning on taking him with you to Sweden? If not, she'd jump at the chance to look after him here if you prefer."

Elijah tried hard not to show the relief he felt. Since the death of the boy's mother, Patrick now sixteen months old, together with his Nanny travelled everywhere with him. Despite his lack-lustre attempts, Elijah was unable to bond with the boy. Carting him around was proving to be a distraction he neither needed nor wanted.

"That'd be good for him, and for me *amigo*. The next few months look like being fairly hectic. Having Elvira provide a home for him would be perfect. Are you sure she won't mind if it lasts a few months?"

"Mind? She's been having trouble settling down here. She'll be in seventh heaven."

***

The wet damp cold of Porjus, indeed of Sweden as a whole, was a shock – bone chilling in a way Elijah didn't think was possible. Heading past the Arctic Circle into the far north of Sweden, the countryside and the weather both grew bleaker the further they travelled. The landscape was an endless expanse of untouched wilderness covered in snow, meters deep, occasionally interspersed by enormous pine and spruce forests and large rivers.

The settlement, sitting alongside the frozen Lule River on the railway-line between the Swedish port of Luleå and the Norwegian port of Narvik had nothing to recommend it. Without either the adjacent mine or the huge hydro electric plant just upstream from the settlement, Elijah determined no-one could live there and still claim to be sane. He grumbled more than once that he reckoned the miners only went underground in an attempt to get warm.

They only stayed two days before heading south once more to the Swedish capital. Despite the heat being piped through the railway carriage, Elijah sat in the compartment, arms folded tightly trying to get warm.

"Shit, this is a miserable bloody climate" he said more than once to Jorge.

"It's those Jamaican roots crossed with the Australian outback" Jorge laughed at him, offering little sympathy even though he privately agreed with him.

"Well just don't expect me to come back here too often and never again in winter. Since you found it; this can be your baby to look after" was the response.

On their second night back in Stockholm they were invited to a government reception. From the moment Elijah entered the room, he couldn't keep his eyes off the six feet tall classic Scandinavian beauty on the far side of the room. He continued to glance in her direction as he was being introduced to other guests, occasionally being met by her cool stare. Finally, he found himself facing the small group of which she was part.

"Mr Hocking, may I present Baron and Baroness Lindforss and Count and Countess Sparre" his host intoned.

"Ah…Mr Hocking, the mysterious Argentine who has bought into our iron ore industry" the beauty responded. "Not at all what I expected. Your wife is not with you?"

"My wife passed away a year ago Baroness."

"I am so sorry Mr Hocking, I had no idea" she said looking anything but sorry. The group stood discussing the mine at Porjus until glancing down at his watch, Elijah excused himself. He headed towards Jorge, when a hand touched his shoulder.

"Mr Hocking!"

He turned to face the Baroness.

"Are you planning to stay long in Stockholm?"

"I'm due to sail for New York in a week."

"Then may I be so forward as to ask you to accompany me to a dinner I'm having with a few friends tomorrow evening? My husband is unable to attend, and I would prefer not to go alone. I'm sure you will find the company interesting and there will be some excellent contacts for you if you're planning further investments in Sweden."

She was holding a cigarette as she spoke, her left elbow cupped in the palm of her right hand. It was as though they were the only two people in the room although he was aware of her husband closely watching the interchange from across the room. That was enough to spur him on. *"If he's fool enough not to spend time with this gorgeous creature"* he thought, *"then why should I miss out?"*

"I'd be very happy to accompany you Baroness; your company alone would be sufficient" he replied.

He thought he saw the trace of a smile. "My driver will collect you tomorrow evening at seven" she said before turning away and heading back to her group.

Joining Jorge, the two men stepped out into the constant drizzling rain and slush of Stockholm leaving Elijah once again feeling numb with the cold.

"I know I've said it before, but what a miserable bloody climate. What do you know of Baron Lindforss and his wife?" he asked his companion.

"Do you mean the Baron or the Baroness?" Jorge asked.

"Both. He must be at least fifty and it's pretty obvious he's not keeping her satisfied."

***

Promptly at seven o'clock the following evening, Elijah was collected from the lobby of the Grand Hotel in Blasieholmshamnen. Stepping into the warm rear of the Hispano-Suiza limousine, he found the Baroness already waiting for him. Attendees at dinner included an armaments manufacturer, a ship owner and a director of SKF, the ball bearing manufacturer. Conversation was lively and Elijah quickly found himself enjoying the company far more than he'd expected to.

Driving away, he commented on the interesting circle of friends she mixed with.

"Then you will enjoy tomorrow night's gathering even more" she replied leaning towards Elijah as he lit her cigarette.

"Your husband's not available tomorrow night either?"

"My husband is rarely available Mr Hocking. We have very different interests. Ours is a marriage of convenience that our friends are aware of and tolerate."

"I see" Elijah replied.

"No Mr Hocking, I don't believe you see at all." The sparkle in her eyes reflected the passing streetlights as she continued. "The Lindforss family is one of Sweden's oldest. Three years ago, there was a possibility of a scandal involving a young man, which would not have been tolerated by the rest of Fredrik's family, or for that matter by the Court. It was forcibly suggested to my husband that he should marry. Fredrik and I have an agreement that allows him to keep company with his young men and allows me to keep company with mine. We work hard to ensure that neither of us embarrasses the other, and from time to time when it cannot be avoided, we attend receptions together such as last night."

Agnota leaned forward and spoke in Swedish to the chauffeur as the car pulled up outside the Grand Hotel. "I assume you're intending to invite me in for coffee" she said to Elijah.

"You took the very words out of my mouth" he replied as the chauffeur opened the rear door for them.

Stepping into Elijah's room ahead of him, she turned and said "Don't bother with the lights...or the coffee" as she shrugged off her dress. It was nearly noon the following day before she left.

"I'll be back to pick you up at six thirty" she said as she left. "Tonight will be a little less formal, but every bit as interesting."

***

"You asked about the Baron" Jorge started to say as Elijah joined him for lunch. "It appears he ..."

"...has a preference for young men" Elijah finished the sentence, "and I'll be grateful to him for ever more."

"As long as you realise his wife will never leave him" Jorge continued. "The pre-nuptials are very specific about this and were drafted by Sweden's foremost legal counsel."

"That suits me *amigo*. After Mercedes and Miranda, I don't intend to become emotionally attached to another woman. Should I be so stupid as to consider marriage again, then I promise you'll get to organise my pre-nuptials."

That evening's dinner was to be hosted by one of Agnota's closest friends.

"Carin was born into one of Sweden's aristocratic families" Agnota briefed him. "Her father was a colonel in the Swedish army and her mother's family brewed beer in Ireland. It's rumoured her grandfather may have once been in the British army. Anyway, Carin married

Baron von Kantzow but left him for her current husband. He's a highly decorated German air ace from the war. He was badly wounded in an unsuccessful uprising against the government in Munich. I think it was about three or four years ago and they had to flee Germany. I've only met him a couple of times. He was recently discharged from a mental asylum where he spent the last year recovering from the effects of morphine addiction."

"Well this is shaping up to be a very jolly evening" Elijah remarked. "Any others whose backgrounds I should be aware of?"

At dinner he found himself seated alongside his host's husband. Elijah quickly found the handsome former air ace to be a fascinating conversationalist. Despite his recent incarceration in a mental asylum, Hermann Göring was highly intelligent and genial, revealing he and Carin were returning shortly to Germany where charges against him for insurrection had recently been dropped.

"I intend to re-enter politics Herr Hocking. Germany is in need of a saviour. The leader of the National Socialists, Adolph Hitler, is the only man who's capable of rescuing Germany from the depths of despair into which it's been dragged. The Fatherland will once again claim its rightful position in the world, so that businessmen like you will want to invest in us and trade with us again."

***

For the balance of that week Agnota rarely left his side by day, and never by night, before Elijah travelled to Gothenburg to board the Swedish America Line's *"Gripsholm"*. Despite the distance from Stockholm, she insisted on travelling to the port and farewelling him there.

"It's been a wonderful week" she told him. "I can't remember when I've enjoyed the company of a man as much. I'm almost tempted to run away with you, the way Carin did with Hermann and to hell with the consequences."

"No Agnota, we both knew it could never be anything more than a fling, but you've helped me come alive again. Should you and Fredrik ever come to New York, there's always room in my bed for you. I'm sure I could find something to keep Fredrik occupied" he quipped.

As the *"Gripsholm"* edged away from the dock, he spotted her in the crowd waving to him and immediately waved back.

"She's very beautiful. You must be extremely unhappy to be leaving her" a sultry voice to his left murmured.

Turning, he found himself standing next to an attractive brunette dressed against the cold in a long mink fur coat and matching hat.

"Well the English say that parting is such sweet sorrow" he responded.

"I'm Kyra Michaelides" she said extending her hand.

"Elijah Hocking" he replied. He looked back towards the dock but she was gone. Later that evening he was handed an unsigned cable which simply read *"You cad. You could at least have waited until the ship disappeared from sight."*

That night at dinner, as Elijah was escorted to the Captain's table, he found he'd been seated next to the woman he'd met on deck. "I recognise the name Miss Michaelides."

"My father is Stamos Michaelides" she replied naming one of Greece's largest ship owners with a fleet of freighters and tankers that traded worldwide.

"Of course; shipping! I'm involved in shipping myself."

"I'm well aware of who you are Mr Hocking. That gives us at least two subjects we can share for the next eight days, although I warn you I get very bored, very quickly, with shipping."

"It's Elijah, and the other subject is?" he asked innocently.

"I didn't think you'd need to ask, but I can assure you we won't need to waste a lot of time talking about it."

Chapter 3

New York, U.S.A.
May 1928

Nancy was at the dock when the *"Gripsholm"* berthed in New York. She had travelled to New York to see Dennis Pratt as the lead in *The Three Musketeers* which was due to open at the Lyric Theatre. Elijah introduced the two women before Kyra departed, promising to meet him again later in the week.

"Who's your friend?" Nancy asked him in the car.

"Daughter of a Greek shipping tycoon" he replied. "She made the voyage a bit more enjoyable."

"I'll bet she did" she remarked before suddenly bursting out laughing. "I'll *bet* she did" she repeated trying to stifle her laughter, but before long Elijah joined her in breaking into loud guffaws. "Isn't Patrick with you?" she asked once she'd recovered.

"I left him in Zug with Jorge and Elvira. He needs a bit of stability and I'll be moving around over the next few months."

"You can't continue to live this way Elijah. If you're serious about basing yourself in New York, you need your own place. Then you'll actually have somewhere you can make a home for him. I'm here for the next few weeks and I'd be happy to help you look if you like."

It was Nancy who found the apartment at Fifth Avenue and 66th Street. For the life of him, Elijah didn't know what he needed with six bedrooms, seven servant's rooms and a dining room which measured twenty two feet by thirty feet, but he recognised the eighteen room apartment as a prime investment.

"Now you need to have it decorated. I have just the person for you."

"For Christ's sake Nancy, it's only four years old. What's wrong with it as it is?"

"Just the answer I'd expect from a man. Leave it with me and I'll organise everything."

She promptly hired one of the city's major interior decorators who proceeded to strip the apartment to its bare walls. It was to be another eight months before he finally moved in. In the meantime, he took a suite at the Hotel Elysée on 54th Street.

***

The serious work of expanding into manufacturing started when Jorge arrived in New York in late June and immediately set about acquiring a number of small steel companies in Pennsylvania with the intention of merging them. The two men had just returned to the Hotel Elysée from one of their inspection trips when the concierge delivered Elijah a letter postmarked Stockholm. He opened it, read it and passed it across to Jorge without comment.

His friend raised an eyebrow. "What do you plan to do?"

"Nothing! You've already told me that she signed a pre-nuptial agreement that doesn't allow her to leave Fredrik, or at least she leaves with nothing. We knew each other for a week; we were great in bed, end of story. She's not asking for anything, just letting me know she's pregnant. If they're smart she and Fredrik will claim it's theirs, even if most people will think it's a joke."

"Swedes aren't known for their natural tans *amigo*" Jorge replied drily. "She better hope that your Jamaican blood-line doesn't decide to make an appearance."

In September 1928, with the United States in the throes of an election campaign, they decided the time was right to merge the five steel companies they'd acquired into one entity. By doing so, they determined that apart from the normal savings to be expected from the consolidation, they could reduce wages by a further twenty percent.

"We can expect trouble from the unions" Jorge commented as they planned the tactics needed to bring the workers into line.

"Then I guess this would be a good time to recall Johnny" Elijah suggested.

"Do you know where he is?"

"Yeah, I have a fair idea. Leave it to me."

He'd first met Johnny at the mission near Brisbane in Queensland when both boys had been plucked from their parents and sent there due to their mixed blood. Johnny, who was substantially darker skinned than Elijah, had settled into the role of minder after they both ran away to sea and disembarked in Buenos Aires back in 1911. When Elijah entered the bootlegging racket in San Francisco following Mercedes' murder, it was Johnny's job to keep the clients in line. He'd been banished from Elijah's presence nearly three years previously[3], when against Elijah's orders, he'd ruthlessly disposed of two of the major oppositions' leaders. In particular, Johnny's part in the de Falangio brothers' deaths was known to the authorities in San Francisco although no warrants had been issued for his arrest. Deciding discretion was the better part of valour, Johnny crossed into Canada and moved to Montreal where he worked with a local racketeer, keeping a low profile. Whilst Elijah knew his whereabouts, there had been no contact between them until Johnny received the call asking him to return.

Slipping back across the border between New Brunswick and Maine on a back road near Edmunston late one night, Johnny headed for New York.

"Great to see you again Boss" he said effusively as Elijah waved him to a seat.

"You too mate" Elijah replied somewhat more guardedly. "You ready to come back to work?"

"Sure thing. Montreal's about worn out its welcome for me."

"Its worn out *its* welcome or the other way around?"

Johnny laughed nervously. "Jeez Boss, you know me too well."

Elijah fixed his former minder with a long cold glare, only speaking again once Johnny looked away. "Things *will* be different this time Johnny. When I give orders they'll be followed to the letter. Step outside the line and next time it'll be terminal. Do we understand each other?"

"Boss..." Johnny started.

"I know about Nick and Giuseppe mate. So do the authorities. Tell me it won't happen again."

"Sure Boss."

"No Johnny, you're not listening. *Tell* me."

"It won't happen again Boss" Johnny quickly replied.

"Good we won't talk of it again. Now we've got work to do."

***

The formation of Mercedes Steel was announced in October, just weeks before the 1928 Presidential election. Politicians from both parties clambered to claim credit for the initiative, issuing press releases highlighting the potential for job increases and growth in Pennsylvania's industrial belt. By mid-November, following the election of Herbert Hoover as President two weeks earlier, winter arrived in the northeast with temperatures plunging and heavy snow falling throughout Pennsylvania and the adjoining states.

During the third week of November, the local union leaders were invited to meet the management of Mercedes Steel in Harrisburg and hear their plans for the new company. Elijah personally greeted each of them as they entered the boardroom, giving no indication of the announcements he was about to make. Little was known of the Argentine businessman other than representatives such as local Democrat Congressman Michael Leveridge spoke highly of him. The coffee, whiskey and cigars that were served helped blunt the apprehension the union leaders felt.

With the introductions completed, Elijah rose and called the room to order. He gave a quick précis of the operations and highlighted the falling production figures. "The facts are that each of these operations would've failed if we hadn't stepped in and bought them. We in turn are unable to continue with the existing cost base that we've inherited. Gentlemen, to survive we're forced to introduce economies across all the operations."

There was a shuffling of feet and the men opposite looked uneasily at each other.

"Firstly, the York mill will be closed and mothballed forthwith and the workforce retrenched."

The feeling of bonhomie that had been created when the union leaders first arrived dissipated immediately. The tension built as Elijah continued unperturbed.

"The workforces at each of the remaining four mills will be reduced by twenty-five percent. Those employees we retain will be required to take a twenty percent cut in wages. In addition, management positions will be reduced across the company by fifty percent. All changes will take effect as of now. The papers you've just been handed list the names of those who've been made redundant. Gentlemen, I must stress that should these measures not succeed in halting the decline in profitability, we will be forced to introduce further cost savings in order to achieve our objectives."

***

He sat down to a stunned silence. The union representatives looked at the list of names that were distributed to them while Elijah was speaking. He calmly lit a cigarette and watched them through the smoke haze before a big man opposite jumped to his feet.

"You wop bastard!" he exploded. "You won't get away with this. Many of these men have worked here for twenty years or more. You try this and we'll take everyone out on strike. Am I right men?" he asked looking at the others seated alongside him. A chorus of agreement ran up and down his side of the table. "We'll close you down you prick. We'll run you out of town."

"Mr O'Reilly I believe" Elijah said trying to make himself heard over the shouting. The attack came from the quarter he'd expected. O'Reilly was of Irish descent with a reputation of ruling the union by fear; speaking first and thinking later.

Johnny stood and eyeballed the ringleader across the table. There was a hush as the union leader looked away before Johnny sat down again and Elijah continued.

"Mr O'Reilly, you strike and I will personally close all the mills myself. There won't be any need for you to do so. It's primarily due to your union's practices that the mills are uneconomic in the first place. The only way the remaining jobs can be saved is to do what we propose. Instead of issuing threats, I appeal to you to work through this together with us. As a first step, my management team will answer any questions you may have."

O'Reilly was still standing. He leaned down and thumped the table to emphasise his words. "There're no questions you bastard! Close the bloody mills down and see how long you survive! Our men are out as of now!" he shouted. Snatching the papers off the table in front of him, he raised his fist at Elijah and shook it vigorously. "Two wops and a nigger ain't going to get much support round here I can tell you. You want war you bastard, you got it." Turning on his heel, he stormed from the room followed by his fellow delegates.

Elijah grinned at the others as the last of the unionists left. "Excellent! Looks like you win the wager Jorge. Seventeen minutes! The stupid prick reacted exactly as predicted" he laughed. "Right, it's action time. Get on with locking everything down as planned. Jorge you take over here. Johnny get the troops on standby. I'm off to Washington to start calling in favours. Oh and Johnny, remember – stick to the script."

***

The news of the mills closing their gates and being barricaded against the union marchers who descended on each of them broke like a bombshell in Washington. Elijah found many of those Senators and Congressmen that he'd extended favours to and financed election campaigns for in the past were initially hostile.

"If you succeed in cutting their wages like this Elijah, then all the other operators will try to do the same" Michael Leveridge complained. "Surely there's another way through all this."

"I can't speak for any of the others Michael but if they're facing the same cost pressures and inefficiencies as me, then of course they'll have to" Elijah agreed.

Initially, Elijah held his forces in check. Publicly he stressed he was prepared to negotiate with the unions while newspapers across the nation reported scenes of striking workers attacking company trucks, attempting to pull down gates and shouting militant slogans outside each of the company's mills.

While legislators reacted nervously, the Federal government, in transition mode between Presidents Coolidge and Hoover, was powerless to act. That rapidly changed two weeks after the meeting with the union leaders.

As a convoy of loaded vehicles attempted to recommence deliveries from the Middletown mill, the striking workers barricading the gate surged forward to stop the emerging trucks and pull the drivers from their cabs. In the midst of the action, a shot rang out and one of the drivers slumped over the wheel of his truck. Eleven strikers were seriously hurt in the ensuing melee as the other drivers panicked, accelerating through the packed mass of men to get out of harm's way.

Shock erupted from all quarters. The Pennsylvania State Governor called out the National Guard while the press roundly condemned the striking workers for the fatal shot. Two days later as Elijah's car was being escorted by a flying wedge of guards into the York mill, more shots were fired hitting the trunk of his car, resulting in the arrest of a number of union leaders.

Later that day Jorge issued a press statement. "We're dismayed that the thuggery you'd normally expect of European demagogues has been allowed to infiltrate a democracy like the United States" he told the assembled reporters. "Since the union thugs are intent on murder, there's no way the company can be expected to work or negotiate with them any longer."

He revealed the company would evict all striking workers and their families from company owned houses, at the same time offering an amnesty to any workers who returned to work the following day.

***

That night a major storm front moved across the north-eastern states as far south as Washington D.C., with temperatures falling to minus twelve degrees. The following morning in near blizzard conditions, pitched battles broke out between the opposing groups of workers forcing the National Guard to open fire on the rioters. Order was only restored after three more deaths and numerous injuries. The following day, a force of men protected by State Troopers, moved from house to house evicting families into the bitter conditions.

The escalating violence between those wanting to return to work and the hard-core strikers continued for a further twelve days with steadily mounting casualties. Finally, at a rowdy meeting just before Christmas, the strikers narrowly voted to accept the redundancies, revised pay rates and conditions. The three men gathered in the boardroom of the Harrisburg headquarters of Mercedes Steel on Christmas Eve 1928 to toast their success in defeating the strike.

"I wouldn't move around this area too freely for some time though" Jorge observed. "It's going to take some time before feelings cool down. I'll wager there'll be a few hotheads out there who'd be willing to have a pot shot at any one of us. In fact *amigo*, it might be a good time for you to get as far away from here as you can."

"Point taken. While we're on the subject of pot shots" Elijah interrupted him, "there's something I've been meaning to bring up, but with all the action I keep forgetting. That hit on my car a couple of weeks back was a bit close for comfort Johnny."

"It had to look real Boss" Johnny laughed. "Andy put the shot exactly where he was told to. We couldn't have the reporters guessing it was a fake. If it hadn't gone near you, they might've twigged. As it was, you ended up being the hero for not even ducking for cover even though the bullets were so close."

"And what about this guy Andy?" Elijah enquired. "What's to stop him squealing?"

"Don't think that's likely to be a problem Boss" Johnny chuckled. "He's too busy learning to crawl like a crab at the bottom of Chesapeake Bay."

Chapter 4

New York, U.S.A.
February 1929

His shipboard companion Kyra had made no contact since leaving him at the docks the previous April so he was surprised to receive a telephone call from her early in the New Year.

"I'm in town. My father's supposed to be meeting me here but he's been delayed in Piraeus for another two weeks. I'm bored and thought you might want some company. I could be there in thirty minutes."

When the concierge called to advise she'd arrived, Elijah anticipated she'd be alone. He didn't expect the two trunks and eleven suitcases that accompanied her.

"What's all this?" he asked.

"It seemed silly to have an empty hotel room full of my clothes, not that I'm planning on wearing many."

"You're welcome to stay Kyra, but I have work to do. I'll be in and out of New York over the next few weeks and I *will* need to be dressed; well at least some of the time" he laughed as she began unbuttoning his shirt.

The two weeks stretched into a month and then a second as Kyra showed no inclination to leave. She accompanied Elijah when he travelled until it became accepted by both of them that she'd moved in more or less permanently.

When Jorge returned from Europe in early May he pulled Elijah aside. "Your personal relationships are your own business *amigo*" he started, "but I think you're making a major mistake with this woman. She's going to bleed you dry if you get tied up with her. She knows rich pickings when she sees them."

"You forget that she's already rich; she doesn't need my money."

"Wrong *amigo*! First the old man might be big in ships, but he's in trouble cash wise. Second, her brother's sole beneficiary of most of the assets if anything happens to the old man. Kyra and her father can't stand each other. She won't get much more than a few trinkets and I'm guessing she knows it. Just promise me you won't get in too deep without talking to me first. Remember you told me that you'd make sure I worked up a pre-nuptial agreement for you before you married again."

"OK Boss" Elijah said saluting him.

"I'm deadly serious Elijah, she's trouble with a capital 'T'" Jorge cautioned him.

A few days later it was Nancy's turn. She was back in New York for the premiere of Eugene O'Neill's *"Dynamo"*.

"She's a tramp! I can't put it any plainer than that. When you're away she's certainly not sitting at home pining for you. I've run into her a couple of times with a young stud on her arm. She's playing you for a fool."

When Elijah challenged Kyra with Nancy's accusation she laughed it off. "That was my cousin Eugenio. He was in town. He's since left or I would've had him join us for dinner one night. You have similar tastes and I think you'd both get on well."

***

A week later Elijah told her he and Jorge were heading to Harrisburg and would be away for a few days.

"I hope you won't mind if I pass this time darling" Kyra told him. "It's not exactly the most scintillating place I've ever been. It'll be nice to have a few days on my own getting my hair done and doing some shopping."

That night she sauntered into a bar on Jerome Avenue in The Bronx.

All conversation stopped as she opened the door and stepped inside. Looking around, her eyes finally rested on a young muscular black man leaning back against the bar, hips thrust forward, his tongue sliding suggestively between his lips. She started towards him when a figure in the booth in the far corner raised his hand beckoning her.

"Nice" she said to the man at the bar, brushing her hand against his groin. "Who knows, I might be back."

"I wasn't sure you'd come" the man in the booth welcomed her as he slid over so she could sit next to him.

"I wasn't that sure myself, but the invitation seemed to have definite possibilities."

"I didn't think the great man would let you out of his sight."

"The great man's out of town. He doesn't own me. Besides I've yet to experience black meat" she murmured, lightly caressing his knee.

"Hey Johnny! You planning to share or you keeping her to yourself?" a voice called across the room.

"Your call" he said looking at her.

"Interesting proposition, but another time perhaps. Let's see what I've got here first" she replied as her hand glided up his thigh.

"Baby, you have no idea what you've let yourself in for."

"Then let's get out of here and find out. I'm not much into talking – I'm more of an action girl myself."

***

She travelled with Elijah to Southampton in June for the maiden voyage of the *"Presidente Bernardino Rivadavia"* to South America. The first of the trio of liners was causing considerable interest as she was the largest and most luxurious passenger ship on the run. From Southampton it would call at Cuxhaven, Lisbon and Cadiz to collect additional passengers before heading to Tenerife, Recife, Rio de Janeiro, Montevideo and Buenos Aires. Kyra was in her element as virtual 'first lady' of the liner. The combination of her position as the owner's companion, and the influence she was able to exert on seating plans in the dining salon, ensured that even the most straight laced madams, who would normally have expressed distaste at her marital situation, were prepared to overlook her sharing a cabin with Elijah.

June 25th dawned clear and sunny with calm seas. The *"Presidente Bernardino Rivadavia"* was sailing between Recife and Rio de Janeiro at eighteen knots when an SOS was received at around seven o'clock that evening from the Portuguese liner *"Rainha Maria-Teresa"* which was carrying 900 passengers and calling for help. The Argentine ship was fifty miles away and immediately turned north towards the sinking ship while the captain increased speed beyond her previous best of twenty one knots set on her trials.

The scene they came across was one of chaos as the sinking ship's migrant passengers, many of whom had never been to sea before were panicking, some jumping overboard without life jackets. Many of the ship's lifeboats had either been crushed as they were being launched or had overturned. Two smaller ships were already on the scene but standing off from the liner fearful that its boilers would explode.

The *"Bernardino Rivadavia's"* captain switched on his ship's powerful searchlights to illuminate the sea and allow him to launch her lifeboats, while bringing his ship close to the sinking liner. As he maneuvered closer, passengers lined the rails ogling at the events unfolding before them. The *"Rainha Maria-Teresa"* finally sank at two o'clock the following morning as the Argentine crew were still pulling survivors from the water. Elijah had immediately turned his suite over to be used for accommodation for survivors while Kyra displayed her previously unannounced skills as a nurse.

"Where did you learn this?" Elijah asked in surprise.

"I volunteered in the Greco-Turkish War in 1919" she said. "I was bored and went to Smyrna with the first of our troops. I spent about a year there before my father ordered me back home."

The *"Bernardino Rivadavia's"* arrival in Rio de Janeiro with nearly seven hundred and fifty survivors was feted by the city. While Kyra was hailed as a heroine for her efforts, Elijah on the other hand refused to allow any details about him or his involvement to be released to the press. However he was privately pleased that his ship should have been close by to the tragedy, as it ensured huge publicity which he hoped would flow on to bookings on subsequent voyages.

"Pity we couldn't arrange something similar every sailing" he commented to Jorge later, "it would save us providing entertainment and give us great publicity we could never hope to buy."

***

After disembarking and spending a couple of days in Buenos Aires they continued on to the *estancia*. Kyra immediately hated the place where the ghosts of Mercedes confronted her at every turn. She plotted to have them leave from the first day they arrived but Elijah would not be shaken.

"What is it about this damned place?" she shouted at him over dinner one night as the maid fled from the dining room.

"I can have Julio drive you to Santa Rosa in the morning" he replied coldly. "I don't see you being kept a prisoner. You're free to leave any time you want to."

"That damned woman disapproves of me; I can feel it and I won't have it." Kyra shrieked. "She's dead but she's jealous of me. It's not healthy the hold she has over you."

Elijah threw his napkin on the table and stood up, his chair toppling on the floor as he strode angrily around the table. He smacked across her across the face with the back of his hand.

"That 'damned woman' was my wife. Everything you enjoy by hanging around me is because of her. She was a lady you bitch, and you'll never sully her name by referring to her again."

He strode angrily from the room leaving Kyra in tears. Normally an habitually later riser, next morning she was already at breakfast when Elijah entered.

"The car will be ready at ten" he said tonelessly.

"Where are we going?" she asked innocently.

"Not we; you. It's up to you where you go. I really don't care."

She stood up and rushed over to him. "Please Elijah; I'm sorry for my outburst last night. It was unforgiveable and it'll never happen again. Please don't send me away."

He stood stiffly at the sideboard, his back to her. "My mind's made up, you leave at ten."

As she broke into tears, he barely heard her next comment.

"I don't know what came over me. It must be because I'm pregnant. I didn't know what I was saying."

"What did you say?" he asked turning to face her.

"I'm carrying your baby Elijah. I've suspected it for the last couple of weeks, but now I'm sure."

He stood staring at her for a long moment before coming to a decision. "There's a number of matters I have to clear up" he said and strode from the room.

***

It took several hours and many attempts before Elijah was finally able to make contact with Jorge in Zug. The connection was terrible, the static constantly interrupting their conversation forcing both men to have to repeat themselves many times.

"*Madre di Dios* Elijah, that's the second one in twelve months" Jorge shouted down the line.

"I don't need the morals lecture" Elijah shouted back. "Just prepare the bloody agreement."

"Are you sure; sure it's yours and that this is what you want *amigo*?"Jorge quizzed him. He was having trouble making himself heard over the static. "We could always get Johnny to get the truth from her" he half joked.

"Don't think I haven't considered it" Elijah shouted back. "Just get on with the paperwork. I'm leaving here tomorrow and will be back in

New York by the end of July. The *"Doña Margarita's"* due to sail from Buenos Aires but I've held her there until we're on board."

Kyra spent the next two weeks at sea being solicitous to Elijah at every opportunity. He made no further comment to her about the baby, although her swelling belly had started to make its presence known. When Johnny met them at the pier, Elijah failed to notice the alarm in Kyra's eyes as his minder climbed the gangplank to the ship.

"Last time we did this together was on the old rust bucket *"Clan Dennison""* he laughed as he embraced Elijah. He merely pecked at Kyra's cheek, deftly avoiding her arms as she reached forward to embrace him. On their return to the apartment, she immediately fled to her room, leaving the two men to talk.

One afternoon shortly after their return to New York, Nancy dropped into the apartment. "I'm heading back to England. I couldn't believe the news. I had to come over to confirm it for myself before I left. Why are you doing this? Her reputation's terrible. People talk about her everywhere. Even if you believe only ten percent of the rumours, she must have slept with everyone in New York, some several times."

Elijah stood at the window looking out at the sunlit New York landscape. He sighed before he replied. "I thought that you more than anyone would understand. You know my background. I wouldn't wish that on any kid of mine. I've already got one bastard out there Nance. I know what it was like growing up under those circumstances. The kid deserves to have a mother...and a father."

"You're assuming the baby's yours..." she started before he turned. She could see the cold steely look that he could conjure up at a moment's notice.

"Enough Nancy! The decision's been made. I don't want to hear any more about it. Understood?"

She silently placed her cup back on the table, gathered her coat and gloves and left the room. A couple of minutes later he heard the front door to the apartment close behind her.

***

A few days later he passed a sheaf of papers across to Kyra at dinner.

"What's this?"

"The marriage contract for you to sign" he said.

"Is this supposed to be a proposal?" Kyra asked while the papers hung in the air between them.

"The best you're going to get from me" he replied as he dropped them on the table.

Kyra leaned back and stared at him. He met her stare unflinchingly until she finally dropped her eyes.

"I'll have my lawyer look at them."

"This isn't a negotiation. You'll sign them as they are. Walk away and I'll disown you and the kid, no second chances. Sign them and you'll both be provided for. It's that simple."

They continued staring at each other again for another minute before she said "You bastard!"

"You got that right darling" he said as he picked up his fork, "but at least my status is official. I don't know how they describe slut in official documents. I must ask Jorge to look that up for me. Now would you pass the salt please?"

She picked up the saltshaker and threw it at his head. He ducked, laughing, as she stormed from the room.

They were married in late July. Elijah refused to consider a religious wedding – his childhood experiences meant there was no way he wanted any priests involved. Neither Kyra's father nor her brother bothered to respond to their invitations. Her wedding present to him was a valuable Greek Orthodox religious icon while he gave her an allowance and her own bedroom.

The wedding nuptials completed, they drove away from City Hall in the drizzling rain. Elijah looked out the window at the passers-by walking despondently, heads down against the wind howling in off the Hudson River as he casually told Kyra he was heading to Europe the following week on the *"Berengaria."*

"Since you're already several months gone, I've assumed you're not in a condition to travel. We wouldn't want to put the baby at risk now would we?"

"When will you be back?" she asked dully.

"Before you're due if everything goes to plan."

She turned away determined he wouldn't see her tears. This was supposed to be the happiest day of her life; after all she'd plotted for this day and succeeded in landing the bastard. It wasn't supposed to be like this; *she* was supposed to be the one in control.

Chapter 5

Zug, Switzerland
August 1929

When the two men met in Zug in mid-August, Jorge started by cautioning against any unnecessary spending for the foreseeable future.

"The markets can't keep climbing like this" he predicted. "Something has to give. I'm planning to dump all our stocks over the next couple of weeks and convert our cash into gold. If we make it into 1930 without some major shakeout happening, then I've probably overreacted and we can go back into the market."

Elijah thought Jorge probably *was* overreacting but he'd learned long ago to trust his associate's judgement calls. Jorge normally preferred direct investment in their own businesses to holding stocks, but over the years he'd still accumulated a sizeable portfolio. By the time Wall Street peaked in early September then took off on a wild roller coaster ride, all their external shareholdings had been disposed of.

It was mid-September before Elijah arrived back in New York. His intention had been to bring Patrick, now two years old, back with him but Elvira had been heartbroken at the prospect of losing him and begged Elijah to leave the boy with her.

"You and Kyra have hardly got off to a happy start" she said tearfully. "Do you really think it'd be smart taking Patrick back to that? You need to sort out where your marriage is headed before you expose him to it."

He was secretly relieved that Jorge and Elvira were prepared to continue looking after the boy. Emotionally, there continued to be a blank. Patrick may as well have died with his mother for all Elijah felt for him.

***

The apartment was empty. Checking her bedroom, he didn't know whether to be relieved to find Kyra hadn't moved out; but then, where would she go and who'd pay her bills? Certainly not Daddy.

It was several hours before she returned home. "You're back" she said standing in the study doorway.

"I told you I would be" he replied without looking up.

"I wasn't expecting you. I have a dinner date and won't be back until late" she said and headed to her room.

As the door closed behind her, Elijah stood up and poured himself a drink. Crossing to the window, he stared off into the distance as his mind wandered back to the life he'd shared with Mercedes and Miranda. How had he been so stupid to allow Kyra to entrap him? Was she God's way of reminding him that at the root of it all, he was still a half-caste kid from Outback Australia; that despite his money and increasing influence, at the end of the day he really didn't control his own life. Was there a greater power than his that could enforce its control over him whenever it wanted to?

He recalled Father Luke saying all those years ago at the Mission when he'd been set upon by one of the priests..."*Understand that God has not abandoned you. You'll find that each visit to purgatory awakens our souls and gives credence to the existence of some greater being.*"

"*Bullshit!*" he thought fiercely. "*What absolute fucking crap!*" There was no place in his life for such clap-trap. He downed his drink, refilled his glass and returned to his papers.

***

Early in the evening of Thursday October 24th Jorge called, excitement brimming in his voice.

"There's something's happening to the market" he shouted down the line. "Get down to Wall Street when it opens tomorrow and see what's going on. All hell's breaking loose here in Europe. I'll monitor things from this end."

The following day Elijah witnessed the vice-President of the New York Stock Exchange place overpriced bids for stocks in what appeared to be a successful attempt to arrest the panic-selling. Elijah left, sure that Wall Street would settle down again.

He abandoned that view when the markets re-opened the following Monday. After the close of the various exchanges in Europe later that night, the two men spoke by phone.

"There's no way I'll ever doubt you again after this *amigo*. Just what type of bloody crystal ball are you holding? If I hadn't seen it with my own eyes, I wouldn't have believed it; traders were literally clawing at each other to dump their stocks. Jesus, I'm glad you decided to get out of ours when you did."

"It was the same here" Jorge told him. "London, Paris, Berlin – they all went mad. This thing's not going to be over in a couple of days *amigo*. We're in the lucky position of being able to sit back and watch what happens next. On the other hand, if this leads to a depression as some are predicting, then it's possible we'll be forced to cut back on steel production in the States and mining in Sweden. It could affect our agriculture and shipping businesses as well. The only good news is that you won't personally have to think about jumping out a window any time soon."

Elijah had just hung up and crossed to the cabinet to pour himself a drink when he was interrupted by a knock at the study door.

The door opened and the maid stood there looking agitated. "It's Mrs Hocking sir, her water has just broken" she stammered breathlessly.

"Well don't just stand there you silly girl; have you called the doctor or an ambulance?" he snapped back.

The maid shook her head.

"Do so at once" Elijah commanded her. "Shut the door behind you and Maria...I don't want to be interrupted again."

Three hours later; Crisantro Hocking, a dark skinned baby boy with jet black hair, entered the world.

"Christ, Jorge was right about throwbacks" Elijah thought when he finally found the time to meet his son. *"What the hell does Agnota's son look like? If he's anything like this, there's no way Fredrik's going to get away with claiming to be the father."*

***

Jorge's premonition was spot-on. As share values continued to decline dramatically, he astutely started buying up stocks again in major US companies for a fraction of their value. He also started snapping up properties in New York City as the market continued to fall and cash-strapped owners were forced to sell at almost any price, resulting in Mercedes Properties becoming the owner of some of the city's prime apartment buildings and commercial properties.

Their own companies weren't immune to the market turmoil. Production at both the Swedish and Pennsylvania operations was reduced to a three-day week and four freighters were laid up as cargos became increasingly hard to source. But if the shipping market was proving difficult for Elijah, others were finding it even worse.

Kyra and Elijah continued to co-exist in the Fifth Avenue apartment, rarely speaking to each other. One evening six months after the tumultuous events of October, she walked into his study and sat down. Elijah kept working at his papers without looking up.

"Out of money?"

"Don't be a pig all the time Elijah, it's not necessary. Anyway, I'm not here for myself."

He put down his pen and leaned back. "So, the boyfriend's out of money is he?"

She stood and turned back to the door. "You really are a pig aren't you? You just can't help yourself."

He wiped the back of his hand across his forehead and rubbed his eyes. "Wait Kyra, I'm sorry. What do you want?"

"Does it always have to be like this between us?" she asked softly. "You really shouldn't be working so hard. Take some time off. There's a son down the hall you should be spending time with. Anyway, it's not us I'm here about."

"So what are you here about then?" he asked again.

"My father's in trouble. He's facing foreclosures on much of his fleet. He won't come to you, he's too proud."

"So he sent you along instead. The loving father who's cut his daughter from his will; the same one who couldn't find the time to attend his only daughter's wedding. Are we talking about the same man?"

"He doesn't even know I'm here. In fact he'd explode if he knew I was having this conversation with you. I just thought there may be some way you could help. Who knows, perhaps you could end up with his ships instead of the bankers."

Elijah whistled. "That's what this is all about? You thought you could get me to move in on the old man and seize his toys. Jesus Christ, I knew you guys hated each other but I had no idea...sorry Kyra, I'm not prepared to play your little game, and besides, I don't have any use for his rotten rusting relics."

He picked up his pen and bent back to his papers.

"Screw you" she hissed at him.

"I think I'll pass up on that one too thanks" he said to her retreating figure.

The following day while Elijah and Jorge were having their daily transatlantic telephone hook-up, Jorge mentioned Nancy's husband was in trouble.

"What do you mean trouble?"

"I got a call from one of his bankers. Seems he's overextended himself expanding into America. They wanted to know if we were interested in taking the media group off their hands. I got them to agree not to act till we took a look."

"*Mierda* Jorge. I haven't seen or heard from Nancy since she walked out when we argued about Kyra. How serious is it?"

"The hounds are gathering. They could lose the lot."

"I'll call him straight away."

"It's more serious than that Elijah. I suggest you go see them."

"In England?"

"*Si*. In England!"

***

In her environment at Elphinbrook House, Nancy looked the perfect embodiment of an aristocratic English lady. You would never guess she was born and brought up on an Australian sugar-cane farm on the far north New South Wales coast. Tall and slim, her complexion was flawless, her skin a delicate pale colour with a slight natural touch of colour about her cheekbones, her dark brown hair set in soft curls cascading to just above her shoulders.

"Elijah, it's so good to see you again" she greeted him, offering her cheek for a kiss.

"It's not just a social call Nance. I hear Montague's having a few problems" he said after several minutes. "I'd like to help."

"You're well informed as usual darling, I hadn't realised that the situation was public knowledge."

"You know..." he started then stopped. "Oh for Christ's sake Nancy, let's cut the crap. If you're still angry about Kyra, say so and let's get it out in the open."

"You're far too good for her Elijah. We both know it. I can't believe you let her play you for a fool. I hope you're not going to try and tell me you're happy."

"I told you, I did it for the kid."

"What about Patrick, or Josefina for that matter? I don't see you being an outstanding success as a father to either of them. What's going to be so different about this one?"

"You have a way with words don't you Nance? With the possible exception of Jorge, I'd never let anyone else speak to me like that."

"Perhaps it's because we're the only two who truly care." She got up, crossed over and sat on the couch next to him and took his hand. "Please, don't let her destroy you. Get rid of her at the first opportunity. Promise me that."

The silence stretched until he finally said "I promise you you'll be the first to know whatever I decide. Now where's Montague?"

***

"The purchase of the U.S. papers was highly leveraged" Montague explained as they poured over a swathe of financial reports. "They haven't been performing to expectation, in fact they've never made money since we bought them. When the crash came, sales fell further. I put this place up as collateral and it's possible I might lose it."

"Your other papers, how're they performing?"

"The British ones are breaking even. Those in Australia and Canada are also bleeding but we could survive if it weren't for the American ones. I've had an offer from Hearst, but it's so low it wouldn't resolve anything."

"So you're saying that if you could get a reasonable offer for the American papers, the rest would survive."

"Yes."

"Would you take a partner?"

"No! Not you Elijah!" Nancy interrupted. "You really are one of my dearest friends. We'd destroy a special friendship if we tried to work together."

Elijah nodded. "You're probably right." He reached into his pocket and glanced at the paper he removed. "By my reckoning, you need close to two million pounds to send the vultures packing."

"You really have been doing your homework haven't you?"

He shrugged. "I'll take them off your hands for two and a half."

"Montague, no!" Nancy exploded. "Don't let him turn you into his charity case! You know they're not worth it and I won't have Elijah spending his money to get us out of trouble."

"Bloody hell woman" Elijah snapped back. "You might have the title, the house and all that goes with it but underneath you're still that bloody stubborn Nancy Marshall from Mullumbimby. I need a paper in New York if I want to seriously influence those in power. I can either start one or buy one. This way we resolve each other's problem."

"Assuming I was to agree, why pay more than you have to?" Montague asked.

"So you can buy yourself a new bloody car. I'm not ready to be buried yet. I also told Nancy a few years back that I'd never forget the way she pulled me back from the edge when Miranda died" he said. "Take it as part payment."

***

The *New York Leader* proved to be exactly what Elijah was looking for. Sitting down with the paper's editor to review the business plan, two problems were immediately obvious; the lack of available cash combined with the concerted opposition from the city's major dailies to keep the *"Leader"* from growing.

Mark Frost impressed Elijah at their first meeting and quickly agreed he'd stay on as editor, but only if Elijah agreed to fund the purchase of new presses and support an aggressive push for advertising revenue. The two men reached agreement within days and met for dinner at Sardis on West 44th Street to celebrate.

Entering the restaurant, Elijah's eyes fell on a woman seated at Frost's table, possibly the only woman whose beauty came close to Mercedes. Throughout dinner, he found himself increasingly drawn to her; not only was she beautiful, she was articulate, knowledgeable and witty. The fact that she was Frost's wife didn't deter his interest in the least.

Several nights later he joined Frost for a working dinner at the editor's apartment when Mark was called to the phone. Left alone at the dining table with Amanda he asked "What do I have to do to get you on your own, really on your own?"

"Nothing. It's never going to happen. I'm perfectly satisfied with Mark. I have no intention of being stuffed and mounted in your trophy case…in fact I have no intention of being mounted by you at all."

"Am I really that bad?" he asked with a grin.

"It's not just that you're bad, I find you sleazy. If that comment's going to cost Mark his job, then so be it but I'd rather be responsible for that than for two marriages. Now would you care for coffee?" she asked as her husband re-entered the room.

Elijah didn't dwell over her rejection. Expanding the paper was too important to him. Besides, he quickly found Mark excellent to work with and totally trustworthy. The new presses were ordered and the price of the paper reduced by one cent, undercutting all the major dailies which in turn attracted additional advertising.

With the *Leader* in New York and a companion paper in Boston, Elijah sensed there was also an opportunity to expand into the Washington market and in late October 1930, he launched the *DC News Monitor*, at the same time appointing Mark Editor in Chief of all three papers.

Amanda pulled him to one side later in the week. "You've made Mark very excited" she said. "It's always been a dream of his to run a national stable of newspapers. It doesn't change anything between us, but thank you."

***

Elijah hadn't heard from Joe Kennedy since the Boston based businessman had tried to buy his film studio back in 1925. The studio had finally been bought by Howard Hughes, but Elijah and Kennedy had established a rapport. The businessman asked if Elijah would meet him next time he was in Boston.

"Be wary *amigo*. Remember how he tried to screw you when you were selling the studio. He hasn't changed by all counts." Jorge warned him. "He obviously wants something."

"That was a fancy piece of work you pulled off in Harrisburg" Kennedy commented when they met at the Lenox hotel on Boylston Street. He was referring to the recent strike at the steelworks in Pennsylvania. "I was employed by Bethlehem Steel a few years back but I'm not sure I could've got away with it."

"Well Joe, it was your deal in forming RKO Studios that convinced me to get out of movies."

The two men continued to size up one another as they exchanged small talk before Kennedy finally broached the reason for the meeting.

"I'm supporting Franklin Roosevelt's nomination as the Democrat candidate next year. I'm looking for support and funds and I'd like to have you in. Your papers could also be pretty useful."

"I'm a foreigner Joe. I don't vote in US elections."

"You do business in the USA; that's good enough for me."

"Then there's my natural tendency to support the Republicans" Elijah continued. "I'm not crazy about your lot's labour leanings. I'd also need to know a lot more about what Roosevelt's planning to do about the economy. Granted Hoover's been a disappointment, but why should I believe Roosevelt would be any better?"

As they parted company several hours later. Kennedy commented "Let me assure you Elijah, you won't regret this, I promise you."

***

"I'm heading to Europe next month" he informed Kyra a couple of weeks later. "I thought you and the boy might want to join me."

She looked up in surprise. It'd been a long time since he'd made any sort of friendly gesture towards her and her first reaction was to make a sarcastic reply. Instead, she bit her tongue and replied demurely. "That would be nice."

They travelled on the *"Ile de France"* to Le Havre in mid September, before boarding the express to Zürich where Jorge, Elvira and Patrick met them. While Kyra headed for a brief visit to Athens, Elijah told Jorge he thought he'd take a look at the operations in Porjus before the weather closed in.

"I thought you said you'd never travel back there, particularly in winter" Jorge laughed.

"It's always bloody winter in Sweden" Elijah shot back, "but if I go now I can at least beat the worst of the weather."

He decided to take the opportunity to experience travelling in one of the "new fangled" aeroplanes, and flew from Zürich to Stockholm before travelling on to Porjus by train. The Junkers aircraft so impressed him, he decided that whenever possible, all his future travel would be by air. He was still in Porjus when Jorge tracked him down to tell him that Carin Göring had died in Stockholm and that the funeral would be held early the following week.

Carin's internment in the family mausoleum on Drottningholm Island in the middle of Lake Malaran attracted a sizeable crowd of mourners. Bereft with grief, the recently widowed German politician stood alongside Agnota who in turn was holding the hand of a young boy. There was no sign of Fredrik amongst the mourners.

"How are you Elijah?" she asked softly once the service finished and he stepped across to her. "Thank you for coming."

"You're looking as beautiful as ever" he replied.

"This is Benjamin" she said introducing the young boy alongside her. He was tall for his age; fair skinned, with auburn hair and brown eyes.

"*How amazing*" Elijah thought, "*that this one should be so fair, yet Crisantro's so dark.*"

She turned to her companion. "Hermann, I am sure you remember Herr Hocking from our dinner in Stockholm a few years back."

"Yes of course." He spoke almost distractedly. "The Argentine businessman who invested in iron ore."

"Correct Herr Göring. I am truly sorry for your loss" Elijah responded.

"Thank you. I appreciate you coming. If you are ever in Berlin Herr Hocking, be sure to look me up. If there's anything you ever need…" He turned away to speak with another mourner.

"Agnota, can we meet?" Elijah asked.

"I don't think so Elijah. Let's leave things as they are. Benji knows nothing and I don't want to complicate things for him at this stage. Besides, Fredrik's currently being rather difficult and it's better I don't antagonise him in any way."

"As you wish, but you know how to contact me if you need me" he said bending and kissing her hand before departing.

***

Kyra was beside herself when Elijah returned to Zug.

"You've been screwing that bitch again haven't you?" she screamed at him as she hit at him with her clenched fists. "That's why you went to Sweden on your own. You think I don't know about you and her bastard son?"

"Why don't you go crawl back into your hole you stupid bitch" he yelled back at her. "You're drunk."

"Why won't you have me? What's so great about some frigid blond bitch?" she kept screaming at him.

Stepping towards her, he snarled back. "I would've thought you'd have been more than satisfied working your way through the male population of New York to be worried about what I might have been up to." He grabbed her by the throat and forced her to the floor. She resisted as he straddled her and pinned her down. "Is this what you want?" When he'd finished, he stood up and looked down at her.

"Happy now?" he sneered. "Christ you disgust me! Fuck off out of here you whore."

He was seated at breakfast next morning when Kyra entered the room and announced she and Crisantro were returning to New York

45

immediately.

"I'll be back when I'm finished here" was all he said in response.

"What, here or in Sweden? Are you having it off with Elvira as well?"

As Elijah jumped to his feet angrily, she ran from the room and a short time later departed the house with Crisantro.

"You're going to have to resolve that soon *amigo*" Jorge commented as they stood at the upstairs window watching the car leave. "You can't take Patrick back to that and it's not doing your other son much good either."

"Leave it Jorge, please just leave it. I'll work it out."

He'd hoped that by spending Christmas in Zug, he and Patrick might finally bond, but it was quickly obvious that his son was far more comfortable in the company of Jorge and Elvira.

"Don't let it get to you Elijah" Jorge said. "He'll come around. Just sort things out in New York so that he can come and live with you as a family."

***

When he returned to New York three months later, he found Kyra waiting for him in the apartment.

"I'm pregnant" she told him dully, forgoing any form of greeting.

"Have you worked out who the father is, or would that be too hard?"

"It's you, you bastard!"

"That's impossible" Elijah replied in his cold hard voice. "You're going to have to do better than that. Don't think for one moment that I'm going to cover for somebody else's bastard."

"Zug you arse-hole; this is what you did to me in Zug" she spat back at him. She crossed the room to the large window, but the picturesque view of the sun shining on the snow covered city failed to register in her eyes. "I want out Elijah. I want out of this marriage."

"Go back and look at the agreement" he said, a nasty edge to his voice. "You leave and you take nothing and I mean nothing, including the kids. It's quite specific in that regard. You signed it. I'll cut you off without a penny and it won't be any use turning to your father for help. Assuming he has any money, and we both know he hasn't, he wouldn't lift a finger to help you anyway."

"Oh God Elijah, has it got to the point where you hate me so much you're prepared to take it out on Crisantro and now this one too?" she cried. "It would be better for me to abort it rather than bring it into this world."

"I've put up with your whoring since the day we met" he snapped back. "It suits me to have a wife for the moment, in name anyway. You can keep spreading your legs wherever you like, but you'll remain my wife until I say it's over. Do we understand each other?

She crossed back to where he was standing, her nostrils flared and her eyes blazing with anger.

"Okay arse-hole. We'll do it your way, but the day will come when you'll pay, believe me you bastard, you *will* pay."

Without warning, she raised her arm and raked her nails across his cheek drawing blood which started dripping onto the pristine white carpet.

"You fucking bitch!" he shouted putting his hand to his cheek, pulling it back and seeing the blood smeared on it. He struck back at her, nearly lifting her from the floor with the force of the blow as she stumbled backwards and collapsed.

"You *ever* touch me again you bitch and you're dead!" he snarled with all the venom he could muster.

***

The Democrat Convention was underway in Chicago in June 1932 when Elijah received an urgent call from Joe Kennedy asking him to travel to the windy city. A voting deadlock had developed between the two rival nominees, Roosevelt and Nance Garner. As he met with

Kennedy, rival newspaper publisher Randolph Hearst joined them.

Hearst was supporting Garner's nomination but Kennedy was leaning on him to switch his support to Roosevelt. Joe hoped Elijah's presence might help. It was in both Elijah and Hearst's interests to have Hoover's Republicans defeated, but the two men disliked each other on sight. In addition Hearst was concerned that Elijah's breaking of the steel workers' strike in Pennsylvania in 1928 would be used by Roosevelt's opponents against him if it was known that Elijah was supporting his bid.

"That's fine by me" Elijah responded. "I'm happy for my papers to support Roosevelt's candidacy. As far as me contributing funds to his election campaign, I'd prefer to remain anonymous just as long as both Roosevelt and the Party leadership are aware of my support."

The long meeting resulted in Hearst finally switching his support to Roosevelt and ensuring his nomination. Elijah would become one of Roosevelt's major contributors throughout his long Presidency as well as a lifelong friend of Joe Kennedy. Hearst and Elijah however were destined to have many public differences in the future.

Once Hearst had left and they were alone, Kennedy revealed that Roosevelt was committed to repealing the prohibition laws early in his Presidency and that Kennedy himself was well advanced in negotiations to become the sole US importer of Gordon's Gin and Dewar's Scotch once this occurred.

Elijah promptly passed this news through to Jorge suggesting that they should do something similar. Despite having exited the bootlegging racket back in 1926, the distillery they had established near Mendoza in Argentina still supplied illicit grog to northern California's biggest bootlegger, Irish Murphy.[4]

"Roosevelt's a shoo-in" he assured his associate. "There's just no way Hoover will be re-elected. We could get back into the liquor business but legally this time. We switch Llyr's operation to supplying us instead of Murphy. Since it seems Prohibition's coming to an end, we're going to have to find a legitimate market for the whiskey. How about

4 The Elijah Trilogy Book 1 – The Half-breed Boy

we talk to Irish about him going legal? We could retain the exclusive franchise and appoint him as distributor. I reckon he'd go for that."

"Not a bad idea" Jorge agreed. "But we'll work through that fancy lawyer mate of his. Remember, Murphy's still nothing but a gangster."

***

Selena Hocking was born on the same day the Dow Jones Industrial Average reached its lowest level during the Great Depression. Elijah was too preoccupied with the second event to be remotely concerned about the first. It was two days before he became aware of her existence. When he finally saw her for the first time, he was immediately convinced the baby couldn't be the result of him raping Kyra in Zug – the kid was closer in skin tones to her Swedish half brother Benji than she was to her brother Crisantro. By the time Kyra was discharged from hospital, all her belongings had been relocated to an apartment Elijah owned on Manhattan Avenue between 107th and 108th Streets.

"Why Elijah? I thought you'd decided we were staying married."

"We are…for the moment. I also told you I wouldn't have someone else's bastard fobbed off on me. She's got my name which is more than she deserves, but that's where it starts and finishes."

"I'm telling you she's yours you cold-hearted bastard; at least give Selena a chance even if you won't believe me" she pleaded.

"The matter's closed" he said walking off.

***

As Kennedy forecast, one of Roosevelt's first actions after taking office was to declare the Blaine Act repealing prohibition in the United States in early 1933. By the time Prohibition was officially repealed by Congress later that year, Jorge had set up the new legal entity to distribute liquor legally imported from the Argentine distillery they had established to supply bootleg liquor to the United States during prohibition.

But if legal liquor was to be a steady contributor to Elijah's increasing wealth over the next few years, it was nothing compared to the other form of liquid gold that he literally tapped into two years earlier. In January 1931, Elijah received a letter from a farmer in Texas seeking financial backing to test-drill for oil on his farm near Kilgore in the east of the state. Oil had already been found nearby, but due to the depth of the reserves, the cost of drilling was prohibitive and out of reach of most small farmers during the height of the Great Depression. Normally Elijah would've forwarded the letter to Jorge but there was something in the way it was written that intrigued him. He immediately travelled to Kilgore and met the farmer.

Deke Newell was thirty-three years old. At first he seemed to be a typical southern dirt farmer, but appearances were deceptive. The Newell family had farmed cotton in the area since the 1880's, but were hit hard by the collapse in both demand and prices as the Great Depression took hold.

His brother Wilson dabbled in geology at school. He'd never graduated but always believed that oil existed in the area. A couple of earlier efforts at drilling in the 1920's were unsuccessful and the costs contributed to the decline in the family's fortunes. In October 1930, when oil had been struck near the neighbouring town of Henderson at a depth of over 3,500 feet, Deke wrote letters to a number of major companies. When he received the letter, Elijah recalled having recently read that there'd been two other strikes nearby in the previous three months.

There was something about the Newell brothers that Elijah liked immediately He decided to place his trust in them and finance a renewed drilling campaign on the Newell farm. He didn't stay long enough to see them strike oil on their second drilling attempt at 3,600 feet, resulting in a gusher that came in at a spectacular 17,000 barrels a day.

"What the hell made you back them?" Jorge asked when Elijah first told him what he'd done.

"It seemed like pocket money. It was an unusual letter. I nearly tore it up, but then I recalled the newspaper reports. Kyra was driving me crazy at the time so I went to Texas to escape from her. When I met them, my first thought was these are honest men. It seemed so long since I'd met one that on the spur of the moment I said yes. It was the luck of the draw; a month either way and I'd probably have binned the letter."

The strike resulted in the formation of Mercedes Occidental Oil in October 1931 which Deke would head for the next fifty years.

Chapter 6

Just as Jorge predicted ten years before when Elijah first moved to the United States, Roosevelt's inauguration in March 1933 saw legislators on both sides of politics seeking Elijah's counsel and favours. That night he did the rounds of a number of inauguration balls. At the Spanish Embassy, he was in conversation with the Argentine Ambassador when they were joined by a woman in her early thirties.

"Señor Hocking, may I introduce Señorita Carrasquillo. She is a Counsellor with the Spanish Embassy here in Washington."

"You are alone *Señorita*?" Elijah asked. "There is no Señor Carrasquillo?"

"It's obvious you're not with the Diplomatic Corps Señor Hocking" she replied, trying not to smile. "You're too direct."

"I apologise. I hadn't meant to be rude. It's just that I'm surprised to find someone...someone of your youth in such a position."

"Surely you mean an unmarried woman don't you? It's refreshing to meet someone who is prepared to discuss it openly. Most people skirt around the subject as though it's an infectious disease. Now it's my turn; I detect that Spanish is not your mother tongue."

It was Elijah's turn to smile. "Guilty as charged. Argentine by marriage *Señorita*."

"Your wife, is she with you?"

"Mercedes has been dead a number of years. My current wife is in

New York."

When he mentioned that he'd been related by marriage to the de Sestao family, she was intrigued and decided to learn more about him.

It was another three months before Elijah bumped into her again at a reception being hosted by his Congressman friend, Michael Leveridge. Once again he was struck by her poise and demeanour; a complete contrast to Kyra but when he asked her to dinner, she declined.

"I'm sorry but I make it a practice not to dine with married men, especially when they're not accompanied by their wives."

When he recounted this to Jorge, his colleague's comment much to Elijah's chagrin was "This woman's not for you *amigo*, she obviously has taste and scruples."

Not about to be put off, Elijah arranged for Mark and Amanda Frost to host a dinner in Washington for a number of politicians and the diplomatic corps, ensuring that Amanda seated him next to Sophia. She left impressed with his knowledge of events in Spain and by his concern for the de Sestao family should Spain descend into Civil War despite Mercedes' death having effectively severed his relationship with the family.

***

Throughout the first half of 1934, they continued to meet at functions but never alone. Elijah could tell she was interested, but she made it clear there was no possibility of a relationship as long as he was married. Finally, she asked him to stop calling her.

"My parents had a very tempestuous marriage" she told him. "My father had one mistress in Madrid and another in Valencia. Because my parents were practising Catholics, neither would agree to a divorce. As a result we children grew up in a climate of constant hostility.

"My father was not in the least subtle about his relationships. He believed that by attending confession regularly and contributing to the church's coffers he would be absolved of all sin. Certainly the priests did nothing to deter him from this belief. My mother on the other hand constantly wore the demeanour of a martyr. She too sought counsel from the priests and the nuns so that our house was never a home, more a place of discord and discipline for the slightest transgression. I swore I'd never allow myself to be put in that position. I won't deny I enjoy your company Elijah, but I can't meet with you any longer."

"But my wife and I live apart" he told her, "it's a marriage in name only."

"Nonetheless" she said, "it's still a marriage." She pulled on her gloves and leaned over and kissed his forehead. "You're a very nice man. I wish there could be more, but there can't."

Rejection didn't come easily. He tried calling her several times but she refused to take his calls. On both occasions he sent her flowers, they were returned.

Finally he called Jorge. "Get rid of the bitch" he told him.

"I warned you before you married her that Kyra was trouble. It won't be easy or cheap. The agreement says she can't leave you but if you push her out, then you're going to have to pay."

"Come on Jorge, she's nothing but a whore. She has been from the moment I met her."

"You'll get no argument from me *amigo*, but you said it yourself… you've known that all along."

"Then it sounds like I'll have to do it some other way" Elijah said bitterly. "Johnny will know what to do."

"Don't be a fool Elijah. Everyone's aware of the state of the relationship between the two of you. If anything happened to her, they'll come looking for you."

Jorge's comment pulled Elijah up short. No-one had dared to call him a fool for years, and he was damned if he was about to start taking it now, not even from Jorge.

"You're the one who set the bloody thing up! You bloody well fix it!" he snapped and slammed the phone down in anger.

***

Kyra threw her head back in laughter when she received Jorge's letter saying Elijah wanted a divorce. It was a long time since she'd felt this good.

"The bastard had his opportunity a couple of times when *I* wanted out and he turned me down flat" she told her lawyer. "He can pay not just for the divorce, but the public humiliation I've suffered from the day I married him…and for raping me. If he thinks I'm going cheaply or easily, then the news is all bad."

After months of bitter wrangling, Jorge finally told Elijah that he'd have to meet her, saying it was the only way it could be resolved.

"Cut off the bitch's funds immediately" Elijah responded. "Put her on the street. I want her out of my life now."

"Hearst's papers will love that. Just meet her and give her a little victory."

"Okay I'll meet, but on her own. No lawyers, no witnesses" he finally agreed. "but she better not get any ideas of any 'little victory'."

Jorge sighed. He knew Elijah well enough to know that he was the one who'd demand the victorious outcome.

Kyra eventually agreed to meet but insisted on doing so publicly. They finally settled on 21 at West 52nd Street for dinner.

"You're looking good" she greeted him, typically arriving late.

"I can't say the same about you" he replied nastily, "You look like you're still plying your trade."

"Well arse-hole" she replied with a laugh as she removed her coat and sat down, "every insult increases the price, so fire away."

He bit his tongue, asking instead about the children while they both ordered. "What's it going to take to have you piss off?" he finally asked.

"Jorge has the figure." She smiled at him, a victorious glint in her eyes. "Tell me *darling*, what's it like not to be in control? I told you that you'd pay. You know, right now it suits me to have a husband, in name only. You can go when I'm ready."

Elijah silently fixed her with his cold hard stare for over a minute.

Involuntarily she shivered as she realised she'd probably pushed him too far. Slowly, he leaned forward grabbing her knee under the table between his thumb and forefinger, digging deep into the joint. While she gasped and flinched at the pain, he spoke quietly so that only she could hear him.

"Listen to me you bitch. You're going to have to watch over your shoulder every minute of every day, and if you can actually get off your back, every night as well. Believe me, *darling*, I can fix it so you'll have an accident that'll satisfy the cops as to its authenticity. You won't be the first piece of filth I've disposed of. You play games with me, then you're going to have to watch every shadow, worry about every car that drives towards you or backfires, be fearful of anyone who gets into an elevator with you or bumps up against you at the counter in Bloomingdale's. You'll have to double guess whether the repairman is legit or really a paid assassin. Not in control *darling*? You couldn't even start to conceive what control is."

"You're hurting me" she cried out. "Please Elijah, let me go."

He applied extra pressure to her knee before releasing it.

"If you think that's pain you slut, believe me, you've experienced nothing yet" he said, suddenly smiling amicably as their waiter approached.

"I expect a cable from your toy boy on Jorge's desk by tomorrow night agreeing the terms of the divorce. You know I'm serious so don't even think about playing any more games. I wouldn't repeat this conversation to lover boy or the cops either. I can have any investigation brought to a stop immediately."

He called for the bill before standing up. Leaning over her, to anyone watching them, he appeared to kiss her on the cheek.

"Nice happy couple aren't we?" he whispered. "I'm right aren't I? You're screwing the boy wonder lawyer instead of paying him a fee aren't you? Have a nice rest of your life Kyra. It's up to you how long it lasts."

She turned white as he said his goodbyes and stayed seated for five minutes after he'd gone, struggling to bring her shaking under control. She realised exactly what he was capable of and genuinely feared for her life.

Elijah left the restaurant seething. For the first time he felt Jorge had let him down.

"I should've met with the bitch months ago and settled things instead of letting the lawyers get involved" he thought to himself as he hailed a cab, *"and it's cost me a shitload of money as well."*

***

The story was carried prominently on page three of the *DC News Monitor* in late October, 1933.

> *Prominent businessman Elijah Hocking and his wife Kyra were granted a Decree Nisi by the New York Supreme Court yesterday on the grounds of irreconcilable differences.*
>
> *Mr Hocking, an Argentine national, is the proprietor of the DC News Monitor and Chairman of a number of companies including Mercedes Steel Inc. He came to prominence in 1928 during the strikes in Pennsylvania following the merger of several steel companies which resulted in 33 deaths. During the strike, shots were fired at his car.*
>
> *Mrs Kyra Hocking is the daughter of prominent Greek shipping tycoon Stavros Michaelides. The couple have two children.*

Elijah still blamed his compatriot of ineptitude in finalising the divorce and waited another month before extracting his revenge.

"Patrick needs a rounded education" he told Jorge on a transatlantic call in late November. "I've enrolled him at Eton College in England. He'll start the New Year term in January. I'll come to Zug and collect him and take him to the school. Now that the whore's finally gone, he can start coming home where he belongs for holidays."

When he returned to Zug in late January from delivering his tearful son to Eton, Elvira was still upset with him. Patrick was the son she and Jorge had never had.

"He could've gone to school here in Switzerland, instead of all the way to England. There's no-one there for him" she sniffed.

"One day he'll come into the business" Elijah replied. "He needs the best education available. There's no better place than Eton. He'll round out his education at Yale or Princeton so that he gains experience from both sides of the Atlantic. He couldn't get that on the continent in the current environment. Just look at the situation in Germany; there's the smell of war approaching all over again."

Jorge took the opportunity to change the subject. "Talking of Germany Elijah, there's a problem emerging in our negotiations to supply additional iron ore from Porjus. The Swedish state organisations at Kiruna are trying to squeeze us out on price. They've also restricted our access on the railway to Narvik. If we could get additional contracts in Germany, it'd put production back onto a five day week and the operations back in the black."

"The last time I saw Agnota's friend Hermann Göring at his wife's funeral, he told me that if I ever needed assistance in Germany I should call him. Perhaps I should go to Berlin since I'm so close and see if he can help" Elijah suggested.

"I was hoping you'd say that. It'd be a good idea to go on to Stockholm as well. I'm sure that Agnota's circle of friends includes someone useful to help resolve the impasse with the railway."

***

Landing at Templehof Airport, Elijah was surprised at the air of prosperity and the number of uniforms to be seen everywhere he looked as he drove into the city. He hadn't been to Berlin since the Nazis had assumed power the previous year. Even though he'd read the press reports coming out of Germany, he was still shocked by the number of shop fronts plastered with anti-Jewish propaganda signs reading *"Buy only at German Shops"*.

The following morning a member of Göring's staff collected him from the Adlon Hotel and drove him the short distance along Unter den Linden to Göring's Kaiserdamm apartment. His own attempts to meet with the German leader had been unsuccessful. Turning to Agnota for assistance, an appointment had been confirmed within forty-eight hours.

Ushered into Göring's presence, Germany's second most powerful man strode across the carpet, his hand extended in greeting.

"Welcome to the Third Reich Herr Hocking. It's good to see you again." He shook hands vigorously, continuing "I haven't forgotten your immense kindness in attending Carin's funeral." Summoning coffee, the Nazi leader continued. "Follow me my friend. I'm sure you'll appreciate the opportunity to show your respects once again."

He conducted his intrigued visitor to an adjacent room which had been set up as a shrine to his deceased wife. A small altar was draped in cloth over which was mounted a photo of Carin. Not sure what was expected of him, Elijah closed his eyes so that he appeared to be saying a prayer. It obviously pleased his host who put his arm around Elijah's shoulders and steered him back to the room next door when he'd finished.

"I usually conduct business at the Reich Air Ministry, but I prefer to receive personal acquaintances here" he explained. "Now how can I be of assistance?"

Elijah explained the predicament PMAB was experiencing in reaching agreement with German negotiators to supply additional ore. Göring listened attentively before turning to his adjutant.

"Fix it!" he said

Turning back to Elijah he asked "How long do you intend staying in Germany Herr Hocking?"

"I was planning on staying several days. I've been most impressed with the changes I've seen since I've been here."

Turning back to his adjutant, Göring instructed him to provide

Elijah a car and driver for the balance of his stay in Berlin.

"You must also have dinner with Fräulein Emmy Sonnermann and me" he said standing to indicate the meeting was over. "I'm planning to make her my wife."

His reunion with Agnota was equally fruitful, thanks to her introduction to the Swedish Minister for Railways.

"I'm sorry Agnota" Elijah said to her as they sat over lunch. "It must be very hard for you."

Fredrik, a heavy smoker, had contracted cancer and terminally ill, rarely ventured from his bed.

"I don't wish to appear heartless" she replied, "but his early death would be the best result for the three of us" referring to Benji.

"And what do you plan to do then?" he asked gently, the intent of his question patently obvious.

"No Elijah" she replied, shaking her head, "before you raise your hopes or say anything, you and I would never work. You're a special friend and always will be. We share a bond in Benji, but I'm happy here in Sweden. I'm not equipped for the life you lead. It would only be a matter of time before we started to drift apart. I'm happy to see you whenever you come to Sweden and to help you any way I can, but that's all. There's also Benji to consider; he doesn't know about you and I want it to stay that way. But I'd love to take coffee with you in your room following lunch" she added with a mischievous gleam in her eye.

Chapter 7

New York City, U.S.A.
April 1935

Once his divorce from Kyra became absolute, he immediately called Mark. "I need a favour. A limited edition copy of the *DC News Monitor*."

"How limited?"

"One copy, special delivery to an address in Georgetown."

Sophia found the paper tied with a red ribbon pushed through the letterbox of her townhouse the following morning. The front page headline read in large bold letters – *"ELIJAH HOCKING DIVORCE FINAL"*. Beneath in smaller letters was the sub-title *"Businessman Free to Pursue Spanish Counsellor"*.

It was mid-afternoon before she managed to track him down at Deke Newell's farmhouse in Kilgore.

"Smooth, very smooth *Señor*" she said when he took the phone.

"So when can I see you?" he asked.

"Call me when you're next in town" she replied, "and I'll check my appointment diary. I'm sure something can be arranged."

It was a very surprised Sophia who answered the door to her townhouse the following evening. Standing with his back to her, was a deliveryman dressed in a uniform and cap.

"Ain't airplanes a marvellous invention?" he said turning around, a grin from ear to ear, two dozen red roses held in his arms.

Despite his divorce, Sophia proceeded cautiously, determined not to be rushed. Equally, she wouldn't enter into a de facto relationship. Using the cover of her work, she kept him at arm's length whilst Elijah chafed at the bit, frustrated at her attitude.

In July, he brought Patrick home with him from Britain on the new *"Queen Mary"* for the boy's summer break and invited Sophia to join them at a house near Hyannis Port recommended to him by Joe Kennedy. For the first three days, father and son roamed the beaches along Nantucket Sound while Elijah tried unsuccessfully to connect with the unhappy withdrawn boy. Patrick had little in common with his father; a distant figure who occasionally visited him at Uncle Jorge and Aunt Elvira's house in Zug. *That* was where he desperately wanted to be.

Sophia arrived the following weekend for several days and immediately took in the sight of the miserable boy and his increasingly frustrated father.

"Thank God you're here" Elijah said, "I'm at my wits' end. Nothing I do is right and the kid's totally non-communicative. Perhaps he might respond to you."

"I'm not his mother Elijah, but I'll see what I can do."

When she left three days later, Patrick had thawed enough to tell her that he missed his aunt and uncle in Zug and that he blamed his father for taking him away from them.

"Why don't you ask if you can split your summer holidays with them?" she suggested. "You know, your father loves you very much. He misses you terribly and he's trying to make up for all the lost time."

"He didn't want me for all those years" Patrick said through his tears, "What's the difference now? He'll only go away again anyway."

"Give him a try Patrick. Would you like me to talk to him about splitting time between him and your uncle and aunt?" she asked.

He hesitated before slowly nodding his head. Sophia's message to his father was similar. "Be patient with him Elijah, after all they're the only family he's known for most of his life."

Reluctantly, he took her advice, travelling back to Europe a week later with Patrick. Before returning to New York, Jorge counselled him. "We'll work on him *amigo*, but this idea of your woman's is worth trying. Why don't you take him during spring term break, we'll have him in winter and split the summer holidays between us."

It wasn't Elijah's idea of the ideal solution but there seemed to be little alternative.

***

From Zug he headed straight to Chicago where Mark Frost was negotiating to buy a small up and coming afternoon daily. Try as he might to focus on the negotiations, Elijah's mind kept wandering during the meetings with the paper's owner, an intense young man flattered by their interest in him.

"You're not really with it are you buddy?" Mark commented as they left one of the meetings. "Can you remember the circulation figures he's predicting for 1938, or the current cost he's paying for newsprint?"

Elijah's ability to understand and retain details was well known to all his associates. "You're right. I'm hindering rather than helping you. I have to admit my mind's elsewhere. From what I've seen, the paper's a good fit. You carry on and keep Jorge and me in the loop. Whatever you decide, I'll back your judgement."

He immediately flew to Washington DC to propose to Sophia, convinced that the obvious synergy between them would lead to her acceptance.

"I'm sorry Elijah" she said over dinner the next evening. "I really like you but I told you before, when I marry it has to be for keeps. I don't want a repeat of my parents' marriage and your own last effort was hardly inspiring from the little I saw of it."

"What do I have to do to convince you you're wrong?"

"I need commitment, total commitment. I don't see it in you. If I even suspected that you were seeing another woman, I'd walk; I wouldn't hang around for the proof. Let's just leave things as they are and see how they progress" she added, "that is, if you're prepared to hang around of course."

He'd hang around all right. "Project Sophia", as it'd become, was taking on all the elements of another business deal; an acquisition he was determined to conclude at all costs.

***

She finally succumbed to his charms in early 1936 not long after he returned from spending Christmas in Zug. The wedding was held in the last week of June. Sophia, despite confessing to being a lapsed Catholic, initially insisted on being married in Church, but with Elijah's recent divorce, this avenue was closed to them. That was fine by Elijah...he had no desire to enter a church, let alone be married in one.

They were honeymooning on the Northern Spanish Costa Verde when the Spanish Civil War broke out in July. For the first few days of the conflict they bunkered down in the small town of Cudillero. Sophia was convinced that since the area supported the government in Madrid, they would be safer there for the moment. Within a week though, their position became more tenuous as the rebel army sought to cut Spain's northern provinces off from the bulk of the government's forces in the south of the country.

Despite Mercedes' death back in 1921, Elijah had remained in contact with her Uncle Carlos. The de Sestao estate near Bilbao, now owned by Carlos, was only about two hundred and fifty kilometres east of where they were staying. After a few days, Elijah decided they should head there to take refuge. The roads were jammed with military traffic and refugees and progress was slow. It took them nearly three days to cover the distance between the two towns.

"We're not hanging around Carlos" Elijah told him on arrival. "I've already spoken to Jorge and one of my ships is in the Bay of Biscay en route to Antwerp. It's been diverted to Bilbao. She's due tomorrow. This uprising's looking serious; why don't you and your family come with us and sit it out?"

"I won't leave Bilbao, at least not yet" Carlos replied. "From all counts the rebel generals expected this coup to be quick and decisive, but something went wrong for them. I believe it will collapse and that the government will be victorious. I will be quite safe here in the north but I would appreciate you taking Alda and the younger ones along with you just to be sure."

"I'm more than happy to, but where will they go to?"

"I followed your suggestion a number of years ago my friend and bought a property in Bayonne just over the border in France. They will make their way there to wait while we see what happens here in Spain. I would have sent them by road already, but I hear that it is difficult to cross the border at Irun due to the fighting."

The following night, Elijah and Sophia along with Carlos' wife Alda, his two daughters-in-law and their children embarked on the *"Doña Consuela"*. Once the ship had docked in Bordeaux, Elijah insisted on accompanying Carlos' family to their house in Bayonne. Only then did he and Sophia head to Zug where Jorge and Elvira were immediately smitten with Sophia.

"She's perfect" Elvira told him as they stood together on the terrace admiring the setting sun mirrored in the glassy surface of the lake beneath them. "She seems to be your equal on so many levels. I could never understand why you went ahead and married Kyra despite all the warnings, or why you insisted in putting yourself through hell for all those years. I predict a long and happy marriage for the two of you. As much as I don't want to lose him, you should have the chance to give Patrick a happy environment to come home to now."

"You understand it was never for either of us" Elijah replied pensively. "Once Kyra told me she was pregnant it was always for the child but that backfired too. Instead of giving Crisantro a stable childhood with a mother and a father, all he got was total warfare. I don't seem fated to be a good father," he continued wistfully. "First Patrick and now the other two."

***

They moved on to England where they stayed a few days with Nancy and Montague at Elphinbrook House. An immediate bond was struck between the two women.

"Has Elijah told you how we met?" Nancy asked over dinner.

"Briefly. Something about you being a petulant spoilt daughter of Australian aristocracy."

Nancy roared with laughter. "Australian aristocracy! My God my mother would've loved that! I didn't know such a thing existed." She looked across at Elijah. "I guess that makes you a Caribbean Prince or something."

Elijah had briefly told Sophia of the story of his childhood and his subsequent search for his parents, but it'd been little more than a synopsis. She sat spellbound as Nancy and Elijah traced his birth on Nanderra Station in outback Queensland, his removal to the Catholic Mission near Brisbane, and how he subsequently ran away.[5]

"I met Nancy on her father's sugar cane farm when I briefly worked there. A more precocious brat you'd never meet."

"It must come with being a member of the Australian aristocracy" she interrupted before breaking into laughter again.

"We didn't meet again until after Mercedes death...my first wife" he added for Montague's benefit. "By then Nancy really was aristocracy. Not long after that I met a woman who it was claimed was my real mother."

"Don't stop there Elijah" Nancy prompted him. "Tell them where you met."

"A lunatic asylum."

"Which one was the inmate?" Sophia asked.

Nancy roared with laughter again. "Sorry" she said seeing Elijah's face darken. "It wasn't funny at the time was it? Anyway it opened a can of worms for my poor darling here."

"Adelaide was white. I'd always assumed my mother was an

Aboriginal woman called Rosie. Even now I don't know the truth" he explained to Sophia.

"I called it my dime-store novel mystery" Nancy interjected. "Anyway after a lot of work by some of Montague's best investigative reporters, we discovered Elijah's father was actually the overseer who'd whipped him and thrown him off Nanderra. He'd been born in Jamaica of coloured parents but was what's called a throwback. The white genes from his ancestors were predominant leaving him looking white. He'd disappeared and taken a new name in Australia. When Elijah was born coloured, he threatened Hargreaves' exposure."

"So he shipped you off to a mission instead?" Sophia asked astonished.

"It seems so" Elijah acknowledged. "I don't think he knew about my birth initially. It seems he was away droving cattle when I was born. Anyway he had me removed from my mother – the Aboriginal one that is – and when I challenged him as to who my mother really was twenty years later, he just laughed at me." He stopped and stared into the distance before continuing. "They're all dead now so it doesn't matter. Just which one was my mother is immaterial since neither of them was ever there for me anyway."

"You've never spoken of this before" Sophia said, a look of astonishment on her face.

"It wasn't important" he said standing up and crossing to the drinks table indicating the subject was closed.

***

Elijah continued to fret over Carlos's safety in Bilbao as the rebel armies turned east towards the city. The fall of the Spanish garrison at San Sebastian and the subsequent barbaric bombing and destruction of the northern Spanish city of Guernica by German and Italian aircraft in April with heavy loss of life alarmed Elijah. Once again, he implored Mercedes' uncle to escape since it seemed only a matter of time before the northern coastline of Spain, including Bilbao, would fall to

Franco's army supported as it was by the Condor Legion of Germany's Luftwaffe.

Sophia's parents who lived near Zaragoza in central Spain were also coming under threat from the advancing nationalist armies. Her father, a Republican supporter, had abandoned his wife and family by fleeing to Valencia into the arms of his mistress. Like Carlos, Sophia's mother refused to move from her house and rebuffed all offers to have her taken out of Spain.

"What is it about these bloody Spaniards?" Elijah asked her in exasperation one night. "They place themselves in danger by staying where they are, but do you think they'll move to safety? I don't understand them."

He'd become quite fond of Mercedes' uncle and still regarded him as family. Later that month with Bilbao now under siege from the rebels, he decided to travel to Bayonne to organise a clandestine rescue attempt when word filtered through of the aristocrat's death from a combined attack on the de Sestao mansion from a German dive bomber and artillery located in the surrounding hills.

Elijah took Carlos's death hard and for many years continued to blame himself for not having been able to convince the Spaniard of the increasing danger and the need to retreat to his family in Bayonne.

***

For the balance of 1936 and the first half of 1937 he based himself in New York, limiting his travel in the main to Washington, Boston and Chicago. Sophia travelled with him whenever he undertook one of his business trips and her sophistication and personality became the talk of the town, particularly in the nation's capital where politicians, diplomats and public servants fell over themselves to have them attend functions.

Time magazine referred to them as the "new power couple" and Eleanor Roosevelt enlisted Sophia to join her Works Progress Association which sought to provide additional employment opportunities for women. With his newspapers supporting the President in his successful 1936 re-election bid, Elijah gained ready access to all levels of government.

Business was also slowly improving on most fronts. As Italian migration to Argentina increased, two of the liners were moved to the Mediterranean to service the migrant trade. Jorge continued to acquire new businesses; a ball bearing manufacturer in New Jersey, a sugar cane plantation in Cuba where they planned to establish a rum distillery and stevedoring operations in Argentina at the three main ports servicing his agricultural interests; Buenos Aires, Rosario and Bahia Blanca. Since the labour situation at the steel mills in Pennsylvania had settled down and Johnny's talents were no longer needed to keep the unions there in line, he was despatched to manage the Argentine wharf operations.

"Conditions on the docks are pretty chaotic" Elijah briefed him. "The only reason we've invested in the stevedoring operations is to bring some sort of order to our exports. The rolling strikes we've been experiencing, particularly in Buenos Aires, are playing havoc with our shipping schedules and we've recently lost customers because of the delays through strikes. It's too easy for them to get their wheat and beef elsewhere. You have a totally free hand in cleaning the wharves up. Jorge has a list of the major labour leaders for you to study and he's set up top level government contacts for you to develop. They'll be beneficial to your operations. You'll find they'll turn a blind eye to your methods as they have their own reasons for wanting to settle scores with the unions...but Johnny, no brothels; you're out of that type of business these days" referring to Johnny's stint as owner of a high-class bordello when he last lived in Buenos Aires.

Even Patrick entered into an uneasy truce with his father as he formed a bond with Sophia. But the boy still remained wary of Elijah, seeing him as someone to be feared rather than loved.

.

Chapter 8

Agnota's message was quite insistent. *"Hermann's asking when you will next be in Germany. He has something he wishes to discuss with you, something that he won't even talk about with me."*

Göring was now head of the Reich Four Year Plan and with PMAB shipping ever-increasing quantities of iron ore from Porjus to Germany, Elijah was intrigued by the message. Discussing the unusual request with Jorge, they both agreed he should travel to Berlin.

Berlin was hardly his favourite city, nor Germany his favourite country. Despite the outward display of prosperity, an underlying stench of evil pervaded the environment. Everywhere he looked there were many more uniforms on display this time around. For the first time since they were married, Sophia didn't accompany him on one of his trips; Elijah couldn't put his finger on why, but he didn't want her exposed to the tyranny of Nazi Germany. Besides, she was midway through her first pregnancy.

An earnest looking adjutant met him at the foot of the aircraft stairs, clicking his heels together and extending his arm in the outstretched Nazi salute before leading Elijah to the nearby Mercedes-Benz cabriolet. "The Reichsminister has arranged for you stay at his estate at Carinhall *mein Herr*. I am to accompany you there" the young man advised him.

Flanked by motorcycle outriders, with a security detail in vehicles ahead and behind, the convoy sped through the countryside scattering all other traffic in its path. Carinhall was a substantial estate set in the forest northeast of Berlin. The large house had been dedicated to Carin Göring and her body moved there from her family burial plot near Stockholm to a specially built mausoleum.

On arrival, Elijah was conducted to the library and advised that Göring would join him shortly. He found himself in a room over seventy feet long and nearly forty feet wide dominated by a huge picture window overlooking the nearby lake. Stepping towards the window to enjoy the view, he was brought up short by a familiar voice.

"Elijah *älskling*, I wondered when you were going to arrive, I was starting to get a little bored waiting for you."

He turned, his face beaming in delight.

"Agnota, I didn't know you were going to be here. What an unexpected pleasure."

"It was Hermann's idea" she explained as they embraced. "He thought it might be fun for us all to meet up together again."

They were standing at the window talking when the massive library doors behind them were thrown open and their host strode in.

"Jesus Christ, he looks like blubber in motion" Elijah thought to himself as Göring crossed the library to join them.

"Mein liebchen Agnota, you look more beautiful every time I see you" he said bowing and kissing her hand, "and Herr Hocking, it's so good to see you again. It's been too long."

He shook Elijah's hand vigorously before directing them to sit down.

"Emmy will join us at dinner" he continued. "She's expecting our first child in six weeks and is resting at present. I'm told your wife is also expecting Herr Hocking."

"Yes Reichsminister; in our case it will be in about twelve weeks."

"Your first?"

"No, our first, but I've had several others by previous marriages."

After thirty minutes of small talk, Göring excused himself saying he had official business to attend to.

**

Dinner turned out to be a grand affair held in a room equally as large as the library where they were joined by a heavily pregnant Emmy. Throughout the meal, Göring monopolised the conversation, launching into a long discourse on the evils of the Versailles Treaty, International Jewry and the rise of Nazi Germany despite the efforts of the treaty restrictions. Since Elijah personally had no time for any form of religion, he found the obsession the Nazis had with the Jews boring and he quickly switched off from the conversation. Since it was little more than a monologue, this proved relatively easy to do. He was wondering how he might excuse himself without upsetting his host, when Göring leaned towards him.

"Do you hunt by any chance Herr Hocking? We maintain magnificent herds of boar and deer here at Carinhall."

"I'm sorry Reichsminister, but I'm a lousy shot."

Göring looked perplexed. "Lousy? What is this lousy?" he asked, a frown forming on his face.

Elijah laughed. "I'm sorry. It is an Australian word that I use from time to time. It means poor, or in my case terrible."

"Ah" Göring replied nodding his head knowingly. "I will remember to use the word next time I'm in a meeting with Himmler discussing his SS. Lousy" he said a couple of times, testing his pronunciation before continuing. "Back to the matter of the hunt. I was planning a shoot tomorrow morning. Perhaps you would join me; just the two of us."

"I would be delighted Reichsminister" Elijah replied although nothing was further than the truth. The evening's conversation had been bad enough, but at least Agnota and Emmy had been present to give some relief, but he didn't know if he could stand another monologue if it was only the two of them. There were sure to be more lectures on the Jews he thought to himself, but perhaps he would also be told the reason he was here.

It was another hour before he was able to excuse himself. He was heading to his room when Agnota caught up with him.

"Coffee?" she asked in a half whisper.

Next morning Elijah found a complete shooting outfit laid out for him on the settee in his room. Once dressed, he proceeded to the courtyard to find his host fitted out in a medieval hunting costume which accentuated his enormous girth. He was surrounded by a phalanx of security guards, beaters, hounds and gamekeepers.

"So much for just the two of us" Elijah thought. *"Just what the hell's going on?"*

The "hunt" proved to be a farce. Elijah had imagined that they would set off into the forest in search of game to shoot. Instead, the retinue of beaters fanned out ahead of them, selecting suitable animals which they drove into the path of the two men. Göring bagged three adult male deer, each endowed with the most magnificent set of antlers, as well as two boars while Elijah managed to down one oversize boar.

It was nearly two hours before Göring lowered his gun and suggested to Elijah they stop and talk. He waved the retinue of followers away out of hearing before lowering his ample bottom onto an adjacent log.

"Join me" he instructed Elijah. Taking a large hooked pipe from his pocket, he tamped and lit it, exhaling deeply before speaking.

***

"I have a delicate request to ask of you" he began. "My wife has some associates from her time as an actress who…" he hesitated a moment before continuing, "…who are Jewish. They mean a great deal to her and she's keen they be assisted to leave the Third Reich."

Elijah sat quietly waiting for him to continue.

"I assumed you have some form of Jewish link and would be able to assist them" Göring continued.

For a moment Elijah was perplexed that his fat companion may have thought he was Jewish.

"You've been misinformed Herr Göring. Elijah is also a name used by Christians from the scriptures. My parents, as many of their generation did, used the Bible as a reference when naming their children."

"I see. However, be that as it may, are you able to assist? You realise that in my position I cannot afford to be involved directly, but in this special case I don't wish to disappoint Emmy. She has her heart set on them being allowed to leave."

"Herr Reichsminister, I've made it my firm policy never to be involved in two matters throughout my life; religion and politics" Elijah replied.

Göring looked sharply at him; a flash of anger flitted across his face and his eyes hardened before Elijah continued. "However I haven't forgotten your kindness in intervening on my behalf four years ago in regards to supplying iron ore. I'd be honoured to assist you, and Emmy, on this occasion. Of course I'll need some assistance with papers which I am sure you can arrange."

As he spoke, the anger reflected in Göring's face disappeared. His host broke into a broad smile as he leaned across and clapped Elijah on the knee.

"My dear fellow," he said. "Of course! Anything you require. You need only ask. I won't forget this my friend. I'll arrange for all their details to be delivered to you. The couple in question are currently in Munich. Once the arrangements are made, I'll have you flown there. In fact I'm flying to Berchtesgarten tomorrow to meet with the Führer. You'll fly there with me so that I can introduce you to him."

He wasn't sure he wanted to meet Hitler, but it was obvious that Göring wasn't about to accept no as an answer. To his surprise, Agnota was also included in the party that travelled in convoy the following day to board Göring's personal aircraft at Templehof.

"I thought your relationship was with Carin rather than Hermann."

"It was initially but after she died, Hermann and I became closer as he was getting over her death. He was also very kind to me in turn when Fredrik died."

"And now?"

"No Elijah, we don't have coffee in my room...or his" she added with a smile, "but we've remained good friends and he finds me useful when he wants to get in touch with mutual friends such as you."

"So what's he trying to achieve by having us here together; and don't tell me that he thought it would be fun for us all to get together for old time's sake. I just won't buy it."

"I really don't know. I've also been wondering, but it's possible that he's just being friendly. What was so important that he had you travel to Germany to go shooting with him?"

"Just that Agnota, he wanted to go shooting and discuss my Jewish heritage" he said evasively.

"You? A Jew?" she laughed. "Wherever did he get that idea?"

He shrugged. "No idea, but he seemed quite disappointed when I told him there wasn't a skerrick of Jewish blood in me."

***

In Salzburg they boarded Göring's private train to Berchtesgarten before transferring to a convoy of cars and setting off up the winding mountain road to Göring's chalet located next to Hitler's Berghof retreat inside a heavily fortified area.

Elijah finally met the Führer two days later. The experience was at once an anti-climax, yet chilled him to his core. Introduced to the dictator by Göring at afternoon tea on the terrace of Hitler's house, Elijah found himself surrounded by a number of the Nazi hierarchy he immediately recognised from photographs; the new German elite including figures like Josef Goebbels, Heinrich Himmler and Robert Ley.

Elijah had an image in his mind from newspaper photos and newsreels, of a powerful imposing figure. He was disappointed to find Hitler stood only around five feet nine inches tall, had a sallow complexion and generally looked unhealthy. But it was his weak limpid handshake that surprised him most of all. The Führer was still exalting in the Anschluss, his successful annexation of Austria the previous month, and for the next hour he embarked on a near monologue on Germany's rightful place in the world and its need for living space in the east. His diatribe was interupted only by his scoffing of a copious quantity of cream cakes to which he seemed to be addicted.

Hitler's captive audience hung onto his words in a near trance. Elijah considered the bulk of what he heard gibberish, and couldn't help but feel that he was in the presence of a bunch of lunatics. While he thought Hitler was mad, his introduction to Goebbels, Himmler, Ribbentrop and others left him convinced that Germany, far from going through renewal, had sunk into a pit of abject evil. He couldn't wait to get away, but was forced to endure the company of this collection of misfits while he waited on Göring's departure.

Following the function on Hitler's terrace, Göring provided Elijah with an open topped Mercedes-Benz tourer, a driver and a Luftwaffe officer to drive him to Munich.

"You have to agree you've been in the company of greatness Herr Hocking; something to tell your grandchildren about eh?" Göring asked him as they parted.

"Incredible Reichsminister, quite incredible" Elijah replied, with his host totally missing the double-entendre of Elijah's comments.

***

The parcel that Elijah requested including forged Swedish passports and identity papers for his two charges was waiting for him on arrival in Munich. The two actors were identified as employees of PMAB travelling with Elijah as guests of the German government en route to Switzerland. A letter signed by Göring instructing Elijah's party be provided free conduct through any security checks they might encounter was included.

Two days later, he collected Günter Cohn and his wife Dana at a prearranged point on Munich's Stollbergstrasse. Both actors had worked with Emmy Göring in her days on the stage. Günter aged around forty, stood nearly six feet tall with a slight stoop and gracious old world mannerisms. His wife was a similar age, short and dumpy, her hair pulled back into a bun giving her face a severe look. She was unhappy at being forced to leave Germany with a stranger about whom she knew nothing. She was even unhappier at only being allowed to carry whatever could be fitted into the two small brown suitcases they were allowed to carry with them.

As Elijah strolled up Stollbergstrasse, he had no trouble identifying his new charges. The two actors stood out as they waited ill at ease on the pavement amongst the throng of people passing them by.

"Madre di Dios" he thought *"Talk about standing out like sore thumbs. If we're not careful, they'll bring the entire Gestapo leadership down on us."*

Drawing abreast of them, he greeted them as old friends, embracing the surprised actor and kissing him on both cheeks. *"Pers alter freund. Es ist gut sie zu sehen.* I hope your meetings went well and that you succeeded in landing the order" he exclaimed for the benefit of anyone who may have been watching or listening to them. "My dear Berta, I hope you've enjoyed your time in Munich. It's not Stockholm, but then some may say that's an advantage" he said with a little laugh before kissing her on both cheeks as well.

They both looked a little stunned at his greeting. *"Jesus Christ"* Elijah thought. *"They're supposed to be the ones with the acting skills. What've I let myself in for?"*

"Anyway" he continued out loud, "it's a lovely day. Let's walk to the station; we still have a little time for coffee before our train leaves for Zürich."

He started walking briskly down the street looping his arm into Dana's. As they walked, he spoke quietly so that only his two companions could hear him.

"Your name is Pers Nilsson from Stockholm. You're the European Director of Marketing for the Swedish iron ore company Porjus Mineralämnen Aktiebolag or PMAB which is situated in Porjus in the far north of Sweden. The company is a major supplier of iron ore to Germany and vital to the manufacturing industry in this country. I'm the Chairman and my name is Elijah Hocking. You've been on a marketing visit to Germany meeting clients here in Munich. We'll board the express train shortly to travel to our corporate headquarters in Zürich. You're Berta, his wife" he said to Dana. 'We'll stop for coffee at the first opportunity where I'll hand you your papers."

***

Once they were seated in a small restaurant, Elijah passed Günter a copy of the *Volkische Beobachter* inside which were two Swedish passports together with identity papers, rail tickets to Zürich, used airline ticket stubs from Stockholm to Berlin, rail tickets from Berlin to Munich, and unused return tickets from Zürich to Stockholm.

"It'll be important to leave the talking to me if we're challenged" he stressed to them. "You're no doubt aware who's arranged for your safe exit from Germany, but we can't assume that security won't stop us, or that we'll be successful in crossing the border. It would also be helpful if you could both use your acting experience to look like Swedes, not frightened rabbits. Right now you'll attract the attention of the authorities just as surely as if you were wearing the word *Juden* sewn across your backs in capital letters."

"Herr Hocking, my apologies. My wife and I appreciate the risks you're taking and you're right to be concerned. We'll do our best to act the part of our new identities. Please tell us a little more of the company and where we come from" the man replied.

Leaving it until just before their train was due to depart, the three of them entered Munich's main railway station. They were stopped at the entrance by a policeman who gave a cursory glance at their passports before handing them back and waving them through. Their documents were checked once again as they stepped onto the platform, this time by members of the Security Police. As before, their inspection was rudimentary once they saw the foreign passports. Günter had started playing his role as a Swedish businessman well, but his wife continued to act in a frightened manner. Finally, Elijah took Günter to one side and told him to pull his wife into line before she was responsible for bringing them all undone. She finally settled down as the train depart- ed Munich and gathered speed through the suburbs. Drawing closer to the Swiss border, both actors visibly relaxed and were dozing when, approaching the small town of Rothenbach, their compartment door slid open and two men dressed in black leather coats entered.

***

"Papers please" one of them asked pleasantly while the other man stood in the doorway watching them.

Elijah pulled out his Argentine passport and passed it across to the Gestapo man who looked at the photograph and then at Elijah, before flicking slowly through the document.

"And what is the purpose of your visit to Germany Herr Hocking?" he asked in a conversational tone.

"My colleague and I are with the Swedish company Porjus Mineralämnen Aktiebolag" he replied. "I am the Chairman and my col- league here is the European Director of Marketing. We've been meeting with clients."

The policeman continued to flick slowly through the passport as Elijah spoke. Finally he passed it back to his companion and put his hand out to Günter.

"Your papers please" he asked.

Günter passed his Swedish passport across to the Gestapo man. Again the passport was scrutinised closely.

"*Namnge något om din klienten Herr Nilsson*" he said as he passed Günter's passport to his companion and put his hand out for Dana's.

"*Oh fuck!*" Elijah thought. "*Just what I need; a smart-arse Gestapo goon who can speak Swedish.*"

The actor sat looking stunned. He had no idea what the man had just said and was trying to formulate an answer when Elijah interject- ed. He removed a document from his coat pocket and passed it across to the Gestapo officer who was now studying Dana's passport.

"Perhaps this will explain" he said quietly.

The officer took Göring's letter of safe conduct from Elijah, looked at it, raised an eyebrow and passed the letter to the man behind him.

"You move in exalted company Herr Hocking" he commented continuing to fix his gaze on Günter.

"More exalted than you realise shithead" Elijah thought. *"If only you knew whose hand I shook three days ago."*

The Gestapo man looked once more at Dana's passport before closing it and passing all the documents back to Elijah.

"I trust you'll reconsider carefully before either of you decide to return to Germany Herr and Fräu Nilsson," he said.

Tipping his hat to Elijah he stepped back into the corridor.

"Have a pleasant trip Herr Hocking" he said closing the door behind him.

There was complete silence for nearly sixty seconds, broken only by the sound of the train passing over the joins in the track before Günter let out a loud breath. His wife had turned white and was shaking uncontrollably in the corner of their compartment. Günter turned to embrace her, when suddenly she burst into a torrent of tears.

"Ssshhh, ssshhh now *liebchen*, it's alright now. We've passed their checks. Settle down now little one, we're safe now."

Dana continued to sob uncontrollably until Elijah spoke sharply. "We haven't crossed the border yet. Shut that damned woman up before we attract the attention of the Gestapo and have them back in here checking out what the hell's going on. They were far from convinced that either of you were who you claimed to be. It was only the letter I showed them that stopped them from hauling us off the train to check us out further. It could still happen so shut her up, and fast."

They sat in silence for the rest of the trip, crossing the border into Switzerland without further incident, receiving only rudimentary checks of their passports by border officials of both countries. Delivering his charges to the agreed address in Zürich, Elijah was glad to be rid of them.

***

"Herr Hocking, we can never thank you enough for your assistance" Günter said effusively shaking his hand vigorously, tears in his eyes. "We appreciate the risk you've taken on our behalf. I apologise for my wife's behaviour but you wouldn't believe the unimaginable strain and harassment we've been under for some considerable time now. I couldn't begin to tell you the indignities we've had to endure merely because we are Jews. We will never forget your kindness and will always be in your debt."

His wife nodded in agreement and grabbed his hands in hers. "God bless you Herr Hocking. He will surely reward you for your kindness."

"God had nothing to do with it Fräu Cohn" Elijah replied sharply. "If there truly was a God, He would never have placed you in this predicament in the first place." With that, he turned and headed back to the station to catch the next train to Zug.

"They were a bunch of bloody maniacs Jorge" Elijah said to his companion as he recounted his meetings with Göring and his afternoon tea with Hitler. "I tell you Europe, possibly the world's in trouble. There's nothing surer than Hitler means to go to war. It could be six months, twelve months, certainly no more than two years tops. We need to start planning for the eventuality. I want you to arrange Swiss nationality for Sophia, Patrick and me, and I suggest you and Elvira should consider it too. Switzerland won't get caught up in this, but it could be isolated just as it was last time around. If war does break out, Britain in particular is going to require massive supplies of foodstuffs. We should invest in additional Empire properties – meat, grains, wool, that sort of thing. Roosevelt will never let America get involved, the anti-war feeling there's too great, but there should be opportunities to sell American manufactured goods or armaments to the Brits if they go to war."

"There's also the case of what do we do about PMAB and our contracts with Germany" Jorge said.

"Right now I've no problem playing both sides off" Elijah replied.

"Their money's as good as anyone else's; possibly better. But I'm going to see if Joe Kennedy can get me an appointment with someone at the State Department. I think they'll be interested in my meeting, and it might turn out to be good insurance for us for the future."

Chapter 9

Before returning to New York three weeks later Elijah took the opportunity to visit Joe Kennedy in London where he had recently been appointed US Ambassador. Whilst Kennedy had only been in the country a few weeks, he was already scathing of the British.

"The Limeys won't fight" he told Elijah emphatically. "Their Prime Minister will do anything to make sure that England doesn't go to war with Germany, and anyway they're hardly in any shape to fight a war even if they wanted to. Have you seen their airforce? It's nothing more than a collection of kites held together with string and baling wire; and the army barely exists."

"I think you're wrong Joe. Anyway the decision won't be theirs; I believe it's already been made in Germany."

A few days after returning to New York, he was surprised to get a call inviting him to Washington. Any meeting at the State Department he expected would be with a senior official, not with the Secretary of State, Cordell Hull, himself. A week later the two men met alone in Hull's office.

"You're convinced then that Hitler's determined to go to war Mr Hocking?" the Secretary asked after Elijah had finished briefing him on the meeting he'd attended at Berchtesgarten.

"Yes sir, absolutely."

"Tell me more of your relationship with Mr Göring."

Elijah explained how they'd first met in 1927, and his subsequent meetings with him.

"He asked you to take these Jewish actors out of Germany?" Hull asked incredulously.

"I believe that his wife may well have put him under pressure. They were friends of hers."

"Most unusual when you consider his public utterances. Now about your Swedish contracts, what can you tell me about those?"

Again he listened as Elijah outlined the basic details of the contracts PMAB had entered into with Germany.

"I'd like a little time to consider what you've told me today Mr Hocking. May I contact you again?"

"Certainly Mr Secretary, I'm at your disposal" Elijah replied before being escorted by one of Hull's assistants to the lobby of the building.

"*Nice legs*" Elijah thought to himself as he followed them down the hall. The woman turned her head and noticed his eyes firmly planted on her.

"Are you in town for long Mr Hocking?" she asked pleasantly.

"That depends entirely upon you Miss" he replied. It was another two days before Elijah returned home to New York.

***

When Sophia went into labour ten days early, Elijah's first thought was that he seemed to be cursed with women who had difficult births; all except the Greek slut that was. She seemed to be able to function no matter what was between her legs. But it was all over within two hours. Sophia insisted that Elijah remain with her throughout the birth. Despite the doctor's objections, she couldn't be budged from her decision. The seven-pound baby that emerged was the spitting image of Elijah.

For the first time since the birth of the twins twenty years before,6

Elijah felt paternal stirrings as he held his newborn son in his arms.

"Rai, I'd like to call him Rai."

Sophia just nodded, Elijah looked so happy.

"It's also time we found a house that's ours, not one full of memories" he said. "Somewhere the kids can grow up with the countryside around them."

"Kids?" Sophia asked. "I've just been through this and you want more? You have any number in mind by any chance?" she laughed.

"Just kids" he replied. "We'll keep at it till we're satisfied with what we've got, but I reckon we better make the house a large one just to be sure."

They eventually found a ten bedroom house on fifty acres near Scarsdale north of New York which they purchased in August 1938. For many years it would be his principal place of residence.

***

August also brought with it a request for another meeting with Cordell Hull. The political situation in Europe was deteriorating rapidly as Hitler demanded Czechoslovakia cede the Sudetenland region to the Third Reich. War seemed imminent as the two men met alone at the Secretary's request.

"I've discussed our last meeting at length with the President" Hull started. "I must admit I hadn't understood the extent of your support for the President and the Administration Mr Hocking. I'm impressed! I appreciate that you're not an American citizen, so what I'm about to request may be unusual. I'll fully understand if you turn me down" he continued. "The President and I would like to take advantage of your friendship with Göring to get an unbiased view of what the German leadership may be thinking. It would be very useful if you could find reasons by way of your business dealings to call on him from time to time and report your findings back to us; that is, back to me. As a citizen of a neutral country, should war break out, it's possible you could still have access to Germany, especially as your company is a major supplier of a strategic product."

"Mr Secretary" Elijah replied, "I stress I'm hardly one of Göring's friends, merely an acquaintance and then only by dint of my friendship with Baroness Lindforss. There's also the matter of trading with Germany should there be war that may involve say Great Britain. As a Swedish company, PMAB would be bound by the laws and policies of the Swedish Government which is even more determined than yours to stay out of any European conflict. I'd need to be assured that if PMAB is directed to supply iron ore to Germany, that I won't be penalised by the United States."

"I can give that guarantee" Hull replied, "although there will be no minutes of this meeting and knowledge of my request to you today is restricted to only the President and myself. With regards to your relationship with Göring, I wouldn't play down the fact that he considers he's in your debt for moving his wife's Jewish actor friends to safety. I'm not suggesting you discuss troop movements or aircraft manufacturing statistics with him Mr Hocking. Just report back to me your impressions of any meetings you may have with him or any other high ranking officials you should meet, together with any relevant information you glean."

The meeting continued for nearly an hour before Elijah departed having agreed to the Secretary's request. Hull also specifically requested that Elijah keep their conversations confidential, in particular that he not advise Joe Kennedy in London.

Meanwhile Jorge had been working on resolving the dilemma of PMAB's trading with Germany by setting up a trust in Switzerland.

"The Trust will be set up here away from prying eyes. It'll indirectly acquire the shares Empresas de Mercedes currently owns." he explained to Elijah. "You'll have no official involvement in the company other than a consultancy agreement for the time being. That can always be severed by either party at a moment's notice if required. Your continued ownership will be well hidden by Switzerland's secrecy laws."

"How do you plan on exerting control?"

"I've already spoken with Agnota. She's agreed to head up PMAB as its Chairman."

"A woman as Chairman. Bit unusual isn't it?"

"That's what Agnota said " Jorge laughed. "Then I reminded her we were talking about Sweden."

***

Christmas 1938 was spent with Nancy and Montague at Elphinbrook House, collecting Patrick from Eton en-route.

"What do you think's likely to happen?" Elijah asked his host as they sat down over a port.

"I think Chamberlain only bought time in Munich. The man hasn't got the stomach for war." Montague was particularly scathing of the British Prime Minister's act of appeasement at his conference with Hitler in Munich a couple of months before when war was averted by agreeing to the breakup of Czechoslovakia. "Hitler's made it pretty obvious" he continued "that he wants to expand east. That means Poland and what's left of Czechoslovakia are sure to be invaded to give him a clear run at Russia. I would hazard a guess that's the main target."

"And England? What will they do?"

"You saw what we did in September. The only man capable of standing up to the German lunatic is Churchill, but the country doesn't have the stomach for him."

"I met Hitler you know; earlier this year. Lunatic sums him up precisely. My business partner reckons they'll all be at each other's throats before we see 1939 out."

Montague nodded. "I'd say he's nailed it on the head old man."

***

In Zug the following week, Elijah repeated the conversation to Jorge.

"Britain can't avoid being dragged into war despite Chamberlain continually giving into Hitler" Jorge predicted. "If that happens, they're woefully unprepared and going to require additional foodstuffs and raw materials. It's a golden opportunity for us. I've been working on some ideas."

He crossed to his desk and picked up two bulky files, passing one across to Elijah. Inside were detailed proposals to purchase a number of agricultural properties in Australia, Argentina, Canada and the USA.

"Just like we were in the last war, we could become a major supplier of foodstuffs if this conflict takes off. This time though, let's spread the risk. In addition to agriculture, I've had a hard look at a number of manufacturing opportunities in Britain, but frankly we have little influence and few contacts there. They're hardly likely to welcome you if you're trading with the enemy either. I also see that if Germany and Britain declare war, they'll immediately blockade each other with the result that both will find it difficult to source raw materials. The opposite is the case in America. You have excellent contacts right to the very top of the tree. We already have oil and steel operations there and there's a ready source of most raw materials. I say let's forget about investing in Britain or Europe and put our money into manufacturing in the United States instead. If you turn to page thirteen, you'll see I've already prepared a list of possible acquisitions in both agriculture and manufacturing for us to look at."

***

Elijah sat back and studied his comrade. Jorge's hair was showing the first hint of silver around his sideburns, and lines, particularly on his forehead and around his eyes, were beginning to be etched on his face.

"You continue to amaze me Jorge. Just where do you get the energy, let alone the resources, to do all this? We really have come a long way since 1916 haven't we?" he mused. "I can remember thinking a few times way back, that you and I could end up owning the world one day. Well we haven't quite got there yet but we're sure as hell well on the way aren't we?"

A hint of a smile flashed across the lawyer's face. "I haven't finished yet" he continued. "All this will need to be shipped. I propose we pick up some additional freighters and tankers. It'll be useful to have Argentine, Swedish or US flagged ships in any conflict, or even a combination of the three. We should also get rid of the passenger liners. They won't be of much use to us if Europe plunges into war, and there's not enough traffic out of the USA to South America to keep them busy. They're still relatively new and in good shape and if nothing else, they'll make damn good troop carriers. The other matter is where each of us should be based if, or rather when, the balloon goes up."

"That's simple *amigo*, you've got the contacts in Switzerland, I have them in America. It wouldn't make any sense us both being in the same place would it? Besides, since we'll both have Swiss nationality, we should both be able to move around on either side."

"My thoughts exactly, so that's settled then."

For the next couple of days the two of them sat secluded in Jorge's office as they poured over balance sheets and forward estimates, debating potential acquisitions and disposals. By the time they finished, Elijah was largely in agreement with Jorge's proposals. Some funding would be required but Elijah would still be operating with minimal debt. Jorge predicted that any borrowings could be paid off pretty quickly once war was underway.

"You know *amigo*" Elijah said as he rose to stretch, "if America does decide to take sides, we're going to have trouble stashing away the money that we'll make. Now before we wrap up, where are we with Swiss nationality?"

Jorge also had this in hand and Elijah and Sophia signed the requisite papers a week later.

***

Göring was unable to meet over the Christmas period, but sent a message promising to make himself available the next time Elijah planned to visit Germany. Privately, Elijah was relieved. There was only so much of the fat man he could take. He was more than happy to space his meetings to once a year. He was also concerned that others didn't see him either as a Nazi sympathiser, or as one of Göring's circle of sycophants. If Germany did go to war and lost, there would be a settling of scores by the victors.

There was one more item to be taken care of while they were all together. Elijah didn't want Patrick left at school in England if war was going to break out. He raised the matter with Jorge and Elvira over dinner. They agreed it would be prudent to move Patrick from Eton at the end of the school year in July.

"Where are you thinking of Elijah?" Elvira asked, dreading the answer she knew must come.

"I've shortlisted two schools in the United States" Elijah replied. "Phillips Academy at Andover in Massachusetts and Horch School in Connecticut. Both have excellent results and neither is associated with any church group. That means the kid won't get his head stuffed with religious crap. He can finish this year at Eton and start his new school year in America. His results have been excellent so either will accept him, especially combined with the dowry I've been discussing with them for future scholarships. I've also had him enrolled at Yale when he completes school."

Elvira burst into tears at the news. Sophia leant across and took her hand.

"I'm sorry Elvira. I know how you must feel, but if the men are right about this war, Patrick will be far safer in America than in England. It's quite possible he could be trapped there and unable to get to either of us. He'll also be able to come home to us for holidays since the new house is not that far from either school."

Elvira wiped her eyes and gave a weak smile.

"It doesn't help that you're completely right Sophia" she said. "I've known in my heart that this was likely to happen, but it doesn't make it any easier for me. Someone's going to have to tell Patrick of course. I would like it to be me."

None of them noticed the boy standing in the hall outside the dining room listening while they discussed his future. He turned and ran back to his room, slamming the door behind him and throwing himself onto his bed, punching at the pillow in frustration. He hated his father. Once again his life had been changed without Elijah talking to him about it. Even in America it seemed, he was not going to be permitted to live at home.

Chapter 10

Buenos Aires, Argentina
March 1939

They hadn't been back in New York long when Elijah decided that with the possibility of war looming, he should review his Argentine operations. It would also provide the opportunity to introduce Sophia to the *estancia*. As the departure date loomed he received a call from Johnny.

"Hi Boss" the voice crackled over the telephone line.

"Johnny mate, it's good to hear your voice. What have you gone and done?. They're not deporting you are they?" Elijah quipped.

Since sending his minder to Argentina the year before to resolve the labour issues they were experiencing on the wharves, those at Buenos Aires and Bahia Blanca had settled down considerably, assisted by the disappearance of a number of the principle agitators. Only the operations in Rosario were still experiencing sporadic strikes but even those were slowly coming under control.

"Nah Boss. Anyway you know me, my tactics fit right in with the way the locals operate down here. Jeez you're suspicious" he laughed.

"With good reason Johnny. So what do I owe the pleasure of the call? I'm sure it's not to enquire after my health or to give me the weather forecast" Elijah replied.

"I've got some news for you. I didn't want to just spring it on you when you got here. I'm getting married. You may remember her; Gabriella."

"You mean *the* Gabriella?" Elijah interjected.

"That's the one Boss" Johnny responded. "Anyway we're looking to get married early next year. I thought you might be my best man" Johnny continued. "That's the real reason for the call."

"You better check she's forgiven me for being banned from *my* wedding back in '16 mate. She may have something to say about that" Elijah replied laughing, referring to when he and Mercedes were married and her grandfather had refused to let Gabriella attend the wedding.

"Nah, she blames the old man for that. You know she reckons he wanted to screw her but she turned him down because he was too old and that's why he paid her back."

"Somehow I don't think so" Elijah thought. He could still recall the genuine look of distaste on the Vizconde's face when he was first introduced to her. The old man had immediately guessed her true profession and there was no way known that he could see Mercedes' grandfather wanting to screw her.

"Well if you're sure it's fine by her then you're on mate. That's really good news Johnny. I'm really, really pleased for you. I would have been upset if you'd passed me over" Elijah replied.

Hanging up the phone his first thought was that with a wife, Johnny might not be so available in his minder role for emergencies. There could well be a few of those coming up with the rapidly deteriorating situation in Europe.

***

The long flight from Miami on board the Sikorsky flying boat was tiring as they hopped between the endless refuelling stops through the Caribbean and down the South American coast to Buenos Aires, but to Elijah it was far preferable to the three week sea voyage he'd been forced to make in the past. They arrived in the Argentine capital to the news that Hitler's troops had marched into what remained of Czechoslovakia. As he read the headlines he was convinced that war in Europe was now inevitable.

Johnny was there to greet them as they completed the customs procedures. Sophia knew of him, but this was the first time they had met.

"It's great to see you Boss, really great" he enthused as he embraced Elijah and shook his hand vigorously. By comparison he was almost shy as he was introduced to Sophia and Rai. "You sure know how to pick them Boss" he said as he kissed her hand and ruffled Rai's hair.

"Where's your fiancée?" Elijah asked looking around for Gabriella.

"She thought it would be best if we met alone and allowed Sophia to freshen up before she joins us later for dinner" he said. The two men had already decided that it would be better if the details of Gabriella's past profession and the fact that she and Elijah had previously met were best withheld from Sophia.

"Boy Johnny, you sure know how to pick them" Elijah said with a grin when Gabriella joined them later that evening. "You told me she was beautiful, you didn't tell me she was gorgeous."

Sophia was somewhat more restrained in her greetings. Over dinner, they swapped notes but while it was not readily noticeable to the others, Elijah could see that she was quieter than usual. He asked if there was a problem when they returned to their room.

"There's nothing wrong with me" she replied. "Of course I presume you already know that she's a tart."

"What do you mean a tart?" he asked innocently.

"Oh Elijah" she replied with a trace of exasperation. "Don't tell me you don't know. A prostitute, a whore, a harlot, *la puta*. It doesn't matter how you say it, Gabriella's a tart. A high class one I'd venture, but nonetheless a tart. I'm going to bed" she said as she headed away from the lounge. "Oh and darling, you can drop the charade. If you know her just admit it, but you better make sure that's all in the past. You know what I said before we got married. Goodnight" she said closing the door behind her.

He followed her into the bedroom. "I don't know how you worked it out" he admitted sheepishly. "I decided since it was way in the past, before I married Mercedes even, there wasn't anything to be gained by bringing it up."

"You should have told me instead of hiding it" Sophia admonished him. "It makes me wonder what other secrets you're keeping from me. And poor Gabriella; she must have been on tenterhooks all evening wondering who was going to say something that would give her away. Just explain to her in the morning so she can relax and be herself."

She headed into the bathroom, when she stopped and turned back. "And you're not off the hook yet mister, you might want to think if there's anything else you've forgotten to tell me while you're at it." The bathroom door closed quietly behind her leaving Elijah standing in the middle of the bedroom.

***

He was out of sorts for two reasons as he headed out of Buenos Aires alone the next day. Sophia had made it obvious that she was serious about him withholding secrets from her. The discussion had resumed when she returned to the bedroom and for the first time in their marriage, she'd turned her back on him in bed.

But that was nothing compared to the unsettled feeling he was experiencing as he drew closer to the coastal city of La Plata the following day. It was twelve years since he'd last seen Josefina on that day when he returned her to the institution. He tried to tell Sophia about her but couldn't, not realising the pain was still so raw. He'd brusquely explained his absence was due to business appointments needing him to travel away from the capital for the day.

His legs felt shaky and his breath was taken away when his daughter entered the small reception room that had been set aside for their meeting. Framed in the doorway, he could have sworn it was Mercedes standing there, so uncannily alike was Josefina. At twenty-two, she was just a little older than her mother had been when Luis Churruca first took him home to the *estancia* in 1912 and Mercedes had emerged from the *casco* leaving him speechless with her beauty.

Try as he might, he could elicit no response from her. When he attempted to hug her, she shrank from him, retreating to the protection of the doctor who'd accompanied her. Unable to speak, she fidgeted, her listless eyes refusing to look at her father. After fifteen minutes as she began to become increasingly agitated, the doctor finally suggested she should return to her room. The last view Elijah would ever have of his daughter was of her retreating from the room with the teddy bear she'd clutched throughout their meeting. It would be 1973 before she would finally be reunited with her mother and twin brother on the little plateau at the rear of the *casco*.

***

Sophia knew the *estancia* in Patagonia held a special significance to Elijah, but little more. That chapter of his life was a closed book and she knew better than to try and intrude on it. Eleven years had passed since he'd last visited the property. After the incident with Kyra he'd promised himself that he would never take another woman there, but he felt sure Mercedes would accept Sophia's presence.

Driving up the poplar lined driveway to the *casco*, Sophia realised Elijah had gone quiet. The car pulled to a stop before the double oak entry doors as they burst open and a family spilled out onto the pebble driveway. A handsome man, bronzed from long exposure to the elements stepped forward to greet them.

"*Bienvenido a casa*; welcome home Elijah. It has been too long."

"Enrique *viejo amigo*, what a sight for sore eyes" Elijah responded as the two men embraced for nearly a minute before stepping apart. "Let me introduce Sophia and Rai."

Sophia warmed to the man at once. There was an inner strength about him. His handsome weather-beaten face exuded honesty and his handshake was strong and firm. She could never recall Elijah greeting anyone with such warmth. The bond between them was palpable.

"You've never met Esmeralda or my children Elijah; Bento, Julio and Conchita" he said guiding each of them shyly forward in turn to shake their visitors' hands.

Over the next few days, the two men headed away from the *casco* on horseback together so that Elijah could inspect the *estancia*. On the second day Sophia, who'd been raised with horses, accompanied them. She noticed her husband was a different man, totally relaxed, as though all his cares and worries had fallen away.

On the third day, she decided to explore around the homestead alone on foot. She was drawn to the only rise, other than the distant snow capped mountains, that broke the monotony of the endless landscape; a small hill behind the *casco* where something appeared to be standing out on the top, etched against the clear blue sky. She was staring at the four graves she found on the small plateau when a shadow fell across her making her jump. She hadn't heard him coming up behind her and turning, she saw Elijah's face contorted in a mask of pain.

"I am glad you've found them" he said quietly. "Mercedes has been calling me since I arrived but I couldn't come here, not alone. I'm sure she approves of you."

Sophia put out her hand and clasped Elijah's in hers. They stood there together as one, neither of them speaking nor moving.

"You must know that it doesn't diminish my love for you in any way" he finally said in a voice that was little more than a whisper, "but I think of her every day of my life. This is one of those secrets I couldn't share with you before now."

He slid down to his knees pulling her with him as he told her of Mercedes and their children, of her brother Luis, of their mother and the events of long ago.[7] When he'd finished, Sophia reached over and brushed her hand across his cheek and lightly kissed him.

"Those are secrets I can live with" she said softly.

Tenderly, he took her face in his hands and looked into her eyes. "If anything happens to me, you must promise that the *estancia* is never allowed out of our family. I would rather lose everything else first."

She nodded, crossing her heart with her finger before placing it on his lips. "I promise" she said.

7 The Elijah Trilogy Book 1 – The Half-breed Boy

For the remaining two weeks they were at the *estancia*, Sophia climbed the hill every day to place a flower on each of the graves. She felt strangely at peace, as though she had known the woman buried there all her life. Both she and Elijah returned together one more time taking Rai with them late in the afternoon of the last day before returning to New York. It was cold and crisp, heralding the onset of winter. All three were well rugged up against the wind which carried with it the chill air from the distant mountains. It was Sophia's idea that they should plant a eucalyptus tree to shade the graves.

"It's my gift to Mercedes" she told Elijah softly as they sat in the lounge one evening. He didn't reply, not in words anyway, but he reached across and embraced her. She could've sworn she saw tears but could never be sure. When he eventually pulled away, the evidence had disappeared.

The tree planting was a solemn affair. Even young Rai seemed to understand there was a special significance to the occasion. The task completed, they sat back, each submerged in their own thoughts as the sun slowly set behind the jagged peaks to the west.

Sophia was happy in the knowledge that Elijah was content, that the ghosts of the *estancia* seemed to have finally been put to rest. Elijah's thoughts were with the day the elder Luis brought him home. He could have sworn they were all gathered there to greet him and to accept Sophia into the fold; Mercedes, the two Luis and the Vizconde. Who could've guessed he thought, that the uneducated half-caste kid from outback Queensland would one day be sitting here in the distant pampas, well on the way to becoming one of the richest and most influential men in the world while far away, the world seemed out of control, as once more it rushed headlong towards war.

***

With the situation in Europe rapidly worsening as Hitler began making demands on Poland Elijah told Sophia one night shortly after their return to New York that he felt it was time to head over and bring Patrick back from Eton. "I wouldn't be surprised if this lot blows up at any moment" he told her. "I also need to touch base with Jorge while there's still an opportunity to do so. I think it would be best if you and Rai stayed home."

"No way" she replied. "We're coming too. I'm not prepared to be separated from you if war breaks out; besides Patrick will be a lot happier if I'm there rather than being alone with you."

He couldn't argue with that. Reluctantly he agreed, deciding they'd travel to Europe by ship and return on the new Pan American trans-Atlantic flying boat service that was to be inaugurated while they were in Europe.

As he and Jorge finished reviewing the long list of transactions Jorge had been working on since the beginning of the year, Elijah mentioned to his partner that he had to travel to Germany to meet Göring. "As much as I don't want to, I can't get out of it. Sophia's insisting on coming to Germany too but there's no way I'm taking her and the boy with me" he said.

"Like your friend Hull, I'm also intrigued to know what Göring can tell you about what's happening" Jorge replied. "Another three months *amigo*...just three more months and we'll be ready. Our gearing will top out at thirteen percent so we can more than manage the debt level. Then we can sit back and see what transpires."

Sophia proved to be as intransigent as ever – she was going with him "and that was that!" The tone of her voice made it obvious that she wouldn't be swayed. Elijah had heard that tone too often before whenever she reached a decision. It usually signified the end of any discussion. This time however Elijah wasn't prepared to be overruled without a fight, but he couldn't shake her.

***

On a balmy day late in June they were collected from Berlin's Adlon Hotel by a member of Göring's staff. The young adjutant explained the Reichsminister had decided he would meet them aboard his yacht due to the weather and the fact that Sophia was accompanying him.

The yacht turned out to be a luxurious twenty-eight metre long wooden motor launch named *"Carin 2"* which had been presented to the German leader by the German motor industry. As the car pulled up to the landing on the River Spree, Göring emerged with Emmy and their baby daughter and stepped ashore.

"Herr Hocking *alter freund*, it is good to see you again" Göring gushed, beaming from ear to ear as he extended his hand in greeting. "You remember Emmy of course. As I recall, you missed Edda's birth by a matter of weeks on your last visit."

"Herr Reichsminister, Fräu Göring I'm delighted to meet again. Please allow me to present my wife Sophia and our son Rai" Elijah replied.

Bending to kiss her hand, Göring quipped "I was beginning to believe that there was no Fräu Hocking, only a figment of his imagination. Your husband always seems to prefer to travel alone."

"Perhaps it's because there have been so many of us...Fräu Hockings I mean" she replied with a glint in her eye. They followed Göring and his wife aboard the yacht. Their host's ample buttocks were barely contained within the traditional German leather breeches he wore, stretching the material to limits unforeseen by its designer as he descended the stairs to the boat's saloon.

While the women swapped notes about their home lives and their children, Göring launched into his usual monologue, lecturing Elijah for over two hours on the situation developing in Europe.

"Poland must relinquish Danzig and the Corridor; this is non-negotiable to the German people" Göring stated emphatically, "otherwise there *will* be war. The Führer is unshakeable on this. The English are sabre rattling and this only encourages the Polish to be pigheaded. The French are buffoons; no one takes them seriously. The English must see sense and convince the Polish to cooperate, then together the three nations can do something about the threat from the communists in the east. Germany does not want war but it seems to be the only way the matter can be resolved."

He continued in similar vein until it became time to leave. As Sophia and Emmy climbed the stairs to the deck, Göring put his hand out holding Elijah back.

"Herr Hocking, I'm aware that you have business interests in America. Perhaps you could pass a message to the politicians there who matter and tell them that it is still possible to stop this conflict. If their President could convince Chamberlain that were the Polish to relinquish Danzig and the Corridor, then we'd have no further territorial demands to make in Europe. You have both my solemn word and that of the Führer on the matter."

"I'm not sure my contacts go that high Reichminister, but I will attempt to pass your message to the right authorities" Elijah promised him.

"Thank you, you have proven to be a good friend in the past, I'm sure you'll do your best."

As they said their farewells, Emmy leaned forward to kiss Elijah goodbye, whispering in his ear "Thank you and God bless you for Günter and Dana."

Driving away from the dock Sophia started to speak. "Well..." she said only to be interrupted by Elijah who squeezed her hand and almost imperceptibly shook his head. He flicked his eyes slightly at the driver and the adjutant in the front seat of the car.

***

He took her hand as they exited the car back at the hotel. "It's a lovely day. Why don't we take a walk in the Tiergarten? It's too nice to be shut up inside."

They strolled in silence down the Unter den Linden past the Brandenburg Gate, across Hermann-Göring-Strasse onto Charlottenburger Chausee and entered the massive park that cut through the centre of the German capital. All around them people were enjoying the late afternoon sunshine; a smattering of civilian clothing amidst the masses of grey, green, black and blue uniforms. Elijah steered them onto one of the side paths that cut through the trees and gardens.

"It's lovely isn't it?" Sophia said. "It's so hard to believe that in a matter of days or weeks, we could be at war. I heard most of what that fat idiot was saying to you. Surely they don't believe all that nonsense."

"Sophia, it's very important you don't say anything where we can be overheard. You have to assume our hotel room is bugged. It's really only safe outdoors like this. I've never told you before but on my last visit, Göring took me to meet Hitler. He's mad, quite mad" he said, speaking softly as they walked slowly through the gardens. Rai ran ahead of them laughing while they watched him. "I can't tell you much of what I'm doing but please trust me darling."

"Just tell me you're not working for them" she replied.

"Never!" he said emphatically. "That's something you'll never have to worry about!"

"Then I trust you."

The sound of Rai crying interrupted them. For a brief moment, they'd taken their eyes off him and he'd tripped over. As Sophia rushed forward, a man dressed in a black uniform with a skull and crossbones insignia on the collar bent down and picked the toddler up.

"Your son *Fräu*?" he asked as he handed him to her.

"Thank you" she nodded. She found she couldn't look the man in the eyes as she took Rai back.

"You should be more careful of him. The children, they are our future!" he said in a clipped voice before snapping a Nazi salute at her and striding off.

She shuddered involuntarily. "Did you see his eyes Elijah? There was no bottom to them; it was as though they went for ever."

"Now you know why I didn't want you to come Sophia; this place is a pit of evil. Do you know, Göring actually called me his good friend. Let's just get out of this goddamn country."

***

102

The Boeing 314 flying boat they boarded in Southampton and flew back to New York in was huge in comparison to the Sikorsky they had flown in to Buenos Aires a couple of months earlier. They had collected Patrick from Eton, but even the prospect of flying in the huge plane did nothing to cut through his cold distant responses whenever Elijah spoke to him.

While Elijah headed to Washington to meet with Cordell Hull, Sophia took Patrick to a nearby horse stud-farm and allowed him to select his own horse. She'd arranged for a riding instructor to give him lessons throughout the summer.

"I loved riding when I was younger. It allowed me to get away from the problems my parents were experiencing" she said reminiscing. "The wind in my hair, being at one with the horse and just the feeling of freedom were intoxicating. It's such a shame we aren't at the estancia in Argentina. That would be really wonderful. Perhaps we can convince your father that you could spend your summer holidays there next year."

"It's no use asking him for anything for me" Patrick responded bitterly. "He'll never agree to it; for anyone else yes, but not for me."

"Patrick, he's not like that. He really does love you you know" Sophia said.

"Well he has a funny way of showing it" the boy countered.

She shook her head sadly. It was obvious she was going to have her work cut out trying to sort out the relationship between father and son.

***

"Did you believe him?" Hull asked after Elijah completed his briefing, ending with Göring's message.

"While I don't think Göring personally wants to go to war Mr Hull, he firmly believes that Danzig is German and should be handed over. But then he's not the one calling the shots."

Hull sat silently studying the floor for a long moment. "And what's your reading of the situation Mr Hocking?" he asked raising his eyes to look at Elijah.

"There will be war sir" Elijah replied without hesitation. "I think Hitler has already decided on war whether it be over Danzig or his next demand, whatever it might be. You only have to see these people in his presence. They hang on every word as though he's the Messiah. No matter what Göring may think personally, he'll never go against Hitler."

"I place great credence in what you've told me Mr Hocking, just as I know the President will. I understand you've taken Swiss nationality. That could be very useful to us. I have the feeling we may wish you to visit Germany again in the not too distant future if possible" Hull replied standing up.

"There's going to be war as sure as night follows day" Elijah told Mark Frost in New York the next day, repeating the comments he'd made to Hull. "The British will be dragged into it along with most of Europe. My contacts in Washington tell me there's absolutely no way that America will get involved and they'll remain neutral. We should support Roosevelt's policy of neutrality. I believe it's also time we had a paper on the west coast, either Los Angeles or San Francisco if you feel that's not spreading yourself too thin."

Mark nodded his head. "It makes sense" he said.

"Jorge and I have decided we should hive the papers off from the rest of the group into a separate company, with you at the head holding some equity. If America does get caught up in all this, it won't look good to have a bunch of the major dailies under the control of a foreigner, especially one who travels to Germany. Jorge's arranging to have the company transferred somewhere the shareholding details will be inaccessible to others. Do you have a problem with that?"

"Not at all" Mark responded. "I've always wanted to be a newspaper mogul. It'll also put a spoke in Hearst's wheel and take away the opportunity for him to attack you as a nasty European. Anything that hobbles Hearst can't be bad in itself" he added with a grin.

***

Throughout the rest of August 1939, Elijah and Jorge spent many hours on trans-Atlantic telephone calls as they assembled the final pieces in the jigsaw of acquisitions.

"We're going to make it" Jorge told him by the third week of August. "Another month and it'll be in place. By the way the British Ministry of Shipping have lodged an offer for the *"Bartolomé Mitre."* They're going to use her as a troopship so that's a good result." Her two sister ships had already been disposed of earlier in the year. The last of the trio had been tied up in Buenos Aires harbour for the past two months as the shipping company exited the passenger trade.

Next Elijah headed to Kilgore to meet Deke Newell and discuss plans for oil production in the event of war. "With Germany sure to blockade the Brits" he briefed Deke "we should be shipping as much as possible in our Swedish tankers. My guess is they'll hit those only as a last resort, whereas US flagged ships may become a target. That's how it happened last time. I also want you to look at how much we can ramp up production if we have to. The next couple of years are going to provide us with a great opportunity to make some good profits since the Brits have no oil of their own."

"For some reason I thought you were pro-Limey" Deke said, "and that you'd offer them some sort of special deal."

"I don't have any particular love for the Brits Deke, although I'd pick them over the Nazis any day. I'm pro-profits first and last. Why shouldn't they pay above the odds for our oil?" Reaching for the coffee pot, he continued. "Someone asked me during the last war what I was prepared to do for England and I answered then that the King had never done anything for me, so why should I do anything for the King. Turns out that while the King has changed, nothing else has" he added with a grin.

They were pouring over production estimates when the ringing of the telephone interrupted them. "It's Mark for you" Deke said passing the phone across.

Elijah's face grew grim as he listened to the newspaperman. "When did this happen?...You're sure of your sources?" he asked and then "Have you spoken to Jorge?"

Deke could hear the sound of Mark's voice speaking rapidly through the phone before Elijah said "Thanks Mark. I'll head straight back to New York. Deke and I have nearly wrapped up anyway."

Hanging up the phone he shook his head and said "The shit's hit the fan, literally. Russia just signed a non-aggression pact with the Germans. I can't believe that arse-hole Ribbentrop actually sat down with Stalin and suddenly the Commies and Nazis are best buddies. War's inevitable! It's going to be on for young and old! Hitler's just cleared the decks to attack Poland."

***

It wasn't the only news waiting for Elijah when he arrived back in New York.

"Rai is going to have a playmate" Sophia murmured as they lay together in bed, the moonlight streaming in through the large picture window that looked out over the landscaped gardens outside their bedroom.

"Oh?" said Elijah half asleep. "Whose kid?"

"Yours you moron."

He lay on his back semi-conscious when the import of her reply suddenly hit him. "You're..." he started to say when she interrupted him.

"Yes silly, early in February."

Chapter 11

New York, U.S.A.
March 1940

"I need to see you Elijah" the caller said, "as soon as possible."

A long silence ensued while Elijah considered his options. He only ever communicated these days with Kyra through their lawyers.

"There's nothing you could say I want to hear" he finally said.

"Please Elijah, I need your help."

"We agree on that. You sure need help, but not mine."

"Please Elijah" she pleaded again. "Have you any idea how hard it was to pick up this phone and ask for your help? Please!"

He could hear her voice break as she spoke. "Manado's in an hour" he said naming a small restaurant on Sixth Avenue near 54th Street. "Try pulling your usual stunt of being late and I'll be gone. That's it."

He found her already waiting for him, nervously smoking a cigarette. She watched him enter and followed his progress to her table.

"It's been a long time" she said trying to be friendly.

"What is it Kyra I don't have much time" he replied.

"You'll never change will you? You haven't seen the children in nearly three years."

"And whose fault is that?" he retorted. "You said you needed my help. If you've brought me to hear an update about your kids, forget it; tell the lawyer."

As he started to stand up she fumbled in her bag, removed a silver cigarette case and extracted another cigarette. "I'm sorry Elijah. You're right. Do you have a light?" Inhaling deeply, she continued. "Petros has been arrested in Germany and charged with espionage."

"Christ Kyra, what's your brother, or any of your family for that matter, got to do with me?"

She pulled a handkerchief from her bag and dabbed at her eyes. "I remembered you had some contacts there and I hoped you might be able to influence them to release him. This isn't about us Elijah; this is about life and death."

"The bloody country's at war Kyra. How am I supposed to exert any influence? What's he supposed to have done anyway?" he asked in his cold dispassionate voice

"He was found near a naval fitting out dock in Wilhelmshaven."

"That's a closed naval port. Is this the same brother who launched that action in Britain back in 1935 and tried to seize two of my ships?"

She nodded miserably.

"Then he can rot in hell. I'm not interested in you or your stinking family. You'd better hope for his sake that he's only been arrested by the Naval Police and not the Gestapo. Anyway there's nothing I could do to help him, even assuming I wanted to. I don't know where you get the idea I have any contacts there but if I did, you can be bloody sure I wouldn't be working with the Gestapo. Anything else I can help you with?" he asked sarcastically.

She shook her head, tears coursing down her cheeks as he stood up.

"Don't bother contacting me again Kyra, I'll be changing my number first thing I get back to the office anyway. Anything you have to say, say it through the lawyers. You should lose some weight too; you're obviously still spending too much time on your back; it's showing" he added nastily before walking away.

"Elijah!" he heard her shout, but he ignored her as he headed for the door. A glass suddenly splintered on a table to the left of him. He didn't miss a beat as called over his shoulder. "You still can't aim straight you stupid bitch."

***

Sophia had been quietly working on Elijah for several months to allow Patrick to travel to the *estancia* for the summer vacation. At first he wouldn't consider the idea due to the war and the distance to be travelled, but she kept chipping away.

"Oh come on darling, the war's nowhere near Argentina, or anywhere else in South America for that matter" she said. "Being in the outdoors at the *estancia* will do him good and spending time with Enrique will also help him to develop."

Elijah couldn't argue with that. Finally he relented, but insisted she would have to accompany him. Then the pendulum swung the other way as she argued that she couldn't possibly travel without him. With the situation in Europe he told her, he couldn't be away for so long. The only way he'd allow Patrick to holiday at the *estancia* was if she and the other children accompanied him. Finally, they reached a compromise. Sophia and the children would travel to Argentina once school broke in late July for the summer vacation. Elijah would join them early in September before they all returned to New York together.

Around the same time, he received a message from the Secretary of State asking for another meeting. He had a premonition as to what Hull wanted but elected to say nothing to Sophia as she prepared for her trip to the *estancia*. Patrick could scarcely believe that Elijah had agreed to let him spend his summer there. As departure day drew close, he could barely contain his excitement. The day before they were to leave, Elijah asked his son to go riding with him. Patrick was flabbergasted since Elijah had never shown any interest in spending time with him in the past.

After about thirty minutes, Elijah reined his horse in and suggested they stop and talk for a few minutes. Dismounting, they tethered their horses and each selected a rock to sit on. "Only the *estancia* beats this place" Elijah commented quietly as he reached into his shirt pocket, removed a packet of Camels and lit up. They both sat quietly taking in the view for a few minutes before he continued.

"Son, you need to understand that the only reason you're being allowed to go to Argentina is because Sophia's going with you although I'm still far from convinced that I've made the right decision allowing you all to go with this war on."

As his son started to speak Elijah stopped him. "Just let me finish please Patrick. I also used to get into trouble for interrupting while my elders were speaking" he said with a small smile. "I know you resent me, but I expect you to show your stepmother total respect while you're in her care. You also need to understand that *gringos*, especially Americans, are not held in high regard where you're going. Enrique is a hard task master. Listen to him, show him respect, don't backchat him. If you want to earn his respect in turn, master the skills he'll teach you, and speak to him only in Spanish. I'd trust him with my life. Your Uncle Jorge is the only other person I could say that about."

His son sat scowling at him. "Is this little father-son chat the only reason you came riding with me father?"

Elijah sighed in exasperation. When he didn't answer Patrick stood and remounted his horse.

"I hoped there might have been something more, but I should've realised you're incapable of any feelings. But don't worry father" he said, a bitter tone to his voice, "I'll be the good little boy and there won't be any need for you to be ashamed of me" before flicking the reins and riding off at a gallop. He didn't speak to Elijah again before leaving the following day, refusing even to say goodbye as he departed.

***

The day after his family flew out of New York for the long flight to Buenos Aires, Elijah took the train to Washington. With the war intensifying, it was time to call in favours from those senators and congressmen Elijah had spent years cultivating and paying backhanders to. His plan was to stay in Washington for at least a week, and possibly longer, as he started arranging meetings with his contacts to ensure that his companies got more than their fair share of military contracts.

One of the primary contacts was his old friend Michael Leveridge, the Congressman from Pennsylvania. They met in a private room at the University Club on Sixteenth Street so that they could talk without being overheard.

"Roosevelt's going to steamroller Wilkie in the election" Leveridge told him as they sat enjoying a cigar and a Jack Daniels. "There's nothing surer than poor old Wendell doesn't stand a chance" referring to Wendell Wilkie who had just secured the nomination as the Republican Party's presidential candidate in the 1940 election. "Care to take a wager how many states Roosevelt will win?" he asked with a grin.

"I'll take forty five" Elijah replied.

"Well he'll win, but not quite that well. I'll wager thirty eight. And the bet?"

"A box of the best Cuban cigars, and a case of Jack Daniels Black Label" Elijah suggested which was promptly agreed to by Leveridge. Elijah duly delivered both in November following the election with a note that read *"Great counting of the numbers Congressman; that's why you're the politician"*.

"We have a consignment of arms that will be ready to ship early next month to an organisation called the Ecuadorian Confederation of Catholic Workers. They're starting to stockpile arms in readiness for action against the military there" Leveridge continued. He and his associates had continued to show interest in political developments in South America ever since Elijah first met him back in 1924. Elijah's ships had carried arms assignments to rebel groups on Leveridge's behalf a number of times.

"Same arrangements as normal I presume?"

"Yes. The payment will be in the bank by August first."

Elijah reached for the whiskey bottle and poured himself another drink. "Michael, I'll waive the fee for this shipment in return for my companies being granted preferred supplier status for defence procurement. In return, we'll pay you five percent of the value of all orders placed with us. I have a list of the companies here" he said passing an envelope over to Leveridge.

As one of the most senior members of the House of Representatives, Leveridge sat on the Congressional Committee that oversaw the U.S. Defence Department and was in a position to influence purchasing decisions. The Congressman stood up and crossed the room. At first Elijah thought he may have gone too far as Leveridge opened the door and checked the corridor outside. Closing the door again he crossed back to his chair and glanced at the list that Elijah had handed him before looking up and nodding. "That can be arranged" he said.

***

His next meeting was at Cordell Hull's house. "I appreciate you meeting me again Mr Hocking" the Secretary began. "Both the President and I respect the quality of your observations. They've proven to be somewhat more on the ball than advice we're receiving from some of our diplomatic posts. You probably wouldn't be aware that Hitler recently offered a peace treaty to the British who rejected it this week. We believe the Germans will now attempt an invasion of England. What we don't know is when, although they appear to be transferring landing craft to the Channel ports in readiness to strike."

Elijah listened intently, guessing exactly where this conversation was heading.

"I recall saying to you once before, that as a citizen of a neutral country, albeit one who does considerable business with the US Government, you have the right to refuse the request I am about to make" Hull continued.

"Mr Secretary," Elijah interrupted, "in return you will recall that it was I who first came to you with my concerns about the thugs running Germany. I don't need to be reminded either of my business links to your government, or of my nationality."

"I apologise" Hull replied hurriedly, seeing that Elijah was visibly annoyed by his comments. "I meant no offence and I withdraw my comments. The President and I would very much like to get an unbiased reading of what the German leadership is considering now that France along with most of Europe is under their control. I'd suggest that Göring will be so elated by their victories, he'll be glad to meet you to boast, possibly letting slip something of their future plans. He's obviously comfortable with you and being in charge of all German war production, he'll want to be sure that his supplies of Swedish iron ore continue uninterrupted. I'm sure you should be able to secure an appointment with him."

"That's all possible Cordell" Elijah said, deciding it was time that he treated the man opposite on an equal footing. "However I've no idea how I'd get to and from Europe, let alone travel within the continent with a war on."

"We'll get you to Zürich and back with diplomatic credentials as a priority. You could leave tomorrow if you wish. Hopefully your people in Europe should be able to arrange onward travel from Zurich" Hull said.

"It's not that simple" Elijah continued. "My family flew to Argentina last week. I have business there and must join them by the end of August. My wife knows nothing of our discussions and I intend to leave it that way. I don't see how I could do this and still be in Argentina as required."

Hull thought for a moment. "If your people can get you from Zürich to Berlin and back, we'll arrange the rest. We'll get you out of Switzerland and back to New York, then down to Argentina. I'll also personally guarantee seats for all the family on a flight out of Argentina so that you're back in the United States by mid-September."

As he'd known he would before walking into the meeting, Elijah finally agreed. He would need to have Agnota arrange the meeting with Göring for him which in turn would determine his departure date. As the meeting came to a close and the two men rose, Hull stopped him "There's another matter Elijah."

The change in the form of address resonated with Elijah as Hull picked up a folder and handed it to him. "You may be interested in this information. It won't be available to the markets for at least another couple of weeks. The folder contains details of two companies; one in Columbus Ohio, the other in McCall Idaho. Both are vital to our armaments programme and both are experiencing serious financial problems. It's important to us that a financially sound purchaser is found for each of them. In return they would be guaranteed government contracts for their total production for the duration of the European war. Hopefully you may know of such a purchaser" he said, completely deadpan.

Elijah accepted the folder equally deadpan. "Thank you Cordell, I'll have a look at it and see what I can suggest."

***

The response back from Berlin was almost immediate. In addition to agreeing to meet Elijah, Göring offered to despatch a plane to collect him in Ravensburg just over the border from Switzerland and then fly him on to Stockholm after his meeting in Berlin thus partially solving the problem of transportation.

Three days later, under the guise of a US diplomatic courier, Elijah flew out of New York to Foynes, then crossed the Irish Sea to England. There he connected with the BOAC flight to Lisbon. Travelling across Spain and Vichy France by train, his diplomatic papers barely rated a glance by either police or customs officials. Switching back to his own identity in Zürich, he finally arrived in Ravensburg, where as arranged, Göring's plane was waiting to fly him onto Berlin.

This time the two men met in Göring's sumptuous office at the Air Ministry on Wilhelmstrasse. It seemed to Elijah that he walked miles in the huge building before finally being ushered into the "great man's" presence.

"It really is amazing" Elijah thought to himself as Göring forced himself to his feet from behind the huge desk which dominated a room of truly gigantic proportions, *"I didn't think he could get any bigger."*

"Herr Hocking, my dear fellow" Göring exclaimed, a huge smile breaking across his face, "As always, it is good to see you." He strode across the thick carpet to Elijah, clasping him by both shoulders. "Welcome back to the Third Reich."

With a wave of his hand, he dismissed the Luftwaffe adjutant and led Elijah to two large chairs near one of the windows.

"May I congratulate you on your promotion to Reichsmarschall?" Elijah replied.

Göring beamed expansively. "Ah, so such news filters even through the enemy's censorship".

"More than that Reichsmarschall, the exploits of the Luftwaffe are well known outside of Germany." Once again Göring heard only what he wanted to hear, totally missing the double meaning of Elijah's comments.

***

As usual, the German dominated the meeting, as he launched into an hour-long monologue, reiterating Hitler's offer to enter a peace treaty with Britain to end the war and boasting of the Luftwaffe's mastery of the skies during the recent Polish and French campaigns.

"What will happen if the British won't agree to peace?" Elijah asked.

"The Führer is determined to smash them. The Luftwaffe will destroy the RAF then we'll invade. Such a force is being readied. Churchill is a fool. We would still be prepared to have him join us and smash the Communists. They're the true enemies of both our nations."

"I thought the Russians were your allies Reichsmarschall" Elijah exclaimed.

"Only for as long as it suits us" Göring replied darkly. "Now tell me what the situation is with regards your supplies of iron ore" he asked, abruptly changing the subject. "With these damnable Englanders refusing to accept the inevitable, we are going to need additional quantities? How long before you can increase supplies?"

They talked for another fifteen minutes before a knock at the door interrupted them. "You'll have to excuse me *mein freund*, there are so

115

many demands on my time these days and I have to leave for my head-quarters in France early in the morning. Emmy wanted you to dine with us while you're here, but my schedule doesn't permit it. Hopefully we can do so next time you visit Berlin."

Declining the offer of a lift, Elijah decided to walk the few blocks back to the Adlon Hotel in the warm August afternoon sun. Allied bombers were yet to reach Berlin and Wilhelmstrasse was full of fellow promenaders enjoying the warm afternoon sun; the vast majority of them in uniforms. But what struck Elijah most were the high spirits of those around him. On past visits, he'd detected an undercurrent of concern as Germany slowly but surely edged towards war. It was obvious that the quick victory over France and the anticipation of Britain's expected capitulation had dispelled the fears that had previously been on display.

***

The following day, Elijah flew to Stockholm in the plane that Göring had arranged for him.

"I have a surprise for you" Agnota told him as they drove into the city from Bromma Airport. "I hope you won't mind but I've arranged for you to stay with me rather than at a hotel. It seemed so silly for you to be there."

"Things have changed Agnota" he said softly, "I'm not sure that's such a good idea."

"I realise things have changed Elijah, but surely as both a friend, and as your representative in Sweden, no-one could possibly object."

He didn't answer for a couple of moments, looking instead at the passing landscape. "As a friend and as my representative in Sweden then Agnota, but nothing more, and thanks. It'll give us time to catch up."

"By the time Fredrik died, the Lindforss fortune had largely disappeared" she told him. "Benji will inherit what's left, but it isn't a lot. Luckily there was still an apartment on Kommendörsgaten which we've moved into."

"I had no idea" Elijah said. "Why didn't you tell me?"

"We're not penniless Elijah" she laughed, "just poor aristocracy. The other thing is that Benji doesn't know anything about you other than I work with you."

Benji was a tall, striking looking boy. He'd inherited his mother's skin, but instead of normal blond Nordic hair, his was auburn coloured. The three of them ate dinner together at the apartment, which turned out to be a large ten-room residence with three bathrooms, filled with priceless furniture and works of art.

"Somehow after your little speech in the car Agnota, I expected bare floor boards and that you may be taking in washing" he joked.

"Believe me, this is poor compared to where we moved from" she retorted.

***

After dinner Benji headed to his room at the far end of the apartment while Elijah and Agnota sat in the lounge sipping their wine. She sat on a couch with Elijah opposite, her feet tucked under her.

"I won't bite you know" she said softly.

"More's the pity" he said before turning the talk to business matters and briefing her on the business aspects of his discussions with Göring. Finally he looked at his watch. "I hope you'll excuse me, I find that flying tires me, particularly when I was half on edge wondering if the Brits might come out of nowhere and attack our plane. If you don't mind, I think I'll head for bed so that I'm fresh for tomorrow's meeting with the Minister."

He went out like a light, falling into a deep sleep, so deep he didn't realise she'd joined him until he woke the following morning by which time protesting seemed futile. What surprised Elijah most was Benji's reaction later that morning. He didn't seem in the least bit surprised at meeting his mother exiting Elijah's room in her nightgown.

Since Jorge hadn't been able to secure a seat for Elijah on the commercial airline flight back to Berlin for another three days, he found himself left with plenty of time on his own with Agnota. On the second night he attended one of her intimate dinners with a small number of her friends where he was introduced to Folke Bernadotte. The Count was responsible for integrating the Boy Scout movement into the Swedish defence plans in the event the country was invaded.

Elijah found him a fascinating conversationalist. Bernadotte in turn was interested in Elijah's background, particularly on learning he controlled a Swedish shipping line. But what started out to be an amiable evening ended in high drama as Bernadotte and Agnota got into a heated argument over the Swedish government's recent agreement to allow Germany access to the Swedish railway system so they could move troops between Norway and Finland. She agreed with the decision; he didn't.

The depth of Agnota's pro-Nazi sympathies surprised Elijah. Whilst he'd always suspected they were there, he'd never before been exposed to the full extent of them. Later, when he replayed the evening back in his mind, he realised her close friendship with Carin and Hermann Göring should've prepared him for this.

***

The return trip to Zürich was uneventful other than for the constant security checks he endured as he travelled by train from Berlin to the Swiss capital. There, after stopping overnight with Jorge and Elvira, he resumed his cover as an American courier and travelled back across Vichy France and Spain to Lisbon.

True to his word, Cordell Hull had organised priority seating on the flights to Southampton and New York and exactly three weeks after he had left, Elijah finally arrived back in New York. The following morning he continued to Washington to keep his appointment with Hull and brief him on his meeting with Göring.

"So they're planning to go ahead with the invasion" the Secretary mused. "That matches other intelligence we're receiving. They're certainly pounding the British from the air. Joe Kennedy tells me that the

Brits can't last and they'll be forced to surrender soon."

"That wasn't the feeling I got from my short time in England" Elijah replied. "I'd give them a lot more resilience than that."

"And this comment about the Russians" Hull continued, "I find that very interesting. This could mean the Germans may well be looking to attack Russia next." As the meeting broke up twenty minutes later, he extended his hand. "As always, I'm indebted to you. You'll find that the United States Government will always be grateful for your efforts. We shan't forget."

"Just get me to my wife before she suspects what I've been up to Cordell; that'll be thanks enough" Elijah replied.

Chapter 12

Estancia Tierra de Abundancia, Argentina
September 1940

By the time he arrived in Buenos Aires several days later, Elijah was thoroughly sick of flying. Checking into the Alvear Palace Hotel in the up-market *barrio* of Recoleta, he fell onto the bed and slept soundly for twelve hours. Emerging refreshed onto the streets, he was dismayed to encounter a feeling similar to the one he'd experienced in Berlin in the early days of Nazi Germany. Johnny confirmed the country was rife with rumours of an expected military coup.

"It's not if Boss, rather it's when. The people are pro-British, but the military is pro-German. Everywhere you look, there are strikes across the board, although our operations are generally pretty good these days. My deputy's brother-in-law is a colonel" Johnny informed him. "He keeps me up to date with events. He says the man to watch is a colonel called Juan Perón who he claims is destined for bigger things."

"I've decided it's time to pull you out of here Johnny. I want you back in the States within the month. I'm seriously considering what to do with the businesses here, but I'd rather have you back in the States than stuck here if Argentina decides to throw its lot in with the Nazis."

He felt disillusioned by the very clear evidence of fascism taking root. He loved Buenos Aires, considering it was where life really started for him after the dark days of his childhood spent in the mission outside Brisbane. By the time he reached the *estancia*, a dark mood had settled over him.

***

In the space of only a month, his son had grown nearly an inch, his shoulders and chest were broader and despite it being winter in Argentina his face and hands reflected the effect from being constantly outdoors. Like his father before him, the boy had immediately taken to the outdoor life of the *gauchos*, spending most of his time with them on cattle drives and learning skills in horsemanship.

"You must be proud of him" Enrique exclaimed. "He's so like you were when I first taught you to ride."

"In truth Enrique, I hardly know him" Elijah sighed. "He won't allow me to get close."

Enrique shook his head sadly. He worshipped his employer. Father and son were so alike in looks and temperament it saddened him to see the chasm that divided them. Patrick's only acknowledgment of his father's arrival was a brief cold hello. Beyond that, he spoke only as required.

Sophia also fretted at the continued antagonism between Patrick and Elijah. She'd hoped the holiday at the *estancia* might help heal the wounds of the past but she could see that Elijah wasn't relaxed in the way he'd been the previous year. He even seemed distant towards her and the two younger children. Two year old Rai doted on his older half-brother and was delighted at the return of his father. He couldn't understand why Patrick suddenly no longer spent time with him, picking him up and throwing him in the air or chasing him through the house as he'd done for the previous month.

Elijah for his part was concerned about the future of his Argentine investments and the direction the country seemed to be taking. He decided not to tell Sophia of his rushed trip to Europe. As the carefree atmosphere that had prevailed before Elijah's arrival soured, she found herself increasingly seeking solace at the little cemetery on the hill. For their own selfish reasons, each of them was glad when the two weeks were up and they returned to Buenos Aires for the long flight home.

Try as he may, he couldn't shake the uneasy feeling he'd experienced during his visit to the city. With the military continuing to sympathise with Germany and its allies, Argentina fell out of favour with the United States. Everything pointed to the possibility of a military coup. Finally in mid-December 1940, Elijah decided he and Jorge needed to talk about the problem.

Despite the limitations caused by wartime phone communications, he was able to convince Jorge that they should start to sell off everything except the *estancia* and the other farming properties.

"I want the *estancia* moved into a foundation out of anyone's reach now or in the future; tied up so tight it'll be impossible for any of my descendants to ever consider selling it. Can you do that?"

Jorge confirmed it could be done.

"That's not all, one of the foundation's articles is to include employment for life for Enrique and his direct descendants for as long as they stay on the *estancia*. I also want Mercedes' name included in the foundation's name."

"How about keeping it simple; say *El Fundación Elijah y Mercedes*?" suggested Jorge.

"Yeah I like that, Elijah and Mercedes. Let's run with that."

It would take Jorge nearly two years to sell off his Argentine assets in an orderly manner. In so doing, he beat the military coup of 1943 that paved the way for the Perón years by just six months. Once again, the pair's noses for trouble had been unfailingly correct.

***

Late one afternoon about ten weeks after returning to New York he was at work in his Fourth Avenue office when his secretary interrupted him. "Excuse me Mr Hocking" her voice came through the intercom. "I have a lady with me who claims to be Mrs Hocking."

It could only be one person. He sat drumming his fingers on the desk while he considered his options.

"Mr Hocking?" his secretary's voice sounded again.

"Show her in Amelie, and ensure we're not disturbed."

The door to his office opened and Kyra entered the room accompanied by his secretary.

"A moment Amelie. First, while this woman was *once* Mrs Hocking, she's definitely no lady. Second, advise security that she's to be denied entry to this building in the future. We'll talk about this later" he said dismissing her.

"I'm sorry Mr Hocking, I didn't realise" she stammered, backing out of the room and shutting the door behind her.

"What do you want Kyra? Make it short and then get out."

"I know all about you and your Nazi whore and your trips to Germany" she said triumphantly, pulling at her gloves as she started to remove them.

"Don't worry about the gloves or even think about sitting down; you won't be here long enough. Is that all you came for?"

"You don't fool me" she replied. "You're a Nazi plant and I'm going to expose you. I've waited a long time for this you arse-hole. Now I'm going to watch the high and mighty Elijah Hocking fall all the way into the cesspool and drown in the shit" she laughed.

"I assume you're finished" he said. "Now get out or I'll have you dragged out."

He pushed the intercom button.

"Amelie, the woman in my office is leaving. Please escort her to the street."

Without looking up he said "Goodbye Kyra, and this time it *is* goodbye." The door opened and his secretary re-entered. Kyra turned on her heels and stormed out as Elijah picked up his phone.

When the other party answered, he said " I have a job for you" before hanging up.

***

As Kyra left her apartment later that night and opened the door of her La Salle sedan, her mind focussed on the euphoric feeling of sweet revenge that was still enveloping her. She not only had the bastard where she wanted him, she was going to destroy him. But that could wait for tomorrow. Tonight was set aside for a celebration with the young muscular Armenian waiter she'd selected for the occasion. He would need at least a week to recover from what she had in store for him she thought gleefully. She slid into the driver's seat and bent forward to push the starter-button when something cold pressed into her neck.

"Hello Kyra, long time no see. Don't turn around; we're going for a drive and a little talk."

Her face registered surprise and then horror as she saw the face framed in the rear vision mirror.

"Just drive and don't do anything stupid."

For ten minutes she did as instructed until she suddenly swerved the car hard to the right, trying to throw him off balance. He reached forward and grabbed a handful of her hair, yanking it hard and making her head snap back as she screamed in pain.

"Do that again and you'll wish you were never born" he said in a conversational tone, releasing her hair before delivering a backhander. Her head hit the door pillar with the force, splitting open her cheek in the process.

She was petrified. She hadn't seen him for years, but could guess what he was capable of. Involuntarily she released the contents of her bladder as she pleaded with him.

"Please Johnny let me go. I won't say anything. Please, think of the children" she cried, choking on her tears.

"Just keep driving till I tell you to stop. Till then keep your mouth shut" he said.

They drove in silence through the Holland Tunnel to the New Jersey side of the Hudson River before he directed her to turn right onto Main Boulevard finally finishing up near the Hamburg-Amerika Line docks in Hoboken.

"This will do" he told her as they cruised along the dark, empty, poorly lit streets among the looming warehouses. She stopped the car and felt the muzzle of the gun press deeper into her neck.

"Who did you talk to Kyra?" he asked.

She sat silently, shivering, before he prodded her again.

"There's still time to save yourself if you speak up" he said softly.

She hesitated a moment longer before saying "No one. I was going to the FBI tomorrow."

"Who were you going to see there?"

"I don't know" she said, "I haven't contacted anyone yet."

He grabbed a handful of hair once again pulling her head back hard against the top of the seat.

"How can I be sure you're telling the truth Kyra? I'd hate to think you were lying to me."

"No Johnny, it's true; on my children's lives I beg you it's the truth" she cried.

"You know, I think I believe you. Such a shame, I've never forgotten those times we spent together while Elijah was away. After all these years, you're still the best."

"Please Johnny" she pleaded, "I won't say anything. I promise. I wasn't thinking. I just wanted to get back at him for everything he's done to me."

"It's okay Kyra, Ssshhh" he replied softly. His teeth were reflected in the rear vision mirror as he smiled at her in the dark, cocked the trigger of the gun and calmly shot her in the back of the head. It took another hour for him to dump the car in a remote section of the Hudson River and clean himself up before heading to his nearby car and back to New York City.

***

Two days later, Elijah's secretary entered his office looking flustered. "There's a Detective O'Ryan here to see you Mr Hocking."

"Did he say what he wants?"

"He's enquiring about Mrs Hocking, I mean the visitor you had the other day."

"Then show him in and ensure we're not disturbed."

Elijah rose from his desk as the detective entered the office "How may I help you Detective?" he asked pleasantly, waving the man to a chair.

"I apologise for intruding but I'm investigating the disappearance of Mrs Hocking" he replied.

"I beg your pardon detective, the *disappearance* of Mrs Hocking? My wife is *missing*?" he asked.

"Yes sir, her housekeeper reported she left home two evenings ago and hasn't been seen since."

"You must be mistaken Detective. I had breakfast with her this morning."

It was the policeman's turn to look surprised. "I'm sorry sir; we received a report and I met with the housekeeper just a couple of hours ago. She tells me that Mrs Hocking had not returned from a dinner engagement two nights ago."

"I'm sorry Detective. I'm finding this discussion somewhat confusing. Are we talking about the same person?"

By now O'Ryan was looking totally perplexed. He removed his notes from his coat pocket and consulted them before looking up again and continuing. "You are married to Mrs Kyra Hocking?" he asked.

"Oh her!" Elijah retorted. "You mean my former wife. We've been divorced since 1935."

"I apologise sir. I wasn't informed. When was the last time you saw her?" he asked.

"We rarely speak and on those few occasions we do we don't exchange pleasantries" Elijah said. "I hadn't seen her for many months, but she called into my office here on Tuesday afternoon. I sent her away and told security not to let her in again."

"If relations between you are poor, would you mind telling me why she visited you Mr Hocking?"

"Certainly detective, her brother has been arrested for espionage by the Germans and she had some half-baked idea that I might be able to get them to release him."

"How did she seem to you?" the detective asked.

"No different to normal. Full of the normal profanities when I told her to get out" Elijah replied.

"What can you tell me about her friends?" the detective asked.

Elijah leaned forward. "Mr O'Ryan, Kyra and I were at war throughout most of our marriage and have been ever since. She has always maintained a wide circle of young male friends but I don't think they spend much time talking. Kyra is more into physical relationships. I stress it's a very wide circle and the young men are chosen for their physical attributes and prowess rather than their ability to provide mental stimulation or hold a meaningful discussion. It was the major reason we divorced. Now if she has not returned home, what about the kids – where are they?"

"At the moment the housekeeper is at the apartment, but I'm not aware of any other arrangements."

"Do you suspect foul play?" Elijah asked.

"Well sir, at this stage it's a missing person's file, but yes we're concerned" he replied.

"Then if there are no further questions it may be best if I arranged to have the children collected by my wife until Kyra turns up" Elijah said standing up. "This doesn't sound like her detective. Kyra may have been a lousy wife, but she was always a good mother. She would never leave them alone like this without having made some sort of arrangements for them to be looked after."

Accompanying the policeman to the door, he added "I'd appreciate you keeping me informed of any developments detective."

***

A few days later the Detective called again. "I'd like to revisit the reason for Mrs Hocking's meeting with you" he started. "As I understand it, you'd had no contact with her for some time. Could you tell me again why she visited you?"

"Certainly. I'm sure you're aware I'm a Swiss national. Before the war, I was Chairman of a Swedish company which did business with the Germans. Kyra's brother had been arrested at the Wilhelmshaven naval base, which I understand is closed to foreigners. Petros and his father own a shipping company so I assume he must've been in Germany on business. She told me that he'd been arrested near a fitting out dock on suspicion of spying. She hoped I still had contacts in Germany who could assist in having him released."

"What was your response?" asked the detective.

"I reminded her there was a war on and that her brother shouldn't have been where he was. For a serious charge like espionage he was likely to be in the clutches of the Gestapo. I certainly don't have any contacts with them."

"What did she do then?"

"Oh I got my usual serving of abuse. Kyra's language could descend to the gutter immediately she couldn't get her way. She called me a prick and an arse-hole and all manner of similar epithets, so I summoned my secretary and had her thrown out with instructions that security were not to let her back in the building at any time in the future."

After asking a couple of additional questions the detective closed his notebook and stood up. "Thank you Mr Hocking, you've been very helpful. We're convinced your former wife has met foul play and her disappearance is now being treated as a homicide. If you think of anything that you feel might assist us further, I'd appreciate you calling me."

"Of course Detective. Likewise if you receive any information regarding her whereabouts I'd appreciate you letting me know."

As the detective reached the door he stopped and turned around.

"One further question Mr Hocking. It's more for my curiosity than anything else. If you could have, would you have attempted to have her brother released?"

"Well detective, that's a rhetorical question but since you've asked; no I wouldn't have. My opinion of Petros and his father is well known. They're both unscrupulous and totally and morally dishonest. I found it unusual that Kyra even came to me for help. You see I think she detested her father and brother even more that she detested me. Perhaps it's true what they say; at the end of the day, blood *is* thicker than water."

***

Crisantro and Selena barely knew their father. Since their parents' divorce in 1935, Kyra ensured they grew up hating Elijah. She spoke out against him at every opportunity convincing the children that their father wanted nothing to do with them. On those few occasions Elijah gained access, it was only possible with a court order. When Sophia called to collect them from their apartment, the children shrank from her. It was only through the power of her personality that she convinced them to leave with her.

Treating them no differently to her own two sons, it didn't take long for Sophia's two new charges to warm to her. As the days stretched into weeks and there was still no news of Kyra, Elijah believed Crisantro should be sent to boarding school. There could be no mistaking the boy's parentage with the throwback to Elijah's Jamaican roots very evident. Most elite schools of the day didn't admit coloured students, but Phillips Academy which Patrick attended was one of the few that did. Patrick was aware he had a younger half-brother, but he'd never met him.

"It's going to be very important that Patrick is introduced to Crisantro properly" Sophia warned Elijah "if they're going to attend the same school. Let me float the idea to him. If you tell him Crisantro's going to attend Phillips then he'll go out of his way to make things difficult as a way of getting back at you."

Elijah knew she was right. The fact was, he'd failed dismally with both boys. Reasoning she should strike before Patrick came home for the holidays, Sophia travelled to Phillips before the end of term. Gently, she explained about Kyra's disappearance and that the police believed she'd been murdered.

"Crisantro and Selena will now be part of our family" she told him. "They've lost their mother, just as you lost yours. They need our help especially as this will be their first Christmas without her, and I'm going to need your help to get them through. I'd like to think that you and Crisantro can become friends and that you'll be able to watch over him for me."

"Why hasn't father ever brought them home before?"

Deciding that truth was the best response she replied "Their parents had a very unhappy marriage and a very bitter divorce. The reason you lived with Uncle Jorge and Aunt Elvira for so long was because the relationship between Kyra and your father was so bad even while they were married, your father decided it wasn't a home he wanted you brought up in. When they divorced, Kyra did everything she could to deny your father access to them."

The boy asked a couple more questions about them before finally agreeing. Sophia leaned forward and embraced her stepson. "Thank you Patrick. You don't know how much this means to me."

But Sophia was not to get off so lightly with Selena. Elijah literally couldn't stand the sight of her, convinced the girl was not his daughter.

"You can't blame me Sophia" he said as she brought up the issue once again. "I look at her and all I see is the result of Kyra's whoring."

"That's hardly the girl's fault Elijah. She's lost her mother and her father's rejected her. How do you think that plays on the mind of an eight year?"

"I'm sorry. You know I'd do just about anything for you, but I can't look at that child with anything but contempt. She's already a carbon copy of her mother in looks and temperament. It's too much to ask. She should be in a school too" he replied.

But Sophia wouldn't hear of it, looking instead for a day school near Scarsdale that Selena could attend.

When Patrick was due to come home for the Christmas vacation a couple of weeks later, Sophia collected him taking Crisantro and Selena with her as a way to break the ice. After a perfunctionary greeting, all three children fell silent on the way home, with only Sophia making any attempt at conversation. She was therefore pleasantly surprised to find Patrick starting to hang out with Crisantro and Selena after a couple of days. She pulled him aside to thank him for making an effort, not anticipating the response she got.

"It was easy" he said. "We all swapped notes on how much we hated father. Once we realised we had that in common, it was easy to be friends."

**

War was highly profitable Elijah discovered, especially when you dealt with both sides. The Germans were paying directly into his Swiss bank accounts for their iron ore, and the British had an insatiable appetite for all the foodstuffs he could supply from Argentina and his Empire farms and ranches. In the U.S., his companies' total production of oil, steel, ball bearings and other manufacturing items were committed for months ahead with production running at double shifts, up from the three and four day working weeks of just a couple of years previously.

He'd bought both companies listed in the file that Hull had handed him. Of the two, the molybdenum mine at Pollock near McCall, Idaho had the greatest potential. With the United States gearing up towards possible war, there was a huge demand for the mineral used in the manufacture of armour plating and stainless steel. The company had been hit badly during the great depression. When it finally started to recover, it was almost ruined through a major embezzlement by its founder. The company's bankers wanted their money back and it was only because of the ore's strategic importance that the company hadn't been liquidated. Elijah wasted no time in repaying the banks and taking control of the operation. The Columbus Ohio lead was almost as good; a piston manufacturer supplying to Boeing, Consolidated Aircraft and Lockheed.

Christmas 1940 brought Elijah's extended family together for the first time as all five children gathered at Scarsdale. Patrick was now approaching fifteen and like his father at that age, looked older. Crisantro was twelve and Selena eight while Rai had turned two and Marcello was already sitting up and showing signs of being an early developer. Despite all Sophia's efforts, Christmas was a strained affair. Try as she may; she couldn't bridge the gap between Patrick and his father. Crisantro and Selena were both miserable, missing their mother terribly. Only the two younger children seemed unaffected by the tensions as they opened their presents with gurgles of delight.

Finally giving into Sophia's nagging, Elijah took Patrick cross-country skiing one morning. The boy only agreed as a favour to Sophia of whom he'd grown quite fond. Father and son skied across a landscape blanketed with thick snow, both silent with their own thoughts for the first twenty minutes. The only sound that broke the still air was the whoosh of their skis in the powder snow. Occasionally Elijah pointed out items of interest or gave directions as they followed the trails through the forests surrounding Scarsdale. Finally he called a halt.

"Is this to be another one of those father-son talks?" Patrick asked. "If so don't waste your breath. I've already promised Sophia that I'll look after Crisantro at school, so I don't need the lecture from you."

"Patrick" his father began. "What is it about me that you hate so much? I'm ready to accept I haven't been the best father, but we've never talked about why I wasn't there or why I sent you to live in Switzerland. Will you at least give me a chance to tell my side of the story? If at the end of it you still feel the same, then I'll have to accept the inevitable."

Patrick stood away from Elijah. He appeared not to be listening. The silence between them stretched until Elijah was convinced his son had decided to give him the silent treatment.

"Where would you like to start?" the boy replied eventually, a bitter brittle edge to his voice. He turned to look at Elijah with the same cold hard look that was a trademark of the older man before lapsing once more into silence. It was Elijah who finally broke the impasse.

"Your mother's death devastated me" he said. "There was no warning; she was full of life, so vibrant and suddenly she was gone." He looked away staring out over the rolling hills that stretched in front of them. "I thought I'd lost all hope of happiness when my first wife and son were murdered. You didn't know that did you?"

He looked back at Patrick as he spoke. Patrick shrugged his shoulders. "Enrique told me and Sophia took me to their graves" he said.

"Yes, I should've guessed they would do that." Elijah replied before lapsing into silence once more. Another minute passed before he cleared his throat and continued. "Miranda showed me what life was again. When she died I was convinced it was all a crock of shit and then Kyra came along and confirmed it. I've made some mistakes with my life son, but she was the biggest."

He looked away again out over the distant hills. "Her legacy is your hatred for me. I thought I'd done the right thing when Jorge suggested you stay with them so that I could clean up the mess my personal life had become. Weeks became months and months became years. I could never have brought you into that den of hatred. But then I don't expect you to understand."

"What is there to understand? You rejected me, and then destroyed *my* chance of happiness when you took me away from Uncle Jorge and Aunt Elvira. Just because you'd loused up your own life, you didn't have to louse up mine!"

"Patrick it wasn't….."

"You've had your turn to speak father" Patrick interrupted him. "You once told me that I shouldn't interrupt when you were talking. Well the same goes for you when it's my turn. Do you know how many times I looked forward to you coming to Zug, but when you arrived I can't remember one hug, or you reading me a story, or just taking me somewhere. Then you turned up one day and announced you were sending me off to a school in a foreign country. I hated Eton but not as much as I hated you by then. Finally just when I started to get used to it, you pulled me out again and sent me here to America."

"The war was coming Patrick, I couldn't leave you at Eton. You would've been cut off from both me and Jorge."

"There's always an excuse isn't there?" the boy retorted, his voice rising in anger. "I'm cut off from Uncle Jorge anyway, and I never see you either since I'm at boarding school or you're away on business. So what's different?"

It was the boy's turn to look away as his voice broke.

"Patrick" Elijah said as he moved closer to his son, his arm extended out to him.

"Forget it father" Patrick said. "If that's your excuse for me, what've you concocted for Crisantro and Selena's little chat?"

The retort brought Elijah up short. His arm dropped and he felt as though his son had punched him in the solar plexus. In that one question Elijah realised he was never going to break through.

"I think it's time we headed back" he said quietly. "There's not much else to say after that is there?"

Silently his son turned his skis and headed back in the direction they'd come from.

Chapter 13

New York, U.S.A.
February 1941

The two boys had been back at school for a week when Elijah received another call from Detective O'Ryan.

"I'd like to meet again Mr Hocking" he said. "There're a couple of matters that have come up I'd like to go over with you. It shouldn't take long."

"Well" Elijah replied, "that would be fine detective except that I'm not in the city at the moment and I'm heading to the west coast the day after tomorrow."

"I'd be happy to head out to your house if that's convenient; Scarsdale isn't it? How about later today?"

"Quite a spread" O'Neil said as he sat in Elijah's study later that morning. "I doubt I'm going to be able to afford anything like this on my salary or pension."

"I think we can both agree on that" Elijah responded. "Now what was it you wanted to talk about?"

"We've been talking to a number of your former wife's friends and associates. You mentioned that Mrs Hocking came to you for assistance to have her brother freed from the Nazis."

"That's correct Detective. Would you please stop calling her Mrs Hocking. We haven't been married for over five years and Mrs Hocking is actually in another part of this house. With regards to Kyra's request, we've been over that a couple of times already" Elijah said.

"Was this the first time she'd requested your assistance in this matter?"

"No" replied Elijah, "as a matter of fact it wasn't. She asked me the same thing seven or eight months previously and I turned her down then as well."

The detective looked puzzled. "Why didn't you mention this to me before? Didn't you think it was relevant?"

"Not at all. Kyra rarely took no for an answer regardless of what she wanted. It's how I got stuck with her in the first place. I have to say I don't particularly like your line of questioning detective, so perhaps you better tell me exactly why you're here."

The detective smiled and shook his head. "That's exactly why I'm here Mr Hocking. I'm surprised that a man of your considerable intellect and ability wouldn't have thought to tell me that this wasn't the first time that she'd asked for your assistance in the matter. There wasn't any other reason that she called on you that perhaps you've forgotten to mention is there sir?"

"No there isn't" Elijah replied with a hint of annoyance. "I hadn't realised you possessed expertise in international relations or I would have made a point in asking your advice. I don't see this has any bearing on your investigation into Kyra's disappearance."

He rose followed by his visitor. "By now I'm sure you've satisfied your curiosity as to my life style and hopefully you've exhausted your line of questioning. Right now you're impinging on the little time I have available to spend with my family. I promised my wife this week would be her's without interruption until I fly to Los Angeles the day after tomorrow. If that's all, let me show you the way out."

"Of course sir, I appreciate you giving me the time you have. I'm sure you realise it's necessary for me to follow up anything which might resolve the mystery of the former Mrs Hocking's whereabouts. It's most peculiar that she's completely disappeared without any trace."

"I assume you've attempted to contact her circle of male associates, although I appreciate that could be a never-ending exercise based on my experience during our marriage" Elijah asked.

"Excuse me Mr Hocking. Is that a Cézanne?" the detective suddenly asked, stopping in front of a painting of some figures on a riverbank.
"It certainly is a beautiful painting."

Elijah smiled. "A detective with a flair for art; I'm most impressed
but no, that is a Seurat; it's called *Groupe de Personnages* to be precise."
He followed the detective's eyes as they moved to another painting
hanging nearby. "That Mr O'Neil is a van Rysselberghe, and before you
ask, the one opposite is in fact your Cézanne."

Elijah pointed to another painting that could be seen through an adjacent open doorway "and that is one of Sérusier's. I'm rather partial to
post impressionism. Now while I'd normally be delighted to give you
a guided tour, my wife will be champing at the bit. Are you married?"

When the detective nodded, Elijah continued "Then with your own
working hours I'm sure you know where I'm coming from."

***

In early May 1941 Elijah travelled to Washington to attend a function
being hosted by Mark Frost at *The D.C. Monitor*. He was on the point
of leaving when he was approached by a tall, blond, typically Nordic
looking man in his early forties. There was a weary look about him as
though he was carrying all the world's problems upon his shoulders,
contradicted by his sparkling clear blue eyes that looked as though
they couldn't stop laughing.

"Mr Hocking" he started, "if I might interrupt for a moment." He
passed Elijah a gilt edged, cream coloured card identifying him as
Count Ludde af Möllevángen, the Second Secretary at the Swedish
Embassy. "I wonder if we could meet somewhere in private to discuss
a rather delicate matter? I'm afraid a gathering like this would not be
suitable."

Intrigued, Elijah agreed on The Owl Bar on East Chase Street in
nearby Baltimore later that night. He had no trouble identifying the
diplomat on arrival since he was the only other customer in the bar.

"Mr Hocking, it's kind of you to meet me" the Count said in clear unaccented English. "You've been spoken of in the highest regard by my associates in Sweden. Please, may I order you something to drink?"

As Elijah shook his hand and ordered a Jack Daniels, he took an instant liking to the man. "And who might your associates be?" he asked.

His host smiled in response. "Perhaps you will allow me to be a little slow in answering that question, although it will come out in the course of our discussion. We have a number of mutual friends, one of whom is extremely well known to you. I speak of course of the delightful Baroness Lindforss who particularly asked me to pass her warmest wishes to you should we meet."

The two men sat and discussed a number of friends they shared in common while they ordered their meals. Once they'd been served, the Count steered the discussion to the situation in Europe.

"I'm sure you'd be aware of the current plight of those of Jewish extraction in Germany and the occupied countries. Already in France, Belgium and particularly Holland, Jews are being rounded up and deported to camps in Germany and Poland. We're hearing the most frightful accounts of the inhumane treatment these people endure while being transported. There are even rumours of people being put to death at some of these camps, although we haven't been able to verify this as yet."

"Are you Jewish as a matter of interest Count?" Elijah interjected.

"No I'm not" his companion replied "and please call me Ludde. May I call you Elijah?" he asked gaining Elijah's ascent with a nod of his head.

Ludde stopped talking to eat a mouthful of his steak before continuing.

"The situation in Eastern Europe is even more dire. The Jews in Warsaw are blockaded inside a ghetto by a wall and the future of those in Czechoslovakia is little better. Even Germany's allies, Hungary, Bulgaria and Romania are rounding them up. It seems only in Italy are they currently safe."

Elijah sat back in his chair. He found the Count's company enjoyable but hoped he hadn't been brought out on a cold rainy night just to hear a discourse on the problems of Europe's Jews. "This is all very interesting Ludde, but exactly what has it to do with me?"

"There are a number of us in Sweden who believe that we can help even if only in a small way" the Swede continued. "While Germany forces Sweden to maintain her neutrality by trading with them, it doesn't mean that we must sell our souls as well. The last time you were in Sweden, I believe you had a discussion with Count Folke Bernadotte over dinner."

"Ah yes, a most enjoyable gentleman as I recall, although I wouldn't have thought that with their opposing views, Agnota and Folke would have been allied in their concern for the Jews of Europe."

Ludde smiled at first, and then started laughing. "A very erudite observation Elijah. They rarely agree on anything, but love to argue and debate about everything. You can always be assured of entertainment at any dinner party which they both attend" he said before becoming serious once more. "Folke is aware of a plan I'm working on to assist Jews to escape by ship to Sweden. He suggested I should talk to you regarding utilising your ships on their return voyages from Germany to Sweden."

***

Elijah put down his knife and fork and sat silently for a long moment before answering. "The first problem Ludde is that while I own the ships, I have no control over where they are shipping from or to. The bulk of the Swedish cargo we carry is from Narvik in Norway so even if I was to agree to your request, I'd be delivering your human cargo from one Nazi territory to another. That seems to negate the whole purpose of your plan. Secondly as I understand it, the ships are searched thoroughly each time they leave port in Germany to ensure there are no illegals on board. I wouldn't want to put my captains at risk of arrest if stowaways were found. Thirdly, what makes you think I'd be remotely interested in such a venture?"

"Günter Cohn also speaks highly of you" his companion replied. "He moved from Switzerland to Sweden just before war was declared and has become active within our group."

Elijah was startled at the mention of the German actor's name. "I hope that this information is not widely known" he said.

"I believe he's only ever mentioned it in confidence to the executive members of our group, and then only when your name was mentioned as a possible source of assistance" the Count hastened to assure him.

"Be that as it may, you haven't addressed the problem of the port or the searches of the ships in Germany."

"We wouldn't want to utilise every return sailing from Germany" Ludde explained. "We'd concentrate only on those voyages that sail back to either Luleå or Oxelösund in Sweden. The escapees would transfer from fishing boats in the Baltic once the ships have sailed from port."

"Why don't you take them across the Baltic to Sweden in these fishing boats yourselves then?" Elijah asked.

"Any small boat found at sea is likely to be stopped and searched by the German Navy" Ludde replied. "Fishing boats are only allowed a certain distance from shore and anyone headed towards Sweden is likely to be fired on or even sunk without warning. Secondly, the weather in the Baltic can be unpredictable. Your ships are well known by the navies of both countries and are on regular commercial voyages. The Germans wouldn't want to create an incident by stopping a neutral ship, particularly one involved in the vital iron ore trade once it'd sailed from a German port. We believe we can ensure the Swedish authorities will look the other way once they reach Swedish waters."

"What sort of numbers are we talking about?"

"Small groups. They'd be limited to the size of the fishing boats; probably no more than twenty five per voyage."

The Swede continued to explain the plan to Elijah over the next hour.

Finally Elijah said "I can't promise anything Ludde. I'll need a month so that I can talk with my own associates before making any decision, but I promise you it'll be seriously considered. I'm guessing that this doesn't have the official approval of your government; correct?"

The Swede shook his head in response.

"So what's a Second Secretary at the Swedish Embassy doing spruiking such a plan then?"

"As I said at the start Elijah, Sweden may officially be neutral but we still own our souls. Armies may go to war; that's the way of human nature since time immemorial, but innocent civilians should not be caught up the way these people are. As for me personally, I can't sit by idly and watch inhumanity on this scale."

Ludde's proposal kept playing in Elijah's mind. His first reaction had been to reject the request. There were few if any positives and too many negatives starting with the fact that there was no money being offered for his involvement. But Ludde's comment that he couldn't sell his soul or watch inhumanity on this scale kept repeating itself. With telephones, telegrams and telexes being tapped, the only way he could talk with Jorge about something of this magnitude was face-to-face. While they utilised a code that had been designed for them by one of Europe's top code breakers, Elijah wasn't prepared to risk something of this nature becoming knowledge to either the Germans or the Allies.

After a week of mulling over the Swede's request, he finally sent a message to Jorge. *"Can you meet me in Ireland sometime in the next two weeks?"* the telex read.

Elijah was sure he could use his contacts to get a flight across the Atlantic to Foynes, but he didn't want to have to run the gauntlet travelling across Europe to Switzerland again. Besides, it was time to let Jorge see first-hand the inconveniences of wartime travel and what Elijah had gone through when he last travelled to Sweden and Germany. A couple of days later, Jorge confirmed he could be in Dublin in ten days time.

***

Meanwhile, in New York, Sophia was experiencing her own problems.

Selena was becoming increasingly withdrawn, and separated from Crisantro, prone to temper tantrums. Elijah's response was to have her sent away to school but Sophia wouldn't hear of it. Her mind was changed one day in late May, when responding to Marcello's cries, she found Selena bending over his cot hitting the toddler with a wooden toy.

"Selena!" she screamed, "Selena stop it! What do you think you're doing?"

She ran across the room, seizing the girl by the arm and dragged her away from the crib. As Sophia turned back to comfort Marcello, Selena sank her teeth into her step-mother's arm before running from the room. Fearful of Elijah's reaction, Sophia gave an abridged version of the event before announcing she'd decided that Selena should be sent away to school as soon as possible.

"Don't say I didn't tell you Sophia, she's got the makings of a little tart written all over her, the result of her mother's genes. *La madre es una puta, la hija es una puta.*"

"Elijah, how could you? This is your daughter you're talking about" Sophia exclaimed angrily, shocked at Elijah's comparison of Selena to Kyra as a whore. "That's not fair, but she needs more professional help than I can provide her."

"You're too soft with those kids Sophia" Elijah said shaking his head. "Their mother had no concept of discipline. School will knock that into her."

Unlike Elijah, Sophia was not looking for a boarding school with a military regime to beat Selena into submission. It took a month, but finally she found a small, newly established residential school in Lake Placid, New York which balanced scholastic studies with an outdoor farming life. She arranged for Selena to board at the school during the week, returning home to Scarsdale for the weekends. While Elijah wasn't happy with the arrangements, he agreed to them in the face of Sophia's steely determination.

***

Jorge was already in Dublin when Elijah arrived from New York two weeks later.

"*Infierno sangriento* Elijah!" Jorge exclaimed as they met in the bar of the Royal Marine Hotel from where Marconi had broadcast his first wireless transmission nearly twenty years before. "I had no idea how complicated it'd become to travel across borders with the war on."

"Can I take it you enjoyed your train trip across France and Spain?" Elijah replied, a huge grin plastered across his face. "You'll enjoy it twice as much heading back home. You'll be very thankful that I talked you into taking out Swiss nationality."

The two men moved to a table in the far corner of the room where they could talk uninterrupted and be able to see anyone who entered the bar. They sat discussing the situation in Europe for some time before Elijah said "Before we turn to our own businesses *amigo*, I want to discuss the meeting I had in Washington."

He briefed Jorge on Ludde's request to use their ships to transport Jewish refugees across the Baltic to Sweden.

"I've obviously had a couple of weeks to think about it and I've formed some views on the matter" he finished. "It's a pretty far reaching decision we have to make. We're potentially putting our captains and crews at risk, not to mention our business with the Germans if we agree to Ludde's request. There's also the question of whether we're a charity or a business. Don't answer me right now, think on it overnight and we'll talk about it tomorrow. In the meantime I know you're busting to talk business so let's do that over dinner."

The next morning his companion joined him clutching a sheaf of notes.

"I've being weighing up the pros and cons of yesterday's discussion. Think me paranoid Elijah, but even though this country is officially neutral, it has pro-German tendencies in high places. It's reportedly riddled with spies from both sides. I've arranged to hire a small yacht so that we can go sailing and talk quite openly."

"I didn't know you sailed" Elijah said surprised.

"Elvira and I took it up over the past year. With the lake on our doorstep, and since we can't travel with the war on, we decided it was time to take up new interests. If you prefer, we could go tramping instead – we do quite a bit of that in the mountains back home these days as well."

"No, no, sailing sounds fine as long as it's sheltered and calm and you realise I've no idea how to make the boat move" Elijah responded.

"Good. I've been able to arrange a boat through my membership of the Zug sailing club and a car will pick us up at ten. You could even pretend you're a Jewish refugee at sea to add some realism to our discussions" he added with a grin.

***

The yacht had a small cockpit where they could sit and talk out of the wind. For the first hour assisted by moderate winds, Jorge sailed them down the coast from the Royal George Yacht Club at Dun Laoghaire to a small bay between Greystones and Wicklow where he lowered the sails and dropped anchor behind a headland out of the wind. Ducking down into the yacht, he re-emerged with a bottle and two glasses.

"Sorry *amigo*, I couldn't put my hands on any Jack Daniels, so you'll have to make do with this bottle of Green Spot Irish Whiskey that's been recommended in its place. The barman insisted it's Ireland's finest."

He opened the bottle pouring a generous measure into both glasses before raising his own glass and toasting "*Salud amigo!*"

"A smooth drop Jorge, I'm most impressed" Elijah commented as he downed the liquor. "Since you've obviously come well prepared, you kick off first."

"You're closer to the decision-makers than me" Jorge began, "so you're more likely to have some indication which way the war might turn. My view is that with the completion of their campaign in the Balkans, the Germans will be the indisputable masters of Europe for the foreseeable future. There's only Sweden, Switzerland, Spain and Portugal who either haven't been occupied or aren't allied to Germany.

None of them's going to oppose the Nazis; they're pretty well told what to do as it is anyway. The Russians have taken themselves out of the game by signing their treaty with Germany and Britain's on her knees. She only survives because America's supplying them with arms and food. The Americans are as far away from joining in as ever and whatever Roosevelt's sympathies may be, the voters won't let him take sides officially. How am I doing so far?"

"You could be a lecturer in politics any time you feel like changing vocations" Elijah said nodding.

"The only way that the status quo is likely to change is if the Russians fall out with the Germans or America enters the war on the side of Britain" Jorge continued. "Neither's likely to happen any time soon. Both countries are on too good a wicket as things stand. Now let's look at us. We're in the unique situation of supplying both sides. If we *were* to start transporting Jewish refugees and got caught by the Germans, we'd put our very profitable Swedish business at risk either because they'll stop dealing with us or more likely they'd lean on the Swedish government to take action against us. If we do carry the refugees, it'll be at our cost and our risk, and the Americans or Brits won't jump in to pat us on the back. You're already placing yourself at risk running Hull's errands as it is. I'm sure that if Göring suspected for one moment that you reported his conversations back to Hull, he'd have you arrested on the spot."

He stopped to take another drink of whiskey before continuing. "That all assumes of course that the status quo doesn't change and Germany remains as master of Europe. However should that change then there could be a payoff from being seen as the good humanitarians, especially in the highly unlikely event that England wins the war and starts a witch hunt of those who traded with the Germans."

"I already have Hull's guarantee that our trading won't be held against us" Elijah responded.

"Hull's yes but Churchill's no" replied Jorge. "Hull's not at war and his cities aren't the ones going up in flames every night from aircraft and bombs made in part from Swedish iron ore. We have an awful lot of investment in Empire countries that could potentially be impounded as payback."

"What about the moral issue Jorge? I've been over most of the arguments you've listed time and time again but Ludde's comment about not selling our souls keeps coming back to me."

Jorge looked away for a moment. *Mierda* Elijah" he swore. "We've both sanctioned things in the past that would contravene most people's interpretation of morals."

"True" Elijah said sharply, "but you can't compare us to these Nazi animals."

"I'm not questioning our past actions *amigo*. I happen to agree with you. All I'm saying is that we could be losers either way." He looked away again before saying *"Debemos esperar y debemos ver quién puede proporcionar el beneficio más grande a nosotros."*

"So you're saying wait and see who can provide the greatest benefit to us" Elijah asked.

Jorge nodded his head. *"Si"* he replied.

"Don't go all dago on me now mate" Elijah said back to him in a broad Australian drawl making Jorge laugh and breaking the tension that'd built up between them. "There's no-one out here to hear you. Okay, then I'll tell Ludde that we'll review it again in say twelve months."

Jorge was in a deep sleep the next morning when he was abruptly woken by a loud banging on his bedroom door. He tried to ignore it but it continued, only more insistent. Snatching up his dressing gown he crossed to the door and angrily pulled it open to be confronted by Elijah standing there grim faced.

"I'm withdrawing your invitation to teach politics" he said.

"What the hell are you talking about?" Jorge asked.

"The bloody Germans invaded Russia this morning and all hell's broken loose. They've just lost the war" Elijah responded. "Guess who can provide the best benefits now?"

Chapter 14

On his return from Ireland, Sophia told Elijah she wanted them to take a complete break as a family. She was determined that the toxic relationship between him and the older children had to change and was insisting that he make an effort. When he asked how long she was thinking of, she told him at least a month.

"It's out of the question" he replied. "With the invasion of Russia, there's too much to do with the government cranking up support for the Allies. Add to that the possibility that Japan and America could actually go to war. I've got a bunch of meetings in Washington over the next month or so and I have to meet with Deke and the others. I'm happy for the rest of you to go, but there's absolutely no way I could be away from the business for that long."

Even as he said it, he knew that she wouldn't accept his refusal without a fight. The debate flowed back and forth for several days before he suggested a compromise.

"Sophia, if I could, I would but you have to understand there's just no way I can possibly be out of contact for that length of time. How about we get a cabin in the woods somewhere in the Catskills for the summer? That way I can be at the office as necessary and still be able to spend some time with you and the kids. Perhaps Patrick could come with me when I go down to Deke's. He could stop with his kids for a week or two. Who knows, it might make up for him not being able to go to the *estancia* this year. Deke's kids are around the same age and I'm sure they'll all get on well."

"Well you better mark February off in your diary. I don't care if the Germans and the Japanese have both invaded, I expect you to be there for the birth and for a couple of weeks after" she told him.

"Again?" he asked

"Again" she replied. "Mid-February."

Elijah's assistant quickly found a cabin near the small town of Old Forge in the Adirondack Mountains about 300 miles upstate from New York City. It was further from the office than Elijah liked but he agreed to it as a compromise. It turned out to be such an idyllic spot that before long he purchased land at nearby Raquette Lake and built a ten-room cabin of his own.

***

Sophia and the four younger children travelled to Old Forge in late July while Elijah and Patrick flew south to Texas. Despite his previous rebuffs, Elijah still hoped that his son might drop his hostility towards him but the boy spoke only when spoken to, and then only in monosyllables, making his feelings towards his father quite obvious.

"Howard Hughes tells me I should get a plane and a pilot's license and fly myself around" Elijah told Deke as they drove from the small municipal airport near Kilgore back to the farmhouse. "It mightn't be a bad idea considering all the travel I'm doing these days. Perhaps Patrick could learn to fly as well" he added looking sideways at his son in the back seat.

Patrick had been staring morosely out of the window, but the comment made him suddenly turn and stare at his father.

"Are you serious or is this just another of your empty promises?" he asked.

His tone and attitude made Deke look sharply at Elijah sitting beside him. This was the first time that he'd met Patrick; in fact Elijah rarely talked about his children to anyone other than Jorge.

He noticed Deke's reaction. "It's alright Deke. I'll explain later." To

Patrick he said "I'm serious. We'll talk about it later."

In the twelve years since he'd first bankrolled Deke's exploration, Mercedes Oil had become one of the country's major oil and natural gas producers with wells in Texas and Oklahoma and substantial reserves recently discovered near Olla in central Louisiana. Despite becoming a multi-millionaire, Deke still drove a battered 1925 Hudson sedan and lived in the same farmhouse where the two men had first met.

"When are you going to get rid of this heap of shit and build a new house while you're at it?" Elijah would tease him, but Deke would just say "What for? The car still drives well, and I don't need any more rooms than I got already."

"What is it with you and the boy?" Deke asked as they sat at the kitchen table a bit later drinking coffee.

"To a large degree I'm paying the price for ignoring him, as he puts it, in his early years. I thought I was doing the right thing at the time" Elijah replied and proceeded to tell him of Patrick's childhood since Miranda's death. "I have to accept that the fault's largely mine. I just can't seem to be able to break through to him. He resents me but I'll keep at it. He's a bright kid and hopefully he'll want to come into the company when he's finished at Yale."

Over the next two days the two men reviewed the operations before Elijah flew back to Washington for another round of meetings. Patrick was to stay another week at Kilgore before joining Elijah in Washington and then travelling together to join the rest of the family at Old Forge.

As his father said goodbye, Patrick commented "You said you were going to talk about me learning to fly. See…another empty promise!"

"No Patrick. You've been out with Deke's kids every day so there's hardly been an opportunity. I haven't decided about buying a plane yet or even if I want to learn to fly, but if it's something you want to do, then we'll talk about it when we're alone. Sophia might also have something to say about it."

With Deke hovering close by, Patrick decided not to push it but it was obvious that he didn't believe his father.

***

In Washington Elijah had a large number of meetings organized with a number of leading industrialists and government officials including the Secretary of War, to discuss the government's requirements for increased production of war materials. There were also a number of Senators, Congressmen and powerbrokers who either owed him for past indiscretions, or who he was bankrolling. Finally there was Miranda's conquest of long ago, his old friend from Mississippi. Senator Horatio Wilson[8] was retiring and wanted to introduce Elijah to his replacement.

Hull had also asked to meet again. He arranged for Elijah to be picked up by car late one evening but instead of heading for either the Secretary's office or his house, the Cadillac limousine proceeded onto Pennsylvania Avenue before turning into the White House driveway and drawing up under the portico where Elijah was met by President Roosevelt's Appointments Secretary.

Escorting him into the mansion, the General advised Elijah the meeting would be conducted in the Yellow Oval Room on the second floor of the President's private quarters. He stressed there would be no official record of their meeting logged. Elijah nodded in acknowledgement.

Hull rose from a settee as Elijah entered and quickly crossed to him exclaiming "Elijah, it's good to see you again" shaking his hand warmly.

Taking Elijah by the elbow, he directed him to where the President was seated in a grey leather armchair. President Roosevelt remained seated as he shook hands saying "It's good to see you again Mr Hocking. Cordell here speaks highly of your past efforts on our behalf. Please, make yourself comfortable."

After a few minutes discussing the situation in Europe, Roosevelt commented "The German attack on Russia was far from unexpected. We tried to warn Stalin on a number of occasions but he wouldn't listen. You yourself reported that Göring made reference to the possibility of such an attack during your meetings with him last year. The German advance has certainly been impressive, but I can't help but wonder whether they've bitten off more than they can chew this time round. History has never been kind to those who've tried to invade Russia. One only has to look at Napoleon's defeat at the hands of the weather to see a clear precedence."

"I'm no military strategist Mr President" Elijah replied, "but when I look at the vast size of Russia and the disparity in their populations, I can't help but wonder at what point Germany will just run out of men or supplies."

"An excellent point. Trying to guess when they'll reach that point is what the Secretary and I want to talk with you about. I'm asking if you would be prepared to make one more visit to Germany and meet with Göring if it could be arranged. With him being so close to Hitler, and as the man who's tasked with the country's war production, his current views on their potential to continue to wage war would be most useful. He appears to have been open with you in the past and your information to us has proven impeccable."

"I'm not sure that I'd be able to gain an audience Mr President" Elijah told him. "I relinquished my shares in the Swedish ore company some time ago. I know Baroness Lindforss who now controls it very well. She's also a close friend of Göring's. I'd probably need to use her good graces to arrange a meeting."

Roosevelt and Hull looked at each other. It was obvious that they didn't know of the arrangements that Jorge had put in place to remove Elijah's continuing involvement in PMAB from public scrutiny.

"I wasn't aware of this" the Secretary said sharply.

Elijah didn't think this was the time to tell his hosts of Jorge's recent acquisition of a Swedish ball bearing manufacturer or of the contracts he'd subsequently entered into with Messerschmitt and Blohm and Voss.

"I felt that I couldn't continue to play both ends off against the middle particularly as my sympathies are with the Allies. It's true that the ships being used to transport ore to Germany are owned by me, but as they sail under the Swedish flag, they could be subject to confiscation by the Swedish government should I refuse to do so. They also carry substantial cargoes for the Allies"

Hull turned to the President. "That certainly takes away any inference that Elijah here is trading with the enemy should your detractors ever wish to raise it. When did this occur?" he asked Elijah.

"Around the time war broke out in Europe. My meeting with Hitler helped make the decision easy. That's when my associate and I decided to get out and invest instead in the United States. Obviously we didn't brief the Germans of our decision either. They seem to believe that I still control the company."

"It would be to our advantage if they continued to operate under that impression" Hull responded.

"I'm aware of the manner you have been assisting our economy in a number of areas Elijah" the President said switching to a first name basis. "Your valuable efforts have certainly not gone unnoticed or unappreciated. Are you saying that you don't believe that you could arrange a meeting with Göring? It's of the highest importance to the United States if it could be arranged. I for one wouldn't be asking you to undertake what I realise is a dangerous and compromising mission if I didn't consider it to be vital to our interests."

Elijah sat back and appeared to be studying the painting mounted over the fireplace. The silence stretched for over sixty seconds before he turned his gaze back to the President and responded. "Well Mr President, I guess there's only one way to find out."

"We'll make the same arrangements for you as before" the Secretary of State added. "I'm assuming you won't be continuing on to Argentina this time?"

"Not this time Cordell" Elijah responded with a smile. "But there will be a price for me making the trip if it can be arranged."

Hull glanced at the President before asking what Elijah expected in return.

"My fifteen year old son wants to learn to fly and I want him to learn from the best. An Air Force instructor would be perfect if that could be arranged."

The President slapped his leg as he let out a loud laugh. "I think that could be arranged, don't you Cordell?"

Hull was also laughing as he nodded his head in agreement. "I'll have someone contact you" he said.

"I'd also need to make the trip before Christmas as my wife's due to give birth in February and believe me gentlemen, I'd rather face your wrath than hers if it meant choosing between her and Göring. Let me contact the Baroness and see if she can expedite a meeting with the great man."

Roosevelt lit his pipe and took a long draw on it. "Elijah, the country and I continue to be deeply indebted to you. Thank you very much" he said extending his hand.

***

Back in 1935, Elijah had bought a house in the DuPont Circle neighbourhood of Washington. He decided he'd conduct his meeting with Ludde af Möllevángen there so that they wouldn't be seen together or overheard. The Swedish Count arrived promptly at 8.30. As before, Elijah was struck by his visitor's tired looking demeanour contrasted by his laughing blue eyes. They talked of the change in the war situation since their last meeting as Elijah served a tossed salad together with venison steaks which had been slowly smoking over hickory shavings for the past couple of hours.

"This is an excellent wine Elijah, my compliments" Ludde commented as he took a sip.

"It's a little hard to get fresh supplies these days obviously. It's a Pinot called Les Boudots from the village of Nuit Saint Georges in the Burgundy region" his host responded. "My wife is the wine expert in our household. She introduced me to it and it's now a staple in our cellar."

"And the steaks, these are hers too?"

"I'm afraid you've caught me out there too. I can't claim those either" Elijah laughed. "My cooking skills match my knowledge of wine. No, my cook prepared those and the salad for us this afternoon."

The two men ate silently for a few moments before Elijah spoke. "I'm interested to know whether your group has any contacts within the upper echelons of power in Germany."

"We have established a dialogue with two generals on Admiral Canaris's staff in the Abwehr... his deputy Hans Oster and the head of Section Two, Erwin von Lahousen plus Canaris himself."

Elijah whistled in surprise. The Abwehr was the German counter-espionage agency.

"All three are absolutely opposed to Hitler." Ludde continued. "We're hearing terrible reports coming out of Russia. While I have yet to sight any supporting evidence, we're told that in Lithuania and the Ukraine, Jews are being systematically killed by squads of SS troops following behind the Wehrmacht. This only makes us more determined to proceed with our plan."

"I've discussed your request for assistance with my associates" Elijah told him. "We feel that we need to consult with our captains as they're the ones who'll be most at risk if the Germans discover stowaways on board. There are only another three months of this season where the ports of Oxelösund and more particularly Luleå will remain ice free and open for shipping. I'm planning to travel to Europe sometime in the next few weeks if it can be arranged, and I propose to meet a number of them then and ascertain their views. It's not something I'm prepared to delegate to anyone else. Obviously if the captains object, then the matter ends there."

"And if they're agreeable?"

"Then we'll meet again. That's the best that I can offer you right now."

***

There was one final task to fulfill before leaving Washington – meeting Horatio Wilson's replacement as Senator for Mississippi. Hiram Sanders hailed from another old southern family but most importantly, he was a cousin of the retiring Senator's wife. Wilson's continuing control of the local party structure and his blatant rigging of the pre-selection process guaranteed he dictated the appointment of his replacement. With Congressman Leveridge and a number of his other contacts in government also considering retirement in the near future, Elijah was keen to ensure that he maintained his level of influence with those who replaced them. Horatio Wilson's despotic manipulation behind the scenes would also ensure that his replacement experienced a meteoric rise in the Senate Committee structure and Elijah therefore viewed him as very important to his plans.

Sanders was a younger version of Wilson in every way. In his mid-forties, publicly he was the very epitome of a Southern gentleman as demanded by his voters. Factually, like his mentor, he was a degenerate prepared to sell his soul for the right sum. The three men met at the Washington Club on K Street where Senator Wilson had arranged a private room. It was immediately obvious that Sanders and Elijah would get along famously.

"Washington won't be the same without you Horatio" Elijah said raising his glass to the older man. "On that note I'm not sure either Mississippi or your wife are ready for you full-time either."

"Yah still a young whippasnappa Elijaah. Ah cud still whup yah if needs be" the Senator responded in his long Southern drawl.

Turning to his compatriot he said "This heah young fella turned up one night with the mos' stunnin' piece a pussy yah eva did see. Pity wus he took her outa circulation after a bit by marryin' her. Never did meet anyone who eva matched up ta Miranda tho'."

He gazed off into the distance, his weak watery eyes lost in the haze of reminiscing. "Hiram here, he's gunna need lookin' afta the same way yah've looked afta me all'a these years" he continued. "Same discretion frahm both sides. Mah contacts tell me he's gunna get a committee in the Senate real quick. Somethung in defence wud be the raht area ah suspect fuh his talents."

"Elijah heah's got the ears a' those alla the way up ta the man at the top" he said to Sanders. "Yah stay close 'n' heed whut he tells yah, 'n' yah'll go far."

As the evening wore on, the old man consumed increasing quantities of liquor leading him to utter several indiscretions relating to his long public record. Elijah could see it was as well that they were dining privately. Finally the Senator could no longer stand, and had trouble holding his head up as he dribbled onto his jacket. The club's steward obviously had previous experience with him. He quietly summonsed an assistant and together they discretely carried the old man to his car waiting by a side entrance. As Sanders got up to follow, Elijah put out his hand and held him back.

"He's out to it for the night. There seems little sense in leaving with him when there's still a great deal of the night left. Am I right in assuming your wife didn't join you for this trip?" he asked.

"That's raht" Hiram replied in a drawl that was a mirror image of the older man. "Da yah have any suggestions Mr Hockin'?"

"Elijah please Hiram. I already feel as though I've known you for some time. Yes, I thought you might enjoy a little company to while away the rest of the evening, but you might want to change out of that tuxedo first. Can I offer you a lift back to your hotel first and then we can see what Washington can offer two upright gentlemen on a Friday night?"

He waited for ten minutes after dropping the younger man off before heading for home. He hadn't expected the new, happily married, upright Republican Senator for Mississippi to reappear; not once he had discovered his "Welcome to Washington" present waiting for him in his bed.

"He won't even have to unwrap her" he laughed to himself, *"and it shouldn't be long before she finds out how just upright he can be."*

***

Patrick arrived in Washington the following day. As the two of them made ready to join the rest of the family at Old Forge Elijah asked him if he was still keen about taking flying lessons.

"I'd forgotten about it. I didn't think you meant it" his son responded in his usual sullen manner.

"I wasn't looking for a fight" Elijah snapped at him. "I'd also appreciate you looking at me when you talk to me however hard that might be for you. I asked, did you still want to learn to fly?"

Patrick put down the book he was reading and looked at his father. "Yes."

"Good! I've arranged for you to take lessons from an Air Force flying instructor and no, before you ask, I haven't enlisted you. A friend owes me a favour and this way I can be sure you're getting the best tutelage possible. I can also look Sophia in the eye when I tell her what I've done. You'll need to come back to Scarsdale with me at the end of the month and you'll take your flying lessons at Stewart Air Force Base. It's about fifty miles from home. You might even want to learn to drive a car at the same time."

Sophia was extremely happy when Elijah told her the arrangements he'd made. She'd already noticed a small change in Patrick's attitude towards his father when they arrived at the cabin but she wasn't so pleased with his next piece of news. They were sitting together in the sun overlooking the lake enjoying a drink while the children swam in the cool waters below them.

"You've just returned from meeting Jorge in Ireland. What's so important that you have to go back to Switzerland?" she asked.

"Believe me, if I didn't have to, I wouldn't be going" he said.

"There's a war on Elijah. There are five children of yours down there and another on the way, not to mention me. The risk is too great. I thought the whole idea of Jorge staying in Zug was so that you could sit the war out here. If it's so important, why can't someone else go?"

"Sophia, I said if I didn't have to go I wouldn't be going" he said again.

She stood up. "That's not good enough" she said angrily. "If you can't trust me with a straight answer then you might as well go back to New York and just leave us here."

She turned to enter the house as Elijah reached out and grabbed her arm.

"Sophia..." he started, but she angrily pushed him away and stormed off, but not before he saw the tears that were coursing down her face.

He leaned over the deck and called out "Patrick!"

As his son emerged from the water Elijah said "Watch the other kids please. Sophia and I need to talk."

***

Before the boy could object, Elijah turned from the railing and went into the house in search of her. He found her preparing to head off for a walk.

"Good. I'll come with you. Patrick can watch the kids. We need to talk but not where the kids can interrupt us."

"Don't bother" she snapped back at him. "I'm not sure I want to listen anyway."

"Don't be so bloody stupid" he responded. "You sound just like Patrick. I'm going to follow you and if need be I'll talk out loud to myself, so you'll hear me anyway. Why not make it easy on yourself?"

After checking on the children, they headed off along a trail amongst the spruce trees. He'd never seen her so angry. As Sophia, followed by Elijah, headed into the surrounding forest, the sun's rays formed shafts of light where they broke through the branches. The silence was only interrupted by the sounds of cicadas humming in the undergrowth and the Palm Warblers singing overhead in the canopy while off to the right, the tapping of a woodpecker resounded through the trees. Ordinarily, the atmosphere would have been magical, but neither of them noticed the display of nature unfolding around them as they headed away from the cabin. Finally Elijah spoke. "I'm going to visit Göring."

Sophia stopped and turned to face him. "What?" she asked, a look of surprise etched on her face. "Why would you possibly want to see him?"

"Because the President has asked me to.".

For the second time she couldn't hide her surprise. "Roosevelt?"

"Well he was still President when I met him a week ago."

"You met with Roosevelt?"

"Sophia, this is going to be a very long explanation if you're going to keep repeating everything I say. Why not let me just tell you the whole story."

While they walked, he told her of his meetings with Göring at the request of the Secretary of State finishing with his meeting in Washington with the President the previous week.

"Why haven't you told me about this before?" she demanded.

"You've seen what Germany and the Nazis are like. I decided that it was better you didn't know for your own protection. The only other person outside the President and Hull who knows is Jorge."

She walked on in silence for a couple of minutes.

"I thought that maybe you were going to see the Swedish woman" she said quietly. "Are you?"

"That was a week's fling back in 1927 Sophia" he lied in reply. "But yes I am, but not in the way you're thinking. There's more to tell you yet. Agnota heads up the Swedish company since we separated it from the rest of the operations back in '39. She's introduced me to a group of Swedes who're actively involved in rescuing Jews from the Nazis."

He went on to tell her of Ludde's approach to him to use his ships to assist Jewish refugees to escape from occupied Europe.

"Have you decided what you are going to do?" she asked

"No. I need to talk with the ships' captains first. I think they should have some say in the matter" he replied.

"There's something else isn't there? This isn't the first time is it?"

"No! I escorted a couple of Jewish actors out of Germany in 1938 at Göring's request. Günter Cohn has since moved to Sweden and is part of this group."

"At Göring's request?" Sophia gasped. "How could that be?"

"They were friends of Emmy's from her acting days."

"That explains the farewell kiss on the *"Carin"*. I've always wondered if she was yet another of your conquests."

"Not guilty" he responded placing his hand on his heart.

"Then you have to go" she said. "You really don't have a choice do you?"

He shook his head in response as he moved closer to embrace her but she put out her hand and held him back at arm's length.

"Promise me that this is the last time!" she said. "You can't win the war on your own! It's not fair that you're being placed at such risk, or that your family should have to bear the cost if something happens to you. You're not even American! I'm serious Elijah; this has to be the last time! Since Jorge is in on the plot, let him do the dirty work in the future."

Sophia spoke with the steely determination that he knew so well when she'd reached a decision that he knew would not and could not be changed. She took his hand and started walking. Elijah sensed she wanted to think and stayed quiet as they walked for over five minutes. Suddenly without warning, she turned and pulled him to her, kissing him with a violent ferocity before pulling back and looking at him.

"Vete a la mierda Elijah Hocking!"

Elijah was genuinely shocked as he had never heard Sophia swear before.

"I can't decide whether you're a hero or a bloody idiot. If anything happens to you, you'd better hope they kill you, because I swear by Almighty God I'll do the job otherwise" she said before sinking her head into his chest and starting to sob.

Chapter 15

Zug, Switzerland
October 1941

Getting approval to visit Germany this time proved to be a lot more difficult. The Nazis' advance into Russia was bogging down and Göring was no longer Hitler's golden-haired boy due to the Luftwaffe's failure to crush the British in the aerial bombardment throughout 1940 and 1941. Just when it seemed Elijah would be denied access, approval arrived.

A light snow was falling when Elijah arrived in Zug late in the afternoon of the last day of October. Once again the trip across the Atlantic and Vichy France posing as a US diplomatic courier proved to be tiring, but uneventful.

"Sophia's right you know" Jorge told him. They were nursing their drinks later that evening as they sat in his study looking out over the peaceful scene of the lake and the twinkling lights of the town spread out beneath them. "This should definitely be your last trip until the war's over, whenever that might be. You'll find big changes in Germany. When I was in Augsburg and Hamburg last month I found the population very apprehensive about this latest campaign. Security's tighter too, and travel's more difficult just with the sheer volume of military traffic heading east."

Elijah nodded. "The problem is, just as Hull threw us Ricardo Minerals as a payoff last time, he could just as easily penalise us by turning off the orders. I've got myself in a bind."

"They need us don't forget *amigo*."

"But they won't always" Elijah countered. "Now, about Ludde's proposal. I need to meet with the captains and discuss it with them, but that's going to be difficult with the onset of winter. Are the Swedish ports still functioning?"

"Most of the ore's being shipped through Narvik right now. Luleå is already icebound until April although there's some still coming through Oxelösund further south" Jorge replied. 'When are you meeting Göring?"

"The seventh."

"The *"Jähn Prinsessa"* is scheduled to sail from Wismar sometime between the sixth and the tenth. Obviously that can change through any number of factors but you should be able to get there from Berlin by train without too much difficulty. Perhaps your fat friend can arrange priority travel for you. Leif Ellström on the *"Prinsessa"* is the most influential of the captains. Get him onside and I reckon he'll sound out the rest of them for you. The *"Jähn Baronessa"* will also be loading in Oxelösund about the second week of November so there's a chance you could also catch up with Isak Stromquist but that's the best I can offer you. The rest of the ships are on the Narvik run and you really don't want to go wandering around there."

***

Elijah could sense the change immediately he crossed the border into Germany at Konstanz. He was closely quizzed at the customs post as to why he was visiting Germany and for the first time, Göring's name didn't command immediate respect. Security on the train to Berlin was the most stringent he'd yet experienced, with his papers scrutinized closely on numerous occasions. Transferring between trains in Frankfurt, he witnessed a Jewish youth being beaten senseless by police before being dragged to a waiting truck and thrown aboard. All the time the beating was being delivered, passers-by stepped around the police, ignoring the incident as though nothing untoward was happening.

The German capital was bitterly cold with a grey sullen sky

162

overhead. Snow was threatening and people were scurrying to get indoors. Around him there was evidence of damage from the sporadic air raids that the city was starting to experience. As Jorge described, the air of confidence that might've been expected after two years of extraordinary victories was missing. The feeling of elation mirrored on people's faces, so evident after the fall of France the last time he was in Berlin, had disappeared to be replaced by a nervousness that communicated itself despite the general lack of conversation. The sombre mood was depressing. He just wanted to get his meeting with Göring over so he could get away again.

Next morning he was collected from the Adlon Hotel by a young Luftwaffe aide. Clicking his highly polished heels together and executing a rigid precision Nazi salute, he introduced himself in a clipped Prussian voice. "*Guten morgen* Herr Hocking. My name is Oberleutnant Ostermann. Reichsmarschall Göring apologises that he'll be meeting with you today at the Air Ministry. He had planned for you to meet at Carinhall, but due to the weather he was forced to stay in the city last evening."

The storm that hit the city the previous evening had dumped a massive amount of snow, and traffic in the Unter den Linden had slowed to a crawl as an army of workers attempted to clear it away. Due to the conditions, the short trip from the hotel to the Air Ministry took them nearly half an hour instead of the usual ten minutes.

As before they seemed to walk for miles as Elijah was led from the massive entry doors facing Wilhelmstrasse to Göring's office. All around them the corridors were filled with a flurry of secretaries and staff of all ranks rushing between offices clutching files or briefcases.

Ushered into the Reichsmarschall's presence, Elijah was once again struck by the man's gargantuan proportions accentuated by the preposterous uniform he was wearing.

"It's always a pleasure to meet you my dear Elijah" he gushed as he crossed from behind his oversized desk to meet Elijah midway across the room. They swapped pleasantries about their spouses and families before Göring steered him to the adjacent settee.

There, he regaled Elijah with a monologue of Germany's successes. "The Russians are in full flight and Stalin's rotten edifice is about to crumble...His government is already fleeing over the Urals...The halt in the advance is only temporary, we'll soon be in Moscow...The British have been forced to their knees by our magnificent Luftwaffe and it's only a matter of time before they surrender...The Italians are useless. If it wasn't for Mussolini's relationship with the Führer we..." This went on for nearly forty-five minutes before he let up.

"When do you feel the Russians will surrender Reichsmarschall?" Elijah asked.

For the first time the look of unabashed gloating disappeared from Göring's face to be replaced by a fleeting look of doubt.

"It's the damnable weather...that's the problem. The current halt in operations is to allow our supply lines to be re-established, but have no doubt, we'll take Moscow, and Leningrad for that matter, by Christmas." He sat back, looking pensive. "We're going to need additional supplies of iron ore. We are indeed fortunate to have good friends like you out in the wider world. Let me assure you, your support is appreciated by the Führer himself."

**

He rose and crossed back to his desk where he picked up a small leather box.

"The Führer has personally approved the granting of this award for your services to Germany" he continued.

Elijah was stunned as Göring opened the box, revealing the gleaming medal that lay inside.

"It gives me great pleasure to award you the Grand Cross of the Order of the German Eagle" he said as he removed it and pinned it to Elijah's chest. He leant forward and kissed him on both cheeks before vigorously shaking his hand.

"Herr Reichsmarschall, I can't possibly accept this" Elijah protested.

"But you must!" Göring responded. "You can't refuse a decoration granted by the Führer himself. He would've presented this to you personally if he wasn't heroically leading our troops in battle. In addition I've had this safe conduct pass prepared for you. With Germany on high alert for saboteurs, spies and fifth columnists, foreigners everywhere in these troubled times are viewed with suspicion. It wouldn't do to have you, the recipient of one of our highest awards, unnecessarily harassed now would it?"

As he accompanied Elijah to the office door, he put his arm around Elijah's shoulders. "You know" he said earnestly, "you will always be welcome in Germany, and in this office."

The snow was falling again as he exited the Ministry. The wind had dropped, leaving the city swathed with a clean, almost virginal look. While he was still stunned at being given the medal by Göring, he realised that this together with his safe conduct pass could be of great assistance should he decide to help Ludde with his plans.

Entering the hotel, he removed his hat and coat, shaking off the snow and crossed the lobby to the lifts aware that staff and other hotel patrons were staring at him. Stepping into the lift, the elderly attendant stared at his chest before snapping a salute. Only then did Elijah realise he was still wearing the medal that Göring had pinned on him.

Since the *"Jähn Prinsessa"* would not complete unloading until late the following day he decided to stay in Berlin overnight before travelling to Wismar the next morning. He wasn't in a mood to mix socially and ate alone in the hotel dining room. He was enjoying a glass of port with his *ersatz* coffee, when the quiet of the dining room was suddenly shattered by the shrill sound of air raid sirens. Staff quickly moved among the diners directing them to the hotel's air raid shelter as the first bombs could be heard exploding in the distance. Unwittingly, Elijah had chosen to stay in Berlin as the RAF mounted their biggest air raid of the war so far.

For over two hours as he sat in the shelter, the ground shook with the force of exploding bombs before the sirens finally sounded the all clear. He couldn't help but wonder where Göring was that night. More to the point, where was the Reichsmarschall's "magnificent" Luftwaffe?

***

Elijah had no sooner boarded the *"Jähn Prinsessa"* the following evening, than the gangplank was raised, the mooring lines cast off and the tugs positioned themselves to assist her away from the wharf. He joined Captain Ellström on the bridge as the ship sailed from port lashed by driving rain and snow and rising winds, heavy clouds scudding across the sky overhead. The storm front that had battered Berlin was centred over the Baltic Sea and a rough crossing to Sweden was expected.

"This is hardly the tourist season Mr Hocking. I'm afraid we can't promise you a comfortable trip, especially since we're only in ballast" the captain apologised. As the ship moved from the shelter of the breakwater and encountered the first wave, it reared up before crashing down again into the trough and then struggled up the face of the next wave.

"It'll get much worse before we arrive in Oxelösund" he added as he turned back to peer through the bridge windows.

Elijah nodded. He could hear the clanging of a bell as the ship passed a darkened beacon tossing in the turbulent water on the starboard side, its sound tolling mournfully into the stormy night. Suddenly they were lit by a piercing light that swept the ship from stem to stern before fixing itself on the bridge.

"That'll be a German destroyer" Captain Ellström called back to him. "They won't want to board us on a night like this."

Standing out of the way in a corner of the bridge, Elijah quietly observed the captain, the first officer and the helmsmen as they guided the ship into the increasing ferocity of the storm. Occasionally the captain would step back to Elijah, speak a few words with him, then rejoin the helmsman at the wheel.

"This is the worst weather we've experienced in years" he said at one point, "worse than the authorities were predicting but still preferable to spending another night in that wretched place."

Finally about three hours after leaving port, Captain Ellström joined Elijah at the rear of the bridge.

"It's going to be a long night Mr Hocking" he said. "I understand you have a matter of the utmost importance to discuss with me."

"It can wait until you have a little more time on your hands Captain" Elijah replied.

"Lars can handle the bridge for an hour or so. There's worse weather predicted ahead and I'll be of more use then; besides there's some real coffee in my cabin, not that acorn shit. I could do with a cup about now. Will you join me?" the captain asked.

After conferring briefly with the first mate, he led Elijah down a small corridor to his cabin where he ordered coffee from a hovering steward. While they waited for its arrival the captain briefed Elijah about the ship's operations.

"What's the weather like in the summer? Do you experience conditions like this?" Elijah quizzed him.

The captain shrugged. "You can get storms any time of the year Mr Hocking, but no, nothing like this. The weather then is invariably fine with longer days and shorter nights."

"Please, dispense with the formalities. Call me Elijah."

His companion nodded as the steward re-entered with a large pot of coffee. "In that case it's Leif."

"Will there be anything else sir?" the steward asked setting the pot and mugs down on the small desk.

"No; that will be all thank you Jacob. You can stand down for the night."

***

Once the cabin door had closed, Elijah said "I'll get straight to the point in case you're called back to the bridge."

The captain listened without interruption as Elijah told him of Ludde's request. "What have you decided?" Leif asked when he'd finished.

"Nothing as yet. I need to know your thoughts and those of the other captains. You're the ones who'll have to take these people aboard. You'll also face the wrath of the Germans if you're discovered".

"I agree with your Count" Leif said. "We can't sit by and allow these thugs to carry out murder if there's anything we can do to stop them. It won't be easy though. We're often challenged by the German Navy, and although we were boarded early in the war to ensure our papers were in order, it's been some time since they've conducted any searches. Our ships are well known to them and we're carrying out a vital trade for their survival. But loading passengers at night from small boats without lights will be difficult and as you saw when we left Wismar tonight, we're vulnerable to being suddenly caught in one of their ship's searchlights without warning."

"The choice is yours Leif; yours and the other captains. Obviously if you don't agree, then I won't proceed. I can't order you to place yourselves or your crews at risk, nor could I enforce it if I was so stupid to try and do so."

"How do you propose to meet with the other captains?" Leif asked.

"With the possible exception of Isak Stromquist who I believe may be in Oxelösund when we arrive, I couldn't possibly meet with them all. I'm hopeful that you'll agree to discuss this with them over the next couple of months. We can't do anything during the winter if tonight's weather is any example, and shipping to Luleå won't start again until the ice breaks up. I'd like be in a position to give Ludde his answer by the end of January at the latest."

"Aye Elijah, I'd be prepared to do that" the captain replied. "I'm no lover of that monstrous regime. Leave Isak to me as well. Let me talk with him."

They agreed Leif would send a coded message to Jorge when he'd completed his discussions with the other captains, and Jorge could then join him on the *"Jähn Prinsessa"* to discuss the decision.

***

"Why on earth did you travel by sea?" Agnota asked when she met him three days later at Stockholm's central railway station. "The weather and the risk of British or Russian submarines make that so risky. Promise me you won't do that again."

"That's easy. I won't be making this trip again until the war ends one way or the other. If the submarines don't get me, Sophia will. I've promised her this is absolutely the last time."

She pouted in response. "What about us?"

"There *is* no us Agnota. We agreed that long ago I think your words to me were something along the lines of *'we would destroy each other and I could not live your lifestyle'*. We're friends and always will be. Nothing will change that, and anyway this war has to end one day."

"We can talk about that later. I hear you've got some celebrating to do" she said. "A little birdie tells me that Hermann had a special present for you."

"Shit! How do you know about that?" he asked, unable to hide his surprise.

"Don't worry darling. It's not common knowledge. I got a message from him telling me what he was planning to do."

"Let's just leave it that way. In the current circumstances it'd be best if it remained our secret."

The following day he met privately with Folke Bernadotte at the Count's estate to brief him on his discussions with Leif Ellström.

"At the end of the day it all depends on the captains" Elijah told him. "Leif will report back to me by the end of January and I'll be in a position to give you a definitive answer then."

"I appreciate the lengths you've gone to Elijah. Many men would have just said it wasn't their problem. May I suggest, it would be best if Baroness Lindforss wasn't made aware of these discussions. While she's a delightful dinner companion, she's altogether too close to the regime in Germany. I'm not suggesting she'd knowingly pass information to them, but she may not treat any information she became privy too as confidentially as say you or I."

"Very diplomatically put" Elijah thought as he agreed to Folke's

request.

To Agnota's disappointment, he was able to secure a seat on an ABA flight to Lisbon two days later. Although there was the possibility of being shot down despite the plane being clearly marked in Swedish colours, he felt this to be infinitely preferable to travelling back across Germany and Vichy France again by rail. Exhausted, he finally arrived back in America in late November 1941 before continuing on to Washington to brief Cordell Hull.

It was early December before he finally returned to New York. He couldn't remember ever being so tired and didn't think he'd have any trouble keeping his promise to Sophia to take a break for the next couple of weeks. That was until she shook him awake just after midday on the following Sunday. He was dozing in front of the fire in his study as Sophia rushed in. He recognised the urgency in her voice as she said breathlessly "The radio Elijah, turn on the radio."

As the valves warmed up, the crackly voice of the announcer could be heard frenetically describing the Japanese attack on Pearl Harbour. The United States had finally entered the life and death struggle that now enveloped the globe.

Chapter 16

Los Angeles, California, U.S.A.
September 1943

The girl rolled over in her sleep pulling the sheets with her, leaving him uncovered. Elijah leaned over and picked up his watch from the bedside table, It wasn't yet five o'clock but he decided to get up and have a cigarette out on the deck. It'd been a hot airless night and he wasn't sleepy anyway. It was too early to send her packing; he'd let her sleep a little longer but he was damned if he was going to shout her breakfast. She'd been pretty communicative in the sack last night with all the right moves where they counted, but the high nasal screech that substituted for her voice was definitely not how he planned to start his day.

Sitting naked, he watched the sky slowly gather light from the sun rising in the east behind him. It was going to be another typically hot Californian day. There was one final meeting out at Clover Field in Santa Monica with Donald Douglas to discuss the supply of parts for Douglas' aircraft before heading back to New York. Stubbing out the cigarette, he headed inside to make himself a coffee.

"Elijaaaaah. Where aaaare you?" he heard a brassy shriek approximating a voice come from the bed. He ignored her, concentrating on making the coffee when once again the shriek pierced the calm.

"Elijaaaaah." This time the shriek was modified into what she obviously considered was a sultry, sexy call. *"Keep that up kiddo and you'll be out on your arse in ten seconds flat"* he thought as he padded back to the deck with his coffee.

Sitting down again, he thought he should call Sophia before

heading off to meet Douglas. Giving birth to their daughter Toya back in February the previous year hadn't been as easy for her as her first two deliveries and was followed by a period of mild post-natal depression. It was the first sign of weakness, as he considered it, that she'd displayed. Then in June this year she'd announced that she was pregnant again. These past few weeks she was constantly tired and hadn't been herself. She'd already made it clear she wanted him to work from home during the final couple of months of her pregnancy.

As the stars merged with the gathering light and the horizon filled with the greens and yellows of the early morning sky, his thoughts turned to Patrick. The boy would complete his schooling at Phillips the following year before moving on to Yale. Despite their continuing differences, Elijah was still hopeful that his son would join the business. He'd taken to flying like a duck to water and easily gained his pilot's licence. Initially his instructor at Stewart Air Force Base hadn't been pleased at his orders to teach some rich snot-nosed kid to fly; but the instructions were clear and unambiguous.

On his second lesson the instructor had asked "Just who is your old man kid? It's not every day an order comes down from the President himself ordering me to teach someone to fly."

Despite his feelings towards his father, even Patrick had been impressed. Elijah decided against getting his own pilot's license but on Howard Hughes' advice, had bought a Lockheed Model 12 Electra. With his contacts, there were never any concerns that wartime restrictions would get in the way of him being able to purchase his own plane.

***

Once again, his thoughts were rudely interrupted by the shrill sound emanating from the bedroom. "Elijaaaaah" he heard her call, lower and supposedly even more sultry this time. He reached behind him and pulled the door to the deck shut. Hopefully that would cut down the racket; it was either that or he'd order a cab and get rid of her.

As the day continued to lighten with the force of the rising sun, he watched a ship slowly growing from a distant blip on the horizon as it approached the coast heading for Long Beach. It looked remarkably like one of his own ships, but then so did half of the ships in the world. His captains had done him proud. All of them agreed to participate in ferrying Jewish refugees to safety across the Baltic Sea from Germany, or as Leif put it to Jorge "There's not a Nazi lover among them". The covert operation had commenced as the weather cleared in April 1942 and continued until the port at Luleå had frozen over again six months later. It then recommenced as the ice broke up again earlier in 1943.

There'd been a couple of scares when German warships had appeared as refugees were being transferred from fishing boats and on one occasion, a fishing boat had been scuttled rather than be discovered as the crew hurriedly boarded the adjacent ore ship.

Just a month ago, Ludde had approached him again. Folke Bernadotte had successfully negotiated a prisoner exchange with the Germans who'd agreed to release a number of Jewish prisoners into his care but had stipulated that they could only be transported on Swedish ships. Elijah readily agreed that his ships could be utilised in the programme and the first of Bernadotte's negotiated exchanges was due to take place at any moment.

Once again he was jolted back from his reminiscing by the caterwauling whine from the bedroom. "Elijaaaaaaaah honey. Where are yoooooooooooou?"

This time she'd gone too far. He stepped back into the bedroom to move her on but it took longer to despatch his overnight companion than he'd planned as she took advantage of his naked condition. He had to admit to himself later that he hadn't resisted too strongly; actually he hadn't resisted at all so that by the time he headed to his appointment at Douglas, he was running late.

***

It was nearly nine o'clock that night before he returned to the Hollywood Roosevelt Hotel. Crossing the foyer, he was intercepted by the duty manager.

"Good evening Mr Hocking. I'm sorry to interrupt you sir, but your office in New York has been trying to make contact. They asked that you call this number regardless of the time you return this evening. They stressed the matter is urgent" he said passing Elijah a telephone number. "Would you like me to place the call for you sir?" he asked. "I'll have it transferred to your suite as soon as we've been able to make the connection."

"What's the problem Amelie?" Elijah asked when the call finally came through nearly thirty minutes later.

"It's Mrs Hocking sir" she said. "She collapsed at home earlier today and has been taken to hospital. The doctors are concerned about her condition."

"And the baby; is it okay?" Elijah asked.

"I don't know sir, they won't discuss that with me, but Dr Preston has asked me to contact him as soon as we'd spoken so that he can call you."

"Never mind that" Elijah responded quickly. "Just give me the number and I'll call him."

It was another hour before the two men were able to speak.

"It's serious Elijah" the doctor began. "She's had a miscarriage. I'm sorry but there was nothing we could do to save the baby. As it is, Sophia's very weak but we've stabilised her. There is another matter but I'd prefer to wait until you're back in New York rather than discuss it over the phone."

"Cut the crap Fred. Whatever it is, just give it to me. I'll be back home just as fast as I can make it but tell me what it is now" Elijah said with a hint of annoyance.

There was a moment's hesitation before the doctor responded. "She has cancer. It's well advanced and it's terminal."

"How long are we talking?"

"Three months, maybe six maximum".

"I'll be out of here at first light Fred and back in New York just as fast as the plane can fly. Can I talk with her?" he asked.

"Not right now Elijah, it's well after midnight here but when she wakes I'll let her know we've spoken and that you're on the way home."

He stood there tightly clutching the phone as the rage slowly built inside him. It was fucking well happening again. First Mercedes, then Miranda, now Sophia. All the decent women in his life just kept getting taken from him and what had he ended up being stuck with as compensation? That slutty fucking bitch Kyra. For Christ's sake, what had he done to deserve this? What did he have to do to get off this treadmill of a shitty life? He suddenly yanked at the telephone, wrenching it from the wall and hurled it across the room, shattering the large mirror on the opposite wall.

"Throw the fucking rule book away. I don't care how you do it but get me back to New York the most direct way with the least delay" he snapped at the pilot as they took off at first light.

The pilot took one look at him and got on with the job. He'd never seen such a cold fury etched on anyone's face before and shrank from looking directly at his boss. Throughout the long trip they sat in silence, Elijah only speaking to ask why the plane wasn't flying faster as they crossed the Rockies, or why they were still on the ground re-fuelling fifteen minutes after landing at Kansas City.

**

Dr Preston was waiting when he arrived at the hospital.

"Any change in the prognosis Fred?" Elijah asked as he sank into a chair.

The doctor shook his head. "It's a cancer of the blood; a rare form that can't be treated. All we can do is to try and make her as comfortable as we can. As I told you on the phone, she has anywhere from three to six months; I can't promise any more than that."

"When can she go home?" Elijah asked. "Knowing Sophia, she won't want to be locked up here, or die in a hospital come to that."

"Within the week. She's been through a traumatic time losing the baby and I need to run some more tests."

"Does she know?"

"She knows about the baby. We haven't told her about the cancer. I thought it'd be better you were here before she had to face that."

"Then let's do it. She'll never thank either of us for keeping it from her."

He was headed for the door when the doctor spoke again. "What about you Elijah? How are you handling this?" he asked.

"Don't worry about me Fred. I've been through all this before, several times. It's destiny's grand plan for Elijah Hocking" he said bitterly.

Sophia opened her eyes as they entered her room. Seeing Elijah, she spoke softly "I'm sorry darling."

He was amazed at how beautiful and composed she looked. There was a serenity about her that was almost saint-like.

"There's always time for more" he said.

"No Elijah and I'm especially sorry for that. I so want to see our children grow up but it's not going to be."

He looked sideways at Dr Preston. "What're you talking about?" he asked.

"Drop it Elijah. I know I'm dying. No-one's told me of what yet, but please, please don't lie to me; not now. I've suspected something's wrong for a while but I'd hoped that I'd get through the birth before I needed to worry about it."

He knelt down beside her and buried his head alongside hers on the pillow.

"It's cancer of the blood" the doctor started telling her. "Inoperative I'm afraid…" as he went on to tell her of her life expectancy, and what she could expect in the coming months, answering the many questions she had for him. As he listened, Elijah realised she must've been quietly preparing for this for some time.

"I won't stay in here Fred" she was saying. "I won't die here."

"We'll set up a full facility at home" Elijah said. "No doubt you've already worked out which room that'll be in."

He was beginning to feel angry that she hadn't shared the knowledge of her illness with him and was struggling to control his feelings.

"Can you leave us alone for a while please Fred?" she asked.

"How could you keep this from me?" Elijah asked as the door closed behind the doctor. "How long have you known?"

"Guessed, not known. You don't really believe I'd have kept this from you do you? A couple of weeks ago I realised something was seriously wrong with me but I decided to wait until you got back home. I didn't have any idea then just how serious it was. And yes, I've worked out where I want to be back at home, but I only worked that out once I knew I'd lost the baby and nobody would give me a straight answer. That's when I started thinking it was possible I was going to die. I only knew for sure when I saw your face when you came through the door."

"Oh shit Sophia, I'm sorry! I should have realised!" he said struggling with his emotions.

She pulled him closer. "I'm so glad you're here" she whispered. "I've been so scared" as she started to weep softly.

***

In the week before she was released from hospital, Elijah had one of the downstairs rooms at Scarsdale converted into a fully equipped medical facility with an adjoining room as his bedroom. His secretary also agreed to move to Scarsdale so that he could run his principal office from home over the next few months.

The day before she came home he was surprised to receive a call from Detective O'Ryan. It'd been nearly three years since they'd last spoken. Elijah thought Kyra's case had been closed but despite his surprise, he was able to keep it from being reflected in his voice

"What can I do for you Detective? Do you finally have some news of Kyra?"

"Sorry Mr Hocking, no such luck. I'm just following up a few loose ends and I wondered whether we could meet."

"I apologise Mr O'Ryan, but that's not possible. My schedule doesn't allow any time for the moment. If you have any questions by all means ask them over the phone but if they're not urgent, I suggest you keep them for another time."

"Well seeing how you've always been most cooperative in the past Mr Hocking, I hoped you might want to help me close the file."

"Nothing would give me greater pleasure than to close that chapter of my life Detective, but as I said, I have other more pressing matters at the moment. I suggest you either ask what it is you want to know now, or mail me your questions and I'll respond as soon as possible. Otherwise this conversation is closed" Elijah told him as his voice took on a hard edge.

O'Ryan remained quiet for a moment before finally replying, "I'm sorry you've taken that attitude Mr Hocking. I'll contact you again to arrange a formal meeting. Good day sir" and hung up.

While Elijah was angry at the detective's attitude, he was angrier still to find that the case was still open. He immediately called the Mayor's office.

"Nick you'll recall you assured me some time ago that you'd get that bloody detective off my back...No, he rang again out of the blue a little while ago wanting to meet to tie up loose ends, whatever that means...O'Ryan...no I don't know which precinct...yeah about Kyra's disappearance...Sophia's coming back home tomorrow from hospital Nick and the last thing I need is some flat foot policeman with spare time on his hands dredging up a case that should've been solved long before now. I suggest he either resolves it or closes it, but keep him away from me."

Elijah listened for a moment before continuing. "I'm sorry Nick, you're not to know. Sophia's had a miscarriage and been diagnosed with inoperable cancer. She's coming home tomorrow and I really don't want that bloody detective anywhere near the house if he's only intent on making mischief."

He listened again before saying "Thanks Nick. Oh and please keep

Sophia's news confidential. We don't want a myriad of callers or sympathy cards. Sophia needs rest and quiet...Of course. I'll pass them on and thanks again."

***

They decided to break the news of her illness to the children jointly. Elijah arranged for the two older boys to be allowed home from school for a long weekend the week after she was released from hospital. None of three older children took the news well whereas the three younger ones didn't understand its full import. For Patrick, Crisantro and Selena, Sophia had stepped into the role of the mother each of them had lost and all three adored her. Patrick turned and walked from the room without speaking as the other two dissolved into tears while Sophia attempted to comfort them.

Elijah found him sitting near the tennis court. He looked up as his father approached him.

"Is this what happens to all your wives? They meet you and get tarred with the death brush?" he asked bitterly. "Is no-one safe around you?"

"You rotten spoilt little shit. That's enough" Elijah responded angrily. "Everything has to be about you doesn't it? Grow up and see that this is about Sophia not you. I'm fucked if I know why, but for some reason she's always thought you were special. Running away like a spoilt brat has upset her even more than her realising that she's dying. For Christ's sake you're almost a man; it's about bloody time you learned to act like one."

He turned and quickly walked away. He'd actually felt like hitting the boy he was so angry. How many times had he bitten his tongue to appease Sophia when faced with his son's outbursts in the past? He was damned if he was going to ignore it this time. The hurt had been written all over Sophia's face when the little shit ran from the room like that. He returned to her still angry at Patrick's reaction.

"Don't push him darling, he'll be fine when he's had time to think about it" she said. "Life was finally settling down for him. Now he's lost his central figure again."

"You're too soft Sophia. You always have been where he's concerned. We'll try it your way but I won't allow his nonsense to affect your health any more than it already has".

***

She passed away early one cold clear February morning in 1944, her family gathered around her. She'd determined that Christmas would be as normal as possible for the children and had last ventured outside on Christmas morning as a light snow fell blanketing the countryside, the boughs of the fir trees close to the house hanging heavy with the weight of the snow from the previous night's fall. Elijah carried her out and placed her in a wicker chair on the verandah; wrapping her in blankets as the children threw snowballs at each other, released the snow from the low hanging boughs and made a snowman for her while she sat there laughing at them. After Elijah's angry words to him back in September, Patrick had become particularly solicitous towards his stepmother and he and Crisantro received dispensation from Phillips Academy allowing them to travel home each weekend. Then early in January, Sophia was confined to her bed and had been bedridden since.

The end when it came was peaceful. She'd opened her eyes and slowly reached for Elijah's hand; smiled at him and closed her eyes again. It was a moment before he realised she was gone.

"Only Sophia could manage an exit like that" he thought later, *"graceful and a lady to the end."* In the period between learning of the cancer and dying five months later, she'd never uttered one word of complaint about her condition.

Her funeral service at Saint Patrick's Cathedral in Madison Avenue was attended by a bevy of political and business figures headed by Eleanor Roosevelt and Cordell Hull. But with her death, the cohesion that bound the family comprising the children from three of Elijah's marriages disappeared.

Once the service was over, Patrick and Crisantro returned to board full time at Phillips Academy. Selena was immediately enrolled as a full boarder at her school as Elijah had always wanted. Despite all Sophia's attempts to broker a rapprochement between Elijah and his daughter, he continued to despise Selena as the reincarnation of Kyra and would have nothing to do with her. The three children from his marriage to Sophia; Rai, Marcello and Toya were the only ones to remain at home with him.

Chapter 17

New York, U.S.A
March, 1944

It took Sophia's death for Elijah to realise how much he'd come to depend on her, or the true depth of the support she'd offered him. Following her funeral, he locked himself away at the house in Scarsdale, refusing visitors and taking few calls. Even Jorge had difficulty in breaking through the barrier Elijah erected to keep the outside world at bay.

About a month after Sophia's death, late one afternoon his maid announced he had a visitor. "I gave specific instructions that I'm not available" he snapped at her sharply.

"I'm sorry sir, but the lady was most insistent. She said to tell you her name is Mrs Frost and she won't leave until you've seen her" the maid replied nearly in tears.

Despite himself, Elijah couldn't suppress a slight smile. He should've guessed it would be her. Standing up, he said "That's fine Julia, you did the right thing. I'll see her. Please prepare some coffee for us."

Amanda was sitting in one of the easy-chairs flipping through a magazine, her stockinged feet tucked under her. She looked up as Elijah entered the library.

"Goodness you surprised me. I thought I may as well get comfortable as I was sure I was in for a long wait. I even brought a sleeping bag with me in case you proved to be particularly stubborn" she added with a smile.

"How are you Amanda?" Elijah replied walking across the room and giving her a peck on the cheek.

"Locking yourself away from everyone isn't going to bring her back you know" she said.

He sat down opposite her. "I have to admit you're a sight for sore eyes. Amanda Frost...my angel of mercy! I would've sent anyone else packing." He waved his hand above his head. "She hasn't gone you know! Everywhere I look, I see her. I'm quite happy here alone."

"Stop it Elijah!" she said sharply, unfolding her legs and sitting up. "Stop it at once! This isn't healthy. I think I preferred it when you were propositioning me. You need to get out of here. Mark has been invited to travel to England by the government and wants you to go with him. I think you should."

Mark Frost had been included in a United States Government mission to Britain to meet with representatives of several European governments in exile to start planning the rebuilding of their shattered economies once the war was over. Elijah had also received an invitation to attend as an observer on Cordell Hull's recommendation, but he'd failed to respond.

"I can't. The kids need me. I loused up badly with the first three, but I'm going to try damned hard to do a better job on the others. I owe that to Sophia."

"Oh crap Elijah! Spare me the histrionics! What a joke! You, the dutiful father playing wet nurse. How long do you think that's going to last? Tell me, have you actually changed Toya's diapers even once in your life?"

"What gives you the right to come in here and think you can tell me what to do?" he asked softly, his eyes hardening. He fixed her with one of his looks, but Amanda refused to drop her eyes from his. The silence stretched and just when it seemed they were at an impasse, the maid entered the room with coffee.

"Leave it on the table Julia. Mrs Frost will look after it."

"What gives me the right" Amanda finally said without moving "is that I know you too damn well. If you're serious about not stuffing up your relationship with Rai, Marcello and Toya then you need to get out of here. Get back to business, but this time remember to come home to them and act as a father. If you stay here like this, then one day those kids are going to be taken out in strait jackets. None of you need to live in a museum dedicated to Sophia. Do you really think that's what she would've wanted?"

"Ah Amanda" he said softening his tone. "You have such a way with words. But I can't leave them here and take off with Mark, it's too soon. When's he leaving as a matter of interest?"

"The middle of next week" she said. "If you'd taken his calls, you'd know that. How many other calls have you been ignoring? As for the kids, I'll look after them as long as you remember I'm not Elvira and my offer stands only for several weeks, not months or years as happened with Patrick."

His face broke into a smile and he slumped back into his chair. "Sophia always said you two were special people. She wasn't wrong. Tell Mark I'll carry his bags, but you'll have to come with me while I tell the kids so that it's not such a big shock."

***

The extent of the damage from the German air raids on London shocked him when he arrived in the British capital ten days later. On the first night, he and Mark were forced to take shelter from one of the last Luftwaffe air raids of the war.

But he couldn't settle. After several days, he decided the trip was a mistake and contacted the Embassy to arrange a flight back to New York. Returning to his suite at the Savoy, he found an envelope on a silver tray in the entry hall.

Elijah darling

Montague told me you were in London. It's been too long. Please join me for tea at 3.30.

Kindest regards

Nancy

An address in Belgravia was printed on the letterhead.

"You're as beautiful as ever" he said as she welcomed him in the conservatory at the rear of the house. He couldn't help but be impressed by her elegant light grey dress and the simple yet flawless white pearl necklace she wore.

She in turn noticed the years had been kind to him. He was older and a little heavier, a touch of grey at the temples, but his looks were still striking.

"I was really quite upset when I heard about Sophia. She was such a beautiful person. Life really can be a bitch at times can't it? How are you coping?"

"There are days I'd prefer not to wake up. I miss her terribly."

They sat silently while the butler entered and supervised tea and sandwiches. Once the servants left the room, Elijah spoke. "And you Nance. How's life treating you?"

"I have my charities. They keep me busy."

"And Montague?"

She sighed. "I don't think we'll qualify as the romance of the century, but we're comfortable. I think back to my dreams when I first came to England, and wonder what went wrong." She looked at him and added quickly "Don't get me wrong Elijah, He's a very good man. I'm not unhappy, it's just that..." Her voice tapered off and she looked wistfully out the window before continuing"...the sparkle seems to have gone out of my life."

They talked for the next hour, bringing each other up to date before Elijah glanced at his watch. "I have to go Nance. I'm booked on tomorrow's flight back to New York and I still have some things to do."

"I thought the delegation was here for another week. Montague intends inviting some of the members up to Elphinbrook House for the weekend and I know your name's on the invitation list."

"I'm only an observer and I've cut most sessions anyway. My heart's not in it."

"Please, I'd like you to stay on and come up for the weekend. I was hoping you'd be there. It'll be all business otherwise. Please say you'll come, I'd really like you to."

***

There were already four other guests deep in discussion with his hosts when Elijah joined them in a comfortably furnished reception room on the ground floor just before nine o'clock. The bulk of Elphinbrook House had been requisitioned as a rehabilitation centre for injured airmen. Montague and Nancy occupied one wing and had been limited to twenty rooms.

"Elijah old chap" Montague said to him as he entered the room. "I believe you already know George Mallenson and of course Mark is a colleague of yours. Allow me to introduce Monsieur Grégoire Lemieux who's representing Belgium at the talks" he said leading him to a small heavily moustached man with pallid looking acne-pocked skin and heavily oiled slicked back hair, "and Meneer Rutger Redeker from the Netherlands" introducing a tall overweight blond man to his right.

The conversation at dinner was lively. Initially, Elijah elected to sit back and observe, listening with some interest to the opinionated remarks from the Belgian in particular. He soon grew tired of the pompous little Belgian who was dominating the conversation and stopped listening.

The plates were being cleared following the entrée of poached salmon accompanied by a superb 1929 Zind Humbrecht Pinot Gris when Montague interrupted Elijah's thought. "I'd be interested in your opinion Elijah. What do you think?"

"I'm sorry Montague; I was elsewhere and not following the conversation. My thoughts on what?" he asked.

As he spoke, he noticed Nancy at the far end of the table. Her eyes were sparkling and she was obviously having trouble keeping a straight face.

"Monsieur Lemieux was commenting that the Swedish ore

producers are acting immorally in continuing to supply Germany, thereby prolonging the war."

"Well Montague, that would all depend on how you define immoral" Elijah replied. "In the case of the Swedes there's a strong and compelling argument that it's kept them out of the war. Should they have elected not to supply Germany, the country would more than likely have been invaded and the Germans would've continued to mine the ore regardless. After all the only reason they invaded Norway was to secure Narvik and ensure the ore would continue to be shipped to Germany when the Swedish ports were iced over. Sweden's neutrality also provides one of the few opportunities that exist for dialogue between the combatants. Mind you, there are some who'd say that the manner in which Belgium administers its colony in the Congo and exploits the resources such as diamonds with little or no regard for the local black population is immoral. You see it's all depends on how you define the word."

Nancy put her hand to her face to hide the smile she was having trouble concealing as the Belgian placed his glass back on the table with a flourish, a flash of anger crossing his face.

"There is no comparison Monsieur Hocking. The monstrous German regime is actively involved in genocide on a grand scale and must be brought to her knees as soon as possible. Sweden is only prolonging the inevitable result" he said heatedly.

"The word genocide is exactly what some use to describe the manner in which the local Congolese workforce is treated by its colonial masters Monsieur Lemieux. It would seem we're playing semantics here to some degree. I totally agree with you that the German regime must be brought to task for its crimes" Elijah replied, "but then I suppose all colonial regimes are going to find a very different world will emerge from this conflict. There's going to be a push for independence across all regions of the world, including the Congo."

"Do you really think so Elijah?" Nancy asked in an effort to diffuse the situation. Grégoire Lemieux looked as though he was going to suffer a heart attack. His face had turned a brilliant red in contrast to his normally pallid skin.

"I do indeed" he replied. "The era of empires has almost expired. Already pre-war, the British were experiencing a strong independence movement in India and I am sure Rutger will agree the Dutch are also facing a potentially serious situation in the Dutch East Indies. Both regions will surely reignite their push for independence as soon as this conflict's over. Malaya and Burma will join them as will French Indo China. Africa may be somewhat slower, but its turn will come."

"Do you agree with that Mr Redeker?" Nancy asked turning to the Dutchman who nodded in agreement.

"Yes Madame. Our intelligence suggests that the rebels are working with the Japanese who are arming them so as to cause us problems when we return post-war" he said.

***

The Belgian jabbed a finger across the table at Elijah.

"Forgive me for commenting Monsieur Hocking, but you seem particularly well informed for a Swiss national. In fact you don't give the impression of being Swiss at all" he said nastily.

"That may well be because I was Argentine until 1939 when I changed my nationality. My principle domicile has been the United States for many years and I have business interests in a number of countries around the globe. I find that tends to give one a truly global perspective of affairs, rather than the narrow introspective views that tend to characterise so many Europeans and has, I believe, been one of the major contributing factors to the situation that led to the global conflict we find ourselves in today" Elijah replied. "And before you ask Monsieur Lemieux, yes...at one stage I owned an iron ore mine in Sweden but I disposed of my interests pre-war. Whilst I have no personal experience with mining in the Congo, I'm sure that with your interests there, you should be able to enlighten me if my comments are incorrect in any way."

The Belgian pushed his chair back and drew himself up to his full height of five feet six inches, livid with anger.

"Monsieur le Marquis, I do not intend to stay here and be insulted in this manner. Madame" he said turning and bowing to Nancy, "please excuse me."

"Please Monsieur Lemieux, I apologise for my poor manners" Elijah interjected. "I shouldn't have spoken in that manner. Please accept my apologies." He turned to the Montague and added "I promise to behave for the rest of the meal."

The Belgian sat down again after Nancy interceded and begged him to stay, but he was obviously angry. For the rest of the meal Elijah contributed to the conversation only when he was directly addressed.

Retiring to the library for port and cigars after the meal was over, Mark Frost sat down beside him.

"What was that all about?"

"It doesn't happen often mate, but the pompous little shit got to me. He could dish out the dirt but not take it back. He knew exactly what I was talking about. His family owns one of the biggest mines in the Belgian Congo at a place called Bakwanga. The methods of controlling forced labour there include cutting off the limbs of anyone who attempts to escape the appalling conditions. He's lucky that Nancy was at the table or I might've gone into details. Those comments about Sweden were obviously directed at me, so I thought stuff it you little shithead, let's play your game."

"You seem very well informed as usual" Mark said.

Elijah shrugged. "I'm sure it'd make an interesting subject for an article in one of your papers" he said. He didn't think it necessary sharing with his companion that Jorge had bought a diamond mining operation about fifty kilometres from Monsieur Lemieux's in the Congo early in 1939 when he was divesting the group's expendable assets. The Belgian wouldn't have been aware of Elijah's involvement in the purchase. They sat quietly talking together while Monsieur Lemieux cornered Montague and his other two guests at the other end of the library, wildly gesturing and stabbing the air with his finger as he spoke excitedly.

"May I join you?" Nancy asked from behind them. Contrary to normal convention, she'd proceeded to the library with the men to partake of the port. "That was terribly naughty of you baiting that poor little man like that Elijah. Terribly entertaining though" she added with a little laugh. "I must have you for dinner more often. It certainly compensates for the dreary wartime rations."

Chapter 18

The small cold windowless underground cell at 8 Prinz Albrecht Strasse was lined with steel walls and lit only by a bare bulb. The small hatch set into the door allowed the occupant to be observed from the outside. As usual, Jorge was proven right. He'd pleaded with Elijah not to make this trip, but the pressure brought upon him to do so had been too great.

"You owe them nothing *amigo*. If anything goes wrong, they won't be able to help you. You'll be on your own. For what?"

But with Sophia gone, he considered the risks were manageable. Now look where he was. He'd been escorted to the cell at around six o'clock that morning after being awoken in his room at the Adlon Hotel half an hour earlier.

The panel in the door slid open and a pair of eyes inspected him as he sat on the bed attached to one of the walls before he heard the sound of the key in the lock. As the door opened, one of the agents who had detained him entered.

"Herr Hocking, you will follow me" he was told in a clipped authoritative voice. The man stepped back into the corridor and waited for Elijah to emerge. Two uniformed soldiers carrying sub machine guns confronted him as he stepped from the cell and watched as his wrists were roughly handcuffed behind his back. They fell in behind him as he followed the agent down the corridor lined both sides with identical cell doors. Eventually they stopped in front of a door on the first floor of the infamous Gestapo prison located in central Berlin. The agent knocked, then entered in response to the command from within.

"*Heil Hitler Standartenführer*" he barked in his clipped voice. "I have Herr Hocking."

"Thank you *Hauptscharfürher*. The cuffs if you please." The man behind the massive oak desk spoke in a voice that almost sounded lazy. The agent removed a key from his pocket and leaned forward, removing the restraints from Elijah's wrists. "Now Leave us."

As the agent backed from the room and closed the door, the man facing him examined Elijah before finally offering him a seat. "Allow me to introduce myself Herr Hocking. I am Standartenführer Kuester of the Geheime Staatspolizei."

He stood, removed a silver cigarette case from his tunic pocket and opened it before stepping around from behind his desk and extending the case to Elijah. "May I offer you a cigarette?" he asked conversationally.

As Elijah removed one from the silver case, the German snapped open a lighter and lit both Elijah's cigarette and his own before resuming his seat. He stood about six feet two inches tall, broad shouldered with short blond hair parted on the left. His face was ruggedly handsome marred only by a duelling scar that ran from just under his eye down his left cheek ending close to his jawbone.

***

Both men sat silently staring at each other as they drew on their cigarettes. Finally, his inquisitor leaned forward and stubbed his out in a large ashtray that sat on his desk emblazoned with the Nazi swastika and eagle.

"You don't wish to know why you are here Herr Hocking?" he asked in his soft voice, raising his eyebrows as he spoke.

"I assumed you'd get around to telling me when you were ready *Standartenführer*" Elijah replied stubbing out his own cigarette.

The man made a conspicuous display of opening and reading the thick file on his otherwise clear desk. "I see you have visited the Third Reich on a number of occasions" he said after a lengthy delay.

Elijah nodded but didn't say anything, deciding to see where the discussion was headed.

"May I ask the purpose of your current visit to Germany?" his interrogator asked.

"I have meetings scheduled with Reichsmarschall Göring and Reichminister Speer."

"You seem to have met the Reichsmarschall on many occasions. Are these of a personal nature, or are they business meetings?"

"Am I to assume that the Reichmarschall is under investigation *Standartenführher*?" Elijah enquired.

A small smile flickered across Kuester's face. "I am asking the questions Herr Hocking. Kindly answer whether your meetings are of a personal or business nature."

"Business. My Swedish company is a major supplier of iron ore to the Third Reich."

"Ah yes, PMAB is it not? Since the Reichmarschall does not have responsibility for procuring such supplies, it seems unusual you are visiting him for this reason."

"Then *Standartenführher*, you would also be aware of my appointment with Reichminister Speer."

The German fixed him with a long stare before reaching forward and thumbing through the file. "In 1938, I see you accompanied two travellers out of Germany to Switzerland. Tell me about that visit."

The Gestapo goons who'd checked out their papers on the train had obviously made notes in his file. "That was the year I was a guest of the Führer at the Berghof. I then joined a work colleague and his wife in Munich and we travelled together to the company headquarters in Zurich."

"And the colleague's name?" the German pressed

"Pers Nilsson" Elijah replied without missing a beat. "PMAB's

Director of Marketing. In case your file doesn't list it, his wife's name is Berta."

A hint of a smile flashed across the interrogator's face. He continued with the line of questioning for over thirty minutes before closing the file and saying. "I have to say I am not satisfied with your answers Herr Hocking. I will need to consult with my superiors before we continue further with this interview. In the meantime you will be returned to your cell. You may care to review your answers before we meet again."

***

Despite it being summer, the warmth from outside failed to penetrate the chill of the underground cell and it wasn't long before Elijah started to shiver. Assuming he was ever released, he wouldn't complain about the weather in Sweden again.

By all counts, it seemed Göring was probably on the nose with the Nazi hierarchy. Elijah could think of no other reason for his incarceration, unless there was a clamp-down on foreigners in general. But being a supplier of a commodity critical for the German war machine, that didn't make any sense. No, it had to be Göring that was the problem. That's why they were so interested in him taking Günter and Dana out of Germany back in 1938.

Twice as he lay there trying to get warm, he heard the panel in the door slide open and sensed, rather than saw, the eyes staring in at him. They'd taken his watch so he had no idea of time, or how long he'd been under arrest, when suddenly the door opened and Kuester filled the doorway. He entered, followed by another man wearing the uniform of a high-ranking SS officer.

"Good afternoon Herr Hocking, I am Brigadeführer Schellenberg." Elijah immediately recognised the name of the head of the German Intelligence Service. "It would appear there has been an unfortunate administrative error which led to you being mistakenly detained in this manner. I must apologise and trust you have not been too inconvenienced. Encircled as we are by enemies, non-German's, even those who are as actively involved in helping our war effort as you, are viewed with suspicion which sometimes results in regrettable errors of this type."

To Kuester, Schellenberg said "Herr Hocking has been awarded the Grand Cross of the Order of the German Eagle for services to the Third Reich on the personal orders of the Führer."

Turning back to Elijah, the intelligence chief continued. "My driver will return you to your hotel to allow you to freshen up and then transport you to Carinhall for your meeting with Reichsmarschall Göring. Once again Herr Hocking I trust you will accept my profound apologies for any inconvenience that may have been caused by this unfortunate incident." He turned back to Kuester. "Have Raufsfangel join us" he instructed the Standartenführer

Almost immediately a young SS NCO entered the cell. "Unterscharführer Raufsfangel is at your disposal Herr Hocking. You are free to go. I trust the next time we meet it will be under more agreeable circumstances" Schellenberg said with a smile, extending his hand once more to Elijah.

After stopping at the Adlon Hotel to allow Elijah to bathe and change, the driver flanked by two motorcycle outriders headed for Carinhall in the forests outside Berlin. It was a balmy summer day and the beauty of the twilight belied the fact that the country was involved in a life and death struggle for survival. The last time Elijah had been to Carinhall had been in 1938 when Göring had asked him to accompany the two Jewish actors out of the country. Sitting in the rear seat of the powerful armour-plated Mercedes-Benz sedan, he thought back to the chain of events which had led to him being detained by the Gestapo.

***

Not long after he'd returned from his trip to London with Mark Frost, he received a call from Cordell Hull. Suspecting that he would going to be asked to visit Germany once again, he agreed to meet but was determined to refuse any such request.

He was ushered into the Oval Office at the White House and

greeted effusively by both the President and the Secretary of State. "I was grieved to learn of the recent loss of your wife" the President started. "She was a mighty fine lady and the First Lady often spoke highly of Mrs Hocking's valuable contribution to her Works Progress Association."

"I appreciate your comments Mr President. Thank you."

"Allow me to introduce General William Donovan" Roosevelt continued as a thick-set man rose from a nearby chair. The stranger shook Elijah's hand as the President continued "The General is the Director of the Office of Strategic Services."

Elijah knew of the OSS, the United States espionage service. He'd also heard of "Wild Bill" Donovan's reputation. The introductions completed, Roosevelt continued. "Whilst I can't be specific as to either dates or details Elijah, we're close to launching the second front in Europe. With the Germans retreating on both the Russian and Italian fronts, this new front will place them under extreme pressure. Knowing the thoughts of the Nazi's inner sanctum could be vital to our success, and possibly lead to shortening the war in Europe. You're our best hope in evaluating this with your links to Göring. Bill here will coordinate all your movements and also outline exactly what we're interested in obtaining from your visit."

Before Elijah could respond, the OSS Director leaned forward in his chair. "We already have a number of assets in Germany and its occupied territories Mr Hocking, but we don't have anyone with a direct line to the highest echelon of the leadership. There are signs that strains are emerging between old rivals such as Göring and Himmler as each positions himself as Hitler's possible successor. There have also been a number of surreptitious contacts made by high ranking Germans recently, seeking out the potential of a separate peace with the U.S. and the British so that Germany can concentrate on its battle with the Russians."

"Obviously we won't negotiate a separate peace. We're committed to fighting alongside the Commies until the Nazis are defeated. But anything that can help us shorten the war in Europe would allow us to concentrate our forces in the Pacific to defeat the Japs" Cordell Hull added.

"Mr President" Elijah began. "I told you at our last meeting that my so-called friendship with Göring is overrated. I'm not sure that I could get an appointment with him for a start. I had extreme difficulty last time."

"Excuse me for interrupting Mr Hocking" the OSS chief interjected, "but I think you might find that more than ever Göring *will* want to meet you. The Nazi leadership, or at least elements of it, must be concerned that defeat is looming. Certainly the recent rash of peace feelers would indicate this, although no-one at the leadership level has come forward to be identified as being behind any of them. With their reverses in Russia and a new front opening up in Western Europe, I think it's highly likely that they'll each be looking to the future and how they might escape retribution once Germany's been defeated. Some of them may even be deluded enough to believe that they could retain control of the country in a negotiated peace, rather than outright defeat."

"I agree with Bill" the President added. "If they think you have the ear of senior officials here in the west, perhaps even the ear of the President himself, they'll want to meet you. Your reports in the past have always been impeccable, and from everything we've seen, it seems Göring is vain enough to think that he might even be able to use you as a conduit to pass messages. After all, you reported back in 1939 that he asked you to pass a message to try to forestall the outbreak of war" Roosevelt added.

Elijah sat back and pressed his hands in a triangle, his brow deep in thought. "You gentlemen have the advantage. You've obviously given this considerable thought, but has any of you considered why I'd want to travel from the safety of the United States to meet Göring in the middle of Germany with a war that it's losing raging all around me?"

"A very good question Mr Hocking" the OSS chief responded. "That's precisely why you elected to travel at this time. We propose that you'd travel to Germany only after the new front has been established in the west, and the German's are being forced back from the

197

beachheads. In this way you can express your concern to Göring for his future safety and offer to assist him should this become necessary."

"I'm sure he'd just laugh that off, or even be offended by it" Elijah replied.

"Our intelligence suggests he's not particularly in favour with Hitler at the moment due to the Luftwaffe's failure to beat the Brits back in 1940, or to stop the bombing raids over Germany" Donovan replied. "He could be looking to restore himself to favour, or alternatively, to save his skin. He may see you as a way of providing him with the possibility of success through either avenue."

The discussion continued as Elijah raised questions and objections and the three men patiently responded, seeking to gain his agreement to their proposal. Finally, he said "Mr President, I should come clean. My participation may be compromised by my involvement in a programme coordinated out of Sweden aimed at rescuing Jewish refugees from Germany, both in an official capacity and covertly in the Baltic Sea."

"I'm not aware of the covert operations you refer to although I'm aware of your involvement in providing ships for transport in the prisoner exchanges arranged by Count Bernadotte Mr Hocking" Donovan replied.

"If *you're* aware General, then you can be sure the Germans are as well. It hasn't exactly been hidden from them, and my company's not the only Swedish one providing vessels, but there will be elements in Germany who wouldn't be pleased that the exchanges have been taking place. I suspect Himmler could be one of them. If the rivalry between him and Göring is as serious as you say, even though Göring's not involved, my visiting Germany could be a prime opportunity for Himmler, or whoever, to embarrass him."

"That's a possibility I hadn't considered Mr Hocking. Perhaps it'd be wise to arrange other meetings while you're there – with the Minister for Armaments and War Production, Albert Speer, for example. We believe he's one of Hitler's rising stars. That may provide a foil to Himmler or anyone else from taking any precipitate action against you" Donovan replied while the President nodded his head in agreement.

"Again General, for what purpose? My involvement with Swedish industry ceased prior to the start of the war. I'm sure Speer won't wish to discuss shipping schedules with me" Elijah said.

"Possibly not, but you've retained your friendship with the current owners and directors of PMAB for example, haven't you? Isn't it possible they could want to make use of your good offices to discuss Germany's requirements whilst you're in the country?" Donovan suggested.

"We'd appreciate you putting out feelers to Göring so that we can move quickly when the time is right" the President added. He nodded and both Hull and Donovan stood up.

"As always Elijah the country and I are both deeply indebted to you for your selfless assistance to our cause" Roosevelt said in his deep booming voice, extending his hand to Elijah before clasping Elijah's in both of his and shaking them vigorously. "I'm only sorry that we can't publically acknowledge the work you're doing for us, and that it must remain strictly within this circle. Good luck. I look forward to meeting you again on your return."

***

That meeting in the President's office had been seven weeks ago, the week before the D-Day invasion. Three weeks later General Donovan had contacted Elijah and he'd set off for Germany seven days ago.

He flew first to England and stayed with Montague and Nancy for a couple of days before travelling north to an RAF base at Leuchars in Scotland where the USAAF in company with the OSS had established a base for courier flights to Sweden. There he'd boarded a converted Liberator bomber with British markings and flown to Bromma near Stockholm to await confirmation of his meetings with Göring and Speer.

Agnota had been ecstatic when he first contacted her and asked her to contact Göring, insisting he stay at her apartment while he was in Stockholm. At dinner on the first night, Benji joined them. Now sixteen and a few months older than Crisantro, the difference between the two boys could not be more pronounced. Where Benji was tall, fair skinned with an unruly mop of auburn hair, his half-brother was short, with Negroid features and the colouring of a mulatto, his hair resembling a loose cap of black curls.

Benji had fired question after question at Elijah about conditions in the United States. As they finished dinner and moved into the lounge, he excused himself and disappeared to his room.

"He's a fine boy. You've done well." Elijah told her.

"He's been a great comfort to me" she responded, "especially in these trying times. But Fredrik's family is threatening to cause problems over his inheritance and the title. They suspect Fredrik wasn't Benji's father. At this stage Benji knows nothing of the threats, but I don't know for how much longer."

"Promise me that you'll let me help you if it gets too much. Don't try to fight on your own" Elijah said.

When she didn't reply he said again "Promise me Agnota."

She leaned over and threw her arms around his neck. "Thank you Elijah, I promise."

They spent several days and nights together while Elijah waited for confirmation of his appointments in Germany. On learning that the *"Jähn Princessa"* was docked at Oxelösund he also took the opportunity to travel to the port and thank Leif Ellström for his and the other captains' participation in transporting the refugees across the Baltic.

***

Finally, a cable arrived confirming an appointment with Göring in Berlin on July 15th and with Speer the following day. Catching the daily Lufthansa flight from Stockholm to Berlin the day before he was due to meet Göring, he arrived at Templehof airport late in the afternoon and booked into the Adlon Hotel.

It was a bright sunny afternoon in Berlin and Elijah decided to follow the route along Charlottenburger Chausee into the Tiergarten that he and Sophia had walked back in 1939. Despite the war, there were a considerable number of people walking in the park. He noticed that the clambering streetcars had become indescribably shabby and that the vehicular traffic was made up mainly of military and official traffic with very few private vehicles to be seen.

He hadn't gone far before he spotted his tails – two men in coats, one making a show of reading a newspaper, the other stopping to tap his pipe on the heel of his shoe. Passing the spot where Rai had fallen over many years previously, he remembered Sophia's horror when she'd been confronted by the SS officer who'd picked the young boy up.

"*Shit*" he muttered under his breath. There was no pleasure to be derived from walking through the park and he decided to return to the hotel. Re-entering his room, he noticed his bag had been moved slightly. Earlier he'd followed Donovan's advice, placing his bag precisely parallel to an adjacent surface. Opening it, it was obvious the bag been searched in his absence. He'd taken the precaution of carrying his briefcase with him when he stepped out for his walk. Even then he'd carried no papers into Germany other than his identification papers along with those he needed to support his meeting with the two ministers.

Deciding on an early night, he'd eaten a light meal in the hotel dining room and turned in before being woken by the loud banging on his door at five o'clock the following morning.

***

The shadows through the forest were long as the twilight slowly edged towards night with the moon and the evening star both prominent in the sky. Elijah was so deep in thought, he hadn't taken any notice of his surroundings as he travelled out from central Berlin to his meeting with Göring.

He felt the car slowing and realised with a start that it was turning onto the large pebble paved courtyard adjacent to Carinhall's huge entry doors. As Unterscharführer Raufsfangel jumped out and opened the rear door for Elijah, the massive figure of the Reichmarschall emerged from the house. He was dressed in bright red riding trousers, a rough loose fitting cotton Russian peasant style tunic topped by an ermine trimmed silk cape and highly polished green leather calf high boots with silver spurs. His florid face was puffed and as he waddled across to meet Elijah, it was obvious that the exertion was making him wheeze.

"My dear fellow. Thank goodness you're safe. How dare they do this to you? Have they harmed you in any way?" he spoke breathlessly. Before Elijah could reply, Göring turned on the driver and bellowed at him, ordering him to get his car off Carinhall's grounds immediately.

"But Reichsmarschall, I have orders from Brigadeführer Schellenberg to wait and return Herr Hocking to his hotel when he has finished meeting with you" the driver stammered in reply.

Göring exploded; his eyes bulging from his florid face. "How dare you be insolent? Get out! Herr Hocking is officially under my protection and will not be returning to Berlin tonight. Now get out before I have you arrested and shot for insubordination!" he shrieked.

The words emerged in a torrent, as he slipped his hand into his pocket and popped something into his mouth. The driver saluted and ran the few steps back to the car and jumped in. Revving the engine, the wheels spun in the loose stones covering the courtyard as he accelerated away down the driveway.

Göring turned back to Elijah, placing his arm around his shoulders. His face had once again resumed its usual colour and he spoke in a normal voice.

"Elijah old friend, I cannot apologise enough for the barbaric treatment which you've suffered. I suspect that pig Himmler is behind this. Believe me I will find out and retaliate if I'm correct. I acted as soon as I realised that you'd disappeared. Come and join Emmy. She's been as concerned as I have. Of course, you'll stay the night here as my guest where I can keep a personal eye on your safety."

***

That evening was one of the most surreal nights of his life as Elijah witnessed the full extent of Göring's decline. One moment the Führer's heir-apparent would be talking to him in a normal lucid manner, when his eyes would suddenly turn up into their sockets exposing the whites and his cheeks would flush red at the same time as his speech became garbled. He would pop a pill into his mouth which immediately calmed his speech and returned his face to its normal composure. The first few times it happened, Elijah looked across at Emmy who returned a tight nervous smile.

The Reichsmarschall was highly uncomplimentary of a number of his fellow leaders; in particular Himmler, Goebbels and von Ribbentrop, but he reserved his most extreme vitriol for Hitler's chief of staff, Martin Bormann. It was obvious there was no love lost between the two men. He was convinced Bormann was working day and night to poison Hitler's view of his deputy. As the evening wore on, Göring now affected by the drugs assisted by the copious quantities of alcohol he was consuming, slowed down and his eyes took on a glassy effect.

"Do you think there's any possibility of Germany being defeated Reichsmarschall?" Elijah took the opportunity to ask.

"None" Göring replied emphatically. "The Führer has commissioned a series of secret weapons that will smash the Allied forces in the west so that they'll have to sue for peace. Then we can concentrate on destroying the Russians for once and for all. Even Churchill and Roosevelt must realise that Germany is the only bulwark against communism and that we're waging a holy war to save civilisation from the eastern hordes."

He popped another pill into his mouth and washed it down with a large mouthful of brandy.

"But how can Germany hope to withstand both the might of the

American industrial machine and the seemingly endless reserves of Russian manpower?" Elijah persisted.

"Simple! Because the Americans and the Russians are going to fall out. You're a smart man. Surely you can see that. England's finished and if Roosevelt ignored the Jews who control his cabinet, he'd see that he should join with Germany in smashing Russia" Göring replied.

"So are you saying that Germany will never seek peace?" Elijah asked.

"*Never!*" Göring said emphatically. "The Führer will never allow it. Germany will fight to the bitter end rather than have another Versailles Treaty imposed on it."

"And you Hermann?" Elijah asked. It was the first time in all the years Elijah had known him, that he'd addressed Göring by his first name. "Given the opportunity, would you seek peace with one or more of the Allies?"

His host sat up sharply. "I hope you didn't express those views to Schellenberg earlier today. I'm no Hess! The Führer and Germany are one and the same. As long as the Führer's in control of Germany, his will is paramount. As his designated successor, I would feel compelled to follow any instructions he left me to the letter should, God forbid, something happen to him."

His host's eyes turned up into his sockets once again as he reached into his pocket for another of the pills he had been taking all evening. It was nearly three in the morning before Göring finally rose unsteadily from the table. His wife had excused herself several hours earlier, kissing Elijah on both cheeks and murmuring her sympathy at Sophia's death.

"She was a lovely lady Elijah, and I treasure the memory of our meeting on the *"Carin 2"* she told him.

"I believe you're meeting Speer tomorrow Elijah" Göring said. "My adjutant will arrange transport for you." He staggered drunkenly to his feet and seized Elijah's arm. "You have many enemies in Germany, people who are either jealous of our relationship, or who view you as a spy. You aren't a spy are you Elijah?" he suddenly asked, his face barely inches from Elijah's.

"You know better than to ask me that Hermann."

"I know my friend, I know" Göring replied, his head drooping as he reached into his pocket and pushed yet another pill into his mouth. He brightened up again as he continued. "No offence intended dear friend, but if I was you I'd stay out of Germany until we've achieved final victory. There are many people who'd like to make an example of you."

The comment was delivered in such a way that Elijah realised the Reichsmarschall was deadly serious.

"Thank you Hermann, I'll remember that" he replied before bidding his host goodnight and heading to his room.

They parted company for the last time next morning. It was a very relieved Elijah who boarded his flight back to Stockholm following his meeting with Speer. Once again, he was aware of being tailed out to the airport and of being watched by several sets of eyes as he walked across the tarmac to the waiting plane. He decided he didn't need Göring's warning to convince him never to return.

After three nights in Stockholm with Agnota, he headed to Bromma airport to board the Liberator for the night flight back to Leuchars. Sitting in the cramped waiting room at the airport he was approached by an American Captain.

"Mr Hocking sir, I've been asked to hand you this message."

It was unsigned and read *"German radio reports assassination attempt on Hitler earlier today. Your return imperative soonest."* He had no doubt who it was from.

He couldn't help but wonder what his fate would've been had he still been in Germany. He doubted that Göring would've been able to help him. For that matter he wondered whether Göring himself was safe with all the bloodletting and score-settling that an assassination attempt on Hitler would be sure to engender.

***

Four days later he was once again seated across from General Donovan in Washington as he was debriefed on his meetings with Göring and Speer.

"He's a drug addict pure and simple Bill" Elijah said. "I'm not even sure that he knows what reality is. One thing's for sure though, Göring won't move against Hitler; he's totally under the madman's spell. There's no way known he could've been involved in the plot on Hitler's life."

"And Speer?" asked Donovan.

"I've only the one meeting to go on" Elijah replied. "He's a very cool character; smart and decisive. I suspect he's made a few enemies by riding rough-shod over others. By all counts he's highly regarded by Hitler. I got the impression he's totally loyal. I doubt he'll make any move to try and broker a peace agreement on his own initiative."

The session with Donovan lasted for more than an hour before Elijah revealed he'd been detained at Gestapo headquarters.

"I get the sense I was detained as a way of getting at Göring" he told Donovan. "He was certainly of the opinion that either Bormann or Himmler was behind it. I doubt I was ever in any real danger. I suspect my detention was a warning to Göring that his mates could be got at. Even the questioning was pretty lame but I did get to meet the head of German Intelligence, Walter Schellenberg…quite an interesting character."

"I'm sorry Elijah. I hadn't realised" Donovan mumbled, but Elijah got the impression that he wasn't sorry at all, rather that he considered it was all part of the risk attached to the brief. After another ten minutes discussion, the OSS chief stood up.

"Your information is most illuminating Elijah and will assist us greatly. I wouldn't underestimate the possibility that there was more to your detention than simple play acting and I'd take Göring's warning about returning to Germany very seriously. I shudder to think what the outcome may've been if you'd still been there during the assassination attempt on Hitler. I know the President's going to be very interested in your report."

Elijah remained seated. "There's something you can do for me Bill" he said.

Donovan sat down again. While his face still remained friendly, his eyes had narrowed. "Name it" he said.

"My eldest boy turned eighteen earlier this year and has just graduated. He holds joint Swiss-US nationality and I'd hoped he would proceed to Yale to continue his studies. We don't see eye to eye and in my absence overseas he enlisted with the Marines."

"And you want it annulled I suppose?" Donovan asked.

"Not at all" Elijah replied "He'd suspect I had something to do with it and would probably re-enlist straight away under a false name. No, I'd rather that his talents be utilised to their full potential. He's a fully trained pilot, courtesy of the USAAF and I'd like to see him moved to flying duties. I suspect joining the Marines as a foot soldier was his way of getting back at me. It's important that it's done in such a way that he doesn't realise or even suspect that I was involved."

Donovan relaxed and smiled. "I'm sure that can be arranged. Leave it with me. God knows we need the pilots and if he's already trained then we'll have him flying for us in no time."

Three months later, shortly before Franklin Roosevelt was re-elected for his fourth term, Elijah received a handwritten note thanking him for his efforts on behalf of the United States, signed simply FDR.

"Sure America's grateful. It's just a pity that little shit Patrick couldn't pick up a bit of that gratitude" he thought to himself bitterly.

***

Patrick had barely communicated with Elijah since Sophia's death. He'd turned eighteen in July 1944; the same day that Elijah sat incarcerated in the Gestapo cell beneath Prinz Albrecht Strasse. Elijah had travelled up to the Phillips Academy to see him before flying to Europe, but the meeting as usual was strained. Patrick made it obvious that he preferred his father hadn't bothered. As they shook hands, Elijah handed him a parcel containing a silver Rolex wrist watch.

"Sophia chose it" he told Patrick.

The boy looked at the parcel but made no attempt to open it.

"My birthday's still two weeks away. Wouldn't it have made more sense to give it to me then?" he asked.

"I have to go overseas Patrick and I'm not sure whether I'll be back by then."

"That's typical. Nothing's changed has it father? I'm amazed you managed to find the time to fit me into your schedule today."

Elijah bit his tongue and continued, speaking of his desire for Patrick to continue his education at Yale and some day enter the company but Patrick continued to make it plain that he was only meeting his father under sufferance.

Finally he rose saying "I have to go. I have a class I can't miss if I'm to move on to Yale and my continued education. Enjoy your trip." He left the room without looking back, his parcel containing the watch still unopened.

Without telling anyone, he enlisted with the Marines the day following his birthday and entered the Marine Corps Recruiting Depot at Parris Island before his father's return from Sweden. As soon as he realised what Patrick had done, Elijah attempted to meet with him at the camp but his son refused to see him. When Elijah asked Amanda Frost if she would try, Patrick spurned her as well.

Chapter 19

New York, U.S.A.
February 1945

As the Allies encircled Germany and the war ground towards its inevitable conclusion, Jorge suggested it was time they met to plan for the post-war era. While Elijah agreed, there was no way he was setting off once again to Europe. His last trip along with his incarceration had killed any possibility of that happening. Pulling strings, he was able to arrange seats for Jorge and Elvira to fly to New York.

While they had managed to meet a number of times during the conflict, he still hadn't realised just how much his old friend had aged physically during the five and a half years of war. Away from Zug and the familiar surroundings, the grey hair and the lines etched on Jorge's face came as a shock. Elvira too had aged, but in a more graceful manner that highlighted her Hispanic roots. The two of them were like children let loose in a candy store as they stared at goods they hadn't seen for years displayed openly in shop windows. Neither could believe the prolific quantities of food available in shops or served up in restaurants compared to the rationing they'd endured as Switzerland was cut off by the conflict that raged around them.

When they finally sat down to discuss business, the briefing revealed just how kind the war had been to Elijah. Whilst Jorge had kept him briefed on most major investments, even Elijah was surprised at the results of his partner's activities. When hostilities broke out, he'd given Jorge total authority to follow up any opportunities that would result in them making money with either of the two protagonists. With the restrictions on communications, much of Jorge's trading was news when the two men sat down in New York.

"We can expect that the Allies are going to pressure the neutral countries into revealing details of their trading with Germany during the war. I doubt the Swiss will assist or that the Swede's will be any more compliant" Jorge started. "It'll take more than an OSS to prove any involvement by you with PMAB since 1939. Of course your relationship with Agnota may cause them to suspect you're still involved, but even she believes that since you 'sold' your shares" and here he punctuated his remarks by making inverted commas in the air with his fingers, "your sole involvement with the company was as a consultant, and that ceased in early 1940."

He looked down at his notes before continuing. "Likewise there's no evidence of any involvement by you in any of our other wartime investments in Sweden all of which are profitable but insignificant in the scheme of things. Our Swedish-flagged ships have carried goods all over the globe for the Allies, in addition to Germany. Having them involved in carrying Jewish refugees from Germany to Sweden is sure to come out and should be in our favour."

"What about payments from the Nazis, where've those been parked?" Elijah asked.

"With the shipping line and PMAB they're in Switzerland but the Swedish Government intervened so that all payments to our other entities there had to be directed to Sweden. In Switzerland itself we own a number of companies linked with heavy industry – steel and small arms in the main plus foodstuffs and timber. They're all owned by a Swiss corporation called GUB. It has Swiss nominee shareholders and directors. Even I don't appear in the documents. Their affairs are managed by a firm of lawyers not easily linked to Perdido and Associates, and not at all with you unless someone has a forensic background. Even then I'd lay money they couldn't prove a link. Any problems we might encounter in Switzerland will come from an entirely different quarter."

"What do you mean?" Elijah asked as the lawyer stopped.

"The art purchases" he replied. "While we've been careful not to buy anything from easily recognisable collections such as a major museum or an art gallery, we still have a large number of pieces that you can be sure were looted from private collections, most of them Jewish I suspect. Although I've met the art dealer socially on a couple of occasions, I've never discussed art with him nor shown the slightest interest in his business so there's no direct link. All communications have been through a nominee bank in Geneva."

"And...?" prodded Elijah

"When they start investigating the Nazi leadership, which they will, then the trail from them will lead straight to Werner von Schultheiss. He's known to have worked closely with a number of art dealers in Germany such as Walter Hofer who's linked to your friend Göring and other top Nazis like Goebbels and Ribbentrop. The bank won't co-operate, it's von Schultheiss who's the weak link."

"I see" mused Elijah. "Where's the art now?"

"Apart from those pieces you have, the bulk of it's stored in the bank's vaults. I plan to release it progressively to private auctions or sales – that is those pieces you don't want of course. There should be a good market for it over the next few years before buyers possibly start getting more discriminating as to where a piece might have originated from. It's just something we'll have to watch and be careful."

"So we need to take care of this Werner character and resolve the problem then?"

"It's not von Schultheiss we need to get rid of *amigo*. His records will be securely hidden. If he was to be knocked over, we'd need to have access to them first or else they could be the problem."

"You seem to have plenty on your plate at the moment. Let me give it some thought. What's next?"

***

"I'll leave America till last" Jorge continued. "We've made quite a few investments in Africa. Gold and diamonds in South Africa, diamonds in the Belgian Congo, asbestos mines in Southern Rhodesia and cocoa and rubber in Nigeria and the Gold Coast. These are all owned under an umbrella company called the Swiss African Investment Corporation which is headquartered in Geneva. One of my associates named Manfred Baer oversees this."

"Talking of the Congo, I met a Belgian named Grégoire Lemieux at a dinner in England a year or so back" Elijah interrupted and went on to recount his discussion over dinner at Elphinbrook House.

"I know of Lemieux" Jorge told him. "His company has a reputation of extreme cruelty that makes the Nazis look like amateurs. They complained to Manfred recently that we're undermining the employment market in the country because we don't treat our workers at the same subhuman level they and a number of the other Belgian companies do."

"It doesn't surprise me. He was a rotten little shit, full of his own importance, with all the symptoms of small man disease" Elijah replied.

"Moving on, Deke's got himself some oil concessions in Arabia we haven't started working yet. They're in a couple of out of the way places called Kuwait and Abu Dhabi both of which are controlled by the Brits. They could be useful assets in future years but right now they're just sitting there. We've also picked up a couple of other concessions in the Mexican Gulf we've talked about previously. We need to think about developing them. Even with the winding back of the war machine, I see a big requirement for petroleum products over the next few years. Over in Argentina we've disposed of everything except the farms and the ships. That was a good call of yours back in '41 with the instability that's been there since. We even managed to get a good price for everything."

"Our Australian operations are pretty small change. There's several farming properties, all of which are performing well and I'm not suggesting any changes. They're owned by a company headquartered in London which also owns a couple of sugar operations in the Caribbean and our beef ranches and wheat farms in Canada along with a salmon hatchery there."

"Salmon hatchery?" asked Elijah. "What the hell are we doing with a salmon hatchery?"

"Centurion acquired it when a debt owed to them couldn't be paid." Centurion was the liquor wholesaling company in the United States which had developed out of Elijah's old bootlegging operation. "Taking it over seemed a better proposition than getting nothing, but it's actually been a great little money spinner. But as I'm sure you've guessed, our really big assets are here in this country, just as the big opportunities are. America's going to be the only country to emerge from the war with its manufacturing base intact. It's going to rebuild the world. This is where we need to be, but there'll be some big changes required as the country moves from a war footing to making consumer goods. We need to be ready when the switch occurs. We're already in steel and oil which are both going to be in big demand but our manufacturing plants are all geared to the war machine. We need to start sourcing opportunities now. I have some ideas which we should spend some time going over. The bottom line *amigo* is that right now you're potentially one of the richest men in the world. But it's not just switching our manufacturing from war to peace that we need to discuss."

"You've obviously something in mind" Elijah said as Jorge stopped and stretched.

"What we need most is a more formal structure. We're spread all over the globe but we need someone controlling the operation."

"No" Elijah replied emphatically. "I've got you. I like it the way it is; I don't want anyone thinking they can tell me what to do. There's only one person who can get away with calling me *uno gilipollas*. No, we continue operating as we are. It's served us well to date even with a war on."

Jorge could see that Elijah wasn't going to budge and decided not to push the point for the moment. After all, hadn't Hitler just shown that you could win the battle, but end up losing the war?

***

The two men fell silent while Elijah crossed to the bar and topped up both their drinks. Walking back he said "There's another matter I want your advice on Jorge."

He sat down and hesitated before continuing. "I had a message from Agnota the other day. Walter Schellenberg was in Stockholm recently trying to broker some peace deal. He got her details from my fat friend and asked her to pass a message to me. He seems to think that his intervention to free me last year from the Gestapo has somehow made us best friends. There's an organisation being set up to help senior Nazis escape Europe to South America. He knew of my Argentine connection and wanted to contact me to see if I'd help, at a price of course."

"*Joder!*" Jorge responded. When Jorge swore he always reverted to Spanish. "Why would you want to get involved in that?"

"Cash, pure and simple. They've got the money, someone's going to do it and get paid. Why not us; preferably in gold? We've got the ships and governments throughout South America are still sympathetic to the German's, even though most of them have finally got around to declaring war on them. But let's face it, that's only been to satisfy the Americans, not because they wanted to. It could be very lucrative."

"And very dangerous" Jorge interjected. "There'll be a witch hunt after the war. Why expose ourselves? What did you say?"

"Nothing yet. I wanted your view."

Jorge sat momentarily staring at the ceiling, before saying "*Tendríamos que estar loco,* bloody mad. We could never hide our involvement. I don't want any part of it. Don't go there Elijah, you owe those bastards nothing."

"My thoughts exactly *amigo,* I just wanted to hear you say it" Elijah readily agreed. "I won't lose any sleep over it."

Jorge's reaction left him in doubt as to his friend's feelings. The last thing he wanted was anything that might create a problem between them. Nor for that matter did he want to be a handler for Himmler or any of the rest of the scum. As far as he was concerned those pricks deserved everything that was coming to them, but being paid to move some of the lesser lights had momentarily piqued his interest.

***

The night before returning to Switzerland, Elvira decided she couldn't leave without intervening over Elijah's treatment of Crisantro and Selena. When she found Elijah alone in his study she pounced.

"Crisantro's due to graduate next year. What plans do you have for him?" she asked.

Elijah frowned. "I guess he could go to university if he wanted to. We haven't really talked about it."

"I remember your plans for Patrick were set by the time he went to Eton. What's so different about Crisantro?"

Elijah stiffened. "He's my problem Elvira. We'll work something out."

"*Your problem*!" she exploded. "He's your son, not your problem Elijah! What exactly has the boy, or his sister for that matter, done to you to make you treat them like this?"

"Leave it Elvira. It's none of your business!" he snapped back.

Elvira rounded on him. "My total life has revolved around your *business* for years Elijah. I moved to Europe because that's what *you* wanted. I hate Switzerland and I've hated being locked up as though I was in jail for the past six years while we've been surrounded and blocked off by the war. I haven't seen my family back in Argentina for eight years. Instead I'm surrounded by cold, arrogant, contemptuous Swiss bitches for company."

She laughed bitterly before continuing angrily, her voice rising. "Patrick was the closest I ever came to having a child of my own, but *you* removed him because it suited *you*! I shouldn't sound too ungrateful; after all you did let me launch a ship once, but then as I recall *that* was to suit you too. For years I've been aware of your affairs and kept my mouth shut. Jorge does God don't know what to serve you. Whatever little time I have with him has to fit in with that *and you dare to sit there and tell me to mind my own business?"*

Her reaction shocked Elijah. This was a side of Elvira he'd never seen. She'd always been Jorge's faithful and compliant partner. Even when he'd taken Patrick from her care and placed him into boarding school, she'd only displayed tears, not anger.

"Their mother whored around" he replied. "There's absolutely no proof that either of them is mine anyway. I look at them, and all I see is that bitch."

"Don't come the pity trip with me Elijah. How many times were you warned not to marry her? We all knew what she was like, but that's no reason to take it out on the children. You say there's no proof they're yours; what proof do you have that they're not?" she asked. Her voice softened. "I don't want to fight with you; I'm just asking that you show them a little warmth and compassion. They're both desperately unhappy. With Patrick in the air force, they've lost both him and Sophia as the counterbalance to your callousness. Will you at least promise me you'll try?"

Elijah realised the only way this conversation could be brought to an end was for him to acquiesce, or at least to appear to.

"And you'll discuss Crisantro's future plans with him?" she pushed.

He nodded again although inside he was seething. What was it about these bitches that they thought that they could control him? Elvira would still be living in some two-room apartment in Buenos Aires while Jorge slaved as a junior partner for a law firm if he hadn't come along. She showed no sign of appreciation that Elijah had rescued him, or for the money that Jorge had made which allowed her the lifestyle she enjoyed.

Chapter 20

Elphinbrook House, Chelmsford, England
September, 1945

It was a perfect summer's day as the group of mourners gathered to farewell Montague Elphinbrook at the family plot behind Chelmsford's Cathedral Church of St Mary, St Peter and St Cedd. All around them stood the gravestones tracing the family's history back to the establishment of Elphinbrook House in the seventeenth century following the restoration of the monarchy. Montague's ancestors had been rewarded with the landholdings by Charles II in return for their support for the King during the Cromwell years.

The crowd that had overflowed the Cathedral and was now gathered around the grave represented a who's who of British society. Prime Minister Clement Atlee and his predecessor Winston Churchill both stood bareheaded near Nancy as the Bishop invoked prayers beseeching God to accept Montague's soul into his care. It was the first time Elijah had seen Churchill in the flesh and he understood the comparison between the British politician and a bulldog. Most of the other faces meant nothing to him, although he thought he possibly recognised at least one member of the British Royal Family.

Nancy stood across from him on the opposite side of the freshly dug grave dressed all in black, her face obscured by a heavy widow's veil as she leaned heavily on her late husband's uncle. Alongside her stood Montague's younger brother; a foppish looking man in his forties with an unruly mop of red hair.

Elijah had last seen Nancy when he and Jorge stayed at Elphinbrook

House just four weeks ago to formalise arrangements for Montague to assume the Chairmanship of Elijah's British interests. Elijah had extended the invitation in early May as Montague passed through New York on his return home from the inaugural meeting of the United Nations in San Francisco, where he'd had been a member of the British delegation.

Winston Churchill's loss in the British elections in July, and the formation of a Labour government under Clement Attlee had been the deciding factor in Montague accepting the offer.

"It's going to be nationalisation all the way old chap" he told Elijah. "There won't be a place for an avowed Tory like me with Attlee's government. God knows it's going to be a long haul for whoever's in power. The country's bankrupt and poor old Winnie copped the backlash. People are tired and want a change, but I wonder if they realise exactly what Attlee and his bunch of socialists have in store for them?"

Montague was to have taken up his new role in the New Year. Until then Atlee had requested him to remain involved in the negotiations with a number of the newly formed governments of Western Europe as they struggled to establish themselves in the aftermath of the German surrender. He was flying from London to Brussels five days previously when the de Havilland Dominie aircraft crashed into the English Channel shortly after take-off killing all on board.

***

Once again this so-called merciful bloody God had thwarted him. *"Now I'm going to have to find someone else to take his place"* was running through his mind when his train of thought was broken. He realised the ponce in the white robes and mitre hat had finished muttering his mumbo-jumbo and Nancy had stepped forward to place the lilies she was clutching onto the coffin before it was lowered into the waiting grave.

He hung back from approaching the widow with his condolences, waiting until the line had thinned before stepping forward.

"Elijah. I hadn't realised you were here. Thank you for coming. It means so much to me" Nancy said as he wrapped her hand in both of his and pecked her on the cheek. "I hope you're staying on" she continued as she leaned forward and embraced him.

"I was planning to return to London" Elijah replied when she let him go. "I'm sure you'll be engaged most of the afternoon with your guests."

She nodded absent-mindedly before suddenly realising what he'd said. "Oh please, no, I really would like you to stay. I have the feeling I'm going to want to escape the throng at some point to keep my sanity."

With the completion of the graveside service, most of the mourners gathered back at Elphinbrook House. As Elijah circulated in the Great Hall he suddenly found himself standing before the former Prime Minister.

"Hocking! Ah yes, I've heard of you!" Churchill barked at him as they introduced themselves.

"Here it comes" Elijah thought. *"Nazi sympathiser, war profiteer, immoral neutral; I wonder which I'll be... probably all three."*

Churchill's next words shook Elijah. It took a lot to surprise or catch him unawares these days but the great man certainly managed that. "President Roosevelt spoke highly of you Hocking! If you have time when you return to London, I'd like the opportunity to meet with you" he said in his gruff voice.

Finally the numbers thinned with the remaining guests segregating into two groups at either end of the huge room. Nancy stood nearby looking elegant in her simple black dress, surrounded by a small knot of people who were obviously close friends. She looked across and saw him watching her, gave a little smile and beckoned him over. As Elijah moved towards her, a loud peal of laughter broke out from the other end of the hall where a larger group of people were gathered in animated conversation.

Another raucous round of laughter broke out from the group.

Nancy winced and an older man detached himself from Nancy's side and strode purposefully to the other end of the hall where he could be seen remonstrating with her brother-in-law. A sulky look came over the younger man's face before he and his group moved into the adjacent garden and the Great Hall once again resumed a sombre ambience more in keeping with the occasion.

Nancy introduced them as the man returned. "Elijah this is Montague's Uncle Rupert. Montague and Elijah were going to work together when he had completed his assignment at the Foreign Office" she explained.

"Ah yes" Uncle Rupert replied. "He talked with me about that. Seems you've done extraordinary things young man" he said, despite there being less than twenty years difference in their ages.

Another hour passed before the numbers dwindled to just Elijah, Nancy and Rupert.

"If you'll excuse me my dear, I think I might retire for a while" Uncle Rupert said. "My gout's giving me gyp from being on my feet all day. You'll be all right with this young fellow won't you? Holler if he gives you any trouble."

He winked at her as he gave her a peck on her cheek and limped off in the direction of the main staircase.

"Would you like to walk outside with me?" she asked. "I need some fresh air."

***

They stepped out onto the flagstoned terrace and down the steps into the manicured gardens that ran across the rear of the huge house.

"I thought they were never going to leave. Do you have a cigarette on you?" she asked.

Off to the left the sound of animated talking and more laughter could be heard.

"Gerald!" she said. "It was always Montague's worst nightmare that Gerald would inherit this."

She walked quietly as she drew deeply on her cigarette. "He can't wait to get his hands on the house. He's already hinted that I might like to start packing up. Thank goodness for Uncle Rupert. He can't stand the little shit and although he can't stop him inheriting the title or the house, he can slow the changeover."

Elijah let her talk as they stepped along the raked pebble paths that ran between the immaculately manicured rose bushes. "He'll go through it all of course" she continued. "He and his friends will plunder everything that Montague worked for until there'll be nothing left."

She stopped and Elijah noticed her eyes were brimming with tears. "Damn him" she said bitterly as she ground her cigarette butt violently into the path beneath her heel. "Damn him to hell!"

Elijah would never be sure till the end of his days whether she was referring to her brother-in-law or to her recently departed husband.

They continued walking as Nancy wrapped her hands tightly around herself as though she was cold, despite the warmth of the sun on their backs. "We could never have children you know. Oh we tried but we..." She fell silent. Elijah was struck by the look of sadness that had enveloped her usually radiant face. "...and Gerald never will. Medical science hasn't yet reached the stage where either he or his male friends could fall pregnant no matter how hard *they* try."

She gave a little laugh as she emphasised the word they. "So it really won't matter to Gerald if he ruins this place. He'll have no-one to pass it on to. He and Uncle Rupert are the last of the line and Rupert never married. The thought of Gerald becoming the last Marquess haunted Montague. He hoped Gerald might get carried away and not survive one of his weird sexual games one day and that would resolve the problem." She stopped briefly then continued. "Welcome to the wonderful world of the British aristocracy my dear" she said.

They continued to walk silently for a few minutes before Elijah asked "What will you do now?"

"I still have the house in Belgravia. Montague used it whenever he had to stop overnight in London and it escaped the bombing. It's very comfortable, although not quite of this standard" she answered.

It made Elijah think of Agnota being forced to "slum it" in her apartment on Kommendörsgaten in Stockholm when Fredrik died and she'd had to leave the family's ancestral home. Once more their solitude was interrupted by the distant sound of laughter forcing Nancy to shiver involuntarily. She looped her arm through Elijah's.

"Take me back inside please. I can't bear the thought of what that degenerate might be up to out here, even on the very day his brother has just been buried."

***

Before winging his way back across the Atlantic to New York, Elijah returned to Chelmsford by train the following weekend and stayed overnight at Elphinbrook House. Uncle Rupert was still in residence offering Nancy moral support against her brother-in-law's increasing demands that she should vacate the mansion.

"There's always been something dodgy about that young chap" Rupert told Elijah as they sat in front of a roaring fire, each nursing a glass of port. "Wouldn't play rugger at school and not in the least interested in cricket. I took him to Lords once, but the bounder sat with his nose in a newspaper. Even did *The Times* crossword instead of watching the game. Now all this is his." He suddenly changed tack. "Young Nancy quite fancies you, you know. Montague and her were quite chuffed when you offered him that Chairman position. She's going to need some looking after and I'm not always going to be around."

"Montague's hardly cold yet Rupert" Elijah chided him, a hint of surprise in his voice.

"I don't mean in that way young man. I understand you've known her for many years. She's hardly going to get any brotherly love from that scoundrel Gerald. I thought that's where you might step in."

"I apologise Rupert. I misunderstood. Of course I'm here for her. She did the same for me when I lost my second wife. I thought I might ask her to join my family for Christmas. With Sophia gone..." He hesitated. "With Sophia gone, it might be good for all of us."

***

"I've decided to move from here as soon as possible" Nancy told him. "Gerald can have the place. It's a pity because I love it so much, but it gets me away from him. He's on the phone daily pressuring me to go."

"You could do with a complete break. Winter's almost here and rationing looks like it's going to be pretty grim for some time yet. Christmas will be summer in Argentina and I'm taking my kids to the *estancia*. Why don't you join us and recuperate?" Elijah suggested.

"Now wouldn't that set the tongues wagging?" she replied with a smile.

"That you should be so lucky" he replied grinning back. "Your morals and chastity will be well guarded. Jorge and Elvira will be there as well. They haven't been back to Argentina since before the war. I'm even going to try and persuade Patrick to join us if possible. Seriously though, give it some thought."

It took little to convince her and it was agreed she would travel to the *estancia* in mid December. Convincing Patrick to join them was somewhat more difficult and eventually Elijah turned to Elvira for assistance.

"You lectured me a few months ago on my need to work on my relationship with Crisantro and Selena" he said, "and I'm trying. But I need your help with Patrick. I'm trying to get the whole family together if possible this Christmas. He'll do it for you, even if he doesn't want to see me. He loves the *estancia* and it'll be good for Crisantro to have him there."

In truth there had been no change in Elijah's attitude to Kyra's children other than he'd secured a place for Crisantro at Stanford University at San Jose in California when he graduated the following year. For Elijah the decision was easy; it was as far from New York as the boy could be sent without sending him overseas.

Chapter 21

Since his meeting with Jorge earlier in the year, Elijah had assumed responsibility for resolving the matter of the Swiss art dealer and his files. He'd not long been back in New York following Montague's funeral when he received a coded message from Johnny advising that the 'Venezuelan Project' had been completed. This was code that Johnny had resolved the problem of von Schultheiss and his hidden records. The matter of the Swiss art dealer was always referred to by this name as Elijah assumed that any wartime tapping of telephone lines into or out of Switzerland would still be in place, especially while the Allies were investigating the Nazi leadership in the run up to the following year's Nuremburg Trials.

Johnny crossed into Switzerland just as the war in Europe came to an end in early May. Making contact with von Schultheiss had been harder than he'd anticipated as the Swiss art dealer went to ground in anticipation that the victorious Allies would be interested in following up the trail of missing and stolen art from throughout Europe. He re-emerged in August once it became obvious that the Swiss government weren't going to cooperate with the Allies by allowing foreign investigators access to its secretive banking laws.

There was another problem making Johnny's investigations difficult. Coloured people were few and far between in the country and not only was he the object of curiosity, but he was also subject to latent racism. He found a remote house high in the pastures in the Alps behind

Grindelwald and retreated there while he waited for von Schultheiss to resurface.

Once it was obvious the art dealer was back in circulation, Jorge sent a message from one of his phantom clients via the Banque Privée Wolff Ehrlichmann in Geneva asking the art dealer to meet with a Venezuelan emissary to discuss purchasing additional paintings that might surface from fleeing Nazis. Johnny then met with von Schultheiss on three occasions at various locations as he established his credentials. The last meeting had been at the art dealer's house at Meilen south-east of Zürich on the edge of the lake where Johnny purchased three paintings; a Matisse and two Cézannes. Satisfied he was genuine, the art dealer had relaxed in Johnny's company giving him the opportunity to surreptitiously run his eyes over the layout of the office he was sitting in. He noted the locks and other security devices on the doors and windows, the possible locations of a wall safe, the Alsatians patrolling the gardens and the barbed wire on the external walls. As the art dealer conducted him from the reception hall up the main stairs to the first floor and down the wide hall to his office, Johnny kept his eyes peeled for possible alarms inside the house, but it appeared that security was concentrated on the exterior of the house and the grounds.

***

Von Schultheiss's office was located away from prying eyes on the first floor at the rear of his house. The expansive gardens were surrounded by a two metre high brick and stone wall topped by rolls of razor-sharp wire. Trees and bushes had been cleared for at least five metres inside the wall on all sides providing a mown grass strip that was constantly patrolled by armed security men accompanied by leashed Alsatians. Inside and outside the perimeter of the wall were hidden trip wires, and at night the perimeter was brightly floodlit. The only entry to the grounds appeared to be by an electronically controlled gate with a manned guardhouse, or else from the lake.

A trip by hired boat revealed that the shore frontage was equally well secured with a guard post mounted on top of each end of the wall.

About two thirds of the way from the western perimeter was a large wooden boathouse with a ramp and a small jetty. As Johnny slowly motored along the shore, seemingly showing little interest in the property, the sun glinted off a pair of binoculars trained on him from one of the guardhouses. The place had all the characteristics of a prison and short of invading it with an army, seemed impregnable.

***

Several nights later, Johnny undertook an exploratory inspection of the jetty and the boathouse. He entered the freezing waters of the lake about half a kilometre from the eastern perimeter of von Schultheiss's property, swimming underwater all the way. The night was windy with squalls of rain clouds scudding across the face of the occasionally exposed moon. Despite the wetsuit he was wearing, the water chilled him to the core and he hoped the weather would hide any tell-tale trail of bubbles from his air tanks.

Coming in close to the jetty, he was relieved to find it'd been dredged to allow larger boats to dock alongside. A set of steps loomed ahead in the murky water attached to one of the pylons. He avoided those in case they'd been alarmed and continued underwater until he was beneath the boathouse which was built partially over the water. Once he was sure he couldn't be observed from either guardhouse, he surfaced quietly. Using a torch with a very fine beam, he inspected the floor of the building above him. As he hoped, outlined above him he found a hatch set in the wooden floor. Pushing carefully, to his delight it moved slightly.

Pushing harder, Johnny felt it move again but there seemed to be something placed on it. Working carefully so as not to create any noise, it took him another ten minutes to displace whatever was sitting on the hatch. Silently he placed his hands either side of the opening and slowly pulled himself up until his eyes were above the level of the floor and he was able to look around. Inside was a wooden launch about eight metres long pulled up and resting in a cradle alongside a three metre long yacht. Two small rowing boats and a canoe were lashed to the far wall, and around him was stowed various paraphernalia for the boats. The object he'd pushed away from the hatchway was a large open topped wooden box inside which were stored coils of rope. Carefully pulling himself into the boathouse, staying alert for any alarms, he inspected the large doors facing onto the lake through which the boats could be launched down the slipway, a matching set at the opposite end of the building, and the two windows and a small door which led out of the building into the grounds. Each of the doors was locked and he was sure they were also alarmed. Turning his attention to the windows, he noted that the panes were large enough for a man of his size to be able to crawl through once the glass had been removed.

Crouching in the dark, he spent the next few hours watching the guards with their dogs pass by, noting that they appeared every fifteen minutes almost like clockwork, always walking from east to west. The same five metre wide expanse of mown grass existed between the boathouse and the main building and there were few bushes to provide him any cover. He would need a dark and preferably rainy night if he was to successfully make it between the two buildings without being seen. Carefully cleaning away any evidence of his entry, and ensuring a loose sail would fall across the hatch as he pulled it closed, Johnny dropped silently back into the dark waters of the lake before swimming away undetected.

***

His opportunity came just over two weeks later as a storm front swept in over northern Switzerland from Austria, bringing with it heavy rain accompanied by thunderstorms. As before, Johnny donned his wetsuit and slipped unobserved into the cold waters of the lake, a pack strapped to his back. Visibility was zero with the surrounding snow covered Alps blocked from view by the combination of the driving rain and the heavy cloud cover. He risked swimming most of the way on the surface, only diving once he'd spotted the boathouse and taken his bearings. Pulling himself through the hatchway in the floor, Johnny entered the boathouse stripping off his wetsuit and tanks and hiding them. He then changed into a lightweight poncho, trousers and jumper, a balaclava, a pair of rubber soled shoes and gloves he removed from his backpack. Next he removed a glass cutter and waited to watch the patrols as they passed by. After forty-five minutes, he was satisfied that despite the weather, the guards were keeping to the same schedule as before. The rain meanwhile intensified as thunder rolled and reverberated around the surrounding mountains. This suited Johnny as it would hide his dash from the boathouse from the guards in the watchtowers, and help to mask any evidence of his scent or tracks from the dogs as they passed by.

Removing one of the panes of glass, he waited for the next patrol to pass by, before carefully climbing through, then replacing and securing the glass. Crouching low, he ran across the grass through the near torrential rain before flattening himself against the wall of the house near a rear door. Satisfied he hadn't been seen, he reached for the door handle and gently tried to pull it open but it was locked. Over the next twenty minutes he carefully crept around the perimeter of the house checking doors and windows until suddenly about two metres from where he was crouched, a door opened. Light flooded out onto the ground as the figure of a short fat balding man appeared rubbing his hands on a striped apron, a cigarette hanging from his mouth.

"Shit, this bloody weather would freeze the balls off a monkey" he muttered out loud to himself. He drew heavily on his cigarette before stepping back inside, slamming the door behind him. Johnny listened intently, but there was no sound of a key being turned, or of any locks being drawn.

He remained crouched low against the ground for another five minutes as the rain beat down on him before quietly rising and creeping to the door. Opening it carefully, he found himself in a small darkened room.

***

Shining his torch around, he found himself facing two doors; one with a slit of light beneath it. He opened that one first to find himself looking into a kitchen in which the man he had seen at the back door was chopping up some meat. Carefully closing it again, he opened the other door to reveal a narrow set of wooden stairs leading to the first floor.

Carefully wiping the water from his legs and shoes with a cloth from his backpack, he stowed his poncho away in a corner of the room behind an umbrella stand, then quietly headed up the stairs, carefully checking each tread for squeaks before applying his full pressure to it.

The top of the stairs exited into the main hall that ran the width of the house. Trying to gain his bearings, a flash of lightning eerily lit the hall revealing the main staircase. Realising that the study was at the far end of the hall he tiptoed quietly, checking each door as he looked for the master bedroom. Opening the third door he was met by the sound of snoring. Creeping into the room, he found two people asleep in the double bed; the art dealer and his wife.

Creeping around the bed, he aimed his torch into the von Schultheiss's eyes. The art dealer woke with a start to find himself faced by a man, his face hidden by a balaclava aiming a Mauser fitted with a silencer at his wife's forehead.

"Not a word" Johnny warned him. "You! Roll over!" he ordered the wife. She stared at him in wide-eyed terror and opened her mouth to scream. "One noise and you're both dead" Johnny said. "Now roll over before I shoot you" he ordered her again.

As she complied, he tossed a cord to von Schultheiss. "Tie her hands and make sure it's tight. I'll be checking. Any nonsense and you'll force me to hurt her." When the man finished, Johnny tossed him another cord. "Now the feet" he said. When he'd finished tying them, Johnny ordered him back before reaching forward and checking the bindings. Satisfied that they were tight enough, Johnny ordered the woman to roll over again, stuffing a wad of cloth into her mouth before dictating her husband to gag her.

"Now pull that chair into the middle of the room and drag her to it" he ordered the art dealer, indicating an upright leather upholstered chair near a small table. When that was done, Johnny ordered von

Schultheiss to tie her to the chair, again checking the knots ensuring they would hold.

***

"Fräu von Schultheiss, if you make any noise, attempt to summons help or make any attempt to escape, your husband will die immediately. Your own death however will be somewhat more prolonged and infinitely painful I can assure you. Nod your head if you understand."

She nodded her head vigorously, her eyes still wide with terror as Johnny leaned forward and kissed her gently on the forehead. "Good, I see we understand each other" he said softly. "Let's make sure it stays that way."

Pointing the Mauser at von Schultheiss, he said "The same goes for you! Any funny business and I'll shoot you first and then amuse myself with your wife for a while, quite a while." He could hear the muffled gurgle behind him as the woman tossed her head from side to side as he spoke.

"What do you want?" the art dealer asked him in a terrified whisper. "You want money; I'll show you where it is."

Johnny leaned forward and slapped him hard across the face leaving a red welt on his pale cheeks. "I'll do the talking. Just answer the questions. Understood?" he asked as he stepped back to the man's wife and gently rubbed one of her breasts with his free hand.

Von Schultheiss took a step towards Johnny who cocked the gun. "I wouldn't play the hero if I was you" he said squeezing the woman's breast a little harder. "I might decide to let you watch what happens to her before I finally kill you both if you try anything again. I want your records – all of them, and don't tell me you don't have them. I know they're here." Johnny actually had no idea where the art dealer kept them. He assumed they would be kept in a safe deposit box in a bank.

"You're bluffing" the man said. "Go to hell."

Johnny pretended to look shocked. Still pointing the gun at von Schultheiss, he looked back and forth between husband and wife before slowly stepping behind the chair. "And here I was, thinking I'd stumbled onto one of the great love matches of the century. It's amazing how the true expression of love is revealed in times of stress isn't it. Obviously you're of no further use to me my dear, or for that matter to him. Pity! I was quite looking forward to us spending some time together." As he spoke, he whisked a stiletto out of his waistband and in one quick motion slit the woman's throat.

***

Blood spurted from her severed artery, soaking her nightdress and pumped onto the carpet in front of her as Johnny bounded across the room to the shocked man and held the stiletto to his throat. "Bluffing? Well your departure from this world will definitely take a lot longer. I get my kicks out of this sort of thing. The longer it takes, the more pleasure I get. Besides, my German paymasters are not about to let your records fall into the wrong hands. Bormann told me that if you were co-operative then he might let you live." Johnny's voice was no longer friendly and he pricked the knife into the man's throat drawing a trickle of blood as von Schultheiss started trembling uncontrollably.

"They're in the bank" he blubbered, "the Eidgenosse Englehart Böschung." Once he started talking, he couldn't stop. The words came out in a gush as he revealed the details.

"The keys, where are they?" Johnny asked.

"My study" the weeping man said. Johnny pushed him towards the bedroom door and they proceeded down the hall to the study where von Schultheiss unlocked a large wall safe and withdrew the safety deposit key. All the time Johnny kept the Mauser pushed into his back.

"Write down the code and all the access details" Johnny instructed him as the man complied. "The cash that's in there, I'll have that too" Johnny told him. He'd spotted a large number of banknotes in bundles in the safe "and those papers" He had no idea what they were but he figured they wouldn't have been locked away in the safe if they were worthless.

"You are going to let me live aren't you?' the still weeping man asked Johnny.

"That all depends on your actions over the next hour or so" Johnny replied. "Is there an internal door to the garage?" he asked to which the man nodded. Johnny's initial plan had been to escape from the house in the laundry van which called at the property early each morning. Now that he had von Schultheiss as a prisoner, he would get the man to drive him away from the property. It was possible that the police might believe he was responsible for his wife's murder and had run.

"Good. We're going for a drive. I'll be on the back floor and my gun will be pointed at your back at all times. Just so you understand, one of the slugs in this gun will tear your guts apart if I'm forced to fire. Behave yourself and you'll get to drive yourself home again. If you don't believe me, just think of your wife back there. I've already told you, I enjoy my work, but I can also show my gratitude to those who do what they're told. The choice is yours."

***

Von Schultheiss climbed in behind the wheel of a dark green Horch sedan and drove slowly down the driveway until he reached the gate where he pulled to a stop.

"Good morning Herr von Schultheiss" the gateman said as he stepped from the hut. "An early start for you today sir." There was a silence and the guard continued "Are you alright sir? You don't look well."

For good measure Johnny pushed the Mauser hard into the seat-back to indicate the man shouldn't attempt to raise the alarm. "It's a touch of the flu I suspect Rafhäusen" he heard von Schultheiss reply. "I have urgent business in the city or I wouldn't be venturing out on a night like this."

"Travel safely sir, there may be fallen trees on the road" the guard responded as he pushed a button and the electric gates silently opened. Johnny felt the car shift into gear and they started forward, accelerating as they turned onto the road. He sat up on the back seat. "Very good. You did very well there. Keep that up and you may yet get to have your great-grandchildren sit on your knee."

At ten o'clock that morning Johnny turned the car into St Peterstrasse and parked half a block from the Eidgenosse Englehart Böschung near the corner of Nüschelerstrasse. He was keen to gain access to the safe deposit box as soon as possible. He was sure that the woman must have been discovered by now, and the police would be looking for von Schultheiss.

Entering the banking chamber Johnny looked around him, his eyes falling on the desks occupied by staff controlling access to the safety deposit boxes. He was keen not to attract attention to himself and noticed a young earnest looking man in his early twenties at one of the desks. Hoping he didn't know von Schultheiss personally, Johnny approached him, produced his key and repeated the instructions that had been given to him by the art dealer.

"Everything is in order sir" the young man said as he completed his paperwork. "If you would sign here please."

To Johnny's relief, the signature he'd been practising for the past couple of months passed the young clerk's scrutiny. The young man smiled, stood up and said "Follow me please sir."

An hour later Johnny returned to the small vacant rented warehouse in Fierzgasse where von Schultheiss had been left tied up. He couldn't believe that access to the art dealer's records could've been so easy. He didn't doubt the young clerk would face serious disciplinary action once the bank realised he'd allowed Johnny access to the safety deposit box. He hadn't bothered to look at any of the papers that he'd found; Elijah would do that. He placed everything into the carry-all that he'd taken with him deciding he would keep the cash and jewellery he'd stolen from the safe in the house. He reasoned that was fair since he'd taken all the risks; besides, Elijah had more than enough money already. There remained just one more task to complete before he disappeared.

Around ten o'clock that night he bundled von Schultheiss into the trunk of the Horch and headed out of Zürich on the road that skirted the southern edge of the lake towards Nuolen at the far end of the Zürichsee. He reasoned that the police would be looking for the car by now, and he was keen to be off the road as soon as possible. Turning from the main road onto Bachtellenstrasse he followed this until he came to the rutted track he was looking for that led into the trees. Finally, the bumpy track came to an end surrounded by the dark forbidding forest where he parked alongside the black Stoewer sedan he'd hidden in the woods bordering the lake the previous day.

It didn't take long for him to transfer the carry-all with the papers from the bank between the cars along with the case containing the contents he'd looted from the safe in von Schultheiss's study. Satisfied that nothing was left behind, he carefully wiped down all the surfaces of the Horch before opening the trunk where the trussed up form of von Schultheiss stared out at him with pleading eyes. Reaching into his coat pocket, Johnny removed the Mauser and calmly pumped four shots into the art dealer's chest and one further shot into his head before closing the lid, hiding the bloody mess inside.

Chapter 22

Washington D.C., U.S.A.
November, 1945

President Roosevelt's death in March 1945, combined with Cordell Hull stepping down as Secretary of State, had left Elijah without ready access to either the White House or the State Department for the first time since he'd first met Joe Kennedy in Boston back in 1928. In addition, a number of his prime contacts in the capital such as Congressman Michael Leveridge, hadn't stood for re-election the previous November. The only person still in power in Washington who was aware of his meetings with Göring on behalf of the United States was the OSS chief, Bill Donovan.

With Japan's surrender bringing the war to an end, Elijah decided a Swiss national could never have too many friends in the right places. The post war boom that was sure to follow would result in a new intake of legislators hoping to share in the booty. For three weeks solid, Elijah worked the capital tirelessly; wooing, cajoling and where necessary entrapping those he needed.

"As I thought, nothing's changed" he told Jorge later. "Greed, opportunity and crooked politicians are as alive and well in America as they ever were."

Journeying north to Massachusetts, he renewed his acquaintance with his old friend Joe Kennedy. They hadn't met since Kennedy had been replaced as Ambassador to Britain a number of years before. Elijah came away impressed with the plans the statesman confided to him to have his son Jack become President some day. Elijah decided it would be smart to stay close to the old fox since he could yet be pivotal to America's future.

Returning to Scarsdale, he arranged for his old friend Michael Leveridge to join him there. Despite his retirement, the former Congressman continued to exercise a high degree of influence within the Democrat Party.

"What are you doing with yourself these days?" Elijah asked as they sat before the fire in the library nursing their drinks. "Surely you're missing the cut and thrust of politics after all your years in Washington?"

"Well I must admit the first few months were difficult to adjust. There were times I suspect Trudy was tempted to cut my throat having had the place to herself all this time. There's a few things I still do for the party, I'm playing a bit of golf and we intend to travel next year when things have quietened down in Europe. I'd hoped for an Ambassadorship once the war was over, but I don't know Truman or the new guys at State that well, and with most of the available positions already allocated, I guess the opportunity's probably passed me by."

Elijah stared into the fire for a few moments before he spoke. "You'd have made a fine Ambassador. I reckon they missed a golden opportunity there." He stared off into the flames again before continuing. "We've worked well together over the years Michael. There's no reason why we shouldn't continue to. My Counsel, who's also my closest friend and has steered the business operations of the group for over twenty years, has finally convinced me we need to put a global board in place to oversee our operations. We're spread all over the world and we've become too big for just him and me to control on our own any longer. I'd like to have you join us."

Leveridge glanced at Elijah as he took a drink of his whiskey. "I'd need to know a lot more Elijah, but I'm flattered to be asked" he replied.

"Excellent" Elijah replied, leaning forward and clapping his companion on the knee. "You'll need to meet Jorge of course, but he lives in Switzerland. Dismal place this time of the year and besides travel to Europe is still too fragmented. What about you and Trudy joining me at my place in Argentina for Christmas? Jorge and his wife will be there along with someone else I have in mind. It'll also be a break from the Pennsylvania winter for the two of you. It's much easier to travel to South America these days than Europe."

"Trudy would kick up a bit of a fuss, what with the kids and grand-kids due for Christmas. With a bit of luck my eldest son should be dis-charged from the Army by then, but if you're agreeable, we could fly down in time for New Year."

"Capital" Elijah said. "Amelie will make all the arrangements. I'll have her get in touch with you next week. Now what about a top up?" he asked as he reached for the bottle.

***

It was amazing what a restorative effect just being at the *estancia* had on Elijah. Wanting the place to himself for the first couple of weeks before anyone else arrived, he flew there with his three younger children, his personal assistant Amelie and the children's nanny in the Lockheed during the first week of December.

Enrique was overjoyed to have Elijah to himself. He had long re-garded Elijah as a friend rather than his employer, and Elijah recipro-cated by always deferring to him in all matters relating to the *estancia*. Rai, Marcello and Toya were immediately adopted by Enrique's wife as her own. It wasn't long before all three of them were running happily with their Argentine counterparts as the *estancia* rang with the happy sounds of children.

Most mornings Elijah and Enrique rode out on to the pampas, only returning close to sunset. It was the tonic Elijah needed. He was able to relax in Enrique's company in a way he found he could do with few others since his old friend made no demands of him. At night, Amelie always had a folder of material requiring his attention. After spending an hour with the three children, he disappeared into the study to attend to business matters. Only on a couple of days did business restrain him from joining Enrique on horseback.

Crisantro and Selena arrived at the start of the third week. Now seventeen and in his last year at Phillips, Crisantro was gifted at mathematics and excelled at school. His relationship with his father was distant, but lacked Patrick's belligerence. There was never any possibility that Crisantro would work for him; in fact his father displayed little interest in the boy's future at all.

Selena on the other hand had grown into a darker skinned carbon copy of her mother. Now thirteen, she was just starting to fill out and it was obvious that she was destined to grow into a beautiful woman. But every time he looked at her, all Elijah saw was Kyra. To make it worse Selena had uncannily picked up her mother's mannerisms right down to the way she flicked her head when she was annoyed. Elijah literally couldn't stand to be in the same room as his daughter and didn't bother to hide his antipathy towards her. She'd already learnt that if she flirted in her father's presence, it sent him into a fury. This only encouraged her since it forced him to notice her. With the arrival of the two older children, the happy atmosphere of the *estancia* soured, at least until Jorge and Elvira arrived several days later.

It was Elvira's first visit to the *estancia*, and Jorge hadn't been to the property since he'd relocated to Switzerland nearly twenty years before. She fell in love with the place immediately and within twenty-four hours of her arrival she and Esmeralda, Enrique's wife, were old friends.

Two days later Elijah flew to meet Nancy in Buenos Aires. He'd briefly considered bringing Josefina back with him, but the doctors at the institution convinced him it wasn't in her best interests.

"I knew this one had to be yours" Nancy said as Patrick stood beside her "as soon as I saw him at the airport in Miami. He's been wonderful company, so much so that the trip has been a blur it's passed so quickly."

Patrick took over the controls of the Lockheed for the flight to the *estancia*. He had topped out at six feet three inches, weighed just over twelve stone and had inherited his father's good looks and his mother's colouring. He spoke little during the flight while Elijah and Nancy chatted together in the rear of the aircraft

"I couldn't wait to get away" she told Elijah. "Gerald made everything unpleasant. I couldn't have managed without Uncle Rupert to help me. I took everything that wasn't nailed down and figured I'd worry about the consequences later."

"I told you Nancy, if there's any trouble, you should contact me" Elijah reminded her.

"I appreciate that Elijah, but it's not just the legalities. Elphinbrook is one of only two uniquely English Marquessates. It is ranked above all the other Scottish, Irish and British ones. The only one that ranks higher is Winchester. Now the thirteenth Marquess is installing his boyfriends, not just one mind you but several, in one of the nation's grandest addresses. It's really too much and there's nothing that you or anyone else can do about it. On top of it all I still officially have the title of Lady Elphinbrook. Heaven forbid anyone would mistakenly think I was married to that" she said with a shudder, matched by the look of horror on her face.

***

The following morning Patrick wandered into his father's office. "Feel like riding with me this morning?" he asked.

Surprised, Elijah looked up. "Sure son, I'd like that. Alone or do you want company?"

"Alone" Patrick replied.

They headed out onto the pampas towards the Colorado River on the *estancia's* southern boundary. After thirty minutes Patrick slowed his horse to a walking pace.

"There's something about this place isn't there? I've always loved it and often thought about it while I was overseas."

Elijah nodded as he leaned forward and patted his horse on the neck. "I never get back here enough. Before Mercedes' death, I spent some of the happiest days of my life here. Every time I come back, I can feel her here looking after me. But I knew she disapproved of Kyra when I brought her here."

"So why did you marry her?" his son asked.

"I was in the process of throwing her out when she told me she was pregnant. I married her for Crisantro's sake, but I got that wrong too" Elijah replied. He glanced across at Patrick. "Do you want to just walk for a while?"

Patrick nodded and Elijah continued talking. "I never wanted you to go to war. I was angry at the time, but I have to say I'm very proud of you son."

Patrick had been awarded the Distinguished Service Cross and the Air Medal for heroism while under fire.

"I'd rather not talk about that" he responded quietly. "You just do what you have to do at the time. I guess I should thank you for having me moved from the Marines although I was angry when it happened. But then someone who was taught to fly on the express orders of the President should've guessed he wasn't going to be allowed to remain in the ground forces."

"So you know about that" Elijah said. "But it wasn't strictly a favour. The President was repaying a debt."

Elijah pulled on the reins, stopping his horse. "One of the biggest regrets of my life is that we never got to know each other. The fault is mine; I acknowledge and accept that. All I ask is that you accept my decision to leave you first with Jorge and Elvira, and then to send you away to school was always taken with your future in mind. But there was no way I was going to leave you in the Marines to die on some godforsaken beach as machine gun fodder at the hands of the Japs if I could do anything about it. I can't apologise for that Patrick. I'm sorry, I just can't!"

They rode on in silence, each of them lost in his own thoughts before Patrick spoke again. "This last year and a half I got to do a lot of thinking. I can't change my life or what's happened in the past. I realise that I've been a rotten shit much of the time, but I also think I had good reasons for my actions. Sophia's death was the last straw for me.

I really loved her. She was so gentle and caring even though she must have gone through hell because of our relationship…you and me that is." He stopped and cleared his throat. "I can't change the past father, but I'm prepared to start again if you are."

"I can't ask for more than that son" Elijah said extending his hand across the void between them. Patrick grasped it, shook it once and then held it for a moment longer before letting go.

"What are your plans for Nancy?" he asked.

"She's my oldest friend. I first met her when she was fourteen. Montague was going to head up our British interests from next month, but he went down in a plane crash over the English Channel. She's had a rough time of it ever since and I asked her here to recuperate. She's a pretty smart cookie and I intend offering her a position on the new board that Jorge's setting up. Beyond that, nothing" Elijah replied.

"Nothing father?" Patrick asked with the merest hint of a grin forming on his face.

"Nothing Patrick. If anything should develop it will be because it was meant to, but right now; nothing!" He changed the subject. "What I'd rather talk about are your intentions. I've never made a secret of the fact that I want you to come into the company after you've finished Yale."

"That's the other thinking I've been doing" his son replied. "I expect to be discharged in another month and I'd like to come back down here until Yale kicks off again in September and then get stuck back into my studies and graduate as soon as possible. Then we can talk about your job offer. I guess I'll compare it with whatever else is going around and make a decision then."

Elijah looked at him sharply but his son just grinned.

"Don't be so jumpy. It's going to be hard remembering we have a truce, and not stir you up from time to time."

With that he flicked the reins and raced off across the pampas.

***

241

By the time Elijah returned to New York in late January 1946, both Michael Levinson and Nancy had agreed to join the new global board of Mercedes Group GmbH as directors. He considered that having a former United States Congressman and an English Marchioness added a certain amount of class and respectability to the letterhead. Now that he and Patrick were finally reconciled, it seemed there were only two immediate problems to be resolved; what to do with the Greek slut's brats. He sure as hell didn't want them hanging around him.

Chapter 23

Stockholm, Sweden
March, 1948

"Thank you for coming Elijah. I don't know how much more I could've taken on my own" she whispered. "I didn't realise just how mean and vindictive these people could be."

He pulled her closer under the covers. "I always told you I'd be there if you needed me"

"I know you did, and I'll never forget your help but it's Benji I'm most worried about. I don't know how he'll react" Agnota whispered back.

"Go to sleep, it's over. Tomorrow you've got to look your best."

"I know I shan't sleep tonight" she replied, "I'm too worried about tomorrow."

Within minutes though, her breathing relaxed and it wasn't long before she fell asleep. He slowly extracted his arm from beneath her and padded across to the window, pulling back the curtain to look outside. The snow was falling gently in huge flakes highlighted by the orange glow of the streetlamps along the Kommendörsgaten. At least the wind had dropped, but he involuntarily shivered standing there naked in the warm room. After all these years, Elijah still wasn't used to Stockholm's bone-chilling cold.

He turned back from the window and looked at Agnota lying in the bed, her face highlighted by the glow of the streetlamps. Still strikingly beautiful, she'd changed little in the twenty years he'd known her. He drew the curtain closed once more and slid back into bed, softly brushing her mane of blond hair as she stirred, murmured something in Swedish and snuggled into him.

***

Sleep eluded him as his mind played back over the events of the past year that had brought him flying to her assistance, and the agreement that had finally been reached earlier that day. That questions were being raised about Benji's parentage was hardly surprising. What was surprising was how long they'd taken to surface considering Fredrik's well known sexual proclivities.

Elijah and Nancy had married in August 1947 in a quiet ceremony in England attended only by a small circle of close friends and his children. Nancy had proven to be an excellent choice on the new board, displaying a good head for business combined with a propensity to tell Elijah what she thought, which he didn't always appreciate. She also had excellent establishment contacts in a Britain that was still coming to grips with the consequences of having won the war.

As though already having six children, not counting Benji, wasn't enough, the cycle was about to start all over again. Despite their ages, Nancy had made it very clear that children were definitely on her radar when they married. Elijah hoped that age would work in his favour and might just start slowing down his reproductive genes, but they were barely three months into their marriage when Nancy announced the news.

She'd also been outspoken when Elijah was asked by Göring's counsel at the Nuremburg Trials, to testify on the Reichsmarschall's behalf.

"You couldn't seriously contemplate it Elijah" she'd said when he told her. "The man's a monster, and represents a monstrous regime."

"I don't intend to" he replied. "I find it intriguing that he even asked me."

His refusal brought with it other consequences. Agnota was

extremely upset at Elijah's decision. She'd written and telephoned him repeatedly imploring him to change his mind. "He looked after you during the war when you needed help" she said. "Now he needs you, you have a duty to help him."

She was already under attack in Sweden for her Nazi leanings and her friendship with Göring. Jorge had even suggested that it was time that she relinquished the public face of the group in Sweden.

"There's no way *amigo*" Elijah replied. "Just as I don't intend lifting a finger to help Göring, I won't allow anyone to harm Agnota. There're too many business leaders and politicians in Sweden who profited out of their links with the Nazis during the war. I don't see any of them moving aside. Why should she be treated any differently?"

***

Two weeks after the request to testify on Göring's behalf, Elijah received a visit at his New York office by two FBI agents. After identifying themselves, one of them launched into the reason for their visit.

"We're investigating your links with the Germans during the war, particularly with Hermann Göring" he said.

"And is there any particular reason that you've chosen to approach me at this time?" Elijah asked.

"We understand that you've been asked by Göring to testify on his behalf at his trial as a character witness."

"It was always my understanding that client-lawyer confidentiality was one of the tenets of American justice" Elijah responded fixing the two agents with a cold hard stare. "I have no intention of answering any questions from either of you. Firstly, I am a Swiss national; secondly if Mr Hoover wishes to solicit information from me, he'd better contact me himself, but only after he's talked with General Donovan at the OSS and the General endorses such a meeting with him." He continued to fix them with his cold stare. "Now I'm busy. This meeting's over."

The two agents sat staring at him, not believing the manner in which he spoke to them. One of them leaned forward. "Mr Hocking, you don't seem to understand..."

Elijah cut him off. "No sonny boy, it's you who doesn't seem to understand! This meeting's over! Now you can both be smart and piss off immediately of your own free will or I'll have you removed, by force if necessary." He reached for the telephone. "Do I need to make this call?"

Four days later, in response to a call from General Donovan, Elijah flew to Washington.

"I hear you were pretty rough on those two FBI agents" Donovan commented as he poured a Jack Daniels for each of them.

"Well they did send a couple of boys to do a man's job. Bloody amateurs!"

"Turns out Hoover didn't like the way you roughed them up. Sending Hoover to see me wasn't the smartest thing you've ever done since he doesn't like me either. He's been fighting to have the OSS disbanded and all the country's espionage and security forces vested in the FBI since we were first set up."

The General tossed his drink back in one gulp, then poured himself another while Elijah waited. It was obvious he had more to say. "Watch him Elijah. Hoover's a slimy little rat and you've made yourself a powerful enemy. He'll be watching you. If you didn't already have one, you can be sure you now have an active file over at Pennsylvania Avenue."

"That all smacks of Nazi Germany and the commies. I thought that's what you guys just spent four years fighting against" Elijah said softly.

"In Hoover's world, anything goes if it results in capturing or exposing the nation's enemies, or more to the point, his own...real or imaginary" Donovan replied. "Anyway I set him straight on your involvement with Göring and suggested if he wanted further confirmation then he should go and talk with Hull, but I also warned him that neither of us would talk with anyone but him."

He took a sip from his glass and broke out into a deep laugh. "Turns out he doesn't like Hull either. I guess when you dig down deep, Hoover doesn't like anyone except possibly himself and the jury's out on that right now too!"

When Elijah recounted the discussion to Jorge later, his companion said "I've never thought of you as naive Elijah. The Americans didn't go to war to fight for freedom, it was all about profits. If the Japanese hadn't attacked them, the Americans would have never gone to the aid of the British or the Russians. They were doing too well out of just supplying them."

"I thought that was our role" Elijah countered.

"The difference is that we admit it. We've never come up with any of that phony 'fighting for freedom' bullshit to justify our actions" Jorge said.

***

Göring was found guilty of war crimes but committed suicide the night before he was due to hang. It was another twelve months before Agnota talked to Elijah about anything other than business matters. But she was facing her own problems and had finally called him in late November the previous year.

"I have to see you Elijah. It's urgent. There's no-one else I can turn to. Can we meet?"

He and Nancy split their time between the United States and Britain, using Elijah's house at Scarsdale and Nancy's townhouse at Lowndes Square in Belgravia as their bases.

"That's fine, but you understand that you'll be staying at a hotel?" He added softly "There won't be any coffee breaks either Agnota."

With her flawless complexion and long blond hair, all eyes followed her as she entered the Dorchester Hotel's Grill Room a week later.

"My God Agnota, you're magnificent" Elijah said admiringly as he rose to kiss her on both cheeks.

After about fifteen minutes she leaned forward. "I'm in trouble Elijah. Oskar has irrefutable proof that Benji's not Fredrik's son."

She was referring to Fredrik's younger brother. She took a small lace handkerchief from her purse and lightly dabbed her eyes. "He first challenged Benji's legitimacy twelve months ago" she continued, "and although I fought it, he successfully petitioned the Court for the release of Fredrik's medical records. These prove that Fredrik was sterile at the time of Benji's conception."

She stopped and dabbed her eyes again as Elijah reached across and took her other hand in his.

"What does he want?" he asked.

"He's demanding that he be recognised as the rightful claimant to the Lindforss title. In addition he's claiming one million kronor as restitution of funds that I've spent since Fredrik's death and as compensation for his 'pain and suffering'."

"Does Benji know?"

"Not yet, but Oskar's threatening to go public and take legal action if I don't agree to his demands."

"And there's absolutely no doubt that Fredrik was sterile?" he asked.

"None' she replied. "We both knew it. That's why I fought against his medical records being released. Fredrik knew Benji wasn't his; he couldn't be since we never consummated our marriage but it suited him to be able to parade a son around, especially with his lifestyle. It also suited Oskar and the rest of the family at the time as it squashed many of the unpleasant rumours doing the rounds about Fredrik."

"So you're saying that Oskar knew all along that Benji wasn't Fredrik's son, but did nothing about it. Why now?"

"Because Benji will turn twenty one next year and he'll inherit the Lindforss title and what remains of the estate. Oskar also thinks that I'm more vulnerable now because of this Göring business. This way he can have me labelled as both a Nazi *and* a whore" she said with a bitter laugh.

"First things first Agnota" Elijah said. "Benji has to be told."

"No!" she said emphatically. "Not yet! I need your help to beat Oskar or at least to salvaging what I can for Benji first. What I really need is for you to meet with my lawyers. You have a far quicker mind than me. Please Elijah; I really need your help in dealing with Oskar."

"Of course I'll help, but on two conditions. First I have to tell Nancy. I won't do this behind her back especially if I am going to acknowledge Benji as mine. Secondly, I have to be there when Benji's told. It won't be enough that he finds out that Fredrik's not his father; he needs to know who his real father is."

***

"Is she still in London?" Nancy asked when Elijah completed telling her the story later that night. When he confirmed that Agnota was at the Dorchester, Nancy insisted they meet. Against his better judgement, Elijah agreed. He'd been in some sticky situations through different stages of his life, but this he decided, was amongst the stickiest. It took all of his powers of persuasion to convince Agnota to agree, but the two women met the following afternoon. The meeting had actually been very civilised.

Returning from escorting Agnota back to her nearby hotel, Elijah found Nancy seated in front of her dressing table mirror brushing her hair. He walked up behind her and put his arms around her and nuzzled his lips against her neck.

"Back off kiddo" she said, "I've still got twenty strokes to go."

As she continued to brush her hair she raised her eyes to meet his in the mirror. "She's very beautiful." She continued brushing before adding "Is it over?"

"We had one week twenty years ago Nancy" he replied. "I've always known about Benji, but she'd never let me take responsibility."

"Then you have to help her" Nancy said. "You've got to salvage what you can for her and her son."

"You know that'll mean me spending quite a bit of time in Stockholm" he said.

"Why should that be a problem?" Nancy asked. "You've already told me there's nothing for me to worry about."

She put her brush down on the dressing table and picked up a bottle of hand cream and started working the lotion into her hands.

"Perhaps you could come as well" Elijah suggested.

"Don't be silly darling. What would I do in Stockholm while the two of you are closeted with the lawyers? Everything I've heard about the place suggests I'd have more fun down by the docks in Liverpool."

***

Surrounded by his phalanx of lawyers, Oskar had been arrogant throughout the negotiations. He relegated everyone in the room, including his own advisors, to the status of subservience, totally ignoring Agnota throughout. Not once during the many meetings, did he speak to her and only addressed her lawyer directly as required. Months of negotiations between both parties' lawyers finally led to the meeting earlier that day.

Only once he was finally convinced that Agnota was serious about carrying out her threat to publicly reveal his family had inveigled her to marry Fredrik for the sole purpose of covering up his overt homosexuality, Oskar dropped his claim for compensation. She knew he was desperate to keep Fredrik's sordid past from public knowledge at all costs.

The agreement resulted in Agnota retaining a substantial sum of money from Fredrik's estate, but in turn she was forced to relinquish all the estate's stocks and other investments including the apartment in Kommendörsgaten to Oskar. Unbeknownst to him, Jorge had already undertaken a detailed inspection of the Lindforss estate and quietly bought up stocks giving Elijah control, through a series of trusts, in those companies which now represented Oskar's primary wealth.

For Agnota, the major stumbling block was being forced to acknowledge Benji's illegitimacy, ensuring he was ineligible to inherit the Lindforss title or estate. On this point Oskar was unshakeable. The title of Baron Lindforss meant too much to him. It'd taken Elijah many hours of patient arguments and discussion before she finally agreed.

As the documents were signed earlier that day, Oskar couldn't conceal the look of triumph that erupted across his face.

"Twelve months you prick" Elijah thought as he escorted Agnota from the room, roughly pushing her brother-in-law aside. *"Let's see if that smirk's still on your face in twelve months."*

***

She was plainly on edge the following morning when they joined Benji for breakfast. Elijah tried to engage her in conversation, but she snapped at him, quickly putting an end to his attempts. If Benji noticed her mood, he didn't comment as the meal dragged on in silence. A couple of times Agnota made as though to speak, but both times she found she couldn't continue.

Finally Elijah stood up, crossed to the dresser and poured himself a coffee before returning to the table where he stood beside her, putting his arm around her shoulder. Before she could shrug him away, he said "Benji, there's something your mother and I need to discuss with you."

The boy sat back in his chair and raised his eyebrows. "I thought you'd got married only recently Elijah" he said solemnly.

"Ah, if only it was that easy" he replied.

"We missed that boat a long time ago" his mother added softly.

The three of them sank into silence again while Agnota frantically searched for the words to say. Finally she gave a sigh. "It's not about us Benji, it's about you. Well actually it's about all of us, but it's mainly you...and me...and Elijah too."

She lapsed into silence once more.

"So *Moder,* what you're trying to say is that you want to talk about something that's really about me and you and Elijah, or possibly about all of us, is that correct?" Benji prodded while trying to look serious.

His mother dissolved into tears, her head cupped in her hands.

Finally Elijah spoke. "What your mother's trying to say, is that Fredrik's not your real father and this is about to become public knowledge."

Agnota looked up expecting to see a look of horror, or at least disbelief on her son's face. Instead he answered quite matter of factly. "I know that. I've known for a long time."

"How could you have known?" she gasped. "Both Fredrik and I were always very careful never to allow any doubts about this to leak out."

"*Moder*, I'm twenty years old. I've known about father for many years. I can't ever recall you sharing a bedroom, although I've seen you and Elijah do so on a number of occasions. And the kids at school spoke about him lots of times. I just learned to ignore it although I had to serve out a couple of beatings to kids who tried to come on to me thinking I might be like him."

Agnota eyes opened wide in horror. "Benji, I had no idea! You never said anything!"

"What could you've done? I sorted it out for myself. So, why's this becoming such a big issue all of a sudden?"

"Your Uncle Oskar's decided he's rightfully the Baron, not you, and he's been fighting with your mother over the past year. Unfortunately both the law and the medical facts are on his side and your mother was forced to sign away your legacy yesterday" Elijah said.

Benji thought about this for a moment before speaking again. "So who am I then?"

"My son" Agnota said vehemently, "and don't let anyone say otherwise."

"I mean what will my name be now?"

"Benjamin Lindforss, the same as before" Elijah interceded. "You just miss out on the Baron bit" he added.

Benji shifted his gaze to Elijah as he carefully chose his next words. "Why are you here Elijah? I mean I appreciate you supporting *Moder* and all that, but why are you *really* here?"

"I think you know that too" Elijah replied. There was a moment's silence while they stared at each other.

"So why don't you tell me what it is that I know then?" Benji finally said.

"Oh for God's sake you two! He's your real father Benji!" Agnota snapped.

Elijah realised that Benji must have been rehearsing this scene for some time. He was impressed with the maturity the young man was displaying and withdrew from the room to allow the two of them to talk privately

***

Nearly an hour and a half passed before there was a knock on the door and Benji entered.

"*Moder's* explained a lot to me, some of which I already knew or guessed, but a lot that I didn't" he said falling silent for a moment. "There's no need to set up a trust fund for me. I'll make my own way."

"You're wrong Benji, there's every need. If your uncle had his way, then both you and your mother would be left destitute on the street. You need to finish your schooling and then we should talk about employment opportunities for you at Mercedes."

"Can I ask why you and mother never married?"

Elijah took a moment before he answered, choosing his words carefully. "In the early days that we first knew each other, it was impossible due to the agreement she'd been forced to sign. By the time she was free, we both realised we were better for each other if we didn't live together. I would've made a terrible husband."

"That's exactly what she said" Benji replied, "although she added that she never met anyone else who could measure up to you. Do you mind if we continue this a bit later? I need to take a walk and think."

He headed to the door but stopped as he reached for the door handle. Looking back he asked "Can we cut the idea of you feeling you need to be my father? I'd rather we were just friends."

***

Barely a month later, Elijah was back in Stockholm, this time accompanied by Nancy. As they were introduced, she reached out and hugged the sombre young man.

"I am so, so sorry Benji. I only met her once but she seemed to be a remarkable woman."

He nodded as he turned to shake hands with Elijah.

"This was all Oskar's doing" he told Elijah as they sat in the Chairman's office at PMAB while Nancy rested in their suite at the Grand Hotel. "When he forced her out of the apartment it all became too much for her. She'd been pretty distraught ever since you went back to London. About a week ago, as soon as the agreement was registered at the court, the bastard gave her twenty four hours to be out of the apartment or he threatened to have her evicted. I found her the next morning. She'd cut her wrists. There was blood everywhere."

He fell silent and looked away, but not before Elijah could see the tears brimming in his eyes.

"Oskar will regret this Benji I promise you. Events are already set in train" he told his son quietly.

Benji turned back facing Elijah. The tears had started streaming unchecked down his face. "I took photographs and mailed them to him; registered to Baron Oskar Lindforss so that he'd open the envelope thinking it was important."

"Brilliant!" thought Elijah. *"Bloody brilliant! I'd never have thought of that."*

He stood up and pulled his son to his chest in a bear hug as the boy broke down and sobbed. They stood like that until Benji pulled away.

"I'm sorry. I promised myself that wouldn't happen."

"Don't be silly boy. I've been the same place myself before. Better that it's done here in private so the arse-hole gets no pleasure from seeing your emotions. I promise you Benji, he will pay."

Standing together at the portal of the cathedral the following day, they both experienced immense satisfaction as they witnessed Oskar's humiliation at being refused entry to Agnota's funeral before a large crowd drawn largely from the Swedish aristocracy, politicians and leading business people who filled Stockholm's Sankt Nikolai Kyrka.

"This, my boy, is just the start" Elijah said as they turned and walked into the cathedral.

***

After the service Elijah and Jorge repaired to the Grand Hotel for a drink.

"I found an apartment for Agnota to buy before I left last month. I'll go through with the purchase because you and I need somewhere to stay when we're in town. I also want an apartment for Benji; he's going to need something for himself and won't want us hanging around."

Jorge nodded in agreement.

"I also want to start turning off Oskar's income straight away. Start as a drip feed operation and slowly build up the intensity. I don't want him to suffer all at once. Let him experience death by a thousand cuts. Make sure there're no profits or dividends from any of his investments. Do whatever you can to force the share prices down making sure we're the only buyers. We can start by dropping a few of our own shares on the market at heavily discounted prices and then snap them up again immediately. I don't care what it costs. I want him to start panicking especially now he has the upkeep of the Kommendörsgaten apartment to look after."

"I thought we might do something about that too" Jorge told him "so he can't get a buyer for it if he tries to offload it. I'll have a word to a couple of people in government here to see if we can't get some sort of caveat placed over the property. I'll find something even if I have to invent it so that he'll have to spend money to fight to have it lifted."

"Why not create some borrowings that Agnota secured against the property? I'm sure you could conjure up some sort of loan agreement." Elijah suggested. "I know she signed the place over as unencumbered

255

in the agreement but let him sue her estate. I'm sure we could convince her executor to be very difficult. Oskar's pretty skint otherwise isn't he?"

"That was one of the reasons he took her on" Jorge confirmed. "The title was important to him, but the estate was even more so as just about everything he owns is hocked. He'd have had an orgasm when he got hold of the Lindforss share portfolio. He really thought he'd dudded Agnota when he let her have the cash while he got the shares."

As the waiter refreshed their drinks Jorge continued. "You know Elijah, you never did tell me how Patrick reacted when you told him about Benji."

"It was bloody difficult. I thought we were going to head straight back to the bad old days again. The fact that his mother was dead before Agnota and I met was all that held it together, but he still wasn't happy. He made me swear there were no other bastards lurking in the closet before he calmed down. I think it's fair to say that our relationship's taken a step backwards."

"And *are* there any other bastards lurking around?"

"Well none that I know of" Elijah shot back. "Christ Jorge, the last thing I wanted after Mercedes and the twins was any more kids. Somehow they just kept popping out. Now I've not only got Benji but Nancy's planning her own brood as well."

Jorge adjusted his glasses so that they sat on the end of his nose. He assumed a scholarly look as he spoke in a mock serious tone. "I'm told on good authority that there are ways and means to prevent such things happening you know Señor Hocking."

"Thanks mate, just what I need; at fifty one years old, some smart-arse finally gets around to giving me a lecture on the birds and the bees and what causes it all."

***

Just when Elijah thought life might finally start to settle down again, he received an angry long distance phone call soon after he and Nancy returned to London. He'd been more than relieved when Selena begged to be allowed to spend the summer holidays at Martha's Vineyard with a school friend; the daughter of a well known Boston society family. At sixteen, his daughter had developed a full bodied figure with long legs and long dark hair. As he took the phone, Elijah was unprepared for the angry voice at the other end.

"Ralph, it's good to hear from you" Elijah said pleasantly.

"You won't think so by the time I'm finished Hocking" was the angry response. "I want that tramp out of here today. I don't care where she goes, just as long as she gets out of my house" the man yelled.

"Slow down Ralph. What's this all about?"

"My wife found that whore daughter of yours in bed with our son this morning. He's only fourteen for Christ sake. It turns out they've been at it most of the holidays. I should call the police and have her arrested for corrupting him."

The man was yelling so loud, Elijah was having trouble understanding him.

"Perhaps it's me who should be calling the police Ralph. Remember, my daughter's underage."

"You have to be joking" the voice exploded. "Raymond says she seduced him. He'd never had sex before she came to stay. Don't even think of pointing the finger at him if she finds herself pregnant. It turns out she's been laying it out for half the teenage boys and probably everyone else on the island over the summer."

"That fucking little slut" flashed through Elijah's mind. "I'll have her collected later today" he said and hung up the phone. There was no way he was bringing her to London. He was so angry that if he saw her, he might end up doing something he'd regret. He was staring at the phone when Nancy came into the room.

"What's the matter?"

In a few short terse words he recounted the call to her. "I've arranged for Johnny to pick her up today and take her back to Scarsdale and not let her out of his sight" he said. "I always knew she was just like her bloody mother. Shit! What am I to do with her? I can't leave her in New York, not even with Johnny."

"Give me an hour Elijah" Nancy said. "I might have an answer. I need the phone so go and find something to work off that anger."

About forty-five minutes later she rejoined him. "I recalled that Susan Boddington-Smythe had a similar problem. She packed her daughter off to a place in Switzerland that calls itself a finishing school. In reality it sorts out girls like Selena. Susan said it was fantastic in dealing with her daughter. The school's called the Institut St Allemande Établir pour Jeune Fille. It's in a remote area of the country near a little village called Riemenstalden in the mountains above Lake Luzern. She's given me all the details. You still have time to call them today if you want to."

***

Three days later he met Selena at Zurich airport. She was accompanied by Johnny since Elijah didn't trust her to fly on her own.

She tried hard to stare him down as he asked "So is it true?"

"You obviously think so or I wouldn't be here" she responded tartly, refusing to avert her eyes from his.

As he raised his hand, Johnny reached out and stopped him. "Why don't I take her on to the school Boss? It might be better for both of you."

"Just get the little bitch out of my sight mate" he snarled back. "So help me God Selena, if you cause any trouble at this school, between them and me you'll wish you were never born. Do we understand each other?"

She continued to try and out-stare him, but this time she saw the same look her mother Kyra had seen many years before during her confrontation with Elijah when he demanded a divorce. She felt a chill wash over her. For the first time she realised her father not only hated her, but could quite possibly cause her harm. She looked away, hoping he hadn't seen the panic registering in her eyes.

258

"Do...we...understand...each...other, you little slut?" he said again in a voice that was little more than a hiss laced with menace.

This time she nodded, but she couldn't look at him again.

"Good. Now get her out of my sight."

Chapter 24

In 1950 Elijah decided to trade his Lockheed for a Douglas DC6 which he then had fitted out with a bedroom and an office. He and Nancy used it to fly from London to Patrick's graduation. His son had achieved a degree in business administration and law and was going to work with Jorge in Zug as his assistant. At twenty-four, he was a serious young man and Elijah hoped that with Jorge's tutelage it wouldn't be long before the boy could be sent out to head up one of the group's divisions. To their surprise, Patrick announced he was engaged. Until then they didn't even know he had a girlfriend. They immediately liked Lucinda who was studying American History at Yale and was the only child of an Episcopalian Rector.

"At least he's not a Mick" was Elijah's only comment when he learned of her father's profession, "but if he thinks he's going to convert me, then all the news will be bad."

Despite Elijah's offer to fund the wedding, Lucinda's father refused to allow him to contribute to the cost saying it was both his prerogative and responsibility. The Rector decided the wedding would be held at the local Episcopal Church where he would conduct the ceremony. The reception would follow in the adjacent church hall. Despite a guest list that included some of the nation's best known powerbrokers and businessmen, Lucinda's father could not be shaken.

Nancy urged Elijah to accept the situation and cease interfering. "It's Patrick's life" she told him. "He's a man now and has to be responsible for his own affairs."

They were journeying by road from Scarsdale to Warwick for the wedding when Nancy casually mentioned she was pregnant again and was expecting the following May.

"Christ Nancy, if we keep going at this rate, there's every chance Patrick's kids will be older than some of their aunts or uncles."

"You're going to have to watch your language over the next few days" she responded. "Anyway I didn't do it on my own. I can always arrange for separate bedrooms once we get home and see if that resolves the problem."

**

The day before the wedding, they met Lucinda's parents for the first time. Based on the Reverend's implacable stance on the wedding arrangements, Elijah already had a jaundiced opinion of the man.

The day started badly and rapidly progressed downhill as the two men took an immediate dislike to each other. Jacobsen was of average height with a large protruding stomach, accentuated by his trouser belt being done up a notch too tight. His complexion was pasty, with pink blotchy cheeks; his hair dull, lifeless and thinning and his handshake limp. To the rector, wealth and power both represented diseases. As far as he was concerned, Elijah was cursed with the worst form of both viruses.

"Jesus Christ" Elijah muttered quietly to Nancy. "Where did they dredge this arse-hole up from? Just what has Patrick got himself into here?"

"May I ask which religion you follow Mr Hocking?" the Reverend asked him immediately after they'd met.

Out of the corner of his eye, Elijah could see his son almost imperceptibly shake his head as though begging his father not to answer the question.

"I don't."

"Surely there must be something you believe in other than material wealth and power" the Reverend persisted, a sarcastic edge to his voice.

"Since you insist Mr Jacobsen, it's my view that religion, all religion, is not just a crock of shit; it's the curse of mankind. All my life I've witnessed too much suffering that's been administered in your God's name, and in the name of many other Gods as well. If you truly believe He's responsible for the world we live in, your God if He exists, which I sincerely doubt, has a lot to answer for" Elijah answered pleasantly.

He saw Patrick look away with a resigned look as he spoke, while Nancy just put her hand to her mouth so that the smile she knew was beginning would be covered from view. The Reverend and his mousy little wife were struck speechless and recoiled in horror.

"Why did you need to say that?" Patrick remonstrated with him later. "Couldn't you just have shrugged him off?"

"The sanctimonious shit had it coming" his father replied. "He couldn't leave well enough alone. Forgive me the pun, but he's your cross to bear, not mine. If there's one thing I want you to remember son, it's that you should always be who you are and say what you feel, because those that matter won't mind and those that mind don't matter!"

Despite his anger at the time, when Patrick had cause to replay his father's words later, he recognised their wisdom and never forgot them, passing them down to his own children in future years.

***

Selena's arrival caused the second stir of the day. She'd recently completed her schooling at Riemenstalden with glowing reports. All conversation ceased as she entered the room. Even Elijah was staggered at how brazenly she was dressed but worse, it was obvious that Patrick hadn't prepared his future father-in-law for the fact that he had a coloured brother and sister. For a second time Lucinda's parents were speechless.

"Do you think I should ask him if God sees her as evil or unclean or perhaps both?" Elijah whispered to Nancy.

"Don't you dare" she hissed back. "You've done quite enough

damage already."

"Pity we didn't invite Benji as well. Now that would've been a treat" he shot back mischievously. But he couldn't restrain himself. It'd been a long time since he'd disliked anyone as much as the Reverend Jacobsen and he was starting to enjoy himself.

Temporarily putting his dislike of his daughter to one side, he crossed the floor and put his arm around her waist. As he did, Selena pulled away slightly; she couldn't ever remember her father showing any form of affection towards her before.

"Teenagers Reverend, God's punishment for enjoying sex wouldn't you agree?" he asked conversationally.

Nancy fled the scene, Patrick groaned and silence descended upon the room broken only by the sound of Mrs Jacobsen's cup shattering on the maple floor and Selena erupting into an uncontrolled fit of giggling.

It was five minutes before Nancy felt she could safely re-enter the room.

"We have guests who are our responsibility arriving shortly Elijah. It's time we left to prepare for them. Mr and Mrs Jacobsen, it's been so lovely to meet you. We look forward to you joining us again this evening" she said as she tugged at Elijah's arm. "You too Selena!" she added.

As he went to say something, she stopped and glared at him. "I'd think twice before I opened my mouth if I was you" she said in a voice so soft only he could hear her.

"But darling, I was merely going to ask Lucinda's mother to reserve a spot for me on her dance card at the wedding tomorrow."

He looked across at Mrs Jacobsen as he flashed his brightest smile at her. "I'm best known for my prowess in the tango you know. Learnt it dancing with the other men while we waited in line in the whore-houses in La Boca."

As he delivered this, he was almost pulled off his feet by a visibly angry Nancy. Disappearing from the room Elijah could be heard saying to her in a wounded voice "Well it's true. The purest form of tango started in those whorehouses."

***

Things were no better when the two families reconvened that night with a number of the wedding guests. Patrick pulled his father aside and asked him to tone down his actions. "Once the reception is over tomorrow, there'll be no need for either of you to ever see each other again" he said.

"That's fine by me my boy, but I'll only put up with so much" Elijah responded, "Get Lucinda to have a word with her father and suggest he pull his head in. I'll hold my tongue, but if he starts sprouting his good old homespun religion, vilifies doing business or launches into a sermon on the ills of the demon drink, I won't be responsible for the reactions of some really good friends of mine who'll be attending."

While Patrick agreed, he walked away with a sense of foreboding for what might transpire before the wedding was over and everyone had departed.

That evening's pre-wedding function was being hosted by the groom's parents at the local hotel. Nancy had arranged for the catering to be carried out by a company based in nearby Providence and had painstakingly chosen the menu and accompanying wines.

"God Elijah, I can't change anything and I know it's all going to be wrong" she said as they dressed.

"No it's not" he said taking her into his arms. "Everything's going to be just right. There's no way I could put up with fried chicken, mashed potatoes and lemonade for my son's pre-wedding bash. We're going to get enough of that crap tomorrow. It's the nutcase misfits that Patrick's getting himself involved with that are all wrong."

"You will behave won't you?" she asked anxiously. It'd taken Nancy most of the day to cool down from that morning's performance.

"I'll behave" he acknowledged, but he worded his guests up before the function that evening. "Hold your tongues for Patrick's sake if you can, but if you can't" he added with a grin, "sex, booze and business are the Reverend's hot points. You should do well on all counts Joe" he said to the elder Kennedy, "and on top of everything else you're a Mick."

***

Part way through the evening, Elijah wandered out into the garden to get a break from Patrick's future in-laws. He'd honoured his commitment to Nancy and behaved himself, but it was hard going. During the afternoon, snow had fallen before the clouds cleared at dusk. The small neatly landscaped garden at the rear of the hotel glowed white in the light of a full moon shining overhead, accompanied by a canopy of stars. He drew on his cigarette, enjoying the solitude of the moment before he had to head back into the function.

"It's beautiful isn't it?" a voice said behind him.

He hadn't heard anyone approaching and was surprised to hear an Australian accent in the middle of New England. He turned to face a woman roughly twenty years younger than himself standing with a coat thrown over her shoulders. He decided she was attractive rather than beautiful, with long auburn hair that was cut to emphasise her high cheekbones.

"I'm Maureen Baverstock" she said. "Could I bother you for a cigarette? Kenneth and Prunella carry on so badly whenever I light up that I have to sneak out of the house whenever I want one."

Elijah took a packet of Lucky Strikes from his jacket pocket and passed it to her as she continued speaking.

"I'm assuming you must be groom's wicked father. Your reputation precedes you. You're all Kenneth can talk about" she said with a grin.

"Guilty as charged" Elijah responded as she extended her hand. "Elijah Hocking" he added giving her hand a quick shake.

"Did you really tell him that you'd learned the tango dancing in some whorehouse with other men?" she asked.

"Guilty again. Not only told him, but it was true as well."

"Oh my God, I wish I could've been there to see his face...and poor

265

Prunella; it's a wonder she didn't take to her bed with the vapours" she said with a throaty laugh. "I'm sorry, I should explain, I'm married to Kenneth's cousin Arnold. I can't stand the Reverend and every so often I need to get away from him before I explode."

"A soul mate, just what I need. You seem to be a long way from home Maureen Baverstock. How did you end up getting involved with that bundle of laughs inside masquerading as my son's future father-in-law?"

"I met Arnold when he was a colonel in the U.S. Army based in Townsville during the war. I lost my first husband at Tobruk in 1941 and met Arnold a couple of years later. He was so handsome and seemed so sophisticated compared to the locals. I moved here in 1946 but somehow the fun's disappeared. Kenneth's by far the worst of the bunch, but the rest of the family including Arnold have similar idiosyncrasies. But I'm sure you're not interested in my problems."

She dropped her cigarette stub in the snow and stood on it. "I'm sure to have been missed by now. I'd better head back inside. It's been lovely to talk with you. I hope that now we're about to be family we get to meet again."

Before he could stop her, she turned and hurried back inside while he stood there for another couple of minutes before following her.

"Where have you been?" Nancy asked him as he entered.

"Outside, avoiding the arse-hole. Just charging up the batteries. Did you know that he has an Australian relative?".

"Yes I met her a little earlier. That's one of the reasons I was looking for you. That's her over there" she said pointing out Maureen on the other side of the room.

"Yes I met her outside. Extraordinary to find her so far from home here in this remote hole."

***

There was a tap on his shoulder as Nancy moved away. He turned to find Selena standing there.

"I know it's probably not a good time Daddy, but I wanted to talk to you about my allowance" she said with a smile she hoped would pass for being sincere.

"Allowance?" he asked arching his eyebrows.

"Yes Daddy. Now I've left school, I'm going to need an increase, and I was hoping you'd let me get an apartment as well" she added quickly.

"I don't have freeloaders on my payroll Selena. Now that you've left school, either get yourself a job or a husband. That'll take care of both the allowance and the apartment. And you were right; this is not a good time."

He left his daughter in shock as he walked away. She'd hoped his attitude towards her might have changed when he'd put his arm around her earlier. Suddenly, she realised she'd been used. She determined he wouldn't see her cry and fought back the tears as a man in his early thirties materialised alongside her.

"You look like you could do with a drink" he said.

Selena was about to tell him to drop dead when she made a split second decision. This could be the way to pay the prick back. "Only if it's a real drink handsome" she replied smiling.

He produced a small silver flask from his pocket, unscrewed the top and passed it to her.

She took a swig, coughed once, then took another. "What is that?" she asked. "It's so smooth."

"Pyrat Rum from the Caribbean. Only the best. How're you mixed up with this lot?"

"I'm Selena, Patrick's half-sister. That arse-hole over there's my father" she replied pointing to Elijah. "And you?"

"Robert van Holme. *That* arse-hole's distantly related" he said pointing to Lucinda's father. "Do you want to get out of here?"

"Perfect, but only if you've got a good supply of rum stashed away" Selena replied linking her arm in his and ensuring they walked close to her father as they departed.

"Where are you off to?" he asked as they passed by.

"I'm doing what you told me to do Daddy" she replied in a sultry voice. "I'm working on my apartment."

"What was that about?" Robert asked her as they exited the function room.

"Private joke. Don't worry about it."

***

In future years Patrick often remarked to Lucinda they must've been meant for each other to have still made it to the altar after those two days of family sniping, feuding, and animosity and then to have remained married to each other. Privately, he detested his father-in-law almost as much as Elijah did. Moving back to Zug immediately after the wedding and then to London for a number of years ensured they rarely saw each other.

Elijah, on reflection after heading home, decided the Reverend's life needed a little spicing up. He had a quiet word with a contact at the IRS in Washington who arranged for an exhaustive audit of the Reverend's tax records going back over many years. He also passed his telephone number to Maureen Baverstock.

"If you're ever in need of help, or just need a place for a smoke, call me" he told her. "I know what it can be like to be a long way from home with no support base."

Chapter 25

Joe Kennedy called him the following January. "Thought I should warn you Elijah, McCarthy's asking questions about you."

Senator Joseph McCarthy was beginning to make a name for himself by naming suspected communist sympathisers and liberals in the Senate, ruining many careers in the process.

"Exactly what am I supposed to be guilty of?" Elijah asked.

Kennedy was a strong supporter of McCarthy and his second son Robert worked for the Senator. "The guy's a patriot and he's doing some great work cleaning out the rabble. In your case I suspect he's been put up to it by Hoover" Joe Kennedy replied. "I doubt they could get you for being a liberal, so you must be a Commie" he laughed. "Anyway I've put a good word in for you, but it might be a good idea if you lay low for a while".

Elijah was ropeable, but decided to take Kennedy's advice. He and Nancy were due to fly back to Britain in late February in any case. Jorge had also advised him that just as Nancy had predicted would happen, her brother-in-law was in financial trouble. Life for Gerald and his friends had been one long party since Montague's death back in 1945. He had managed to run through the estate's cash and was disposing of family heirlooms, many of which Elijah quietly bought up and stored away. Elphinbrook House had been heavily mortgaged three years previously and Gerald was now in arrears on his repayments.

***

When he returned to London, without telling Nancy his intentions, Elijah visited Barings Bank. How different his reception was compared to his visit in 1915 when posing as a Brazilian representing an Argentine company hoping to sell beef to the British, he'd been courteously received by a middle ranking manager.[9] Now he was positively fawned over by a high ranking member of the executive.

"It is indeed an honour to be able to welcome you to Barings Bank" the bank representative gushed. "The Chairman extends his apologies that he was not available to receive you personally Mr Hocking."

With the pleasantries completed, Elijah stated the reason for his visit. "You may be aware that I'm married to the former Marchioness Elphinbrook" he said. "It's my understanding that the current Marquis is experiencing liquidity problems and that Barings is concerned at their exposure."

The banker smiled back. "You would appreciate Mr Hocking, that I am not at liberty to discuss another client's affairs."

"Yes Mr Dowding, I appreciate that, but I'm a busy man. I'm here to make an offer to resolve your problems by paying out the mortgage you hold over Elphinbrook House. But I want it resolved immediately and confidentially."

"As I said Mr Hocking, I apologise but I cannot possibly discuss the Marquis's details" the man opposite him replied.

"Pity!" Elijah replied standing up. "I was willing to pay full price for the property, whereas you'll be lucky to recover a fraction of its value with the current state of the economy. Since I am obviously wasting my time, I'll just have to wait until the bank is forced to place it on the open market. Mark my words Mr Dowding, I *will* buy Elphinbrook House."

Four days later, Elijah received a call from the Bank's Chairman asking to meet. Citing work pressures, Elijah agreed, but only at his own office in Lawrence Poultney Lane in The City.

9 The Elijah Trilogy Book 1 – The Half-breed Boy

"I'm afraid Mr Dowding may have been a little hasty Mr Hocking," the Chairman began.

"Somewhat officious would be my take on it" Elijah replied.

The Chairman smiled weakly. "I believe you wish to purchase the property with immediate settlement at market value."

"That was the situation a week ago. However I'm now attracted by the thought of waiting for the house to go on the market" Elijah replied as he watched the man opposite squirm. "Initially I was planning to give it to my wife as a present. She was disappointed when the property passed to her brother-in-law following her late husband's death. But since her birthday is not for several months and Christmas is still ten months away, I may have been a little hasty…much like your Mr Dowding" he added almost as an afterthought.

"Mr Hocking, I'll place my cards on the table" the Chairman replied. "The bank has advanced a substantial sum to the Marquis secured against Elphinbrook House. He is not in a position to service the loan and it's extremely unlikely that he will find an alternative source of finance. As I believe you noted to Mr Dowding, in the current depressed conditions it's also unlikely that we will be in a position to recover the outstanding loans if we are forced to place the property on the market. You obviously have a prime interest in purchasing the property whereas we want to be rid of it. I appreciate you're upset at the manner in which the matter was dealt with by Mr Dowding, however I'm prepared, subject to the agreement of my board of course, to come to an arrangement with you to both our advantages."

"I would have paid the full price you know Jorge, even though I could have waited for a forced sale" he told Jorge later, "but the bastard was just too keen to get rid of the loans and I was the only option he had to do a deal. I saw an opportunity to ensure that Gerald got nothing from the sale. Anyway, I offered to pay seventy five percent of the bank's exposure and the prick jumped at it. Christ, I thought I might have to send out for a new pair of trousers for him he came so close to shitting himself with relief."

***

The paperwork was prepared with almost indecent haste and it wasn't long before title to Elphinbrook House passed to Elijah. The day following settlement, he drove up to Chelmsford unannounced in his Bentley Mark VI. The house was just as he remembered it but as he drove down the long drive, it was obvious that the upkeep of the gardens had long been abandoned. The grass was long and the formerly meticulously trimmed trees and bushes were in disarray. Ringing the doorbell, he was forced to wait for some time before the door was finally opened by a footman.

"I'm here to see the Marquis" Elijah advised the man.

"Is his Lordship expecting you?" he was asked.

"I doubt it, I would hardly be his type" Elijah replied drily.

It was nearly fifteen minutes before Gerald entered the reception room where Elijah had been ushered to wait. Dressed in a flamboyant red silk Chinese dressing gown decorated with golden embroidered dragons, unshaven, his hair uncombed; it was obvious he had just emerged from his bed.

He looked closely at the visitor before saying "We've met before I believe."

"I'm Nancy's husband" Elijah replied, "and the new owner of Elphinbrook House." He enjoyed watching the shock register on Gerald's face as he received the unwelcome news. "I had considered employing the services of a bailiff, but then I decided why should I deny myself the pleasure of evicting you personally?"

"Evict?" Gerald stammered. "What are you talking about?"

"You have precisely one hour for you, your personal belongings and any of your male floosies that may be around to be off the property counting down from now" Elijah told him.

"How dare you?" Gerald squawked. "You can't do this. I'll have the police called immediately."

"Fifty eight minutes and counting" Elijah replied pleasantly, looking at his watch. "You may care to check with Barings Bank if you wish, but this is all eating into your remaining time. I took the liberty of bringing a copy of the letter from Barings transferring the title to me in case your solicitor hadn't briefed you yet."

Gerald turned white, snatching the letter from Elijah's hand and tearing it open with trembling hands.

"They can't do this to me" he said almost to himself.

"They can and they have you miserable little turd!" Elijah snapped back at him. "You're now down to fifty-five minutes and eating into what little time you have left to pack. I promise you that if you are as much as one second late in departing, I intend to personally remove you so fast that your mincing little feet won't have time to touch the ground. I sincerely hope you don't intend to deny me that pleasure. Now, where can I get a cup of tea while I'm waiting?"

***

Spying a bell cord in the far corner of the room, he crossed over and pulled it. "His Lordship will be leaving permanently in precisely fifty-two minutes. He requires some assistance in packing his things; personal items only mind" Elijah told the butler when he arrived. "In the meantime would you please be so kind as to arrange some tea for me?"

The butler turned his head to seek confirmation from Gerald who was still standing in shock, holding the letter from the bank. He looked back to Elijah who continued. "Lady Nancy will be returning to Elphinbrook to live. She's the new owner; I am her husband" he said by way of explanation.

"Of course sir" the butler acknowledged. "Welcome home." Elijah could have sworn there was the merest suggestion of a smile on the butler's otherwise impassive face.

When Gerald hadn't reappeared at the end of the allotted time, he summoned the butler once more.

"Where will I find the Marquis?" he asked.

Following the directions, Elijah found the room and made a show of throwing open the door. Gerald was slouched in a chair still wearing the red dressing gown while a maid and a footman were packing suitcases. Beside him were two men in their mid twenties, all three of them drinking from a bottle of gin.

"Your hour's up chum" Elijah said as he entered. "Out! Now!" he ordered.

"Piss off" Gerald responded. "I'm not finished packing."

"Oh yes you are" Elijah replied as he crossed the room and grabbed him.

"I say" one of the other two men interjected, "steady on old chap" as he grabbed ineffectually at Elijah who responded by giving him a backhander that dropped him to the floor.

"I told you one hour, and the hour's up."

Elijah turned to the two house staff who had retreated to the corner of the room wide-eyed.

"Close those cases and follow me" he ordered. "I'll be back for this garbage" he said indicating Gerald's two cowering companions "once I've disposed of this heap of crap...unless they're smart and get out first."

He yanked Gerald from the chair and physically dragged him from the room into the adjacent passage where they proceeded towards the main staircase.

"Stop, stop!" Gerald implored him struggling to get to his feet only to be ignored. As they reached the head of the wide curved staircase Elijah suddenly let the quivering man go.

"You can get down by yourself or be dragged; your choice."

Gerald stared up from the floor to be confronted by the cold hard look that Elijah developed when he was at his ruthless best. As Elijah bent to grab him once more, Gerald suddenly scrambled to his feet and started descending the staircase.

"Move it" he heard the command from behind him, "I haven't got all day and you're already eleven minutes late."

Morgan the butler, despite his impassive face, was obviously enjoying the spectacle. He held the door open as Gerald crossed the Grand Hall, hesitating as he reached the threshold. Elijah was immediately behind him and took the opportunity to place his foot squarely in the middle of Gerald's backside and with all the force he could muster, he sent the thirteenth Marquis of Elphinbrook sprawling onto the front portico, as he was unceremoniously ejected from his former ancestral mansion.

"Hold that door" Elijah instructed Morgan as he turned and took the three cases the maid and footman were holding, throwing them out behind Gerald. "There's still a couple of other lumps of shit to dispose of" he said.

He turned to re-enter the house just as Gerald's two companions scuttled out the door keeping well out of Elijah's reach.

"Have the garbage dumped beyond the front gate" he ordered. He continued issuing instructions over his shoulder as he re-entered the hall "and get in the local fumigator. Her Ladyship couldn't possibly be expected to return to this shithole until it's been cleaned up."

***

When he returned to London and handed her the title deeds to the mansion registered in her name and told her of Gerald's eviction, Nancy was overcome.

"Whatever happens, it's yours. No-one can take it away from you again unless you get frivolous with your money like Gerald" he said. "I had hoped that you would be able to give birth to number three up there, but it's pretty run down."

"I'll never be able to express my gratitude" Nancy told him though her tears, "you really don't know what this means to me. So what if it's run down? I'm sure we can have a couple of rooms prepared for us. I think moving back there is a lovely idea."

"There's a huge amount of work to be done" he warned her. "The house and the gardens have deteriorated as Gerald ran out of cash.

Morgan tells me the roof is leaking badly in a number of areas and the section of the house that was used by the Army during the war has never been reopened. That's particularly derelict. But there's some good news" he added.

"Good news?" Nancy asked.

"Good news…Gerald has been disposing of some of the heirlooms and paintings progressively for the past few years. Sotheby's and Christies knew to contact Jorge when anything came up for sale from Elphinbrook. There are quite a few pieces in storage to be returned to the house" Elijah replied. "With a bit of luck we'll have it restored back to its former glory."

Olivia Hocking was born at Elphinbrook House in a remarkably quick and uncomplicated birth in late May. It would take another fifteen months before restoration of the house was completed by which time their fourth child Victor was also born there. By then, courtesy of Patrick and Lucinda, Elijah had become a grandfather in September 1951 when Clement was born in Zug, fulfilling Elijah's prediction that Patrick's children would have aunts and uncles younger than themselves.

Chapter 26

New York, U.S.A.
August, 1951

As 1951 unfolded, Elijah wasn't destined to spend much of the year in Britain. Events unfolding in the United States forced him to spend the bulk of his time there. McCarthy's investigation intensified so that by August 1951, Elijah realised if he was going to stop him, he would need to return to Washington. He found to his chagrin that the Senator from Wisconsin had become increasingly powerful and feared with few of Elijah's contacts prepared to cross swords with him. For the first time since he'd arrived in America thirty years before, Elijah found himself sidelined by those in power.

Frustrated, he sat down with Mark Frost to plan a campaign against McCarthy in their papers which now included dailies in Miami, Atlanta and Houston. Walking back from one such session at Mark's office, he was standing on the corner of Nassau and Liberty deep in thought, waiting for a break in the traffic, when he felt a hand on his elbow and a familiar voice.

"Well, there's a sight for sore eyes."

Turning, he was surprised to see Maureen Baverstock standing next to him.

"Well if it ain't the Aussie sheila" he replied in a broad Australian accent.

"Not bad for Swiss cheese" she countered with a smile. "You'd almost think you were dinky-di Aussie yourself."

They stopped in a little bar in Maiden Lane where Elijah ordered his normal Jack Daniels along with a martini for Maureen. They'd been talking for half an hour before she looked at her watch.

"Goodness, I must rush. I was due to meet Arnold five minutes ago and he doesn't like to be kept waiting. I can expect one of his lectures. Perhaps you'll join us for dinner later?"

The thought of dinner with Arnold held no appeal and he begged off suggesting a rain-check, telling her he already had a business dinner arranged.

***

The following weekend he was at home alone at Scarsdale, when he was interrupted by the sound of a powerful engine roaring up the long driveway. The house was set back half a mile from the main road and whoever was approaching had their foot to the floor. Moments later he heard the squeal of brakes as the vehicle skidded to a halt on the large paved area in front of the house.

"Bloody fools" he thought angrily. *"They'll get a piece of my mind."*

He opened the front door to find Selena emerging from behind the wheel of a dark green Jaguar XK120 sports car. He hadn't seen her since Patrick's wedding nearly twelve months previously...but then he hadn't thought about her either.

"Hello daddy" she called cheerfully.

"Do you always drive like a bloody maniac? What if one of the kids had been playing out there?"

"Oh don't be silly. We both know they're in England."

"Where did you get that?" he asked pointing to the car. "Last time we spoke you were begging me for a handout."

"Robert gave it to me. It was my birthday present."

Geez he'd forgotten the little bitch's birthday. Hardly surprising when he had no idea when it was. "Robert?"

"The man I met at Patrick's wedding. We're very much in love."

"Bloody hell" he thought. *"The stupid prick's paying top dollar for his pussy. The little tramp's no better than her mother."*

"Aren't you going to invite me in?" she asked.

He hadn't moved from the front step. "Depends on whether this is a social call."

"I just came to say hello. I heard you were alone and thought you might like some company" Selena explained.

Grudgingly, her father stepped back and held the door open for her. "So can I assume you've got yourself a job?" he asked as they crossed the hall to the library.

"Not really, I'm studying acting. Robert's being very supportive and says I'm star material."

"Yes but what at?" he thought. "Who's this bloody Robert? Am I to assume you've shacked up with him?"

"Robert van Holme. He's a movie producer and he wants to marry me" she purred. "He's letting me stay in his apartment."

Elijah stood up. "I'll be back in a couple of minutes. I was in the middle of something when you arrived. Call Mrs Turner and ask her to make some coffee. Better still if you know how to do it yourself, I assume you haven't forgotten where the kitchen is."

He stepped into his study and picked up the phone. "Jorge" he said after a couple of rings. "A film producer name of Robert van Holme. I need to know everything about him in the next ten to fifteen minutes. Thanks."

Nearly twenty minutes later the housekeeper interrupted Elijah who had returned to the library and was talking with Selena.

"There's an urgent call for you Mr Hocking" she said.

Elijah crossed back to the phone in the study. "Yes Jorge." He listened as the lawyer briefed him on Selena's lover. "That's it?" he asked as Jorge finished.

Hanging up, he immediately placed another call. "Robert van Holme. Pick him up! A one-way ride on a garbage barge sounds good. Today!" he said and hung up.

***

His daughter could see the anger on his face as he re-entered the library. He crossed to her and grabbed her by the hair, yanking her to her feet.

"You stupid little slut. You're your bloody mother all over again. Film producer my arse! Your next answer better be truthful or by God you'll wish you were never born. Have you acted in any of that arse-hole's films? Think very carefully before you answer."

Selena had never seen him so angry. All the bravado she'd been displaying deserted her.

"No daddy. No, I haven't, I haven't! Why are you doing this? I've done nothing wrong" she cried.

He let her go, slapped her hard across the face and pushed her back into the chair.

"That shit is a goddamned pornographer. And married you bloody little tramp. If I find out you've lied to me" he snarled, "I'll kill you myself. First thing Monday morning you'll report to Mark Frost at the *Monitor*. Dress properly. By that I mean keep your tits stuffed inside your dress. You'll work for him at a real job. Johnny will move you into a new apartment tonight. You'll pay for it out of your salary. And get rid of that heap of crap in the driveway. Don't you ever let me see it again. Now get out before I really lose my temper."

As Selena ran from the room sobbing, her father's words followed her. "Your mother may have been a slut you little bitch, but compared to you, she was a class act."

***

It seemed nothing could go right for him. When the United States entered the Korean War, his businesses had initially prospered, increasing production to meet the renewed demand for war materials. But in recent times, he appeared to have become a pariah in the nation's capital. Even Joe Kennedy took to avoiding him.

In mid-October he got a call from Deke Newell. "I don't know what's going on, but the Defense Department has just cancelled another order" he said. "This is the third time in two weeks. Seems they've decided to source crude from Venezuela claiming it's cheaper."

"That doesn't make any sense Deke. With the war in Korea they should be looking for all the oil they can get."

"That's my call too" Deke replied, "but I'm not getting any straight answers. It's almost as though the people I've done business with at Defense for years are avoiding me."

"Tell you what Deke, cut production by a further twenty percent immediately. We'll replace the orders from somewhere and turn it up again when we have them. Also go and look over the situation in Venezuela, we might want to invest there. I'll cover it off with Jorge."

It happened again two weeks later when Mike Tewson, the President of Mercedes Steel called. A definite pattern was starting to emerge.

"We've just had a batch of steel orders cancelled from Newport News. It's crazy; just a couple of months ago they were here begging us to increase production. My man told me off the record that he's been given orders to treat us as the supplier of last recourse."

Once again Elijah's response was to cut back production and start laying off workers. He also called Michael Leveridge to see if he could find out what was happening.

"Seems I'm tarred with the same brush" Michael told him when he called back. "Give me some more time to get to the bottom of this. The Board meets in late January; I'll definitely have some answers by then."

It had been Elijah's intention to spend Christmas 1951 at the *estancia* but Nancy refused saying it was too far. She felt it made no sense to fly all that way when nearly everyone was close to them in Britain. She wouldn't budge and so instead the expanded family gathered at Elphinbrook House. As Christmas approached, he found himself in a very dark mood. It could've been worse. When Lucinda suggested to Patrick that her parents could join them, he'd firmly quashed the idea.

"Don't go there darling" he counselled her, "not even as a joke."

Elvira on the other hand was in her element. With Patrick and Lucinda living in Zug, she'd found a newfound purpose in life as she resumed her role of mother to Patrick and relished being pseudo-grandmother to young Clement.

Even Selena was invited. There was no way Elijah was leaving her to her own devices in New York where he'd appointed a watcher to ensure there was no possibility of her entering into another liaison like Robert van Holme. This was also the first year that Benji would join them. His existence by now was known to his half-brothers and sisters. Unfortunately, most of them also knew the definition of the word bastard. Few were preparing to welcome him to the family.

Despite the size of the house, finding privacy to talk proved impossible, so Jorge and Elijah took a number of long rambling walks in the countryside surrounding the mansion.

"Drew Harrison tells me that he received a cancellation for pistons the day they closed for Christmas" Jorge told him as they walked. "It's obvious there's a concerted campaign to get at you."

"Well perhaps we should just do what we did in the war and sell our stuff to the commies and be done with it" Elijah responded, kicking viciously at a rock lying on the path.

"Assuming you're serious, and apart from the fact it would be blocked by the Commerce Department, that wouldn't be very smart" Jorge replied. "It'd play straight into their hands. No, we have to think smarter than that."

***

The Board of Mercedes Group gathered in Zug in late January 1952. Its members had been selected with great care by Elijah. The Board comprised Elijah, Jorge, Nancy, Michael Leveridge, Dutch businessman Dieter van Rjyks, Swiss philanthropist Helmut Eichel, South African mining magnate Robert Grieves, British industrialist Sir Percival Partington-Compton and former US Ambassador Leroy Harrison.

Elijah briefed them on the problems they were experiencing with the cancellation of orders from U.S. Government agencies. When it came time for Michael Leveridge to speak, the former Congressman removed his glasses, leaned forward, crossed his arms on the board table and fixed Elijah with a long look.

"Simply put Elijah, the problem is you. The word around Washington is that you're anathema to the government and that anyone or anything associated with you is to be avoided at all costs. There're all sorts of rumours doing the rounds as well. Supposedly you were a Nazi sympathiser during the war and it's only a matter of time before they charge you. McCarthy's going to come after you but that will most probably wait until after the elections later this year. Hoover's name is also bound up in all of this. Apparently you bounced him and he's looking for payback." Leveridge sat back. "The smell's so bad Nancy and gentlemen, that anyone on this Board is automatically caught up as well. Is there anything you can add to that with your contacts Leroy?"

The former Ambassador shook his head. "No that's pretty well the way I'm getting it. I had an opportunity to meet with former Secretary of State Hull who tells me he knows you well" he said looking at Elijah. "Also said the scuttlebutt was all bunkum but other than that he wouldn't comment."

Elijah sat silent for a moment. "Thanks Leroy. Like Cordell I can't comment further either but if either you or Michael feels that you want off the board, in the circumstances I'd quite understand."

"Don't be so stupid" Leveridge retorted. "I hope you know me better than that. No I say don't let the bastards get you. Apologies Nancy" he added smiling at her.

"In some ways this could be seen as a golden opportunity" Jorge interjected. "This boom isn't going to last forever. It's also pretty obvious the Ruskies aren't going to let the war in Korea escalate into something major. Right now too much of our business is committed to the American military machine. When this conflict is over, there's going to be a lot of excess capacity on the market. This could prove to be a golden opportunity to wean ourselves off our dependence on the military."

"I couldn't agree more" Sir Percival agreed. "Not only source new customers old chap, but also new businesses situated away from the United States. It may also be a good time to divest ourselves of some that aren't performing so well. With this nonsense hanging over our heads, we should be looking at spreading our risk. Look at the oil division for example. They're sitting on leases in the Arabian Gulf but doing nothing with them. Let's get on with developing those for example so that we aren't totally dependent on the Yankee wells."

The Swiss philanthropist added his agreement, suggesting that the Board direct each of its executives heading up the individual companies to identify opportunities for the group to expand into.

"Good way of seeing which of them cuts the mustard" Sir Percival agreed. "Might find some dead wood we can cut there too."

As the Board completed its deliberations and the meeting prepared to break up, Elijah called for order. "Gentlemen and Nancy, I want to thank you each for your support and confidence in me. I suspect we've facing a pretty rough year, but as Jorge has so rightly reminded us, they may well yet have done us a favour."

***

In his role as Jorge's assistant, Patrick was now attending the global board meetings as an observer. His father was working to a long-term succession plan that would see Patrick eventually appointed a full director but he considered that was still some way off. As the board meeting broke up, he asked Patrick and Jorge to stay back.

"It's time to tell the boy a few facts Jorge" he said looking at his old friend.

His associate nodded.

"Sit down son, there were a number of things that Michael mentioned that you have the right to know about. But I need your promise that what I'm about to tell you will go with you to your grave. You can't even tell Lucinda. Jorge and I are sworn to secrecy as are the few others who are aware of the details I'm about to tell you."

He then outlined his relationship with Göring, how he'd first met the Reichsmarschall and how he'd subsequently approached him in 1934 to seek assistance in gaining additional orders for PMAB. Patrick listened with amazement as Elijah described Göring's request that Elijah accompany Günter and Dana Cohn out of Germany, his meeting with Hitler at the Berghof and his subsequent meeting with Cordell Hull. As he detailed his meetings with the Secretary of State and President Roosevelt, and finally with OSS Colonel Donovan, a small smile fleeted across Patrick's face.

Elijah stopped. "Did I say something humorous?" he asked.

"No" Patrick replied. "But I just realised where my flying lessons came from."

The comment broke the tension that'd been building as all three men laughed at Patrick's comment. Finally, Elijah told him of his visits to Berlin during the war, his detention by the Gestapo and Göring's subsequent request for Elijah to appear at his trial at Nuremberg as a character witness.

"That's when that arse-hole Hoover sent in his boys to try and make a case against me. Bill Donovan warned me that Hoover would try to strike back at me and that's what this is all about" Elijah concluded.

In telling his son the story, he left out Agnota's role, any mention of his involvement in the rescue of Jewish refugees from the Baltic or his being awarded the medal by Göring.

"Because of secrecy issues with the government, the Board can't be aware of any of this, but I wanted you to be so you might understand some of my actions in the future as we fight this. Because of your role supporting Jorge, you might be asked to carry out some tasks which I will expect you to do without question. Have you any problems with any of this?" Elijah asked.

"No sir. Thanks for taking me into your trust."

Patrick was actually feeling quite emotional but trying not to show it. On the one hand his father had never taken him into his confidence like this before; on the other he realised that many of Elijah's absences when he'd treated him like shit, could now be explained.

Chapter 27

New York, U.S.A.
May 1952

The two major U.S. political parties were in the midst of their primaries leading up to the mid-year conventions when he returned to New York. His natural inclination was to support the Democrats, but he felt he'd been stabbed in the back by a number of the party's prominent members starting with Joe Kennedy. Supporting the Republicans would be no easier since McCarthy was a Republican Senator from Wisconsin. After discussing his dilemma with Mark Frost, they decided to wait on the selection of the respective presidential nominees before they threw the weight of the papers behind either party.

A couple of weeks later, Elijah was interrupted by Amelie announcing a call from a Mrs Baverstock. "She's called a couple of times but you haven't been available."

"Maureen, great to hear from you" he said taking the call.

"We're having a small dinner next week at home" she told him. "Arnold's been promoted in his job and we're celebrating. Would you join us?"

She almost appeared to be pleading and against his better judgement, Elijah accepted her invitation. "Just as long as Patrick's in-laws won't be there."

"You're in luck. Even Arnold can't stand Kenneth socially. His only family functions are officiating at weddings and funerals and saying grace for Thanksgiving. Even then most of the younger ones won't let him marry them because they reckon that fast tracks them to the divorce courts."

***

Home for Maureen was the wealthy New Jersey suburb of Hunterdon. This allowed Arnold to commute to Philadelphia where he'd just been appointed a vice President with one of the big three American insurance companies. It also gave Maureen the opportunity to drive to New York City to shop and escape her oppressive family life.

Dinner was a small gathering of a dozen people, none of whom Elijah knew. It was a very stilted affair with Arnold monopolising the evening with a display of his military upbringing; clipped speech, lack of humour and total control of the conversation. It didn't take long for Elijah to realise why he'd been invited. With her open gregarious manner and Australian accent, Maureen was like a fish out of water, while the other guests were very much in Arnold's mould. Elijah couldn't understand what had possessed her to marry him, but one thing was for sure, the marriage seemed to be rapidly approaching its use by date.

He contributed little to the discussion at the dinner table speaking only when spoken to, preferring instead to listen to the offerings of his fellow diners. Every so often he would glance at Maureen and receive a small smile in response. He could see she was desperately unhappy but it wasn't his affair. He could hardly wait for the evening to draw inexorably to its close and put this mob behind him. Not only was this his first dinner party at the Baverstock household…it would also be his last. While he enjoyed Maureen's company and the openness that came with her being Australian, there was no way he was getting mixed up in whatever was going on between her and Arnold.

Elijah suddenly realised that the table had fallen silent and all heads had turned to him as though he was expected to speak. "I apologise" he said. "I missed that."

"I was telling the others how you had a funny story about your dancing lessons" Maureen said.

Out of the corner of his eye he could see that Arnold's face had gone rigid and was suffused with anger. "I don't think Elijah would want to go into that here Maureen" he said sharply.

"What the hell; may as well liven things up for her" he thought to himself. "On the contrary Arnold, I suspect it's a story best told at the dining table rather than the board table" he replied, launching into a long and humorous discourse of how he'd learned the tango in a whorehouse, first having to overcome his repulsion at the thought of dancing with another man.

To his surprise, he soon had the others in fits of laughter; all except Arnold who sat glaring at him, only allowing a false wisp of a smile to cross his face as the tale came to an end. At Maureen's urging, Elijah then followed up with another story involving Miranda and a former Congressman, cleaning it up for the gathering.

"How many times have you been married?" one of the ladies asked him.

"My eldest son says five and still counting ma'am" Elijah replied with a straight face.

Maureen had a choking fit as she tried to suppress her laughter while her husband's face darkened and his thin lips tightened even further.

As he bid his farewells, Maureen whispered "Thank you Elijah. I think you saved me from drowning in there."

Arnold's handshake was perfunctionary and Elijah noted he didn't endorse Maureen's invitation for him to return another time.

"Well I wouldn't mind being a fly on that wall tonight" he thought as he headed back to Scarsdale.

***

As his business problems intensified, he soon forgot the evening. Not only had he effectively been blackballed by government, but a number of companies were also being pressured to sever their links with him. At Mercedes Oil, Deke Newell was successful in sourcing new markets but the other businesses were hurting. It was against that background that they decided to exit the steel business. Michael Leveridge, aware that Elijah was seriously considering mothballing two or even three of the mills in Pennsylvania resulting in thousands of people being thrown out of work, engineered an offer from a consortium of companies to purchase all the mills allowing Elijah a modest profit. Not normally one to retreat under fire, the potential to realise a profit was too alluring and the sale was finalised in early July.

Around the same time Maureen called again. "Arnold's away for a few days and I'm staying in the city overnight. I was hoping you might join me for dinner?" she suggested.

"I'm also staying over in town at the apartment tonight" he replied. "Why not eat with me there? I'll organise for something to be brought in."

The 'something' turned out to be a meal prepared by one of his favourite restaurants and served by one of their staff in the apartment's high vaulted dining room: Florida Rock Shrimp, Stuffed Alaskan Black Cod followed by Pumpkin and Pepita Strudel.

Maureen leaned back as she pushed what remained of her strudel aside. "I'm full" she said. "You're a man of many talents Elijah Hocking. That was delicious."

Elijah also enjoyed her company immensely, affording him a break as it did from his business travails. "I wish I could say I'd prepared it myself, but even boiling water is beyond my scope" he replied.

"I suspect you have many talents. What's more, I'm sure you know exactly what they are. That's what I like about you; your self confidence and self awareness. You exert control without appearing to do so. So unlike Arnold! He's always got to be seen to be in command, issuing orders. My God always issuing orders" she added as she looked sadly into her glass.

"It's none of my business Maureen, but there has to have been some attraction for you to have married him."

"When Alex was killed at Tobruk I was left with nothing. Both my parents died in the thirties. It looked like I was doomed to forever be a clerk in an obscure state government department. Townsville was some forgotten hole which only came alive with the influx of American troops. I wasn't interested in them. I went to a couple of dances with a girlfriend, but apart from the money the G.I.'s flashed around, most of them seemed even more bushie than the local Aussies…and only interested in one thing. Anyway one night I was invited to an officers' only dance and that's where I met Arnold. He seemed so worldly, so in command…there's that word again…so manly. I fell under his spell. He thought he'd found someone he could manipulate and order around; I thought I'd found my ticket out of Townsville."

"So what's to stop you leaving him, or perhaps you don't want to?" Elijah pushed.

"He provides for me. You've seen how we live. I could never hope to live like that in Australia. He doesn't abuse me or anything like that, although it can be very punishing mentally to live with him. But I've cast my lot; I have to accept it. He travels a lot and that will only increase in his new role so I get regular breaks, although it seems harder to steel myself for each return home. I don't have too many options because without Arnold I have nothing and if I were to leave him, he'd leave me destitute."

As he put her into a cab half an hour later Elijah told her "No-one's ever without options Maureen. You just have to recognise what they are."

***

After a month in England with Nancy and the family, Elijah was back in New York by mid-August. Eisenhower's success in gaining the Republican nomination over Taft gave him some confidence. All the advice he received was that Eisenhower was against McCarthy's attacks on individuals under cover of the Senate. He hoped that if elected, Eisenhower might clip the Senator's wings. He'd also met Adlai Stevenson, the Democrat presidential nominee and thought him weak. Consequently, for the first time Mark's papers endorsed Republican candidates across the country with the exception of Wisconsin where McCarthy was standing for re-election.

The Board met again in New York in late August to review the proposals from the group's executives. The meeting agreed that the Group should progressively withdraw from manufacturing in the United States, seeking instead opportunities in Europe, oil exploration in the Middle East and Venezuela, expand its agricultural interests further and enter into minerals exploration. In future years with the rise of the Japanese juggernaut and the slow decline in production and competitiveness of the United States manufacturing sector, Elijah often gave thanks to McCarthy for forcing the Board to completely re-evaluate the Group's businesses and direction.

Now, it was his turn to call Maureen. It was the first time he'd done so but he felt like celebrating.

"As it turns out, I'm actually coming to the city tomorrow and was planning to stop a couple of days to go to a show or two" she told him. "Arnold has to fly to San Francisco and Seattle so he'll be gone a few days."

They met the following evening at Elijah's Fifth Avenue apartment. Once again he arranged for dinner to be catered for and once again the restaurant had excelled.

They sat talking in the lounge with its floor to ceiling windows taking in the Manhattan skyline. It was a clear evening with a near full moon reflected in the nearby East River, the lights of the buildings stretching into the distance along Long Island.

"This is just magical" Maureen said. "It's as though the real world can be put aside for the evening."

"It can you know" he said softly. "You don't need to go to a hotel tonight. I've got seven bedrooms you can choose from."

"There's only one I'd be interested in Elijah. You must know that" she responded.

She put her glass down carefully on the nearby table and crossed over to him, stepping out of her skirt as she did. They met weekly after that until Elijah had to return to England. It was Maureen's idea to spend the last night together before he flew back.

"I feel like being just a little bit scandalous if I'm going to be a scarlet woman" she said. "I'd like to stay with you somewhere away from the norm. How about Boston?" she suggested.

If it'd make her happy, that was fine by Elijah. He'd have his plane repositioned to depart from there instead of Idlewild. It was actually closer to the first re-fuelling stop at Gander. She went out to the airport to see Elijah off before returning home to Hunterdon. An embrace at the foot of the stairs, with a quick wave to Maureen, he bounded up the steps into the plane.

"See you next month" he called as he disappeared into the aircraft and the door shut behind him.

***

The election resulted in a landslide to Eisenhower as predicted. Elijah was pleased, believing that with the former general in power, McCarthy would be brought under control. A number of Senators and Congressmen assured Elijah that McCarthy would be sidelined when the new Senate decided on its committee structure in the New Year. Relieved, he believed the worst was over. Of course there was still the matter of Hoover, assuming he was also behind the blacklisting.

Returning to New York from the Christmas break, he resumed his affair with Maureen For her, it provided relief from a situation she was finding increasingly difficult to cope with; for Elijah it gave him the female company he craved due to Nancy's continuing absence since she wouldn't join him until later in the year when the three eldest children broke from school for the summer holidays.

In mid-March two bombshells dropped in swift succession. Growing wary of McCarthy's continuing abuse of power, and believing they could control him, his fellow Senators appointed him as Chairman of a minor committee. As it turned out, the rules were sufficiently flexible to allow the Senator to turn the committee into a personal vendetta against those he decided to pursue. That clearly included Elijah.

First Elijah received notification that McCarthy's committee intended to call him to give evidence. Then Mark Frost called him.

"It's urgent I see you" Mark said. "Can you stay put? I'll be right over."

He arrived about thirty minutes later. "Damned traffic's a mess out there" he said passing across a large manila envelope. "These were delivered to *The Monitor* this afternoon. I don't know if any other papers got them or just us because of your involvement. Certainly none of our other ones have received copies…not yet anyway."

Elijah opened the envelope and removed nearly twenty foolscap sized black and white photographs. Each of them featured him and Maureen…in a restaurant sharing a meal, walking in the street together, Maureen entering and leaving the apartment on Fifth Avenue, in bed together in Boston and embracing at the foot of his aircraft at Logan Airport before his flight back to England the previous October.

"Have you decided which one you're going to run?" Elijah asked drily without looking up.

"My guess is either you've been tailed by the FBI, or else someone's got a private detective watching you" Mark said ignoring him. "They obviously intend to fight dirty. Perhaps none of the other major dailies would run any of these but they sure would run the story."

"I have to warn Maureen" Elijah said. "Arnold will go ballistic when he sees these and she has to prepare herself. And then there's Nancy." He threw the photos on the nearby table. "This has to be Hoover. He's got the resources and the motive."

He rang Maureen and in a few words explained what'd happened.

"You need to get away. Where's Arnold at the moment?"

"In Philadelphia." '

"Then you have to assume that if he doesn't already have his own set of photos, he soon will. Is there somewhere you can go?"

"No."

"Well you can't come here, it's the first place they'll look for you. Pack a bag and head to Idlewild. The plane will be re-fuelled and waiting for you. You'll be met at the hangar and escorted to a place I have in Argentina. No-one will be able to get near you, not if they value their lives anyway. Just take the basics that you need and get out before Arnold comes home" he stressed.

Next he issued instructions to his Personal Assistant before turning back to Mark who'd remained waiting while Elijah made his calls.

"Nancy's next" he said with a grimace, "then Jorge."

"I'll get out of the way" Mark said. "We'll obviously suppress this in our own papers, but we need a response if it does go public. In the meantime I'll speak with Hearst and a couple of others and see if they have any inkling of it. If they do and I can't get it suppressed, then at least I'll try to get it buried somewhere way back in their papers."

***

There was silence on the other end of the telephone when he finished speaking. Finally, he asked if she was still there.

"You bastard!" Where he'd expected tears, instead there was a cold fury in her response. "I put up with the Swede, but there's no way I'm prepared to put up with this. What is there about you? Can't you keep the bloody thing in your pants?"

"Nancy, I'm sorry. I guess with all this trouble over here, and you over there…"

She cut him off. "So that's supposed to make it right is it? That's the green light for me to go off and have a fling too? I should have realised, you're nothing but a prize prick!" and slammed down the phone.

***

"Don't go near that hearing Elijah" Michael Leveridge warned him. "This is a witch hunt designed to ruin you. You've certainly stirred up a hornet's nest the way you treated Hoover, and right now he's virtually untouchable."

They were sitting in Elijah's office with Jorge who'd flown in urgently from Europe.

"There's no way I'm going to let them get away with this Michael. It's nothing more than blackmail" Elijah replied vehemently.

294

"Those photos were a warning *amigo*" Jorge replied. "Obviously they can be used at any time."

Amazingly, they still hadn't surfaced in the press three days after being delivered to Mark Frost.

"You don't want to get on that stand" Michael continued. "Even if you take the Fifth, the mere fact that you refused to answer questions would make you look guilty."

"So you're suggesting I just sit back and grin and bear it. That still doesn't resolve the problem with Hoover. I've already got the feeling I'm being tailed. Perhaps we should arrange for someone to take a pot shot at the arse-hole."

"Jesus Christ, I hope you're joking. That'd be like starting World War Three" Michael exclaimed. "It'd put Korea in the shade by comparison."

"That's the problem Michael, I don't think he is" Jorge interjected shaking his head. "Put it straight out of your mind *amigo*, it won't work. Anyway you haven't been summoned by the committee yet. Before they do, get out of the country until this blows over. The businesses here are in good hands and don't need you."

"I endorse that" Michael said. "There's nothing to be gained by taking them on under their own rules. Right now McCarthy and Hoover are holding all the aces. Not even the all-powerful Elijah Hocking can fight that."

"Have you heard back from Nancy yet?" Jorge asked.

"No. She's refusing to take my calls. Once the plane gets back I'll fly over and see if I can't sort things out."

"I wouldn't bother" Jorge said. "She called me earlier today to say she'd received her own package and asked if I'd be representing you when she serves the divorce papers. She intends using the photos as evidence if you contest."

"So I don't appear at the Senate hearing" Elijah said, turning the conversation back to business. "Doesn't that make me appear guilty anyway? What difference will it make whether I appear or not?"

"Because if you're not here, they can't serve any notice on you for one" Michael answered. "If they can't serve a notice, then they can't question you or have the press on hand to try and embarrass you. I know there's a bunch of leeches in both houses who've welshed on you up to date, but I still have sufficient influence and dirt on enough of them that I could get your name suppressed. That way there'll be no public record of their interest in you. But you step in front of a hearing and there's no way I could guarantee that."

The three men talked back and forth for several hours discussing a number of options before Amelie interrupted them to advised that Mark Frost was on the phone.

"*The New York Evening Enquirer*'s planning to go to press with you and Maureen front page. They're printing at the moment. You might want to get a suppression order going pronto before they start distributing" he suggested.

Jorge immediately commandeered both Amelie and a telephone, contacting one of Elijah's pet judges and requesting an injunction banning the publication of the story. An hour passed before he returned to the meeting.

"That holds them overnight Elijah, but they'll appeal the order in the morning. I doubt we can keep them at bay. We have a couple of days at the most before your affair with Maureen is made public."

"I really don't give a shit about the affair Jorge, I'm more interested in what the bastards are trying to do to me in Washington" Elijah said. "You tell me my marriage is finished anyway, so there's not much else they can do on that front."

"They're one and the same *amigo*, don't you understand that? This is all about crippling or ruining you" Jorge said. "Please, just jump on that plane as soon as it returns and go somewhere and regroup. Let's plan our counter attack tactically away from all this. Come to Zug and stay with Elvira and me."

"No, if I'm forced to run, then it'll be to the *estancia*" Elijah replied bitterly.

"Not wise with Maureen there" Jorge counseled him. "That'll just give added evidence to the divorce proceedings."

"Worse than those bloody photographs? Come on man, she's the innocent party in all this. Right now she appears to be the only person, other than you two and a couple of others, who's standing by me" Elijah said his voice rising. "Just leave her out of this."

***

His attempts to contact Nancy continued to be fruitless. Finally she relented and took his call. As Elijah tried to apologise, she cut him off. "My mind's made up. I expected better of you Elijah. I knew of your past, but thought we were above that. Don't bother calling again" she told him and hung up.

It was late the following afternoon before Elijah flew off to the *estancia* to lick his wounds. Running from anything was total anathema to him, but he finally recognised that he was never going to win a battle with Hoover on the lawman's turf, or by fighting under his rules. Bitter at the desertion by a number of Senators and Congressmen he'd helped personally, Elijah determined his own dirt files were going to get considerable airing, he would see to that. There were a lot of scores to be settled personally, and settle them he would. In the meantime Michael Leveridge would have free use of the information to ensure Elijah's name was suppressed from any Senate records of McCarthy's committee.

No-one could have foretold at the time, but it would take a change of President before Elijah would return to the United States and when he did, it would once more be on his own terms.

Epilogue

Estancia Tierra de Abundancia, Patagonia, Argentina
June 1953

As far back as he could remember he'd always been in total control, buying and using people and dispensing favours at will; disposing of those who were of no further use to him. That it could have happened to him; that it should be *he* who was now the victim, was beyond comprehension. His bitterness knew no bounds as he retreated to the *estancia* to lick his wounds. He didn't know how to handle defeat; for him there was no other word for what had happened to him.

He hardly spoke to anyone when he arrived at the remote pampas property. He'd only been there for a week when without warning, he suddenly packed some supplies and headed away from the *casco* towards the distant Andes. Mounting his horse, he told Maureen he'd be back when he was back.

Esmeralda held her hand as together they watched the dust cloud accompanying Elijah diminish as he rode onto the pampas.

"He will come back a better man *Señora*" Enrique murmured softly behind her. "It is his way."

For the first few days Elijah spurred his horse on hard into the mountains, climbing over the lower passes into neighbouring Chile. On the third and fourth days he rode through blinding snow as winter storms lashed the Andes before turning back and setting up camp in the canyons at the foot of the western side of the mountain chain, taking care to avoid the one where he'd pegged his father-in-law out to die back in 1921 following Mercedes' murder.

Once the snowstorms cleared and the sun returned, bringing with it cold crisp days where the air was so clear that he could pick out every individual ridge line etched like cardboard cut-outs against the deep blue sky, he headed further north.

Late one afternoon he shot a mountain deer for supplies, then as the shadows were lengthening, sat in wonder as he watched a puma traverse the slopes above him. It stared back warily at the human below before disappearing from view over a ridge. On an impulse he left the skinned and gutted deer on the ground for the giant cat as he packed up and moved away from the puma's territory.

It took fifteen days before Elijah finally turned and headed down from the mountains back onto the pampas towards the distant *casco*. Maureen heard the commotion from the cattle yards as the *gauchos* spotted the distant figure on horseback drawing closer. She rushed outside to greet him as he slowly reined in his horse and dismounted. Her heart was in her mouth, unsure what mental state he might have returned in. For her, the past fifteen days had been a torment as she battled with her doubts, not knowing whether he would want her to stay.

He approached her and gently put his arms around her drawing her into his chest. "I'm back. I need a drink but first there's one more thing I must do."

Taking her by the hand, they headed up the path that climbed the small hillock behind the *casco*, stooping to pick some white daisies blooming alongside the path. Heading to one of the well tended graves, he knelt down and gently placed the flowers on the grave.

"Mercedes" he whispered. "This is Maureen. We need your blessing."

THE ELIJAH TRILOGY

BOOK 3

Elijah's Will

Elijah Hocking lies dying, his dysfunctional family gathered around his bedside. They despise him and each other and the feeling is entirely mutual. As they wait with barely concealed impatience for him to die, they don't realise that even though he lies in a coma, he can hear every word they speak as their hatreds, rivalries and prejudices are displayed for all to see.

Forced to leave the United States during the McCarthy era, Elijah has once again retreated to his beloved *estancia* situated in the Argentine pampas. Down but not beaten, he moves into the world of illegal arms trading, establishing a redoubt hidden deep in the Paraguayan jungle headed by a former Nazi, high on Simon Wiesenthal's wanted list.

From the Six Day War to the invasion of Kuwait, the supply of uranium to South Africa and the loss of his art acquisitions, *Elijah's Will* moves through the annals of history as Elijah regains his place as one of the century's richest and most influential men. Along the way he continues to be a complex character, as his many wives and children can attest.

But Elijah has not yet played his last hand, and as the tension mounts, so too do the rivalries and hatred as Elijah's children restlessly await his death and their share of his wealth.

For them the waiting has already stretched for too long, as finally the day dawns for the reading of Elijah's Will.